DREAM

THINGS

TRUE

DREAM THINGS TRUE

Marie Marquardt

ST. MARTIN'S GRIFFIN ☙ NEW YORK

DREAM THINGS TRUE. Copyright © 2015 by Marie Marquardt. All rights reserved. Printed in the United States of America. For information, address St. Martin's Press, 175 Fifth Avenue, New York, N.Y. 10010.

www.stmartins.com

Designed by Molly Rose Murphy

The Library of Congress Cataloging-in-Publication Data is available upon request.

ISBN 978-1-250-07045-6 (hardcover)
ISBN 978-1-4668-8024-5 (e-book)

Our books may be purchased in bulk for promotional, educational, or business use. Please contact your local bookseller or the Macmillan Corporate and Premium Sales Department at (800) 221-7945, extension 5442, or by e-mail at MacmillanSpecialMarkets@macmillan.com.

First Edition: September 2015

10 9 8 7 6 5 4 3 2 1

For Chris

PART ONE

ONE
Machete Moments

If you grab a machete blade near the bottom, just above the handle, it won't cut through your skin. That's what Alma was thinking, riding in her dad's truck way too early in the morning on the last Wednesday of summer.

Alma knew a lot about machetes—one of the perks of her summer job, if you could call it that. So, pondering the machete wedged behind her seat, she composed a list of facts in her head, hoping that a mind full of machete facts wouldn't have room for anxiety.

Machete hooks are great for pruning blackberry and blueberry bushes.

She pulled her knees to her chest and wrapped her arms around them as her dad maneuvered the pickup truck from their barrio into the rich part of town.

In the traditional dances of many Latin American countries, men wear machetes as part of the costume: the cumbia *in Colombia, capoeira (which, technically, is a martial art) in Brazil, and Mexican Matachines, to name just a few.*

Alma hugged her knees tighter and sucked in a deep breath. Her stomach started to churn, and her hands got clammy.

Her dad always said that if he could only have one tool, it would be a machete.

"*Papi*," she said tentatively, "there's something I need to ask you."

Her father shot her the look—the one that told her she'd better switch into Spanish if she knew what was good for her.

"There's this anthropology class at the community college I want to take. It's after school on Tuesdays and Thursdays," she said in Spanish.

In five days—on August 20, 2007—Alma would start her junior year of high school.

She had been dreading the day for months. Now that it rapidly approached, she knew of only one way to lessen the pain. If she was fated to waste her time at Gilberton High School every day, she could at least take college classes after school.

One problem: she knew her dad would say no. Wasn't this supposed to be any parent's dream?

"*¿Y cómo lo vas a pagar, hija?*"

"I've saved enough money to pay the tuition."

"*¿De verdad?*" He said this with a knowing grin. "Do you know how much those classes cost?"

"I looked online, and—"

"*¿En la tarde?*" her dad interrupted.

She saw exactly where this was going. Sometimes, Alma couldn't believe how absurd her life was.

"*Sí, Papi,* in the afternoon, but—"

"But what about your *primas*?" He chuckled softly. "Will your cousins come to class with you?"

Now he was making fun of her. Fantastic.

"Can't Uncle Rigo watch them for a couple of hours? I mean, he *is* their father!"

"Your *tío* Rigo is recovering from a severe back injury, Alma."

Alma considered asking why, if Uncle Rigo was in so much pain, he went out fishing with his buddies every weekend. Remembering that success was her goal, she kept her mouth shut and considered alternative strategies.

"What if I ask *Tía* Pera to adjust her schedule at the plant?"

"Pera is lucky to have gotten her position back at the plant, Alma. She can't go to her boss asking for special favors."

How could she possibly be lucky to spend eight hours a day as a backup killer at the poultry plant, Alma wondered. Her aunt spent her days gripping a lethally sharp knife in each hand and watching an endless row of headless chickens move slowly by, dangling from their feet. Her job was to chop off the heads of the lucky chickens that made it through the killing machines alive.

Sometimes Alma felt as helpless as those chickens.

Alma was not even seventeen yet, but she had experienced enough to know that there are certain days in a life—moments, even—when the unexpected happens. Just like the swift swipe of a machete, it cuts through your life and leaves behind something entirely new. Sometimes good, sometimes bad, sometimes both at once.

Like that morning in eighth grade, when Mrs. King pulled Alma into her office. Mrs. King was the new middle school counselor, and probably the largest small woman Alma had ever met. She was the kind of woman with wrists so narrow that her bones stuck out, but somehow everything about her seemed oversized, all the way down to her deep and resonant laugh. She transferred in halfway through the year, and brought with her the perfect strategy for luring middle schoolers into her office. The smell of unusual homemade sweets wafted through her door: devil's food cake, buttermilk pie, candied pecans, sweet potato cheesecake. No chocolate-chip cookies, no brownies. They were "too ordinary."

The office was filled with bookshelves and the distinctive aroma of roasted peanuts. A degree from Spelman College covered the narrow strip of available wall space, just above a certificate of recognition from the Association of Black Psychologists. Apparently Mrs. King was part of something called the "Disaster Relief Task Force." Strangely, that made Alma feel hopeful.

She sat Alma down and offered her a hefty chunk of homemade peanut brittle.

"I have a plan," she told Alma. "And I know you're gonna like it."

Alma bit off a piece of peanut brittle and let it slowly melt in her mouth as Mrs. King began.

"We're going to find another high school for you—a good one."

The local school, Gilberton High, wasn't a bad school, but it was the kind of place where Latino boys were funneled into classes like Fundamentals of Construction, and the girls wasted their time in glorified home economics classes, carrying around eggs for a week as a way to practice caring for babies.

"Really?" Alma asked, wiping the crumbs away from her mouth. "I mean, is that even possible?"

Until that day, no one had ever told her there might be an alternative.

Mrs. King pulled out a map of north Georgia.

"Show me where you've got family, sweetheart."

When Alma's sticky finger landed on north Atlanta, Mrs. King set the plan into motion. She laid out a future filled with possibilities: top-ranked teachers, advanced placement classes, college admissions counselors, scholarships and university degrees. Alma would live with cousins in Atlanta and attend one of the best high schools in the state— if they could convince her dad.

Mrs. King, Alma soon discovered, was a very patient woman. Or hardheaded. First, she tried reason with Mr. García, bringing a stack of standardized test scores over to Alma's house and sitting at the dining room table with Alma's dad. The conversation went something like this:

Mrs. King: "Are you aware of how unusual it is for a child to score consistently in the ninety-eighth percentile?"

Alma's dad: "Yes, and my Alma will have this score next year again, here with her family in Gilberton."

Mrs. King then suggested that Alma resort to "good ol'-fashioned bribery." Here's how that conversation went:

Alma: "I'll work for you every summer if you let me go, *Papi. Te lo prometo.* I promise, every single day, all day."

Alma's dad: "Yes, you will, just like your brother, as soon as you turn fifteen."

Alma: "So I can go? To Atlanta?"

Alma's dad: "No, *hija.* How will you work for me here in Gilberton if you're living over there in Atlanta?"

Apparently Alma was expected to do the work anyway, not only in the summer but every weekend during the school year, too—which, by the way, is why it would be a big stretch to call this her "summer job."

When Mrs. King told her to give it one last try, Alma even tried guilting her dad by bringing up her mother. That conversation was so painful that Alma had blocked it out of her memory. Basically, her dad insisted that Alma's mom would have wanted their family to be together, no matter what. It looked like Alma would be heading to Gilberton High School.

But then came another machete moment.

Alma met Mario at a family party three weeks before the start of high school. He was a *recién llegado*—recently arrived from their hometown in Mexico. He was probably a third cousin or something since everyone from their hometown seemed to be related. Anyway, he followed her around all night while she was taking care of her little cousins.

The two of them stood and watched boys throw themselves against the mesh walls of the trampoline, and Mario looked so pathetically sad and lonely that Alma decided to make conversation.

"How do you like Gilberton?" she asked in Spanish.

"It's OK," he replied.

That was all he said. Squeaking trampoline springs filled their awkward silence.

"Are you working at Silver Ribbon?" she asked.

He nodded once but said nothing.

Alma already knew that, like almost everyone else who came from her hometown in Mexico, Mario had a job at the chicken plant. Her *tía* Dolores always scored the newcomers a job there.

"What's your station?" she asked, not having any idea how else to make conversation.

"Killing floor," he said, focusing intently on the pack of boys as they hurled themselves from the trampoline. "Cleanup."

So he spent his days mopping blood and feathers from the killing floor. No wonder he was miserable.

Alma felt so sorry for him that, when he cornered her against the rusty trampoline and tried to kiss her, she let him. He groped at her body with clumsy hands while forcing his tongue into her mouth and swirling it around in swift circles. It felt like she was on some crazy roller coaster ride. To make matters worse, he was chewing Big Red gum, which filled her mouth with an overwhelming burning sensation.

She should have known that the burn would foreshadow worse things to come.

Her dad showed up just as she was disentangling herself from Mario's roving hands. Glaring at Mario, he took Alma by the forearm and pulled her away. They marched directly to his Bronco without exchanging a single word. He opened the back door and pushed her in, not roughly but definitely not gently either.

"Stay here," he grumbled, his eyes burning with anger.

She watched as he slammed the door, trapping her in the car. He went inside and came out moments later with Raúl, Alma's older brother. The two of them found Mario cowering behind the trampoline. To their credit, Alma's dad and brother used only their words to make Mario retreat from the party. As Raúl headed toward the car, her dad went to exchange words with his sister, Alma's *tía* Dolores. Presumably, he was trying to guard Alma's purity.

Raúl jumped into the passenger seat and looked back at her, grinning wickedly.

"Jesus, Alma," he said. "If you're gonna hook up in front of the entire family, you should at least pick a guy who's willing to throw a punch at your brother."

"I'll keep that in mind," Alma replied.

"That guy was a loser," Raúl said. "And you, my little *hermanita*, are in deep shit."

No one endured the killing floors for long, but Mario's move was quietly expedited by *Tía* Dolores. He was long gone by now, probably working construction in another state.

For years, Alma had dreamed that her first kiss would unlock the meaning of that weird English word "swoon." Instead, it resulted in constant mocking from her big brother, several brutal days of nonstop chores, and the need to avoid anything cinnamon flavored for life. To this day, Alma couldn't stand the smell of Big Red.

Here's the miracle, though—the unexpected outcome: After Alma's dad caught Mario kissing her, he was terrified that she would start clandestinely dating the eighteen-year-old. So he called Mrs. King.

Within a week, Alma was packing her bags for Atlanta.

Now, two years later, Alma was back, riding in her dad's crappy work truck through this crappy town and facing, five days from now, the start of her junior year at Gilberton High School, home of the Fighting Red Elephants. How appropriate. Alma's misery at this return was the big red elephant in the room that her father refused to acknowledge.

She was going to make her dad see things her way.

"OK, Dad, listen . . ."

Her dad sent a fierce glare in her direction.

She tried again. "*Papi*, it's just not fair that I have to be the one to fix all of this. Things were going so well for me, *Papi*, and now I have to come back to Gilberton and probably ruin my chances to get into college, all so that I can take care of my cousins."

Her father opened his mouth to speak, but she pressed on. "Wait, *Papi*, please let me finish. I just wish you'd work with me to make this situation better for *me*. If I can take classes at the community college, I just might keep from losing my mind at that lame excuse for a high school."

Her dad jerked to a stop and killed the ignition. He turned to face her squarely, and deep creases took shape across his forehead.

"Alma Julia García-Menendez, I have heard enough from you," he growled angrily. Then he switched into rapid-fire Spanish. "You think I haven't done everything I possibly can to make your life better? You think Gilberton is a 'lame excuse' for a high school? Try growing corn on your dad's small plot of land for prices that have plummeted so far you might as well give it away, while your father spends every week in the city struggling to earn enough money to put some kind of food on the table."

He stopped to catch his breath, but Alma didn't dare say a word.

Her father shook his head slowly and squeezed his eyes shut. "Not once did I complain to my father. Not once did I grumble about making *my* life better."

He pressed his hand against his forehead, rubbing at the deep creases.

"Where have I gone wrong, Alma? Tell me, what have I done to give you the impression that this life is all about *you*?"

Alma said nothing. She just hugged her knees tighter, wanting to disappear.

Her dad took in a long breath and closed his eyes.

"You, Alma, are not a child," he said softly. "You are a sixteen-year-old woman, and you need to start acting like one. You *will* come directly home from school every afternoon to take care of your cousins. End of discussion."

He restarted the truck, and they drove in heavy silence.

He turned off the four-lane highway into the manicured Lakeshore Heights neighborhood. They pulled into a steep driveway leading to a stately colonial home. He lightly touched her arm, pulled the machete from behind her seat, and stepped out of the truck.

"I'll get started on the lawn," he said. "Why don't you take a few minutes to finish your coffee and then prune the roses here in the front?"

Maybe for a couple of years, she had been lucky. But her luck had run out.

Damn, it was hot.

Running in Georgia in August was brutal. It sort of felt like running through the steam room at the club, but without a cold water dispenser nearby.

Sprinting toward his house, heart pounding and legs aching, Evan fixed his focus on the crest of the hill. When he reached the top, he lengthened his gait and shifted into an easy jog. A vaguely familiar red pickup truck was parked in his driveway, with two lean, tanned legs dangling from the open passenger window. They wore black Chuck Taylor high-tops that swung to a slow rhythm, but no music was coming from the truck.

Evan wanted to meet the girl attached to those legs.

He heard the sound of metal crunching against metal and then saw that the truck was beginning to roll backward, toward the street. The legs flailed, and he heard the girl calling out as she clamored over to the driver's seat.

"*¡Pinche troca!*"

Against his better judgment, Evan ran toward the truck, which was slowly gaining speed.

He saw the girl balancing a coffee mug precariously with one hand as she banged the other against the steering wheel.

"*¡Es mierda!* You are such a useless piece of crap!"

The truck began to move fast.

"Pull the emergency brake!" Evan yelled, cupping his hands around his mouth.

She swung around to look at him and gasped.

"Where is it?"

How was he supposed to know? He'd never even been inside a Ford truck.

"Just push the foot break!" he called out.

"I can't find it!"

The truck had almost reached the street. Its momentum would slow on the level road, but it would soon hit a steep downhill slope and head directly toward the Crawfords' house, with the girl still inside.

Evan ran faster.

"Open the door," he yelled.

"No!" she replied. "Are you nuts?"

"Let me in."

When the truck hit the street, the door swung open and Evan flung himself toward it. Grasping the window frame, he slid into the seat. His foot found the emergency brake and pressed down. The movement felt familiar, just like sliding into a goal, except that he had landed on a girl and knocked the coffee out of her hand.

The truck came to an abrupt stop, and Evan jumped out. The girl bolted out behind him, escaping just before the coffee made it to the edge of her shorts. She whipped around, swiping at her rear.

Evan watched, feeling both annoyed and, he had to admit, entertained by the jerky motions of her coffee-avoidance dance.

Her cheeks flushed a deep red as her dark eyes met his.

"Sorry," she said. "I don't drive."

"Yeah," he replied, "I figured that out."

She had to be at least sixteen. Trying not to let himself look at the parts of her body that gave it away, Evan stepped closer and held her gaze.

"You're not too young to drive, are you?"

"No," she said. "I'm almost seventeen. I just never learned."

Evan grinned. "You prefer to be chauffeured?"

"Yeah," she replied, nodding toward the beat-up landscaping truck. "It's all part of my glamorous lifestyle."

This girl had no shortage of sarcasm, but he could keep up.

"So," he asked, bowing slightly, "might I offer my services and maneuver this fine vehicle back into the driveway?"

"I guess," she said, grabbing an old towel from the bed of the truck. "Just let me clean the seat for you."

He watched her wipe the towel across the seat to sop up spilled coffee. Her silky hair was pulled into a ponytail that fell to the middle of her back and he felt the urge to touch it, to let his hands trail all the way down her body.

She turned around and caught him staring at her legs.

"It's all yours," she told him, arching her eyebrows into a murderous glance.

Busted.

Evan climbed in sheepishly, mashed on the clutch, and turned the key in the ignition. The truck was a stick-shift, and very old. This had the potential to be bad.

The girl hopped into the passenger seat.

"Well, Jeeves?" she asked. "What are you waiting for?"

Evan forced the car into first and slowly released the clutch. The truck eased forward, up the driveway.

"This a good spot?" he asked.

"Yeah, thanks," she replied. "I'm Julia, by the way."

Julia was a weird name for her. Or maybe it was the way she said it—sort of tossing it out like it didn't matter.

"Sorry I interrupted your run," she said.

"I was done," Evan replied. "I'm just trying to get back in shape after a long, lazy summer."

Evan saw a wry smile curl onto her lips.

"Right," she said. "A long, lazy summer. Sounds nice."

He wasn't sure how to reply, so he just shrugged. She probably was here to work, which was strange. She didn't look like a landscaper. Plus, it was the last week of summer. It would suck to be working, Evan thought, especially in this insane heat.

"So, do you play a sport or something?"

"Yeah, soccer," he said, "at Gilberton High. It's kind of my obsession."

"You play soccer at Gilberton? I bet you know my brother. Raúl García?"

"*Hell, yeah,* I know Raúl!"

Raúl García was a scoring machine. He'd never met anyone in his thirteen years of playing soccer who drilled balls into a goal the way Raúl did.

"You're Raúl's sister?" he asked, not trying to mask his surprise. "You don't go to Gilberton, do you?"

He would have remembered seeing this girl.

"No—well, yeah. I'll be starting this year, as a junior. I was at school in Atlanta, but I'm back."

"So what happened with Raúl?" Evan asked. "I heard he was still around."

"His scholarship offers fell through," she said. Thin creases formed across her forehead as she spoke, and she lifted her hand to rub them. "He's here, going to the community college and working for my dad," she said. "He plays soccer over at Grant Park."

It made no sense that Raúl was playing on the torn-up city fields. He was a Division I soccer recruit. He wanted to ask her more, but something about the expression on her face let him know that she didn't want to talk about it. What he really wanted to do was reach out and touch her forehead, to make it smooth again. But he didn't. He just shrugged and said, "That sucks."

"It's not a big deal," she said, forcing a fake smile. "It doesn't stop him from acting like he's the next Ronaldo—God's special gift to the *fútbol* universe."

"Yeah, that sounds about like Raúl," Evan said, smiling. Raúl *was* sort of a cocky bastard when he played for GHS, but he deserved to be.

"He's leading my dad's team to overwhelming victory in the Liga Latina," she said, sarcasm creeping into her voice again. "You know, where all the Mexicans and Central Americans play to bring their hometowns to glory?"

Evan didn't know. He'd never heard of the Liga Latina.

"Alma," a man's stern voice interrupted them.

Evan jumped and stood awkwardly by the truck as Mr. García, the landscaper, came around the corner with a machete in his hand.

The girl threw a nervous glance at Evan and then stepped out of the truck. He felt like a kid caught playing spin the bottle. Not good, considering the man who'd caught them was wielding a very sharp weapon.

"My dad," she said, nodding toward Mr. García.

She and her dad spoke in rapid-fire Spanish. Evan found himself concentrating intently, wishing that he studied Spanish in school instead of French. His friend Conway had convinced him to take French. Before they started at Gilberton High, Conway's older cousin Bo told him the teacher was hot. Madame Jones *was* hot, at first. But then she got pregnant and her ankles went all spongy. When she had the baby, she disappeared. Now he had to suffer through Madame Gillespie.

Yeah, he should have taken Spanish.

He watched as Mr. García turned to walk away and she started to rummage in the bed of the truck.

"So what's that word mean?" he asked, moving close to her again. "The one your dad kept saying? Something that started with 'all'?"

"'*Alma.*' It means 'soul,'" she replied matter-of-factly.

"You and your dad were having some pretty deep conversation," he said.

The girl laughed. "Alma is my name."

"Didn't you say your name was Julia?"

"Uh-huh," she replied slowly.

Then she started talking fast.

"OK, so here's the deal. My name is Alma Julia García-Menendez." This time, the Julia sounded different. It sounded like "hoo-lia."

"Most everyone calls me Alma, but in school or whenever I meet, well, a *güero* like you"—she smiled—"I just use the name Julia, pronounced the English way."

"*A what?*" Evan asked.

"A *güero*—you know, a white boy."

"White boy? Is that, like, an insult?"

"No. It's a statement of fact," Alma answered.

Evan smiled in spite of himself.

"I still don't get it," he said. "Why do you use Julia, if it's not your name?"

"It *is* my name, sort of. It started in elementary school, when my teachers would look at the class roster, try to say Alma, and butcher it. Well, maybe not butcher it, but I couldn't stand the way they made it sound—like a character from *The Flintstones*."

"Wilma!" Evan broke in, proud to have made the connection. "Weeelmaaa," he enunciated.

"Exactly! It drove me crazy. So on the first day of third grade, I took charge of the situation. When my teacher called on me, I told her my name was Julia. Not 'hoo-lia' but Julia, you know, as in Julia Roberts— pretty woman."

She paused and then continued, deadpan, "More information than you needed."

"No, it's cool," said Evan, "but I'm not into nineties hooker films. So, can I call you Alma?"

"You can call me anything you want," she replied, shrugging. "But if you want to call me Alma, you have to learn to pronounce it."

Her face broke into a wide, mocking grin.

"OK, I'm at your mercy," he said. "Teach me."

Alma tried to have him repeat her name, and he thought it sounded pretty damn good, but she was not impressed.

Her father called out in a stern voice from the side yard.

"Listen, I have to start pruning roses or my dad will kill me."

"I get it," he said. "But I'm gonna go inside and get you another cup of coffee—you know, since I spilled yours."

Evan watched as Alma's eyes darted toward the house. The soft edges of her smile fell, leaving her face completely expressionless.

"This is your house?" she asked, looking past him.

"Yeah," he said. "I mean, last I checked."

She bit her lip and glanced down at her shoes. When she looked up, a stony expression had replaced her smile. Evan didn't get what was happening. All he knew was that he missed her smile.

"My dad doesn't let us accept drinks from clients," she said, her tone now lacking any of its earlier playfulness. "Thanks for the offer, though."

Evan could almost see the energy being sucked out of the air between them. He felt lonely, suddenly—which was strange, since she was still standing right beside him. He watched in silence as Alma pulled a pair of dirt-stained gardening gloves from the bed of the truck.

"Thank you again for stopping the truck," she said formally as she turned to walk toward the rose garden.

Without thinking, Evan stepped forward and reached out to touch her shoulder. He stood close to her—too close, probably. Close enough to notice her scent, bright and buttery warm. She smelled like rays of sunshine would, he thought, if they ever carried a scent.

"Hey," he said. "If I come help with the roses, will you teach me how to say your name?" It was a desperate move, but he had to try something. He couldn't let her walk away. Not yet.

She turned back, examining his face carefully. She was all seriousness, so he didn't even try to smile. He just held her gaze for a few seconds and left his hand resting lightly on her shoulder until he saw an almost imperceptible nod of her head.

He'd take that as a yes.

TWO
Drive

Evan tossed a pillow off the bed, glancing at the red marks on his wrists.

Pruning roses was harder than it looked.

He sighed and stood up. His feet shuffled along the carpeted floor, where at least six more pillows were heaped. They were covered in shimmering fabrics that his mom insisted were "complementary on the color wheel." As if he cared. He brushed his teeth, pulled on a pair of soccer shorts, and headed toward the kitchen, taking the stairs two at a time.

His mom leaned against the breakfast bar in her workout clothes.

"Hey, Mom. What's up?" he asked.

"Well, my goodness, *you* are!" she chirped with exaggerated shock pulling through her Southern drawl.

"Yeah, couldn't sleep. What *is* that?" he asked, nodding toward a half-filled glass.

"A Hoodia Cactus Smoothie—great for burning fat. Want to try some?"

"I'll pass," he said. The last thing Evan needed was to lose weight.

Evan glanced at his mother's toned arm—skin sagging slightly, age spots beginning to appear. She was already impossibly thin.

"Evan, pumpkin, while I've got you here—"

"Mom, *please* stop calling me pumpkin," Evan said. By some miracle, his hair wasn't orange anymore, and he'd prefer to forget that it ever was.

"Well, all right, sugar. I'll do my best," she said. "Now, I need to ask you about the menu for the party. Should I order Caesar salads from the club?"

"It doesn't matter, Mom," Evan said absently. "Anything's fine."

"Oh, Evan," his mom said, letting out a long sigh, "sometimes you can be just like your father."

Evan sank onto a stool. Not this again. She shot him the look that, without a single word, convinced him to do stupid things like stop at a flower shop and pick up centerpieces for a luncheon—things that seventeen-year-olds didn't do for their mothers. Except for Evan, apparently.

If he had to blame this ridiculous behavior on something, it would be a dinner conversation at the end of his sophomore year. His parents were about to host a charity ball, and Evan's mom was stressing about who should sit where.

His dad looked up from an empty plate. "BeBe," he announced, "I couldn't care less where people sit. When is this party, anyway?"

"Honey, it's next Saturday. You *know* this."

Evan's dad pulled out his phone and punched some buttons.

"Looks like you'll have an extra seat," he said. "I'll be at a conference."

Evan still remembered the way his mom's entire body had stiffened. Her face took on a strange, forced smile.

"Oh, sweetheart," she had said, all sweetness, "you'll just have to miss the conference."

Evan's dad stood up from the table.

"For fifteen years, I have endured your charity events," he said.

He actually used the word "endured."

"But someone in this family needs to work," he announced. "How else will you write those thousand-dollar-a-seat checks?"

They all knew that Evan's mom had inherited plenty of money. No one needed his dad's paycheck.

Evan had wanted to pummel his dad. Instead, he took a tip from his mom's playbook.

He turned calmly to his mother and put a big happy grin on his face. "Hey, Mom. If you need a date, I'm free. What's it for?"

"The local Boys and Girls Club," she replied, a few tears running down her face, forming subtle streaks through pressed powder. "They're raising money for a youth scholarship program for underprivileged students."

"Count me in," he said.

"I'll have the most charming and handsome date at the party," she replied, standing to clear plates from the table.

That was sort of the beginning of the end.

After that night, Evan's dad quietly boycotted the charity network, and Evan started his new routine: dressing up in his tuxedo, enduring hours of soft jazz music, and helping his mom bid in live auctions for ugly art and random trips they always forgot to take.

At least he got to flirt with the cute waitresses. Sometimes they even snuck him drinks to numb the pain.

Evan was nothing like his father. And he would do just about anything to prove it, no matter how boring or painful.

"Definitely order a Caesar salad from the club," Evan said. "Those salads are good."

"That sounds just perfect, pumpkin, and don't forget brunch with your uncle Sexton next Sunday. He wants to talk to you about college."

Evan filled a glass with cold water and chugged it, pretending not to notice she'd called him pumpkin, pretending not to care that his uncle always stood in for his absent dad.

———

Alma should have said "No." A simple "No, thanks," and she would have avoided the agony of the past several days.

"*¡Hija!*" her *tía* Pera whispered sharply in her ear.

Alma bowed her head, trying to look reverent, as she joined her aunts in praying the rosary.

"*Dios te salve María, llena eres de gracia . . .*"

Why had she done it? Why had she let Evan come back to help her in the garden?

Tía Pera grabbed Alma's hand and held it firmly.

Alma squeezed her eyes shut. "*El Señor es contigo.*"

Every time she closed her eyes, she saw Evan, with his deep-green eyes intensely focused and his smooth chin thrust slightly forward, struggling to pronounce her name.

"*Bendita tú eres entre todas las mujeres . . .*"

She saw him take a long chug of cold water and then throw his head back. That was how she had taught him. She had him say "ahhh," after quenching his thirst with water, and then told him to follow it with the simple sounds of "ll-ma." It worked beautifully.

"*Y bendito es el fruto en tu vientre, Jésus.*"

She was supposed to be praying for the repose of her mother's soul, but she couldn't even hear the words tumbling from her mouth. All she heard was Evan repeating her name while his hands gripped the rose-bushes, their thorns tearing red lines into the soft flesh of his wrists. She told him to wear gloves, but he said he didn't have any. He refused the extra pair she offered from her dad's toolbox.

"*Santa María, Madre de Dios . . .*"

She smiled, remembering how clueless he had been, trying to chop the roses off just below the bud. He leaned into her as she explained how to follow the stem to new growth and cut carefully at an angle, just above it. And then she watched, warmth spreading through her, as he ran his fingers gently down the stem.

"*Ruega por nosotros pecadores . . .*"

Ay, Dios, she thought. Alma didn't think her mother really needed help getting out of purgatory, and even if she did, Alma's stiff prayers couldn't possibly offer much.

"*Ahora y en la hora de nuestra muerte.*"

Tía Dolores opened her eyes and shot a withering glance toward Alma.

"*Amen.*"

Tía Pera and *Tía* Dolores continued mumbling unintelligible prayers. Alma squeezed her eyes shut, trying not to see so clearly the way that droplets of water had clung to Evan's slightly parted lips, and trying not to imagine tasting them. Was this a venial sin? God, she hoped not. Alma hated going to confession.

The three of them were kneeling on the hard wood floor of their living room. They all faced the little home altar that was set up in the corner. It had dozens of prayer cards and statues, but the centerpiece was Our Lady of *La Leche*—a statue of the Virgin Mary breastfeeding the baby Jesus. Every family had a favorite, but for most Mexicans it was Guadalupe (the queen of Mexico and empress of the Americas), or *La Virgen de San Juan de los Lagos* if they were from the north. Not Alma's *tías.* They had a special thing for *La Leche*, this obscure *Virgencita* from St. Augustine, Florida, that no one else had ever heard of.

Alma prayed to her sometimes, too—just kind of spontaneously, when things got bad. After all, the Virgin's name was Spanglish, and she was sort of a Spanish immigrant to Florida. According to legend, she came over with the first Spanish settlers. She hung out in her little chapel while the city around her went from being Spanish to British to Spanish to American. Alma figured, with a history like that, Our Lady of *La Leche* probably knew what it felt like to not really have a country. She should be given some special title like the Patroness of the Immigrant's Daughter, or the Queen of the Kids Stuck in Between.

But Alma didn't get the point of these stiff, old-fashioned prayers. It had been fourteen years since her mom left this world, and every year, near the anniversary of her death, Alma's aunts guilted her into praying the entire rosary together for nine straight days. They wanted to be sure her mom would make it to heaven. Alma barely remembered her mom, but everyone described her as a saint, so she was pretty sure her mom should be comfortably ensconced in heaven by now. Even so, Alma always went along with the prayers. She probably just did it because she was afraid of *Tía* Dolores. Or maybe it was because *Tía* Pera knew exactly how to entice her out of bed: with the smell of freshly brewing coffee.

Wiping the sweat from his eyes, Evan glanced down at his stopwatch.

1:32:15

He had been running for an hour and a half, and the summer sun was high in the hazy sky. He willed his body to turn onto another dead-end road and pumped his arms as he sprinted up a hill. When he reached the top, his eyes scanned the pavement. Neither of the two landscaping trucks parked on this road was Mr. García's.

About thirty minutes into his run, Evan began to realize—with more than a little amusement—that he was casing his own neighborhood. Surrounding his house were hilly dead-end streets, each wandering onto a finger of land that jutted into Lake Lanier. Typically, he stuck to the main road, which hugged the edge of the golf course. It seemed pointless to wander down a bunch of dead-end streets and then have to turn around and go back. This morning, though, he turned onto every road he passed, searching for the red Ford truck.

As he watched steam rise off of the asphalt soaked by a broken sprinkler, Evan wished he had started this run at six thirty instead of ten thirty.

He jogged toward the broken sprinkler and paused underneath, letting the cool streams of water run over his head and seep into his sweat-soaked shirt. Revived, Evan shook the excess water out of his hair and turned to go home. Then he saw it. The red Ford pickup was headed straight for him.

***

Alma squinted and stared ahead. Was that Evan Roland stepping away from the sprinkler her dad had been called to repair? He turned around and her stomach lurched. Yes, it was Evan. And yes, he was sopping wet, with his shirt plastered to his chest and shaggy hair falling across his forehead, sending streams of water down his flushed face.

She gathered herself and called out, "Hey, Evan. There's not a shower in that big fancy house of yours?"

Laughing, Evan walked toward her window. "Good morning, Mr. García," he said. "Good morning, Aaaahhhlllma."

"*Ya es tarde,*" grumbled Alma's father.

Alma glanced toward the clock on the dashboard. Her dad was right. It was almost twelve fifteen.

"Man, it's hot today, huh, Mr. García?"

Evan was trying to make small talk with her dad—a lost cause.

"Yes, it is," her dad replied curtly, stepping out of the truck.

"Get that boy some cold Gatorade from the back of the truck, Alma," her dad said in Spanish. "He looks like he's about to pass out."

Evan looked pretty amazing as far as Alma was concerned. She went around to the truck bed and dug in the cooler as her dad grabbed a toolbox and made his way to the backyard.

"Do you want a Gatorade?" she asked.

"Yeah, thanks," Evan replied absently.

When she came back, Evan was holding one of her books. She always brought books to work. Reading was an easy way to pass the time as they drove across town, from one client to another.

He turned the book toward her and pointed at the cover. There was a charcoal drawing of a young woman with downcast eyes and a white flower in her hair.

"I like the picture. She looks like you," Evan said, glancing up at her.

"That's sort of offensive, Evan," she replied, scowling. "That girl's from the South Pacific. I'm from southern Mexico."

"Didn't mean to offend, Miss García," Evan replied, throwing his hands into the air in a gesture of surrender.

"'*Coming of Age in Samoa*,'" he read from the cover. "So Samoa is in the South Pacific?"

"Yeah."

"And why, exactly, are you reading about Samoa?"

"One of my teachers from North Atlanta High let me borrow it," she said. "It's written by a famous anthropologist."

"A famous *what*?" Evan asked.

Since he was grinning in a way that made butterflies rush through her gut, Alma wasn't so focused on his intelligence at this particular moment. Trying to hold herself together, she took the book and opened it to a dog-eared page.

"Read this part," she commanded.

"Really?" he asked.

"Yeah, really. I mean, unless you want to stay ignorant."

"Ouch," he replied.

He grabbed the book and leaned against the door of the truck. He read slowly, " 'In our own civilization the individual is beset with difficulties which we are likely to ascribe to fundamental human traits. When we speak about the difficulties of childhood and adolescence, we are thinking of them as unavoidable periods of adjustment through which everyone has to pass.' "

Thankfully, Alma had read the lines several times before, since she was completely distracted by the way his hands grasped the book. She imagined touching the thick veins that ran along his forearm.

He looked up at her, squinting.

"OK, so *why* are you reading this?" he asked.

It was a legitimate question. The book wasn't exactly *Gossip Girl*.

"It's interesting," Alma replied, shrugging. "Just keep reading."

" 'We feel, therefore, grateful to Miss Mead' . . . blah, blah, blah." His finger skimmed along the page and then he picked up reading again. " 'The results of her painstaking investigation confirm that much of what we ascribe to human nature is no more than a reaction to the restraints put upon us by our civilization. Franz Boas, 1928.' "

He looked up from the book.

"That's anthropology," Alma said, "studying different cultures to see how they vary. Margaret Mead thought learning about other cultures helps us better understand our own."

"Just to be clear, Alma," he said, grinning a perfect grin, "is this book saying there's no such thing as adolescence?" He ran his hand slowly through his hair and stepped toward her. "That would have been great to know three years ago, when I had pimples and all the girls were a foot taller than me."

Alma felt herself blushing as he came closer. She didn't believe Evan's skin had ever been pimply.

"No," replied Alma, stepping back to lean against the truck. "It exists, but it changes in different times and places." Evan moved toward her again, which made her heart start thumping fast.

"I mean, look at us," she said, hoping that her voice wasn't shaking. "We're standing here talking without a chaperone, which wouldn't have happened a couple of generations ago."

They both looked at her dad, who was now crouched in front of the sprinkler but watching them like a hawk about to swoop in for the kill.

"Well, in my case, not exactly," Alma said, shrugging. "But I'm sure *you* can hang out with girls without a chaperone."

She felt a heaviness in her gut as she saw her dad stand up from the sprinkler. "*Ahorita vámonos, hija,*" he called out, heading through a gate and toward the back of the house.

"Dad fixed the sprinkler. We've gotta go."

Her chest pulled tight.

"Alma," he said, looking directly into her eyes.

She had to look away.

"I'm having a ski party tomorrow. Or I guess I should say my mom is having a party for me. But she won't be hanging around. She just likes planning parties for other people. Can you come?"

She knew what she had to say, but her mouth would not form the words.

Evan filled the awkward silence. "I can pick you up."

"I have to work," she said.

"It's the last weekend of summer, Alma. Can't you get an afternoon off?"

"Not really," she replied, shrugging. "I need the money."

"So, come after work," he said.

Alma had to find a way to explain.

"The truth is, Evan, there's no way my dad will give me permission to come to a party at your house. Ever."

"Seriously?" he asked.

Alma nodded once.

"Could I maybe call you," he said, grinning, "or is that not allowed either?"

Alma's eyes darted toward the backyard. No sign of her dad yet.

"Do you have your phone?" she asked.

Evan shrugged, stretched out his arms, and looked down at his still damp body.

Alma didn't dare follow his gaze. She already felt her cheeks turning red.

"Dumb question," she said, turning to rummage in the truck's glove compartment. She found a pencil and an old Walmart receipt. She looked once more toward the backyard and then scribbled her number on the back.

"Text before you call."

Evan looked down at the phone number written neatly on the paper.

"You have a cell phone?" he asked.

"Of course, idiot. Everyone has a cell phone."

Evan shrugged and bit his lip.

"But unlike you," she said, "I have to pay for mine."

"How do you know I don't pay for my phone?" he asked.

Alma shot him a withering look.

"Yeah, OK," he said.

Alma stepped sideways, her back still against the truck. She was afraid of the way her body might react if she let him any closer.

"Do me a favor."

"What kind of favor?" He leaned in toward her and rested his hand against the truck. His nearness produced another strange sinking sensation in her gut. She sucked in a deep breath, grabbed the wheel hub, and replied.

"You can text me whenever you want to, but don't butcher the English language by doing annoying things like using the number two for 'to,' got it?"

Evan chuckled. "Right. Complete sentences, I promise."

Alma heard the back gate swing open.

"Put it somewhere, Evan."

His eyebrows arched as he shot her a puzzled look.

"The phone number. Now."

Evan nodded once and tucked the scrap of paper into his waistband.

THREE
Night Swimming

Evan was standing with his friend Logan at the far end of the pool when he saw the French door open. He watched as two amazing legs carried Alma toward him. Evan took in every inch of them, from her ankles all the way up to a very revealing black bikini. Set off against the jet-black fabric, her slim body was the color of milky coffee. Her dark, shining hair flowed down to the middle of her back, but a few strands fell forward to brush her perfect breasts. Her smooth stomach moved perceptibly with each long breath. And her cheeks blazed red with shame.

"God, Logan, stop gawking," he heard Logan's girlfriend, Caroline, say.

Without thinking, Evan set off toward Alma, pulling his T-shirt off over his head. He caught Alma's gaze, training his eyes steadily on hers as he passed by groups of friends gathered around the pool. Arriving next to her, Evan resisted the overwhelming temptation to look down at her vulnerable, almost naked body. Instead, he held her gaze and blindly pressed his T-shirt toward where he thought her hand might be.

"You look a little cold," he heard himself say roughly.

As soon as he said it, he knew he sounded like a complete idiot. It was August in Georgia.

"Thanks, Evan," Alma replied, shrugging his shirt on. "Uh, your mom, she, uh . . ."

"I get it," Evan broke in. "She's not exactly the one-piece type."

After his run the other day, Evan had made the mistake of mentioning Alma to his mom. She immediately decided that it was her personal responsibility to ensure Alma's social success at Gilberton High, and that Evan's ski party would be the perfect place to begin. Evan tried explaining how strict Alma's father was, but that didn't keep his mom from accosting Alma and Mr. García an hour earlier. Evan and his mom were driving home from the grocery store with supplies for the party when they saw Alma and her dad working at a house down the road. Evan's mom launched herself from her Escalade and demanded that Alma be allowed to come to the party, while Evan watched from the driver's seat.

Alma explained that she had to work, but Evan's mom said she should "live a little." When Alma said she didn't even have a bathing suit, Evan's mom said she had dozens that would look great on "that cute little body." Alma's dad, clearly frustrated, gave in to his client's wishes. He said that Alma could go to the party as long as she got home by eight thirty. *Eight thirty.* Did that even count as a curfew? It was more like bedtime for a kindergartener.

The whole thing was humiliating for Evan. He couldn't even manage to get out of the Escalade, much less come to Alma's aid. So now here he was, desperately wanting a girl who was wearing his mom's bikini.

Gross.

Alma pulled her hair out from the neck of his shirt and let it fall forward. "She even made me take my hair down," Alma said, throwing her hands into the air. "I was completely at her mercy."

"When my mom sets her mind to something, there's not much you *can* do," Evan said, trying his hardest to stop imagining what it might feel like to touch her body underneath his own shirt.

Evan reached out to take her hand. "Let's go skiing."

Evan led her onto the dock, where a dozen people she didn't know were climbing into ski boats. She watched as all of these strangers, presumably students at her new school, casually distributed themselves into boats.

Do teenagers own boats? Alma wondered. Evan led her onto his boat, where two other people were already rummaging around under the seats for life jackets. An athletic-looking girl with long brown hair threw her one.

"I'm Caroline," she said, "and that's Logan." She motioned toward a short, muscular guy with a shaved head. He had his back to Alma, and was untying ropes from the boat. Hearing his name, he turned and grinned.

"*¡Bienvenidos!*" he said in terrible, Southern-accented Spanish.

"Just ignore him when he acts like an idiot," Caroline said. "That's what I do."

Evan got behind the wheel and started the engine. Just as he was backing out, an amazingly beautiful girl came running down the dock.

"Evan, hon! Wait for me!" she called out.

The girl reached the edge of the dock and, without hesitating, leapt gracefully across the water and toward the boat. She was wearing nothing but a bright-red string bikini. Her sandy-blond hair bounced and shone like a model's in a shampoo commercial.

Evan pulled her safely onto the boat, and she collapsed into the passenger seat.

"Thanks, sweetheart," she said to Evan.

"This is Alma," Evan said, nodding in Alma's direction. "She'll be starting at Gilberton next week. And this is Mary Catherine," he said, grabbing onto the beautiful girl's shoulder and squeezing hard. "She's my perpetually late neighbor."

"But he loves me anyway!" Mary Catherine proclaimed. Then she smiled, revealing perfect teeth to match her perfect body.

Were they flirting? Alma felt a tightness in her chest, knowing that she was no competition for this girl.

The engine rumbled, and the boat lurched forward from the dock. Evan grasped Alma's arm to steady her and then pulled her toward him. "Ready to learn how to drive?"

"You're mocking me," she called out above the noise of the engine.

"I don't think you even need a license to drive a boat," Evan said. "Plus, no brakes, so we're safe."

Keeping one hand on the steering wheel, he wedged her body in front of his and guided her hand to the throttle. "Do you want to go faster?"

"No." The wind pressed her back against him, and she felt the heat of his chest through the T-shirt.

"Are you scared?" His lip brushed her ear as he spoke.

"Yes," she said. Her body was off balance, as if the floor of the boat were shifting under her.

"Get over it," he replied, lifting her hand gently and placing it on the throttle.

Together, their hands guided the throttle forward. She tried looking across the lake, in the direction that he was steering, but all she noticed was his hand on hers. The floor kept shifting. She wondered if this was what it felt like to be drunk.

He slipped out from behind her.

"I'm gonna dig out the skis. Just keep going straight, Alma. It's easy."

She grasped the wheel hard to avoid falling back. The boat skittered over the water, and the wind fused Evan's T-shirt to her practically bare skin. Alma tried hard to ignore the dull ache spreading at the pit of her stomach.

After a few minutes, Evan took the wheel. Caroline and Logan both dived into the water and began to swim fast as Evan tossed a ski rope in their direction.

"This should be entertaining," he said as they wrestled with their slalom skis.

"Entertaining?" Alma asked.

"Yeah, they'll both show off."

"Are they, uh, a couple?"

"Most of the time. They fight all the time and break up every couple of months."

Evan shoved the throttle forward and the boat lurched.

"Logan gets bored easily," he said. "He's always looking for a rush."

Logan and Caroline both popped out of the water, crisscrossing each other as they leapt and dived over the wake.

"So they just break up for fun?"

"Yeah, I think it runs in his blood. Everybody says his dad was the same, back in the day. He stole boats and stuff, just for the hell of it." He shrugged and continued, "Which is weird, since he's the sheriff now."

The sheriff. Evan said it like it was nothing, like he was describing the color of Logan's dad's car, or his height—not like he knew this man had the power to throw people in jail and keep them there.

Evan gestured toward Logan and Caroline and winced. "That's gotta hurt."

Caroline was spinning in rapid circles as Logan did strange contortions with his arm.

Maybe, Alma thought, they were all so used to being around powerful people that they didn't even notice it anymore. Maybe they never had.

"Come back here, Alma!" Mary Catherine called from the back of the boat. "I can't hear what y'all are saying and I'm lonely."

Alma glanced at Evan and shrugged. She made her way back and settled into a bucket seat next to Mary Catherine.

Alma wasn't sure how to make conversation with Mary Catherine. She seemed so unapproachable—this girl who wore a bikini confidently, like she was hanging in comfy sweats. But within moments, it became clear that Mary Catherine—or M.C., as Evan called her—was not your typical Southern belle.

"So, when did you and Evan start hooking up?" she asked.

For starters, she was excruciatingly blunt.

"Uh, we're just sort of friends," Alma replied, shrugging.

"Alma, honey," she said, "I've known that boy forever, and the way he looks at you, he doesn't wanna be your friend."

M.C. let out a deep, bellowing howl that sounded like it should come from a balding white guy with a beer gut. Alma was so surprised by M.C.'s laugh that she forgot to be embarrassed.

"OK." Alma shrugged. "Maybe we're not exactly friends. But we're *not* hooking up."

"Makes sense," Mary Catherine responded, sort of talking to herself. "Evan doesn't really hook up. Plus, I would have known."

Confused and desperate to change the subject, Alma asked, "So how did you two meet?"

"Meet?" M.C. asked. "We've been neighbors for as long as either of us can remember. I mean, we used to play doctor together! I was the doctor. I always made Evan be the nurse."

Mary Catherine bellowed again.

"So when you and Evan do hook up," she said, "you can thank me for his gentle, nurturing touch."

Now Alma was blushing.

"You mean, you and Evan were, uh . . ."

"Together? Lord, no. He's like a baby brother to me, Alma. I think I went through puberty something like four years before he did."

Alma and Mary Catherine turned to look at Evan, his perfectly toned arms casually gripping the steering wheel, his broad shoulders gleaming in the sun.

"My baby's all grown up," Mary Catherine continued. "Now, he's what my grandmomma calls a 'tall drink of water.' "

They both laughed, catching Evan's attention.

"What are you ladies talking about back there?" he asked.

"Nothing that concerns you, Ev, sweetheart," Mary Catherine replied. "You just drive the boat."

"Not unless Alma gets back up here to finish her driving lesson," Evan said, reaching his arm out toward her.

Mary Catherine laughed and nudged her out of the seat.

"You heard him," she called out. "You better get on up there, darlin', because I'm sure as hell not driving."

Alma closed her eyes and stood up slowly, her head spinning and her legs quivering.

He took her hand and pulled her body back toward the wheel, and she realized, finally, the meaning of the word "swoon."

When they pulled up to the dock, it was already dusk. The other boats were tied securely, and everyone else was getting ready to leave for a free concert on the square—some country band Alma had never heard of. She and Evan started to gather towels and drinks from the floor of the boat, but M.C., Logan, and Caroline just jumped out and began making their way toward the house.

"Hey!" Evan called out. "Thanks for all your help cleaning up. I really appreciate it!"

"Come on, man! We already missed the opening act," Logan replied. "We'll clean up later."

"I'll catch up to you there," Evan said, glancing at the empty cans and plates of half-eaten food scattered around the dock. "My mom will kill me if we leave her dock looking like this."

As they watched everyone else head up the hill, Evan sighed. "My friends are useless."

Alma figured it was best not to comment on his accurate observation.

"Alma, I know it's getting late, but can you help me get the boat out of the water before I take you home? It's a pain to do alone."

"Just show me what to do," she said.

They worked quietly to clean the dock and hose down the boat. Evan hoisted it into the boathouse while Alma held the bow steady.

"I think this boathouse is bigger than my house," Alma said as they watched the boat rise.

"Yeah, there's sort of a keeping-up-with-the-Joneses mentality when it comes to boathouses—the bigger, the better."

"I'd say that's a general principle around here, wouldn't you?" asked Alma. "I mean, have you noticed the massive SUVs?"

Evan laughed heartily. "You mean, like the two in our driveway? Yeah, I've noticed."

They both glanced around the dock, looking for something else to do.

"I guess we're done," Evan said.

Alma didn't want to be finished. She wasn't ready for it to end.

"So, do you want to see the upstairs?" Evan asked.

Apparently, he wasn't ready either.

They walked up a wooden staircase to the second floor of the boat-house. Evan casually flipped a switch to reveal a screened porch encircled with twinkling white lights. He pushed the door open with one hand and lightly touched Alma's waist with the other, guiding her through. The porch was huge, with cushy lounge chairs and tables arranged in groups. Evan led her in the direction of a bed-like lounger, and Alma felt her hands begin to tremble. What, exactly, was he expecting from her?

"Evan," she said tentatively. She wasn't sure she could handle getting horizontal with him. She could barely manage to keep breathing when his hand touched hers.

He turned to look at her, grinning, and then leapt onto the lounge chair.

"See that trap door?" he asked, standing on the lounger and pointing his finger to the ceiling. "That takes us to my favorite spot. It was sort of my floating tree house when I was a kid."

Relieved that she would have a bit more time to pull herself together, Alma felt the tension release from her shoulders. She hopped onto the lounge chair.

"Just pull the cord," he said.

The trap door released easily, bringing with it a sturdy rope ladder. Touching the small of her back, he gently nudged her up the ladder and onto the roof. She emerged—breathless again—into a small alcove, surrounded by fragrant flowering vines overflowing from huge terra-cotta pots. The alcove had a panoramic view of the lake, rolling gently under the evening sky.

Evan stood next to her, so close that she could feel his arm warm against hers. They both looked out across the lake, saying nothing. It felt right just to be quiet next to him, feeling her heart beat strong, watching the darkening sky.

"Do you want to sit down?" Evan asked, breaking the long silence.

"Sure," she said, quietly.

He reached into a wooden bin, pulled out two towels, and spread them onto the roof of the boathouse.

———

Evan watched Alma lie down on a towel and look up at the sky. It was getting late, and Evan knew that he was supposed to take her home, but they were finally alone and he didn't want it to end.

"Thanks for coming today," Evan said, lying next to her but not close enough to touch her. "I'm still sort of mad at my mom, and my friends can be total idiots, but, uh, well . . . it was great to hang out with you."

He wanted to reach out and take her hand, but he didn't.

"I had a great time," she said. "I mean, sort of. At least, I had a great time with you."

"Me, too," he said. It was so quiet that he could hear the water lapping against the dock.

"And I'm the one who owes you thanks," she said. "You rescued me when I arrived at the party—where I knew exactly one person— wearing your mom's skimpy bikini."

Evan turned onto his side and propped his head into his hand.

"So, Alma, I guess I have a confession to make about that," he said, looking directly at her. He couldn't believe he was about to tell her this, but it seemed right. "As soon as I saw your face, I knew that you felt, uh, naked."

"For good reason!" Alma broke in, sitting up. "I mean, does your mom actually wear this thing?"

Evan shrugged. He didn't want to think about that. Ever.

"So, what's the big confession?" she asked, turning to face him directly.

"I guess what I'm trying to say," he said, tracing his finger along the edge of the towel, "is that when I saw you in that doorway, looking so . . . so amazingly beautiful. I mean, your body, Alma. Uh, it's not exactly what you'd expect to find under the baggy shirts and cutoff jeans."

Alma wrapped the towel tighter around her. Evan's heart started to beat fast. He didn't want to screw this up.

"I didn't want anyone else to see it—to see *you*. I wanted to cover you." He felt a flush rise to his cheeks as his gaze fell to the floor. "I think maybe it was some weird jealousy or protectiveness, maybe."

Evan looked up and his eyes met hers. The words tumbled out.

"I don't know. I'm sounding so old-fashioned. It's not that I have a problem with bikinis or anything. I mean I've never even thought about it. But you just—I mean, I just, uh, I just couldn't take them looking at you."

Christ almighty. He was mangling this. He should have kept his mouth shut.

"Were you embarrassed of me?" Alma asked.

"No, Alma, not embarrassed. In awe."

Evan forced his eyes to meet Alma's.

"Did you want to see me? To look at me like that?"

"I could have stared at you for hours," Evan replied, with a strong, steady voice that he didn't even know he had.

—

Alma knelt and let the towel fall from her shoulders. She slowly pulled his T-shirt over her head. As it dropped to the floor, Evan knelt to face her. Alma remained perfectly still and Evan's gaze trailed along her body. Breathing slowly, she took in the honey scent of the flowering vines and the distant hum of a boat's engine. He wasn't touching her, but her skin, so alive, felt as if it were being caressed in a thousand different places. Alma was vulnerable and strong at the same time, not at all like the cowering girl she had been earlier, when all eyes turned toward her at the pool.

His gaze spread heat over every part of her.

After a long while—she had no idea how long—Alma reached out and let the tips of her fingers graze his chin. She lifted his deep-green eyes to meet hers, and saw them, questioning, as his hands gently rested on the bare skin of her waist.

"I want to kiss you, Alma."

Quiere besarme, she thought. *He wants to kiss me.* Had she imagined the words?

Alma leaned in toward him. The space between them lessened, and she felt the warmth rising from Evan's chest. She ached to press her entire body into his.

Breathe, Alma, she told herself silently. *Respira.*

She took in a trembling breath. Brushing her skin softly, his hands fell to her hips. He gripped her body more firmly, as if he sensed how dizzy she suddenly felt. She wrapped her arms around his waist and held on tightly.

"EVAAAN! AOWWLMA! Are you still down there?"

Calling out from the house, Evan's mom broke the lush silence.

Alma turned toward the sound, opening her lips to form a reply, but Evan lifted a hand from her back and pressed his finger against her lips.

"Shhh," he whispered, almost inaudibly. "Let me kiss you."

Quiere besarme, she told herself again. She hadn't imagined it.

His hand slid from her lips to the base of her neck, and he wound his fingers into her hair. She felt her heart thrumming and Evan's breath warm against her face.

Alma closed her eyes.

"ALMA! *¿Dónde estás?*"

"Sweet Jesus!" exclaimed Evan, pulling his hand back so quickly that he tugged her hair from the roots. "Is that your *dad?*"

Alma's eyes shot open, and her hands fell to her side. Evan's body spun toward the house.

"What time is it?" asked Alma urgently.

Evan grabbed his T-shirt from the ground and thrust it once more into her hands. She scrambled to pull his shirt back over her head.

"Ten," Evan said, looking down at his phone. "Oh, good Lord, Alma, I'm so sorry."

Alma leapt up and scrambled down the boathouse stairs. Forcing back hot tears of anger and frustration, she ran toward her father.

FOUR

Trouble

Evan shaded his eyes and tried to focus on the white ball hurtling silently through the air. It curved sharply off to the right and landed in a stand of pine trees.

"Dude, you are *such* a hacker today."

Logan shoved a tee into the ground.

"Yeah, looks like I'm in jail again."

"No worries, man," Logan said, poised for a swing. "We'll press them on nine."

Logan loved to play golf; Evan tolerated it.

When Evan was a kid, he used to come to the driving range with his dad on Saturday afternoons. They stood side by side and sent ball after ball sailing across the wide lawn. Evan's dad gave him the occasional tip, but mostly they just listened to the *thwack* of metal hitting polyurethane.

Logan and his dad sometimes came out to play nine holes with them. It was a good way to break the silence. Their families were close enough that Evan called Sheriff Cronin his uncle even though they weren't related.

All those hours spent on the golf course with Logan, Uncle Buddy, and his dad had made Evan a reasonably good golfer, but he never enjoyed it. Today was particularly painful. Evan felt trapped inside this perfect green landscape. He imagined scaling the high metal fence surrounding the club and landing solidly on his feet, like a cat that narrowly avoids losing one of its nine lives. These nagging thoughts threw Evan's game off, so he kept ending up "in jail"—hooking and slicing his ball into the pines that lined either side of the fairway.

Logan crushed the ball off the tee, and it sailed three hundred yards down the center of the fairway, landing with a soft *thud* just short of the green.

"It's a good thing I'm so on fire today," Logan said. "Maybe I'll save us from losing a boatload of money to those guys."

"Not a chance," Peavey replied, gesturing toward Evan, "not with that duffer."

Peavey and Conway—friends from the neighborhood whom almost everyone called by some version of their last names—were giddy with the thought of all the money they'd win.

Logan hopped in the golf cart, and they sped off to search for Evan's ball, nestled somewhere in the thick carpet of pine needles.

"So, did you and that Mexican girl hook up last night, or what?" Logan asked, stepping out of the cart to search for Evan's ball.

"Her name is Alma, and it's none of your damn business."

Logan looked up and examined Evan's face carefully.

"So this explains your brutally bad golf game," Logan replied, nodding slowly as his face broke into a knowing grin.

"Shut up, man," Evan said as he turned his back to Logan and crouched down, pretending to look for his ball.

"That girl is easy on the eyes," Logan said.

Evan glared at Logan, a sense of protectiveness welling up again.

He spotted the ball nestled against the trunk of a tree and half buried in a clump of twigs.

"Perfect," said Evan sarcastically. "Just perfect."

Evan noticed the familiar sound of a lawn mower coming toward them. Conway jumped out of the cart and watched the mower approach.

"Is this guy gonna stop?" Peavey called out.

"Hey, cut the mower!" Conway yelled.

The mower turned but didn't stop. Instead, it lowered its blades and began to cut the already close-trimmed grass of the fairway.

"What's wrong? No speak-a *inglés*?" Conway yelled again, angry.

They all watched as the mower continued in their direction.

"Y'all just cool. The guy's probably new," Logan said, trying to break the mounting tension. "I'll tell him."

Evan watched in silent disgust as Conway loudly cleared his throat and spat onto the ground. He wanted to say something to Conway, but his throat felt tight, and the words wouldn't come.

Logan jogged toward the mower, and the other three watched silently. The mower's engine immediately cut, and the driver jumped out of his seat to talk with Logan.

After a minute, Logan headed back toward the green.

"He's new," Logan announced. "We got it worked out."

"What?" Peavey asked. "No one told him you're not supposed to mow while people are hitting?"

Logan shrugged and dug into his golf bag.

"Doesn't even speak English," Conway said.

"Jesus, Conway. He spoke English fine," Logan said.

Conway cupped his hands around his mouth and yelled in the direction of the mower. "Go back to Mexico," he called out, "and mow your own goddamned grass."

"Quit being such an asshole," Logan said, shoving Conway back into his cart.

Peavey leaned back in the cart and laughed like an idiot.

Why could Logan say it when all Evan could do was stand there and fume in silence?

"Well, boys," Logan announced, clearly trying to lighten the mood, "no more putting it off. You're about to get your little white asses kicked clear down to Tifton."

———

Alma filled a glass with cold water from the tap and chugged it. Glimpsing her reflection in the kitchen window, she sighed and placed the glass on the counter. Her face was smeared with mud and sweat. She grabbed a kitchen towel and wiped off the grime. She'd been working since dawn, and was only halfway through the grueling list of chores that her dad had given as punishment. She glanced out at the lawn she'd just finished weeding. At least she had that behind her.

"Ooooh, you are in TROUBLE!"

Alma turned to see her cousin Selena behind her, still wearing her yellow SpongeBob pajamas.

"Mind your own business, Selena."

"I know what you did. I heard Uncle Lalo talking to *Mami* about it before he went to work."

Alma was tempted to ask whether Raúl had been there to hear it. If her brother knew, there would be more hell to pay when he got back from work, and too many questions that she wouldn't know how to answer.

"Please, Selena. Just go back to your TV show."

Selena's sister, Isa, called in from the other room, "Did you kiss him?"

Alma felt a warm blush rise to her cheeks as her lips recalled the tug toward Evan's. But then she remembered the harsh voice of her father, tearing them apart.

"Enough questions," she said to her cousins. "It's none of your business."

Selena huffed, shoved her hands onto her hips, and spun away.

Alma walked to the living room, where Isa was sprawled on the couch, eating Doritos from a large bag.

"Why don't you make yourself useful and feed the dog, Isa?"

"You're not my mother," Isa said angrily. "Plus, I fed Pelé yesterday. It's somebody else's turn."

In Isa's thirteen-year-old mind, it was always somebody else's turn.

Alma opened the cabinet under the kitchen sink and pulled out a bucket and some soap. She dug around, looking for the big yellow sponge that her dad used to wash his Bronco.

How was it possible that the best night of her life could be followed by this day? She probably should be grateful that her dad hadn't woken her up with her bags already packed and thrown her in a bus headed for her *abuela*'s house in Mexico.

The house phone rang. Knowing her cousins wouldn't get up to answer, Alma dropped the bucket and ran to get it.

"*¿Bueno?*"

"Alma?"

"Mrs. King? How did you know I was back?"

She felt her heart expand, and a smile made its way across her face.

"I saw your brother at the Dollar General."

"I'm sorry," Alma said. "I mean, you worked so hard to get me to North Atlanta, and now I'm back where I started."

"Good Lord, child. You had two years of excellent schooling. You're coming back to GHS with a perfect grade point average. Don't you *dare* go telling me that it was all for nothin'!"

Oh, how Alma loved Mrs. King.

"So, how are you?" Alma asked.

"Bored to tears, that's how I am. The county finally forced me to retire."

"What?" How could they force Mrs. King to retire? She was the best middle school counselor ever. "I bet they'll be begging you to come back after the first day, Mrs. King."

"Oh, I reckon they'll muddle along without me."

Alma wasn't so sure.

"On the bright side," Mrs. King continued, "I have more time for *you*."

"For *me*?" Alma asked.

"I have a plan——"

Another plan. Maybe this one actually would work.

"——to get you into college, and we're gonna find you a big ol' scholarship."

Alma loved this plan. "I'm all ears."

"Can you meet me tomorrow?" Mrs. King asked.

"Yes, ma'am. I mean, I have to ask my dad, but I think it will be OK. Can we meet after church?"

"That sounds just fine. I'll pick you up at Holy Cross."

"OK, sure," Alma said. "And Mrs. King?"

"Yes, sweetheart?"

"Thanks."

"Oh, good heavens, child," Mrs. King replied. "It's me should be thanking you. The good Lord knew I needed a project somethin' awful. So he brought you on back home to me."

"Then I guess I should thank the good Lord," Alma said, laughing. And then, just for old times' sake, she threw in some Spanish.

"*Hasta mañana*," she said.

"Haabsta mayntanya," Mrs. King replied.

She always begged Alma to teach her Spanish phrases, but that woman was a lost cause.

FIVE
Dream in the Desert

Cold flesh pressed against her cheek. The distant, droning noise came closer. Metal sliced through air. Dogs barked as a blinding light cut through the sky. Sand pelted against her exposed skin—searing, burning.

The men leapt from a helicopter and lunged toward her, arms outstretched, heavy guns dangling from their shoulders. The dark-eyed man pulled her close, pressing her body against his chest. His uniform chafed against her hot skin. Into the heat that enveloped her, Alma screamed a silent scream.

"*Alma, Alma, despiértate, hija.*"

Alma flailed, pushing away the heat of the man's hands—clinging to the cold.

"*Es un sueño, hijita. Es un sueño. Solamente un sueño . . .*"

Alma shot up in bed, disoriented. She flung herself away from the arms that encircled her. But these were not the arms of the dark-eyed man. It was her aunt, begging her to wake up, assuring her it was just a dream.

"*Ay, pobrecita,*" her *tía* Pera said, grasping Alma's shoulders. "*¿El mismo sueño?*"

"*Sí, Tía*. No big deal."

"I wish you would tell me, *hija* . . ."

"What? About the dream? Why would I tell you?"

"*No sé, tal vez . . .*"

"*Tía* Pera," Alma said, sitting up on the edge of the bed, "dreams are just the random firing of neurons. Nothing more, nothing less."

Tía Pera raised her eyebrows. "If they're so random, then why do you keep having the same one, *hija*? Tell me that, *sabelotodo*."

Her aunt was calling her a know-it-all, which she probably deserved.

"We're going to be late for church," Alma said dryly.

Tía Pera glanced at the phone on Alma's bedside table and let out a squeak.

"*Tienes razón, hija,*" she said. "We have to pick up your *tía* Dolores from the plant on the way. *Ya nos espera.*"

Alma jumped out of bed and began to dress quickly. If *Tía* Dolores waited at the plant for even a moment longer than she had to, they would all suffer.

Alma's aunt Dolores believed that all their relatives owed her their lives since she was one of the first to get a job at the poultry plant. Over the years, *Tía* Dolores had scored jobs there for most of her family members, which the family perceived as fortunate. They needed jobs, and the work at Silver Ribbon offered steady pay. She would never tell her family this, but Alma thought it sounded awful. She just couldn't imagine pulling apart dead chickens all day. Or, even worse, chasing live ones. Her cousins who worked as chicken catchers spent all night scrambling after those birds—apparently they were more docile at night, but her cousins still came home in the mornings with bruised knees and less than a hundred dollars pay. No matter how desperate she got for work, she would *never* agree to work at Silver Ribbon. Never.

As Alma tugged on her jeans, *Tía* Pera shook Isa.

"*¡Apúrate, hija!* Hurry up!"

Not wanting to stick around for the theatrics of her thirteen-year-old cousin, Alma grabbed her phone and headed toward the kitchen.

A text:

It's Evan. I miss you (but definitely not U).

Swoon. Again.

"*Hija*, let's go," her *tía* called from the front door.

Alma moved through the kitchen in a daze until *Tía* Pera grabbed her arm and yanked her toward the car.

Spooning a huge pile of grits onto his plate, Evan glanced toward Willis, hard at work in his puffy chef's hat and white uniform.

"One western omelet for our soccer star!" Willis called out cheerfully as he slid a four-egg omelet onto Evan's plate.

Willis knew everything about Evan and his family, down to the minute details of their favorite omelet ingredients: cheddar cheese, but not too much; two slices of crumbled bacon, extra crispy; red and green peppers. Evan liked Willis, but truthfully he knew virtually nothing about him.

"You're holdin' up my line, boy!" Willis called out, teasing.

Evan stepped back as Willis moved efficiently on to the next omelet.

Weaving his way through the crowded room, he wished, for a moment, that he and his rapidly cooling western omelet could become invisible. It always bugged him that Sunday brunch at the club seemed—despite the fantastic grits and expertly prepared omelets—to be more about chatting with the people at surrounding tables than eating. "Evan, my boy!" Mr. Watson's booming voice dispelled his fantasy. "How are you this morning?"

"Great," Evan replied. "I'm looking forward to graduating."

"You planning to follow your uncle Sexton to Wake or your daddy to Washington and Lee?"

"I'm not sure . . ."

"Well," Mr. Watson broke in, his face broadening into a wide grin, "if you decide to aim for a *superior* school, my offer's still open to write you a letter for Vandy."

"Thanks, Mr. Watson. I'll keep it in mind."

"The dean up there is an old tennis buddy of mine."

"Great," Evan said as he glanced involuntarily toward his heap of cooling grits.

"Well, go on, son. Don't keep your uncle waiting," Mr. Watson said, shooing him along with his hand.

"Uh, enjoy your breakfast," Evan replied, turning toward his table.

Evan finally sat across from his uncle Sexton. Evan's uncle was a U.S. senator. He spent most of his time in DC, but whenever he was back in Gilberton, he made a point of meeting Evan for brunch at the club. That was pretty cool of him since approximately ten thousand people sought a meeting with him every time he crossed over the Georgia state line.

"So what's the plan, son?"

Evan didn't have to ask for clarification. He knew this was to be another college talk. He decided to ease into it.

"I'm seeing some real interest from Wake Forest, which is great, and also from Chapel Hill. I'm pretty sure Georgia and Auburn are safety schools. The coaches like me."

"Well, that's just fantastic, son. I'll go on and call John Stapleton. He's a big alum at Wake. And I've got about a dozen Tar Heels up in DC that I'll get to put in a good word."

"That's great, Uncle Sexton," Evan said. But it wasn't. If a dozen people wrote a letter, he'd be expected to accept an offer.

"What about your daddy's school?

"W and L? Uh, it's too small, and, uh, the soccer program . . ."

"No apologies needed."

Evan took a deep breath and launched into the hard part.

"Uh, Cal's recruiting me, too, which is pretty exciting. I think I wanna go there."

"To Berkeley, California?" his uncle asked, a bit too loudly.

"Yes, sir. Berkeley. It's a great program. And, uh, the school is really good, too."

"And I'm guessin' your momma's not too pleased?"

"No, sir."

"Well, you know she could hardly survive livin' out there after she married your daddy."

"Yes, sir, I know."

Evan's parents met when she was a sophomore at Sweet Briar College. She and her sorority sisters spent many evenings at the University of Virginia libraries, working on what they actually called their "MRS degrees." Most of her friends liked to hang out at the law school, looking for future husbands, but Evan's mom preferred the medical school library—she thought there were already too many lawyers in her family, and the last thing she wanted to do was marry a politician. Her family line was filled with them.

As soon as his mom graduated, his dad gave her what she thought she wanted: a husband as far away from the world of Southern politics as possible, and a ticket to join him in Northern California, where he had begun a medical residency. She didn't last long in California, though. Californians, she learned, lacked Southern manners and courtesy.

Still, the "left coast" (the disparaging phrase Evan's dad always used when discussing the San Francisco area) seemed to have a magnetic pull for Evan. Evan wasn't really sure why. He just knew that the world was a whole lot bigger and more interesting than this town, and he needed to see for himself. For years, he had watched cousins and friends go away to college a couple of hours away and then come back to marry the girls they grew up down the street from. They all just settled so easily into their parents' patterns—same club, same neighborhood, same church, same vacation spots, same lies. It made him sad to think that all those people couldn't come up with anything else to do with their lives— anything even remotely original. He would do something else— anything else. He was absolutely sure of it.

Evan's uncle took a bite of his omelet and chewed slowly.

"Damn, son," he said, letting his fist fall to the table, "I don't think I can help you out there."

"It's OK," Evan said. "I mean, I understand if you don't support my decision, Uncle Sexton."

His uncle leaned back in his chair. "Well, of course I support you, son," he said. "I can handle a little grief from your momma. I'll even run some interference for you."

Evan felt his shoulders relax as relief coursed through his body.

"I just don't think I've got any good connections out there."

It came as no surprise that a conservative U.S. senator from the South was not well loved in Northern California.

"I'm gonna do my best to come up with somebody to call, but you may just have to wow 'em with your fancy footwork."

"I can do that," Evan said, smiling.

"Oh, I know you can, boy. I've seen you out there enough times to be absolutely sure of it."

That was another cool thing about Evan's uncle. Every season, he made it out to at least a couple of home soccer games, which was always a couple more than Evan's dad.

His dad preferred baseball.

Crammed into the bench seat of the minivan with her cousins, Alma watched as they turned the corner and entered the country road that led to the Silver Ribbon chicken processing plant. Dozens of American flags flew on the corner, lining the property of U.S. Auto Sales, a used car company that sold junky cars under the bilingual motto, "Buy here, pay here/*Compra aquí, paga aquí.*" Its location a block away from the plant gave U.S. Auto a brisk business among the bone poppers, cartilage removers, breast cutters, chiller hangers, and backup killers.

Alma knew the details of every job at the plant since members of her extended family had done almost all of them. She knew that it was always freezing cold inside, that workers had to stand still on their feet for hours without talking or listening to music; she knew cleanup was one of the worst jobs, but that skin puller was one of the hardest. She knew that machine operators had the best jobs, and that working as a thigh inspector was unusually exhausting. But she also understood that this plant was the reason her family even knew that Gilberton, Georgia, existed. Without it, and without Americans' apparently inexhaustible appetite for chicken parts, they might all still be farming the rocky soil of San Juan, their little town in Oaxaca, Mexico.

Alma usually heard the plant before she saw it. A loud horn would announce the opening or closing of the gate in the barbed wire fence that surrounded the entire facility, and then another high-pitched bell would signify the end of the night shift.

But something was wrong: she heard none of the normal sounds today. Smokestacks rose above the scrubby pinewoods that surrounded the plant, but no smoke rose from them.

They pulled to the edge of the fence. The gate remained closed. Normally workers would be spilling out by now, and others would be lined up to enter.

"Alma, look," Raúl said. Her brother nodded toward a line of buses inside the empty yard. They were dark blue, with a gold seal on the side.

Department of Homeland Security.

Alma suddenly felt dizzy, as if she were standing on the edge of a cliff, looking down.

"*Madre de Dios,*" Alma's *tía* Pera whispered.

The buses stood empty, and so did the yard, eerily empty. Men, still as statues, lined the perimeter of the gray building. They wore dark-blue uniforms, black pith helmets, and tall combat boots. Three letters stretched across the back of their bulletproof vests: "ICE." And below those letters: "POLICE."

Alma swallowed hard and squeezed her eyes shut. *Was this really happening?*

Raúl leaned forward. "Keep driving, slowly," he said to their dad. "Don't stop."

Alma forced herself to open her eyes and watch.

They drove by, in heavy silence. Alma's cousin Selena crawled over her to press her face and hands against the window. She stared out the window, mesmerized. At six years old, even she knew exactly what this was. How many times had they seen it on television? How many times had it haunted their dreams? An ICE raid. Immigration and Customs Enforcement would put anyone working at the factory without a legitimate Social Security number onto those buses, take them to detention, and then send them out of the United States.

When they passed the building, Alma's father pulled into an empty driveway and turned the car around. They had to go back. They had to see with their own eyes what they all felt in the pit of their stomachs.

They drove by a second time. The metal doors of the plant rolled open, and the workers emerged in two orderly rows. The poultry plant seemed like a prison already, except that the inmates still wore their white hairnets, long white coats, and knee-high waterproof boots. The yellow cloths that covered their mouths when they worked hung limply around their necks. Handcuffs bound their wrists, and they walked flanked by more men in dark combat gear—dozens of them, with guns and sticks slung low around their waists. But no one struggled, no one ran, no one even tugged against the handcuffs. The workers all walked slowly, eyes down, staring at their rubber boots. They boarded the windowless buses that awaited them.

Alma felt tears sting the corners of her eyes. Maybe a hundred workers. Maybe more. Something about their lack of resistance made her feel helpless, too.

"I see her," Isa called out. "*Tía* Dolores. There." She leaned forward and pointed toward the long line of workers.

"She's coming through the door."

Tía Dolores emerged, barely distinguishable from the others, hunched over, deflated. Alma saw that she was crying. Her hands were bound, so tears flowed freely down her cheeks, nothing to catch their fall. Alma felt the tears on her own cheeks, but she couldn't bring herself to wipe them away.

They watched Alma's proud *tía* Dolores, always in charge, always right, step onto the bus without resisting. An ICE agent took her elbow and led her up the stairs. She never even looked up from the ground.

Tía Pera released a deep sob. It tore through the car.

One cry of agony, and then silence.

"We should go," Raúl said.

If they drove by once more, they would recognize neighbors, cousins, friends. They would recognize too many of them. It would be too much to bear. So they pulled away.

Selena's head fell onto Alma's lap, and Alma stroked her hair softly.

"*¿Adónde?*" Alma's father asked. Where would they go now? The question seemed to carry more meaning than he may have intended.

"*A la misa,*" said *Tía* Pera.

"Mom," Isa called out, "you want to go to Mass now? We need to *do* something."

Raúl nudged her sharply in the rib. "Shut up, Isa."

"*Tienes razón,*" Alma's dad said. "You are right, *hermana. Padre* Pancho will find someone who can help us. *Padre* Pancho will help."

The parking lot of Santa Cruz was full. Families rushed into the building, heads down and shoulders hunched, as if they were avoiding a heavy rain or a worse catastrophe. Today the church was a safe space, a place where no dark buses would arrive bringing ICE agents in combat gear.

The scene inside was pandemonium. Children darted around the room unattended, while adults sought friends and consulted one another, sharing whatever information they had. Selena clung to Alma's leg and watched, in awe, as Alma's father and aunt disappeared into the mob.

"*Muévanse adentro del santuario, por favor.*"

Señor Fernandez, who usually served as an usher for this church service, had climbed onto a table at the back of the hallway. He clutched a microphone attached to a portable speaker and begged for order.

"*Por favor, la misa va a comenzar.*"

He repeated a string of gentle commands in Spanish, again and again, but the anxious frenzy did not subside. The hallways continued to pack with people.

"*Señores y señoras, siéntense por favor.*"

He jumped down and started pushing people through the doors and into the sanctuary.

Alma watched people jam into the space around her and glance nervously at the large doors that separated them from the dangers of the outside world. She knew what they were feeling because she felt it, too. Suddenly, their own neighborhood seemed threatening, and their lives seemed dangerously precarious. Alma followed the crowd into the pews of the church and knelt beside her brother.

When the scripture readings started, Raúl took a pencil from the pew in front of him and scribbled on the back of an offering envelope. He showed the envelope to her.

Chino

Javier

Susie?

Xiomara

Loyda

Rafael?

Arturo

They were the names of cousins and friends who were probably working the first shift at the plant. *Tía* Dolores's two sons, her niece, Alma's cousins on her mother's side, and her brother's friends from the soccer team. Thank God Chino's wife quit work when her first child was born a few years ago. Otherwise, what would happen to the kids? Alma felt her body slump. She studied the names. Would they all be deported? Then she remembered.

"Loyda quit, remember? She's working with her mother-in-law, at the Chinese restaurant."

At least there was that. At least he could cross one of them off the list.

Just as *Padre* Pancho was heading to the podium to begin the Gospel reading, Alma's phone vibrated, heavy in her pocket.

Are you in trouble?

It was Evan again.

Another text came in.

I'm really sorry if you're in trouble.

Alma's marathon day of yard work and household chores seemed insignificant now, and the month of restrictions that lay ahead was the least of her concerns. Yes, she was in trouble, but this wasn't the sort of trouble Evan had in mind.

It was impossible to concentrate on *Padre* Pancho's homily. A woman wailed in the pew in front of her, and Alma wondered: Could Evan even imagine this scene?

She had to reply, but she had no idea what to say.

A few minutes later, her brother nudged her sternly and glared at the phone. She shoved it back into her pocket, and went forward for the Eucharist. Then *Padre* Pancho began his announcements. Usually, he talked about church picnics and free English classes. Not today. Instead, he explained that he was gathering volunteers to help families find the locations of their loved ones and seeking attorneys to answer their legal questions.

Padre Pancho offered a final blessing, and the Mass ended.

As Alma walked out of the sanctuary and into the crowded vestibule, someone shoved a blue flyer into her hand. There were so many people mobbing the stairway that she just grasped the paper and pushed her way out into the fresh air.

She and Raúl stood together, blinded by the bright August light. Her eyes came into focus, and she saw Mrs. King standing among the crowds gathered in the parking lot, waving her arm above her head and calling out Alma's name.

Oh, crap. Alma had forgotten all about Mrs. King.

SIX
Delete

The air conditioner was running on full blast in Mrs. King's Buick. Alma got in without saying a word and sank into the velveteen seat. She closed her eyes and let the cool air stream across her face.

"My heavens, that's a popular place to be on Sunday mornings," Mrs. King announced, shifting the sedan into reverse.

"Yeah," said Alma. "It's always packed."

Mrs. King drove slowly past two sobbing women locked in a tight embrace.

"Is it always so . . . emotional?"

Should Alma tell her and risk disapproval? She had never talked to Mrs. King about her family's legal status—or lack of status—in the United States. Would she still want to help? Or would she give up on Alma and find a more practical project?

"Did somethin' happen, sweetheart? You look a little shocked."

"Yes, ma'am. I mean, uh, something happened."

"Well? Go on."

"You know the big Silver Ribbon plant up on the north side of town?"

"*Everyone* in town knows the Silver Ribbon plant."

"There was a raid, and they took people away. In buses."

"Who exactly do you mean by 'they'?"

"ICE. Immigration and Customs Enforcement. A lot of people were working there with false papers, you know?"

"Yes, Alma. I know."

"Including my aunt and some of my cousins."

Mrs. King reached over and took Alma's hand. "Oh, Alma. I'm so sorry."

"Yeah," Alma said. "Me, too."

Mrs. King pulled into the parking lot of a Krispy Kreme, and they got out of the car.

"What will happen?" Mrs. King asked.

"They'll get deported. It's happening all over the country." Alma said.

"Just for trying to work?"

"Most people think it's against the law just to *be* here illegally, but it's not," Alma replied. "I mean it's not a *crime*. But the people who are working at Silver Ribbon, they're using false identities. You know, fake Social Security numbers."

"And that's a crime," Mrs. King said.

"Yeah," Alma replied. "A serious one."

"What will your aunt and cousins do?" Mrs. King asked.

"I don't know," Alma said. "They're definitely not going to find a job in my family's hometown. There's no work there. Maybe they'll go work in the city."

"I'm so sorry," Mrs. King said.

Alma shrugged as they walked into the shop and stared at an array of sweets. Mrs. King pointed to two cream-filled doughnuts glazed in chocolate. Alma ordered black coffee, and they sat down in a booth.

"Alma, we can hold off on discussing your future," Mrs. King said. "I mean, I understand that you're shaken."

She paused to take a sip of her tea.

"But I'd like to go on and dive in," Mrs. King said. "It just might help you feel better." She pulled a thick envelope from her purse. "I have some scholarship opportunities I want to share with you."

Alma figured she might as well just get it over with. She leaned forward and spoke quietly.

"Mrs. King. I'm so grateful for all that you've done for me, but you need to know something."

"What is it, Alma?"

"I'm not legal. So there's no point. I really don't have any way to get legal status. Believe me, I have researched it."

"Good Lord have mercy, Alma. Stop talking such nonsense. I already knew—or I figured, at least—that you were undocumented. That doesn't mean we quit trying, child."

"It doesn't?"

"Heavens, no. It's just another challenge, and you know I love a challenge."

"Really?"

"Of course, really," Mrs. King said, shaking her head. "Silly child. Some scholarships are available to students regardless of their *status*."

"OK, then," Alma replied, feeling her first glimmer of light all day. "Let's see what you've got for me."

While Mrs. King separated stacks of paper into neat piles, Alma thought back to the day she learned that she wasn't *in status*—that she was a person who was here but not welcome, embedded in this place but also somehow apart from it. It was middle school; she was twelve and already suffering the disorientation of puberty. At first, she didn't understand why her father kept brushing aside Raúl's requests to take him to the Department of Driver Services to get his learner's permit.

She assumed her father was just too busy with his work, or that the cost of the permit was too high and Raúl would need to save more money.

But one afternoon, Raúl and several of his friends from the soccer team were sprawled across the furniture in the living room, watching a match between Mexico and Honduras. She decided to tease him, hoping that this might erase the awkwardness she felt in the presence of these older boys.

"What, Raúl?" she taunted. "Your friends all have to come here now since you can't drive?"

"Shut up, Alma," he said.

"Are you too scared to take the test?"

"Alma, *cállate*," he said, standing to face her.

"You *are*, aren't you?" Alma said, thrusting her shoulders forward.

With his jaw clenched and his eyes dull, Raúl reached out and violently wrenched her arm behind her back, dragging her into the bedroom.

Slamming the door shut behind them, Raúl yelled. "Don't you get it, Alma? We're illegals. I'll never get a license, and neither will you. It doesn't matter how good a driver I am, or how goddamned smart you are. It will never happen."

Raúl never yelled at her. He never treated her roughly. He always handled her as if she were one of those porcelain-faced figurines of the Virgin Mary—precious and very fragile.

For a while, she hoped that his fury and frustration were simply the result of Mexico's terrible performance on the soccer field that afternoon. They weren't. She now knew, because fury and frustration had come to live intertwined with hopelessness and despair on her own interior landscape. Alma now understood, too well, exactly how Raúl felt that afternoon. But Raúl had let himself be defeated. Two years later, when the scholarship offers dissolved just because he didn't have a Social Security number, he simply settled for the community college.

Back then, Alma told herself that she would not let herself be defeated by the absence of nine numbers. But now?

She pushed aside her thoughts and picked up the first stack of information.

"That's a scholarship that the Boys and Girls Club offers," Mrs. King told her. "It's very competitive, and we need to look into whether you need to be, uh, 'in status' to be eligible, but I think you've got a great chance. It requires some public speaking. Are you OK with that?"

"What kind of public speaking?" Alma asked.

"The finalists are required to speak at a banquet at the end of their junior year. You'd just be asked to tell a bit about your life and your goals. It's very inspiring."

"Sure," Alma said. "I'm up for that."

She knew there were plenty of things she couldn't tell—things she'd never tell a room full of people—but she would come up with something to say if it meant a four-year college scholarship.

As they made their way through each of the stacks of information, Mrs. King assured Alma that she would research the "problem" of her "status," and that something would work. Alma had nothing to offer except a whole lot of thank-yous. So she said it, over and over, until they got back into the car.

Mrs. King saw the blue flyer from church, and she picked it up from the floor of the Buick.

"What's this?" she asked.

"I don't know. Someone gave it to me after Mass."

Alma stared down at the sheet of paper. In bold print it read, "Tell Senator Prentiss to stop separating U.S. citizens from their parents. Ask him to stop the deportations."

"He's one of our Georgia senators," Mrs. King said, reading over her shoulder. "Looks like he's also the chair of the Senate Homeland Security Committee."

She looked up at Alma. "You know he lives right here in Gilberton, don't you? His family goes way back."

Alma shook her head. She didn't know.

"You should call his office, Alma. Let your voice be heard," Mrs. King said.

"This flyer says that he needs to hear from his constituents," Alma said, pointing toward the bold print. "Doesn't that mean voters? I'm not a voter."

"I'm guessin' he doesn't want to hear from any of us. He probably has his mind made up, but that won't stop us now, will it?"

"Us?" Alma asked.

"Oh, yes, ma'am, you can guarantee he will be hearing from Mrs. Bernice King. And it won't be the first time, either."

She shook her head and chuckled.

"Do you think it will make a difference?"

"Probably not, but we'll go on ahead and do it anyway, won't we?"

She smiled so broadly that her teeth gleamed. Alma couldn't resist this woman.

"Yes, ma'am," said Alma, smiling back. "We will."

After she got out of Mrs. King's car, Alma finally gave herself permission to look at Evan's texts.

> If I got you in trouble, I'll make it up to you.
> Promise.

And then,

> Say something! Im dyin over here.

Her heart thumping and her hands shaking, she stood poised to reply.

Should she tell him that she missed him, too? Should she tell him that three days ago Gilberton High School had been the last place in the world she wanted to go, but now she got butterflies—the good kind— every time she imagined walking through the doors? Or should she tell him what had happened today? How would she even begin to explain?

She groaned and shoved the phone back into her pocket. Pulling out the crumpled blue flyer, Alma entered her house and headed straight toward the computer. Maybe if she distracted herself for a few minutes, the answer would come to her.

By the time Raúl came to stand at her side, Alma's anxious mood had turned to despair.

She stared blankly at the press release posted on the senator's Web site: "Roundup of 200 illegal immigrants in Sexton Prentiss's hometown of Georgia protects 200 American jobs." The senator's staff was prais- ing the work of ICE, celebrating that her aunt, cousins, and friends had just been handcuffed and loaded onto an armored bus. This senator didn't have any interest in immigrant families like hers. According to his Web site, he was all about raiding factories, building bigger fences on the bor- der, and adding a bunch of cameras, radars, and unmanned vehicles—as if crossing the border weren't dangerous enough. Feeling queasy, she closed the press release and opened another. This one described a pol- icy that he called "catch and return." It was, the Web site explained, supposed to be better than the "catch and release" way of dealing with "illegal aliens."

"What are you doing, Alma? I need the computer," Raúl asked, impatiently.

"Reading about this senator. He thinks we're fish."

"Huh?"

"Yeah. It says here, 'No more catch-and-release.' Isn't that what people do to fish?"

"Why are you reading about a senator, Alma? I mean, besides the obvious reason that you're a total nerd."

He tried to give her a playful shove in the arm, but she pulled away.

"Mrs. King told me I should call him." She shoved her chair away from the desk. "But there's no way I'm doing that. He doesn't even think I'm human!"

Raúl stepped forward and looked more closely at the screen, focusing his gaze on a photograph of the senator. He wore a gray suit and ice-blue tie. He sat perched on a table, reading a storybook to a group of schoolkids.

"Hey, I know that guy," he said, his voice rising.

"Keep dreaming, Raúl," Alma mocked. "Where would you meet a U.S. senator?"

"He used to come to our soccer games at GHS. I'm not kidding."

Alma laughed. "You are so full of yourself, Raúl. Why would a U.S. senator come to Gilberton High soccer games?"

"I'm telling you, Alma. It was him. His nephew was on our team. Skinny kid. Tall. He was a sophomore when I graduated. But, dude, he was *good*."

"Do I know him?" Alma asked. "What's his name?"

"Evan."

The word tore a gaping hole into Alma's chest.

"Evan Roland. This guy's his uncle."

Raúl pointed a finger at the head shot on the computer, while Alma tried to focus her blurring vision on the glare off the senator's forehead. She examined his ruddy face and shifty eyes, his thin, pursed lips.

Raúl kept talking. "Yeah, Evan. His mom's the one with all those damn roses, over on Lakeshore Drive. Dad does her yard, remember?"

Yes, Alma remembered. She willed herself not to cry.

"Are you sure?" Alma asked, fighting back tears.

"Yeah, I'm sure. I'm telling you," he said, pointing at the screen, "he and Evan were tight. He came to a bunch of our soccer games. He was pretty cool, actually."

It didn't matter how "cool" he was. Alma would have nothing to do with this senator or his family. She couldn't. It was too risky, and just the thought of being near this man's life made her feel sick.

"You can have the computer now," Alma said. "I'm done."

But she wasn't quite done.

Alma walked onto the deck and pulled her cell phone from the pocket of her jeans. With her hands poised on the keypad, she stared at Evan's messages one last time.

Her thumb hovered over the key for a moment and then hit delete.

SEVEN
Red Elephant

You can do this.

Alma stepped off the bus and headed across the pavement, toward the huge silver *G* suspended above the entrance to Gilberton High School. A red elephant with unfurled ears, powerful legs, and sharp tusks was seared into its center.

Welcome to Gilberton High School, home of the Fighting Red Elephants.

Alma considered making a list of all the things she knew about elephants. Making lists usually calmed her, but the first thing that popped into her mind was politics—donkeys and elephants—which made her think of Evan's uncle in his ice-blue tie. So, instead, she just repeated her mantra for the day:

You can do this.

Maybe if she repeated it enough, she would believe it—as long as she didn't run into Evan.

"Alma, over here!"

Alma turned to see three comforting faces, girls she had known since elementary school, standing near the door to the cafeteria.

"What's up, *chicas*?" Alma asked. She walked toward them and entered their circle as Monica and Magdalena opened space.

"Not much, girl," Maritza said loudly. "Just wishing I didn't have to be here."

"I hear that," Alma said. Her need to escape this place was so real that she tasted it like cold metal on her tongue.

As soon as Alma came near, their bold energy vanished, and the three of them leaned in close to her.

"I heard about your *tía* Dolores," Magda whispered.

"Chino, too?" Maritza asked.

"Yeah," said Alma, "and Javier."

Maritza just shook her head slowly.

"What about Arturo?" Alma asked Monica.

Monica nodded slowly. "Yeah, he's gone."

"At least Loyda quit a couple of weeks ago," Alma said.

"And Susie wasn't working that shift," Maritza broke in. "That's what my cousin said."

A girl came up and joined their circle. Alma didn't recognize her.

"Y'all ready for this?" the girl asked, nudging Maritza in the rib.

"Nope," Maritza said. "Just counting the days till I graduate."

Maritza's tone made clear that they were finished talking about the raids. Alma knew that—even though they knew they shouldn't—they all felt ashamed. She knew they didn't want other people at school to know about their connection to the "illegals" who had been taken to jail.

Maritza's friend, a light-skinned black girl with dark hair braided into long cornrows, nodded toward Alma. "I'm Briana," she said. "I don't think we've met."

"I'm new," Alma said.

"So, Alma, what happened to that fancy school in Atlanta?" Monica asked, "Did they kick you out for being too *mexicana*?"

"What, you think they'd rather have *salvadoreñas* like you?" Magdalena broke in.

"Not a chance, Monica. Down there in Atlanta, they think all you Salvadorans are either in MS or the Eighteenth," Alma said, trying hard to fit naturally into their banter. MS and the Eighteenth were Salvadoran gangs. They were mostly in LA, but everyone in Atlanta was terrified that they were migrating east.

"*¡Órale, ese!*" responded Magdalena as she folded her arms into an exaggerated gangster pose.

They all laughed. It felt good. Being here with her girls, making fun of the way other people sometimes saw them. With them, she didn't have to worry.

"No, really," said Alma. "My *tía* had to go back to work, so she needed me to take care of Selena."

Alma tried not to think about the fact that her aunt's job at the chicken plant was probably history now.

"Why can't your other cousin do it—Isabel. Isn't she like fourteen or something?" Monica asked.

"Isa's thirteen, and she's too busy chasing boys, which means I have to take care of her, too."

"*Ay, chicas.* Did you hear that my little cousin Flor is pregnant?" asked Magda, shaking her head slowly. "Fifteen years old. And she won't even tell anybody who the guy is."

"I guess it's safe to say he's not planning to step up?" asked Briana, arching her eyebrows.

"*Pinche* guy," Magda said, almost spitting out the words.

Maritza's body shifted into a defensive pose, as if the *pinche* guy were standing right in front of her. Alma felt sorry for any guy who crossed Maritza.

"My aunt and uncle shipped her off to South Carolina to live with our cousins," said Magda. "They live on a farm, out in the middle of nowhere."

"Where nobody can see her," Monica said.

"Yeah," Magda replied. "She might as well be in a convent."

"I bet she's, like, dyin' over there," Monica said.

"Flor deserves it," Maritza said, anger in her voice. "It's not that hard to prevent, you know."

"You better watch your cousin, Alma," said Magda. "Your *tía* Pera would just keel over on the spot if Isa got herself knocked up. I mean, she would *die*."

"Damn, y'all," Maritza broke in. "It's not Alma's fault if her little cousin wants to make stupid-ass choices."

Alma conjured an image of Isa, pregnant, wearing a tank top stretched over her swollen belly and those short shorts Isa stuck in her purse every time she snuck out to be with her friends. The image terrified her so much that she closed her eyes and shuddered.

When Alma looked up, Briana, Monica, Magda, and Maritza were all staring past her, gawking.

She turned to see Evan jogging toward her, his face bright with anticipation.

"Alma!" Evan called out.

You can do this.

He arrived at her side and wrapped his arm around her shoulder. Alma willed herself to step back.

"What's up, Evan?" she asked, trying to sound casual and distant. She wanted to feel revulsion, or anger, or anything other than this deep pain of longing.

"Not much. Just looking for you," he said, smiling broadly. "Did you get my texts?"

Alma glanced toward Magda, who was now in full-on jaw-dropped shock, and shrugged.

Maritza broke in, "Damn, Alma. What happened to your manners, girl?"

"Yeah, who's your friend, Alma?" Monica said, thrusting a hand onto her hip. "Aren't you going to introduce us?"

"Oh, sorry. This is Evan. My dad mows his lawn," Alma said, using every ounce of her will to gesture casually toward Evan—to make it seem like he didn't matter.

"These are my friends. We go way back," she said in his general direction.

She couldn't look at him. One look and she would be done.

"Hey, don't you play soccer?" Monica asked.

"Yeah," replied Evan. Alma knew he was confused, or maybe angry. She heard it in his voice.

"My cousin's on your team—Jonathan."

"Mendez? He's a good guy." Evan replied absently. Then he reached out to grasp Alma's arm, his soft touch overwhelming her senses. "Alma, can I talk to you?"

"Um, maybe later," she said hesitantly. "I've gotta find my class."

Alma pulled her arm back and turned to walk away. "Later, *chicas*," she said, waving casually toward her friends.

But then she felt Evan's hand again, warm on her shoulder.

"I'll walk with you," he said.

Her mind told her to find a way out of this, but her body refused to listen. She needed to be near him. So she let him walk beside her in silence, and they made their way together through the huge glass doors and into Gilberton High School.

———

Evan was lost—completely bewildered. When they reached Alma's locker, Evan turned and spoke.

"Alma," Evan asked slowly, "why did you introduce me to your friends that way?"

"What do you mean?"

"Your dad cuts my lawn? What was that?"

"The truth."

The way she said it, it was like she was trying to hurt him. What had he *done*?

"What's wrong, Alma?" he asked.

"Nothing's wrong. I'm just preoccupied. You know, first day at a new school and all that."

He knew she was lying, but he couldn't figure out why. Was she mad at him about Friday night? Embarrassed, maybe? He stared at her intently and replied, "You don't strike me as easily intimidated, Alma."

"You don't know what it's like here," she said, looking down. "I mean, for me."

Of course Evan knew what it was like here. He had been at this school for three years. His mom and his uncle went to school here. He was pretty sure his grandfather did, too.

"I'm not sure I follow," he said, trying to sound sympathetic.

"Do you know what my so-called adviser suggested I take when I met with her last week?" Alma was fiddling with the combination on her locker. He watched her hands closely. Even with her fingernails cut short, there was dirt under them. They were still beautiful, and he loved that she didn't wear neon polish like most of the girls he knew.

"Intro to Fashion?" Evan asked tentatively. Conway and Peavey had tried to convince him to take that class. They told him the teacher looked like Gisele Bündchen. But after the whole experience with French, Evan wasn't inclined to take Conway's advice on the Gilberton High School curriculum.

"You've got to be kidding me!" she exclaimed. "There's a class at this school called Intro to Fashion?"

"I guess so," Evan said. "A couple of my friends are taking it."

"My so-called adviser probably teaches it," Alma said. "She looks the type."

"Is she tall and blond?" Evan asked. "With long legs?"

As soon as he said it he started to blush.

Crap. What are you thinking?

Alma glared at him.

"Forget I said that," he said, cringing. "It's just that my douchebag friends were talking about her and—"

Alma broke in. "You should stop talking, Evan."

"Yeah," he said, running his fingers through his hair.

"Anyway," Alma continued, "first, my so-called adviser asked if I was in ESOL classes—which, obviously, I don't need since I speak better English than she does. Then, she suggested I enroll in food science and early childhood care."

"Seriously?" Evan asked. That was a little over the top.

"I. Kid. You. Not. Then I shoved my transcript from North Atlanta in her face. I knew this would happen. I was prepared."

She was so angry that her body started to tremble. Evan reached out and touched his hand to her arm. He couldn't stop himself.

"It worked out in the end, though, right? I mean, you got the classes you wanted?"

"Yeah, but . . ."

"It was just a mistake, Alma." He squeezed her arm gently and then let his hand drop, even though he didn't want to. He wanted to trace his hand along her arm and across her exposed collarbone. He wanted to feel her hair in his hands again and pull her in close. He had to stop thinking about what he wanted to do with her. Now.

"Doubtful," he heard her say.

"She probably thought you were someone else," he said, grasping for something that might calm her down.

"No, Evan," Alma said. "She thought I was a Mexican girl."

She yanked a book from her locker and slammed it shut.

"I'm sorry, Evan," she said. "I've gotta get to class." She spun away from him and took off toward her first period class.

This was not going to be easy.

Alma made it almost to the end of the day before she saw him again. Evan was standing across the hall, laughing with two of his friends. She recognized them from his party but couldn't remember their names. All she remembered was that everyone called them by their last names—Piedmont and Connor? Something like that. Evan's friends were classic "prepnecks"—part khaki-pants-wearing Southern preppy and part Confederate-flag-waving redneck. Alma knew their type, and she preferred to keep her distance. Evan was way more "prep" than "neck." He definitely wasn't a redneck, but he didn't really work at being preppy, either. He was just sort of effortlessly Southern, wearing those no-pleat khakis with leather flip-flops and a worn-out T-shirt from some South Carolina beach resort. She'd never really thought of beach preppy as her type either. Until now, apparently.

Evan was definitely her type.

She slid into a desk in the front row of the classroom, relieved to have slipped by them unnoticed.

Alma pulled a notebook out of her backpack and, realizing that someone was coming toward her, glanced up. Evan was looking straight at her as if no one else was in the room.

She just couldn't get a break.

He slid into the seat behind her and leaned close to whisper in her ear, "What are you doing here? This class is for seniors."

She took in his scent—faintly metallic. It reminded her of just-turned soil.

"What? You think I can't handle it?" she asked, feeling the anger and frustration return.

"I wouldn't dare think that, Alma," Evan replied with a smile. "But shouldn't you be in American?"

His bare forearm brushed her shoulder.

"At my old school, I took AP World History in ninth grade, so it put me a year ahead of this place."

She sounded fine, not like someone who was crumbling inside.

"Wow," said Evan. "AP classes in ninth grade. You *are* an overachiever."

Alma leaned forward in her seat, needing to create more distance between them if she was going to keep the promise she had made to herself.

Dr. Gustafson entered the room, balancing a large stack of books in his arms. The books tumbled onto his desk as he cleared his throat loudly. Alma had heard from her brother that he was notorious at GHS, mostly for having been there forever.

"Students, let's begin, shall we?"

Everyone shifted into seats, and the room fell silent. Alma tried to focus on the teacher standing in front of her, but all that registered were the intense waves of energy pulsing between her and Evan.

This was seriously going to mess with her concentration.

Dr. Gustafson began to call the roll. When he came to Alma's name, she braced herself.

"Garrceea?" She cringed in her seat as he continued in his deep Southern accent, "Aaooowlma Garrceea."

Ready to explain that her name was Julia, Alma raised her hand and launched in. "Excuse me, Dr. Gustafson, I prefer to be called by my middle name—"

She felt Evan's gentle touch between her shoulders and turned briefly to take in his encouraging nod.

She began again, "Um, Dr. Gustafson, if you don't mind, uh, my name is pronounced Aaahhhlma."

"Ah, yes. Let me try that again."

He spoke her name again, and it sounded just about the same as the first time. Alma sank low in her seat. Then she noticed that he was looking over her head, directly at Evan. She turned back to see that Evan was raising his hand eagerly.

"Yes, Mr. Roland?"

"Um, sir? You might want to think about pronouncing her name this way: You get home from a frustrating day of teaching *us* and you sink into your favorite chair. Let's say, maybe, you've got a bourbon on the rocks—Knob Creek, something good—and you take a long, slow sip."

Giggles erupted from the rest of the class, and Alma felt the heat rise in her cheeks.

Evan continued, undeterred. "So you put the drink down and let out a long 'aaaahhhhh.' Then just add the end 'llma.' And there you've got it: Aaahhhlma. It's simple."

The rest of the class tittered. Alma felt her cheeks turn beet red.

"Why, thank you, Evan, for that vividly illustrative bit of advice," Dr. Gustafson replied.

Alma sank deeper into her desk when Dr. Gustafson tried it again. Astoundingly, it sounded pretty good.

"Aahhlma, I see that you're a junior?" asked Mr. Gustafson.

"Yes, sir," she said, sitting up tall.

"And you've already had AP American History?"

"Yes, sir. I just transferred from North Atlanta, and I took AP American as a sophomore there."

"With Mr. Billups, no doubt. He's an excellent teacher."

"Yes, sir. With Mr. Billups. It was a great class."

"Well, we're certainly glad to have you join us, Aahhlma."

A teacher was welcoming her, calling her by her real name, and pronouncing it reasonably well. Maybe this year wouldn't be quite as bad as she expected.

Dr. Gustafson ran through the rest of the roll and then outlined what they would be learning in the class. When the bell rang, the students gathered their books to head out the door.

"Evan, may I speak with you for a moment?" Dr. Gustafson called out.

"Sure," Evan replied.

Turning to Alma, he asked, "Will you wait for me?"

Alma figured she should stay since he was probably about to get in trouble for speaking up about her name. So she hovered in the doorway, hugging her history book to her chest.

"Evan, I'd like to speak with you about a way that you might help enrich your classmates' learning experience in this course," Dr. Gustafson said.

"Come again?" Evan replied.

Alma smiled. She loved that expression.

"I'm wondering if you might speak with your uncle—Senator Prentiss—about visiting our class at some point during the semester," Dr. Gustafson replied.

Of course Evan wasn't in trouble. What had she been thinking? Guys like Evan—people with money and powerful connections—they didn't get in trouble. Dr. Gustafson continued speaking, but Alma didn't hear the words. A deep sadness rose in her gut and coursed through her constricted chest. Before the crumbling could begin again, she walked away.

EIGHT
Fire Alarm

"*¿Le ayudo, señora?*"

Alma's *tía* Pera stood at the kitchen counter. She was trying to pack lunches but instead quietly crying over a package of processed ham.

"*Sí, gracias, hija,*" Tía Pera replied, wiping her eyes with her sleeve.

Alma grabbed a bag of Wonder Bread from the pantry.

"I'm sorry it's all so hard," Alma said.

Tía Pera's sister and nephews would be deported in a few days, and *Tía* Pera no longer had a job.

Alma laid out six slices of bread and dragged the ham away from *Tía* Pera's clutch.

"*Ay, hija,*" her *tía* sighed as she dropped oranges into paper sacks. "*No sé. ¿Y qué vamos a hacer con tu prima?*"

The problems with her cousin Isa had started three weeks ago, just after school began. After dinner on the second day of school, *Tía* Pera and *Tío* Rigo broke the news of their plans. They would return to Mexico with the girls in time for Christmas. They'd been sending money for years to build a house and a little *tienda* back in their hometown of

San Juan, and the construction project was almost complete. If they moved home, *Tía* Pera could run the small shop. They didn't have any other options.

Isa's body began to shake, and quiet sobs escaped her lips. *Tía* Pera and *Tío* Rigo chastised her with their eyes, darting glances toward Selena. Selena silently played on the floor, yanking a brush through a plastic horse's tangled mane. Isa was supposed to be strong for her *hermanita*, but she wasn't thinking about her little sister. She was thinking about her ruined life. Isa stood up and ran into the room she shared with Alma and Selena.

Then *Tía* Pera turned to face *Tío* Rigo.

"*Ay Dios mío. Y por eso—¡por eso!*" She threw her hands into the air. "This is exactly why we need to go back to Mexico, *amorcito*. You see?"

Her hands flailed wildly as she spoke.

"Our Isa has become the Typical American Teenager." She grasped the edge of the table to steady herself.

Tío Rigo placed his arm on her shoulder, whispering, "*Cálmate, mi vida.*"

But she didn't calm down. She just kept calling out random phrases: "No respect! So selfish! All she cares about is her *teléfono*! And those short shorts!"

The next day, Isa went on a hunger strike. Well, sort of. She refused to eat any foods prepared by her mother. She sat sullenly at the dinner table every night and then returned to the room to raid her secret stash. For the last three weeks, Isa had subsisted on Doritos, Pringles, Snickers, and Dum Dums. Alma was starting to worry.

So she had woken up early this morning to help her *tía*, hoping they'd have a chance to talk.

"*Tía*," Alma said, "I think Isa is just worried, and she doesn't know how to tell you."

"We're all worried, Alma."

"I know, but Isa hasn't been to Mexico since she was three. All her friends are here. Her life is here. She's scared."

Alma understood all too well how Isa must be feeling.

"Maybe you and Uncle Rigo could stay until the school year is out? She could graduate from middle school, and Selena could finish kindergarten."

"We need to earn a living, *mamita*," *Tía* Pera said as she dropped a bag of chips into each lunch bag. "We can't afford to live here any longer."

"They could stay with us. With me and *Papi* and Raúl."

Alma's aunt grasped her shoulders and turned to face her.

"That's a wonderful offer, Alma. But you have a future to worry about—scholarships and college. I can't leave you in charge of a family of five."

Her aunt had a point. It was one thing to watch her cousins for a couple of hours after school, but it was quite another to shop, cook, and clean for everyone. Alma would like to think that her dad and her brother would chip in, but that was wishful thinking.

"*¿Sabes qué?*"

"What, *Tía?*"

"Sometimes I wonder if it was all worth it, you know?"

Alma knew, but it physically pained her to hear her aunt say it.

"But then I think about you and your brother." She looked directly into Alma's eyes, still gripping her shoulders. "And I imagine Raúl playing soccer for a college team someday. I think about you at some fancy university, studying to become a doctor or a lawyer."

"Or an anthropologist," Alma said.

"Or that," said *Tía* Pera, leaning in to hug Alma tight. "I think about you two, and I know it was worth it, *mi vida.*"

"*Gracias, Tía,*" Alma said. She wished that she felt so sure.

"So enough about that," *Tía* Pera announced, turning back to the half dozen lunches she needed to finish making.

"You're right," Alma said. "I mean, not about the doctor part—but if the girls stayed, I'd need some help."

Selena bounded out of the bedroom, singing the ABCs. Even though Selena could be a royal pain, Alma couldn't bear the thought of living in this house without her. It would be so *quiet*.

"I have an idea," Alma said, grabbing a box of cereal from the pantry for Selena. "Why don't we see if *Abuela* Lupe can come stay with us for a while."

"But, Alma—"

"She's always wanted to visit." It had been fifteen years since Alma had last seen her grandmother.

Tía Pera lined the lunch bags along a table by the kitchen door.

"Yes, but she doesn't have a travel visa. You know how hard it is to get one."

She had heard that U.S. officials didn't want people to come as visitors and stay as "illegal" workers instead of returning within a few months as they were supposed to do. So the United States almost never issued tourist visas in Mexico, except to people who had boatloads of money in their bank accounts. Needless to say, *Abuela* Lupe did not have a boatload of money. She didn't even have a bank account until five years ago.

"It's worth a try," Alma said.

Tía Pera stopped filling plastic bags with corn chips and watched Selena fiddle with the straps of her backpack.

"*Sí, mamita,*" her aunt said. "It's worth a try."

Just then Isa stormed out from their room, grabbed her backpack, and flung the kitchen door open. She left without grabbing her lunch. Isa still refused to accept nourishment from the woman who was about to ruin her life, but if Alma's plan worked, maybe that would change.

Alma gave *Tía* Pera a quick hug, grabbed her lunch, and rushed out behind Isa.

The conversation still lingered in Alma's mind as she reached first period. But now her worries were mixed with the anxiety and longing she always felt when she knew Evan was nearby. Alma stared blankly at her open textbook, unable to focus on the equations. She already knew them, anyway. Three weeks at Gilberton High School, and—with the notable exception of Dr. Gustafson's class—she had learned absolutely nothing new. That is, unless you counted strategies for avoiding the beautiful boy you have a massive crush on. She had learned lots of those. Most of them involved girls' bathrooms, the only places where Evan couldn't track her down. Even so, he often waited for her outside, and then she had to come up with other excuses—talking to her teacher before class, finishing math homework, taking gym clothes to her locker. With a knowing smile and a patient nod, Evan always let her pass, but never before finding a way to touch her. "All right, Alma," he would say, resting his hand on her lower back or gently touching her shoulder. "I'll just be right here waiting for you."

Once he even touched her face. That about did her in.

Why couldn't she forget him? Her family was falling to pieces, she had a precalculus test tomorrow, and all she could think about—all she could *ever* think about—was when she might see him again. So far, she had kept the promise she made to herself on the day of the raid—to avoid Evan and all of the complications he and his family would cause. But he was not making it easy.

Alma slammed the heavy textbook shut, got up from her desk, and approached Mrs. Tanner.

"Can I have a hall pass?"

Mrs. Tanner glared at her.

"Uh, it's that time of the month."

"All right, Miss García, but be sure to finish the problem set before the test tomorrow."

When had Alma ever *not* finished a problem set?

Resisting the urge to point out her perfect record and perfect scores, Alma smiled and replied, "Yes, ma'am."

Alma left the building and set out across the football field. She needed to get some fresh air. She knew of only one place to gather the jumbled fragments of her mind, and she came here often. It was a small dock that jutted into the lake across the street from school. For Alma, there was something about balancing at the very edge of the water that soothed her nerves and eased her racing thoughts.

Alma walked slowly out and stepped up onto a wood piling. She fixed her gaze to a point on the horizon and then slowly lifted one leg off the piling. She stretched her arms wide and balanced on the standing leg, carefully inching her raised leg out. Holding steady for a few moments, Alma felt a calm descend. She allowed herself to breathe slowly and deliberately. Her mind emptied and her body settled. She had read somewhere that stillness was strength. That made good sense.

After a few minutes, she stepped off the piling and sat at the edge of the dock, dangling her feet over the water. She savored the stillness that lingered in her body and the new awareness it gave her.

Suddenly, a jarring noise broke her serenity. A fire alarm—and she was off campus. Alma jumped up and sprinted toward the football field.

Weee-ooooh! Weee-ooooh! Weee-ooooh!

A loud siren broke into Evan's daydream. Since Alma featured prominently, Evan wondered whether her father was policing his mind as well as his actions. When everyone flooded out of the classroom, he realized it was a fire drill. Evan stood, half dazed, and followed the mass of people heading toward the football field.

He saw Alma immediately, running across the parking lot on the other side of the field. Evan nudged Logan.

"Cover for me," he said, and then peeled away from the crowd.

As soon as she saw him, Alma stopped running. Her face was flushed, and thin tendrils of hair clung to her cheek. She watched him intently as he came nearer. When he approached, neither of them said anything. Alma leaned against the nearest car, which happened to be Conway's Hummer. Evan grasped the roof rack with one hand and pressed in toward her, his face just a few inches from hers.

"Alma," he said softly.

"Yes," she replied, so quietly that he barely heard her above the hum of the students gathered on the field.

"Why won't you let me near you?"

"You're near me now, aren't you?"

Her whisper almost did him in. He wanted to be closer.

"You know what I mean," he said.

Alma nodded, keeping full eye contact.

"I know this place looks like the set of some lame high school movie, but it's not. I'm not the captain of the football team, and I'm not playing around."

"No, you're the captain of the soccer team," Alma said, looking away. Her face crumpled, as if she were in pain.

"This is the South, Alma. No one cares about soccer."

"Except Mexicans," she replied, her voice hardening at the edges.

Evan never knew how to respond when she said stuff like that. He wished he could just brush the comments off, or even get angry and defensive. Instead, he just felt confused, knowing there was some truth in them but not knowing how to acknowledge it. Right now, though, all he wanted was for her to stop avoiding him.

"The point is, Alma, I want to be with you," he said quietly, "and I'm pretty sure you want to be with me,"

Alma shrugged.

"So why can't we just *do* this?"

Alma paused, and then she looked directly into his eyes. "You can't handle me."

He leaned back, reeling. Alma didn't know what he could handle—what he handled every day. He absolutely could handle her—if she would just give him a chance.

"What the hell is that supposed to mean?" he asked, anger rising in his voice.

Alma sank against the Hummer, arms hugging her chest.

"It's complicated, Evan."

She sounded vulnerable and sad. His anger gave way to something else as he leaned in close, almost touching her, with one hand still raised, gripping the rack. With his other hand, he gently pushed a strand of hair from her face.

"Try me," Evan whispered, tucking her hair behind her ear. "You'd be surprised by what I can handle."

She raised her chin and touched Evan's hand, which lingered below her ear. He stepped back, hearing the scratchy voice of the principal calling for students to return to their classes.

"I should get back," Alma said. "I can't afford to get in trouble."

"Can we talk tonight?"

Alma hesitated.

"I guess," she replied. "I'm still grounded for another week, but my dad gave me my phone back. Just don't call late. I have to be up by six to catch the bus."

"Six?" Evan asked. "Why so early? You don't strike me as the primping type."

Alma laughed. "No, I'm not waking up to flat-iron my hair every morning. The bus comes at six thirty, something about busing schedules for the middle school. We get here an hour before school starts."

"Bummer," said Evan.

"It's not so bad. It gives me time to do homework. I just wish the bus would stop downtown at the Dripolator on the way to school. A double cappuccino would make the morning way more bearable," she called out as she took off toward school.

Evan leaned against the Hummer and watched her perfect legs carry her across the field, and a plan took shape in his mind.

"Hey, Mr. Country Club!"

Evan heard a stern voice behind him. He turned to see a Latino guy about his age with a shaved head and tattoos snaking up from under his wifebeater and around his throat. If he hadn't been in Gilberton, Evan might have thought this guy was a gangster.

"Are you talking to me?" Evan asked, turning to face the guy. He didn't mean to sound aggressive.

"Yeah, I'm talking to you," the guy said, slowly approaching. "Do you see anyone else in this parking lot?"

Evan didn't answer.

"That your Hummer?"

"Who wants to know?" Evan asked.

This guy was pissing him off.

"I *said*, is that your Hummer?"

The Hummer was Conway's. Evan drove a hybrid, a constant source of mocking from all of his SUV-driving buddies. In Evan's world, driving a hybrid was an act of rebellion. But he had no intention of sharing this information with the asshole standing in front of him.

"It's none of your damn business."

"And what if I tell you it *is* my business?"

The guy was up in his face.

Evan laughed involuntarily. "Are you trying to pick a fight with me?"

The whole scene was absurd.

"If this is your truck, then your feeble-ass mind can't even imagine what I'm about to do to you!" The guy grabbed Evan's collar.

Maybe Evan had been wrong earlier. Maybe this school *was* the set of some bad high school movie.

"I need to know whose truck this is," the guy spat in his face. He was so close that Evan smelled his breath. The smell was unmistakable: Juicy Fruit gum.

"Are you planning to volunteer the information?" the guy asked. "Cuz I'm planning to get it out of you one way or another."

Pondering the fact that a guy who smelled like Juicy Fruit might very soon kick his ass, Evan didn't notice the football coach approaching.

"Manny García," Coach Kelley called out, "correct me if I'm wrong, boy, but—as I recall—you are no longer enrolled at Gilberton High School."

Manny—if that was his name—released his grip on Evan's collar.

"In which case, you are trespassing, Mr. García."

The guy turned and jogged toward the street.

"Yes, sir," called out Coach Kelley, "you just keep on running because there's nothing I'd rather do than call Sheriff Cronin down here to escort you to jail."

Coach Kelley's reaction seemed a little extreme, but Evan had to admit he was relieved.

"Shouldn't you be in class, Mr. Roland?" Coach Kelley asked.

"Yes, sir."

"Well," he called out, leaning against Conway's Hummer, "get on along, boy."

"Yes, sir," Evan said, bewildered, as he set out toward the school.

NINE
Addictions

Alma stepped off the school bus and walked toward Evan, who was holding a cup of coffee out as a sort of offering.

"Double cappuccino?" she asked, taking the cup from his hand.

"We've got to feed that addiction."

"No sugar?"

"No sugar."

He watched the contours of her neck as she tilted her head to sip the hot coffee. Relieved to be standing alone with her, studying her at close range, he wondered whose addiction he was feeding.

For almost a week Evan had been meeting Alma at the bus drop-off with coffee made exactly the way she liked, and every day, he got more jittery when she stepped off the bus. She seemed to relax a bit more each day, however, to soften. It was all so strange, like an old-fashioned courtship. Evan had never needed to work so hard to be with a girl, or maybe he just hadn't wanted to. He tried to avoid the girls in his very small world—they came with too many strings attached. He wasn't completely inexperienced, though, thanks to his mom's charity events. Waitresses seemed to like him—or at least to take pity on him. They were easy to hang out with—usually in college and not really expecting anything except a quick escape from the boredom of their jobs. They also had the virtue of keeping things secret so he didn't have to worry about the whole town weighing in on his romantic entanglements.

Until now, he had never really thought about how to get a girl to like him, or to trust him. Alma was a different story. He wanted her too much. It wasn't just desire, though. There was something else.

"Do you want to sit down somewhere?" he asked.

They both glanced toward the cluster of benches that lined the courtyard. Each bench had a word etched into the stone at its base: "Respect," "Restraint," "Honesty," "Fortitude." They glanced toward two girls already sitting on the "Honesty" bench.

"Looks like we'll have to go with 'Restraint,'" she said, leading him in the direction of the empty bench.

Sounds about right, Evan thought.

He settled onto the "Restraint" bench next to Alma.

Evan picked up a book that had fallen from her bag.

"Still reading about random people in the South Pacific?" he asked, grinning broadly.

"Yeah," she said, "and a bunch of other places I'm sure you couldn't find on a map."

"You're probably right," he said. "Why do you read this stuff, Alma?"

"I had this great teacher at North Atlanta," Alma replied. "He got me into it. On the first day of tenth grade, he told us to ditch the textbook."

"What did you do instead?" Evan asked. "Watch movies?"

"No, he passed out a great essay called 'Body Ritual among the Nacirema.'"

"The *what*?" Evan asked.

"Nacirema," she said. "It's 'American' spelled backward. It talks about Americans like they're some exotic North American tribe of people. Most of the kids in my class thought the essay was weird. It described doctors as 'medicine men' and prescriptions as 'charms' written in an ancient language. But I thought it was hilarious."

Evan shook his head slowly. "You have a strange sense of humor, Alma."

"Yeah. That's what people tell me," Alma said. She took a sip of her coffee and gave him a gentle nudge. "And it taught me something about you."

"Huh?" Evan asked. He had no idea what she was talking about.

"It says bathrooms are like shrines. And you know who the more powerful people are by how many 'shrines' they have."

"And what does this have to do with me?" Evan said, arching his eyebrows.

"How many people live in your house?"

"Three. Well, if you count my dad. He sort of lives there."

"And how many bathrooms do you have?"

Evan looked down and counted on his fingers.

"Seven," he said, triumphantly. He stood and stretched his fists to the sky. "I feel so powerful."

———

Alma laughed, watching him pump his fists into the air. It felt so good to laugh, and to feel the caffeine making its way through her body.

"You're lucky that I got that coffee this morning," Evan said, nudging her.

"Why?"

"There were a bunch of yahoos on the town square for some kind of protest. They had the roads closed off completely."

"A protest?" Alma asked. She took a deep swig.

"Yeah, they had a bunch of signs about illegal immigrants and some state law. Anyway, I had to fight through crowds for your coffee."

Alma should have known something like this would happen today. She'd had the dream this morning. Maybe it was superstition, but whenever Alma had the dream, it seemed to usher in misfortune.

Against her will, the searing burn of the desert heat returned to her skin. She saw the blinding shine of a spotlight and heard the deafening roar of a helicopter's propeller slicing through the sky. This morning, she had endured the strangest, most haunting part of the dream. Strong arms encircled her and tore her away from the coolness pressed against her own flesh. When she looked back, Alma saw her mother lifeless on the ground—eyes closed, black hair surrounding her head like a crooked halo entwined with the desert sand, white shirt opened, revealing swollen breasts with broad, dark nipples.

Whenever the dream went this far, she awoke with a sugary sweet taste in her mouth. The burst of sweetness made Alma queasy. How could such a horrifying set of images produce this taste?

She took another deep swig, relieved by the bitter taste. Alma never added sugar to her coffee.

"Are you with me, Alma?" Evan asked, taking her hand into his.

"Oh, sorry. Just lost in thought." Alma squeezed her eyes shut. "It was probably about SB 529."

"What's that? SB whatever?"

"It passed last year. It's supposed to, you know, make Georgia 'tough on immigration.' The anti-immigrant people are freaking out that counties and cities aren't paying enough attention to it."

They sat for a few moments, and Alma felt that familiar dread creep into her gut. She knew it would have to happen eventually—Evan would learn that she didn't have legal status and then everything would change. Alma felt pretty sure that the nephew of a notorious "catch and return" senator would have some strong feelings about "illegals." But she hoped that he might at least give her a chance to explain.

"Hey, Alma," Evan asked, "do you know any? I mean, illegal immigrants?"

Alma shot a glance at Evan. She hated hearing those words come out of his lips. They sounded so *ugly*, and he was—he was too beautiful.

"You know," he continued, "those guys who stand out by the Home Depot looking for work."

"You mean day laborers?" she replied.

"Yeah, I guess."

"Are you asking me whether I know any day laborers or whether I know any, uh, 'illegal' immigrants?"

"Um . . . I guess I thought they were sort of the same thing."

Alma bit her lip hard.

"Did I say something stupid?" Evan asked.

She sucked in a deep breath.

"No, Evan. It's OK."

This was it—the moment she wanted so much to avoid. She just had to gather the courage to tell him. If she couldn't trust him—if this was going to be the thing that finally pushed him away—she figured she might as well get it over with.

She spoke fast. "I do know some day laborers, mostly from my church, and, uh, I'm an 'illegal' immigrant, but I prefer to use the term 'undocumented.'"

"Come again?" he said, his head tilting almost imperceptibly, as his eyes narrowed.

"I don't like to use 'illegal.' It's more accurate to say 'undocumented,' or 'unauthorized to work in the United States.' The government calls it 'unlawful presence.'"

"Wait. *You* are illegal, or undocumented, or whatever?"

Alma couldn't read his tone. Maybe it was just confusion—or maybe it was revulsion.

"Yeah. My whole family is, except my cousin Selena. She was born here. And one of my dad's brothers is a citizen. His wife and kids have status."

Evan rubbed his temple, concentrating hard.

"I don't understand. How can your dad be illegal? Hasn't he been here for, like, twenty years? I thought, I mean, he owns a business, and a house. I, uh . . ."

Alma watched Evan searching, trying to make sense of what she was saying. A big part of her wanted to revert to sarcasm, to make some biting remark about Americans' apparently insatiable desire for boneless, skinless chicken breast. But this was Evan and he was different, so she leaned in and spoke gently.

"I can try to explain. I mean, do you want me to?"

"Yeah," he replied. "I'm not following."

Alma took a swig of coffee.

"Here's the deal. After my mom and dad got married, my mom got pregnant with Raúl. Dad wanted to build a house. He didn't have the money. Typical story, right?"

"Right," Evan said, nodding.

"We're from a really small town. People used to farm, but nobody makes money farming anymore. And there weren't other jobs in our town. So my dad, he had a lot of cousins and brothers working in the U.S."

"Here?" Evan asked. "In Gilberton?"

"Actually, in Los Angeles at first, but it was pretty rough over there, gangs and violence and crappy jobs. So one of my uncles heard about the poultry plants in Georgia."

"You mean somebody in LA knew about this town?" Evan asked.

"Yeah. 'Gilberton, Georgia: Chicken Capital of the World,' right?"

"Right. I mean who wouldn't want to live in the chicken capital?" Evan said, grinning.

He kind of had a point, but really, it *was* the chickens that brought them.

"So he moved over here, and then my *tía* Dolores came up from Mexico to check it out. It was good work, and the supervisors loved hiring Mexican workers. What wasn't to love? Most of them worked hard for low wages and didn't complain."

"But why didn't they just come legally?" Evan asked. "I mean, is that a dumb question?"

"Here's the thing: To come legally, you either have to get the company you work for to sponsor you, or you have to have an immediate family member—like a husband or wife—who's already here legally. Companies like Silver Ribbon wanted workers, but they couldn't—or wouldn't—sponsor them. So people just started crossing over and using false papers. Everyone knew they were doing it. I mean, Silver Ribbon actually sent people to recruit workers right at the border. They told my aunt to bring her whole family."

"So did your dad come to work at Silver Ribbon?" Evan asked.

"No, he came to work for my uncle at first, in landscaping. My dad was nervous about using false papers."

"Is your uncle illegal?"

"You mean 'undocumented'?" Alma couldn't bear hearing the word "illegal," especially coming from Evan's mouth.

"Sorry," Evan said. "Undocumented."

"No. There was a law passed in '86 that gave my uncle amnesty. After that, he could apply for his wife and kids to be here. They had to wait a long time in Mexico, but now they're all legal residents. My uncle is a citizen, actually."

Thinking about her uncle's son, Manny, made her blood boil. Alma clenched her fist tight.

"Is this too hard to talk about?" Evan asked.

"No," Alma said. "I was just thinking about my cousin—he's Raúl's age. He's legal, but it's a total waste. He dropped out of GHS and now he runs around Gilberton pretending to be a gangster. It pisses me off. He has all these opportunities, you know? But he throws them away."

"Yeah," Evan said. "I have a cousin like that, too. I mean, he's not a gangster . . ."

"Thanks for clarifying," Alma said, nudging Evan gently. "I was worried preppy gangs were starting to crop up around here—you know, instead of the Crips and the Bloods, it would be, like, the Navy Blazers and the Bow Ties. Maybe they'd use golf clubs as weapons."

She stood up and pretended to take a swing.

"Shut up, Alma," Evan said, pulling her onto his lap and laughing.

This was going fine. Evan hadn't walked away. In fact, he was holding her pressed up against his chest. That had to be a good sign.

"So was Raúl born here?" He hugged her tightly as she struggled playfully against his arms.

"No," Alma said, breaking free of his grasp.

"Your dad came alone?"

"Yeah. He was here when my brother was born, and my mom wouldn't let him go back to see my brother. It was getting dangerous at the border, and she didn't want him to risk coming back. My dad started going crazy, though. So he just showed up to meet Raúl on his first birthday without telling my mom."

"Was your mom pissed?"

"I don't know. I think she was just happy to see him."

"But he came back?"

"Yeah, he wanted to stay home, but by that time, everybody needed the money my dad sent."

"Does he still send money home?"

"Every week. *Migradollars.* I'm telling you, Evan, we're all addicted to them. Migration's like a bad drug habit: Once it gets started, it changes everything on both sides of the border. Americans are addicted to cheap labor, and Mexicans are addicted to the *migradollars* cheap laborers send back home."

"I'm not addicted to cheap labor," Evan said.

"Do you like tomatoes?"

"Yeah, good ones."

"Do you eat boneless, skinless chicken breast?"

"All the time."

"Is your room carpeted?"

"Yeah."

"Then you're addicted to cheap labor." Alma paused and leaned away from Evan. "Well, maybe you're right. Your family could afford that stuff even if it cost four times as much."

Evan stood up and threw his hand to his head. "Why do you say stuff like that?"

He started to pace and rub his forehead.

"It's habit," Alma said.

"Yeah," he said, stopping to look at her. "It's getting old, Alma."

"I'm sorry, Evan," Alma said. She reached out to take his hand and pull him back to the bench. "It's just that sometimes I think you don't see it, you know?"

"See what, Alma?" Evan asked, not letting go of her hand.

"How easy you have it," she said. "How charmed your life is."

"Maybe you're right, Alma," Evan said, turning to face her. "But my life doesn't really feel all that charmed."

———

When Evan came home from school, Whit was sitting at the breakfast bar.

"What's up, Evan?" his cousin asked casually, as if he belonged in Evan's kitchen—as if he wasn't supposed to be in school several states away.

"Aren't you supposed to be in New Hampshire, Whit?" Evan asked, opening the refrigerator door.

"Virginia," Whit replied. "New Hampshire was two schools ago. Really, you must try harder to keep up."

Whit was like a modern-day Holden Caulfield—sick smart and completely incapable of staying in the same boarding school for more than a few months.

"Whatever," Evan said. He chugged some Gatorade and then picked up the remote to switch on the news.

"Really, Evan?" Whit said, in his most annoyingly whiny voice. "The local news?"

Evan glared at him and tried to focus on the perky voice of the anchorwoman.

"Seeking vital information about the most recent house fire, are we?" Whit asked. "Or perhaps we need a preview of the most riveting reality TV programs?"

The young female anchor broke into Whit's monologue.

"In Gilberton's town square today, more than two hundred anti-illegal-immigration activists gathered for what they called a 'No More Amnesty' rally."

"I stand corrected," Whit said, turning intently toward the TV.

The television showed a rough-looking white man in his fifties, with a gray beard and wide-brimmed hat. He held a handmade sign that said "<u>WE</u> ARE AMERICA!"

"Ah, behold the dregs of humanity," Whit announced.

"Shut up, Whit," Evan said. "I'm trying to listen for chrissake."

"Activists are pressuring city and county government to enforce the state's tough new immigration bill, SB 529." The cameras cut to the television studio, where the anchor sat across from a balding, middle-aged white man in a polo shirt and blue blazer.

She introduced the man as John D. Barnes, the head of a local organization called Save This State. "Illegal immigration is organized crime," the man said. "When we fail to enforce the law, we're basically offering sanctuary to illegal aliens."

"I stand corrected," Whit said. "Local news *does* cover real issues, with the assistance of racist idiots posing as experts."

"Why don't you go annoy people in your own kitchen?" Evan asked.

"Because my parents and I can't bear to be in the same room for more than ten minutes," Whit said.

"Oh, yeah," Evan replied. "That."

"Activists will continue to press for local enforcement," the anchorwoman concluded, "while also putting pressure on U.S. senators and congressional representatives to enact tough new border-enforcement laws."

"And the fearless Sexton Prentiss will lead the charge," Whit called out. He grabbed a pewter flask from his pocket, unscrewed the cap, and took a long swig. Then he walked toward the kitchen door.

To his shock, Evan didn't want him to leave yet. He wanted more information.

"Wait," he said. "So, uh, your dad's not a big fan of undocumented immigrants?"

Whit turned to face Evan. "You mean *illegal aliens*? Uh, no, Evan. Here's a little civic education: your dear uncle Sexton has introduced three border-enforcement bills in the past four months."

"Why does he care so much about the border?" Evan asked. "I mean, we live in *Georgia*."

He knew he sounded clueless to Whit, and he hated it.

"Uh, votes? It's *always* votes, Evan."

He threw open the kitchen door.

"It's been lovely. Give my regards to BeBe, will you?"

Then he sauntered out, taking another swig from his flask.

How was it possible that he and Whit had the same blood coursing through their veins?

———

"So, how long was your dad here alone?"

It was Friday, and Evan and Alma were back on the "Restraint" bench before school. He had been drilling her with questions for twenty minutes. It wasn't easy to answer his questions, but it also was an enormous relief. Evan knew about her "status," and he hadn't turned away. In fact, he seemed pretty desperate to understand her situation. Of course, it helped that he was still bringing her double cappuccinos. Alma could face any challenge as long as she had a good, strong cup of coffee.

"Five years. I was born down there. When I was about two and Raúl had just turned five, my mom and dad decided we should all move to Gilberton."

"Man! I can't believe it took him five years to bring y'all up. He must have been so lonely."

"He was, I think. It was my mom's decision. Her sister was sick with cancer, and treatment was too expensive. She knew it would be easy to get a job here, and she wanted to make money to help her sister."

"Wow." Evan sat back down beside her. "Did it work? I mean, did the treatments work? Is her sister OK?"

Alma stared at the plastic lid on her coffee cup, wanting to prolong the moment a bit longer, wanting to avoid this part of the story. She imagined how Evan would respond. He probably would give her what everyone gave: sad expressions, hollowly sympathetic words, and then a subtle pulling back, an instinct to separate from the pain of tragedy. Alma had seen this instinct in the body language of those few people she had told, and she always sensed it in her cousins, aunts, and uncles. For them, Alma was a constant reminder of the danger and precariousness of life, a well of deep sorrow that they desperately wanted to avoid sinking into.

Evan's quiet voice broke into her thoughts: "Alma? Are you with me?"

"Sorry," she replied. And she *was* sorry—sorry that she had to tell him all of this, but knowing that it needed to happen.

"No, I mean, my mom couldn't help her."

"It was too late?" Evan asked.

"My mom died trying to get here, in the Sonoran Desert."

"Damn," Evan replied, drawing out the word in a tone that was not exactly sweet and sympathetic. "Damn," he repeated, his shoulders slumping.

Alma wasn't sure what to do with his reaction, so she kept talking. "The coyotes—you know, the guys people pay to guide them through the desert?—they abandoned her and another woman. They had fallen into a ravine. They couldn't get out. It was summer, which was a stupid time to cross a desert, but my mom wanted Raúl to start kindergarten in August. The other woman survived until the border patrol found her. My mom died of dehydration."

Evan stood up without speaking. Alma watched, confused, as he stepped toward her and then past her. She stared again at the lid of her cup, noticing the drops of coffee pooled near the opening. She should have known better than to tell him. It was too much.

But then she felt his touch, his chest against her back, his arms wrapping around her waist and pulling her toward him. He sat behind her with his legs swung across the bench, nestling her body between them.

And it felt so good inside his arms. The way he held her was so right that she wanted to cry—not from sorrow but from relief, a profound relief that someone finally understood her. Evan knew exactly what she needed when she hadn't even known it herself.

After a long silence, he rested his chin on her shoulder and asked, "Where were you? And Raúl?"

"In Phoenix, waiting in a hotel with my uncle."

She took a swig of coffee and allowed her body to rest completely against him.

"For kids back then, it was easy to cross. We rode through a border checkpoint with a distant cousin. He's legal, and his kids were born here. We just used their birth certificates."

"How old were you?" he asked, almost whispering.

"Almost three. I don't remember any of it."

"Do you remember her?"

"Not really. No."

She closed her eyes and took a sip of coffee, tasting its soothing bitterness and feeling the subtle movement of Evan's chest against her back. After a few moments, Alma reached forward to put her cup on the bench. She wanted to say something to make him know that she was OK.

"Hey, guess what tomorrow is?" she said, brightly. "It's one month from the day of your party."

A broad smile spread across Evan's face.

"You mean, no more house arrest?" he asked, leaning in toward her.

"I'm a free woman," Alma replied. The words stuck in her throat.

What did it mean to be free, she wondered, when she lived under the rule of her father, and in constant fear that the people she loved would go to jail?

"Or, at least, I'm not grounded anymore," she said, forcing a smile.

"Let's celebrate," Evan said, standing. "Tomorrow night. Where should we go?"

Alma grabbed his hand and pulled him back to the bench. "Evan, hell will freeze over before my dad lets me go on a date with you."

"Seriously?" Evan said.

"Yeah, seriously."

Evan looked at her intently and pulled his lower lip between his teeth. She could tell he was thinking—trying to come up with a way around these insane restrictions.

Watching him think, seeing him like that, Alma realized how tired she was of resisting him. She knew it was time to give in completely. Something inside her told her that she didn't have any other choice.

"I have an idea," she said. She jumped up from the bench and giddy weightlessness spread through her body.

"Should I be afraid?" Evan asked.

"Yes, definitely. Have you ever been to a *quinceañera?*"

Was she actually doing this? She had imagined it, but she'd never thought she would have the nerve.

"A *what?*"

"A *quinceañera*—you know, the elaborate coming-of-age parties that people in Latin cultures have for their daughters' fifteenth birthdays."

"Oh, you mean a keeen-say," Evan said. "Like on MTV."

"Something like that," Alma replied. Apparently, everything Evan knew about *quinceañeras* came from *My Super Sweet 16*. She hoped that was about to change.

"If you want to see me tomorrow night, you need to find your teammate Jonathan and get him to invite you to his sister's *quinceañera.*"

"Come again?"

Alma stood up and pointed toward the school entrance. "Just go in there and score yourself an invite to Yazmín's *quince.*"

"And you promise you'll be there?" Evan asked, standing to face her.

"Yeah, I have to be there. I'm a *dama*."

"A what?"

"Never mind. I'll be there. And don't worry. I'll be hard to miss."

Evan wrapped his hands around Alma's waist and leaned in to whisper in her ear.

"Done."

TEN

Snow White

When Alma saw Evan crossing the street, her stomach lurched and her heart started to beat fast. His shaggy bangs, which usually hung over his eyes, were sort of haphazardly gelled back, framing his high forehead and bewildered face. He looked adorably preppy, in khaki pants, a navy-blue blazer, a light-blue shirt, and a striped bow tie. He also looked utterly out of place.

Alma was so busy gawking that it took her a minute to notice Mary Catherine by his side. In a short, strapless red satin dress and high-heeled sandals, she was hard to miss. Her sandy-blond hair was swept into a neat twist, and a short strand of white pearls stood out against the smooth skin of her throat.

With M.C. looking like that, Alma knew their plan would work.

She and Mary Catherine had hatched the plan at lunch on Friday: Mary Catherine would come as Evan's date. When Evan protested, Alma patiently explained that M.C. wasn't just *any* date; she was a drop-dead beautiful date. This would keep her dad and all of the nosy *tías* from thinking, even for a moment, that the country-club boy might be there to see Alma.

Mary Catherine enfolded Alma in a tight hug. When she stepped back, Alma noticed Evan's eyes scan her own outfit, a puzzled expression on his face.

"Snow White," Alma said, trying not to sound as idiotic as she felt.

Mary Catherine burst into joyous peals of laughter. "You have *got* to be kidding me! You're dressed up as Snow White?"

Alma glanced down at the bright yellow bustier and puffy electric-blue tulle skirt that dropped almost to the floor.

"Would I kid about this?" She swept her hand along the edge of the skirt. "It's a princess theme. Disney Princess."

"Awesome," Mary Catherine said, and then she let out one of those crazy bellowing laughs.

"We each had to pick a different Disney princess. Obviously, I chose last."

"You make a pretty sexy Snow White," Mary Catherine said. "Doesn't she usually have puffy sleeves? That strapless bustier definitely helps."

Mary Catherine turned to Evan, who was trying to look away. "And doesn't her skin tone look fantastic against the butter yellow?" She took his chin in her hand and forced his eyes to rest on Alma's chest.

Alma was surprised to see a splotchy blush cover the edge of Evan's cheeks. His eyes trailed up to meet hers.

"You look beautiful, Alma," Evan said. "You *always* look beautiful."

She mouthed a silent "thanks."

Raúl came toward them, eyebrows arched as he took in Mary Catherine's body. It was hard to ignore.

"Hey, Evan," he said, "why don't you and your friend come sit with me?"

Mary Catherine threw a devastating smile in his direction. "It's great to meet you, Raúl. Alma says you're going to take care of us?"

"I'll take care of you," he replied, with a wink.

Alma grabbed Raúl by the elbow. "Behave," she hissed in his ear. She shot a quick glance at Evan, smiled reassuringly, and turned to join Maritza, who was working a sexy midriff-bearing Jasmine costume.

Maritza always got her way.

———

Raúl led them to their table. A DJ was talking in rapid and very animated Spanish on the dance floor. He sounded like one of the guys on the Spanish radio station, where Evan's dial occasionally paused on the way to some other channel.

Mary Catherine nudged Raúl in the side. "What's he saying?"

"Just welcome and what a special day this is for Yazmín and her parents. He's about to introduce the court."

"The what?" Evan whispered loudly.

"The court. You know, the *damas* and *chambelanes*." Evan must have looked as clueless as he felt because Raúl continued explaining. "It's like bridesmaids and groomsmen at a wedding."

Scanning the room, Evan saw Alma's dad sitting with a bunch of men at a table by the dance floor.

"Do I have time to go say hi to your dad?"

"Bad idea," Raúl said. "Trust me."

"But—"

The DJ's booming voice broke in.

"Too late," Raúl called out. "It's starting."

Evan and M.C. watched in awe as the event unfolded. Seven couples processed somberly down the center aisle of the room. All the girls were dressed like Disney princesses. The guys wore electric-blue fedoras and vests with white crosses stitched onto the backs. The crosses looked more like tattoos than church symbols. Evan looked down at his dull khaki pants and wondered if he stood out as much as he thought.

When the *quinceañera* entered the room, the couples turned toward each other, raising their arms to create a sort of tunnel. The girl was dressed like Cinderella in a powder blue dress with a huge puffy skirt. Her skirt barely made it through the human tunnel.

Mary Catherine cut her eyes toward Evan, trying to get his attention. He knew that if he looked at her, they would both start laughing, so he stared ahead, stone-faced.

The girl walked to a carriage-shaped throne surrounded by hundreds of blue and white balloons. She sat down gingerly, looking more embarrassed than excited. Yazmín's face looked so young, even caked with makeup and framed with stiff curls. To Evan, she looked like a child playing dress-up, except that she seemed to be having a lot less fun.

A man and a woman who must have been her parents came toward her. The dad was carrying a shimmering pillow of sorts. Evan shot Raúl a surprised glance.

"Just watch," mouthed Raúl.

Yazmín's mother lifted the layers of skirt to reveal Yazmín's white Keds. Her father leaned down to remove one of her socks and shoes, and then lifted a shimmery silver stiletto from the satin pillow and carefully slid it onto her foot. He repeated the ritual with her other foot. Once both stilettos were firmly placed, Yazmín stood, shakily, and her mom and dad both offered a hug and kiss before leaving the dance floor.

Just then, booming music filled the room. Evan had never heard music like this. The word that came to mind was "polka." Was that right? There were lots of horns and men singing in harmony. All seven couples did a sort of choreographed dance, swinging around the dance floor, repeating the same simple back-and-forth step. Alma wore a stiff, uncomfortable smile that made Evan wish the whole thing would end soon.

When the song finally ended, Alma and her friends Magda and Maritza headed toward their table. Evan watched Alma intently, trying not to look as bewildered as he felt.

Pulling up a chair, Alma leaned in and whispered in his ear, "Weird, huh?"

Evan just smiled and touched one of the stiff ringlet curls that trailed the side of her face. He let his hand brush her chin for a moment and then dropped it under the table to take her hand. Yeah, it was weird, but he didn't care. He just wanted to feel her warm hand in his and study the flushed skin of her cheeks and throat.

"What *was* that music?" asked Mary Catherine, not even trying to hide her aversion.

"Doesn't it suck?" Maritza replied. "*Banda*. Uggh."

The DJ said something else, and a new song filled the room. Maritza stood, shook her hips rapidly, and said to no one in particular, "Merengue. Now that's what I'm talking about."

A girl emerged from behind the balloon arch, dressed in a skin-tight black micro-miniskirt and a red tube top. Evan saw the long expanse of her bare legs ending with the same silver stilettos Yazmín had been given.

"What the hell?" he heard himself say. "Is that *Yazmín*?"

Alma laughed and leaned in toward him. "Yeah, she changed clothes. This is the 'surprise dance.'"

"As in, 'Surprise! Your sweet Disney Princess is a prostitute'?"

"Something along those lines." Alma laughed. "I think it's meant to show that she's an adult now."

Evan looked around the room in amazement as Yazmín's parents, uncles, aunts, grandparents, and friends smiled sweetly and watched her bump and grind, in no particular order, with every one of the seven guys in her court. He had to admit, she was a good dancer. But she still didn't look like she was having any fun.

"Ev, hon, isn't this *awesome*?" Mary Catherine asked, leaning in from the other side. "I was thinking it's kind of like a wedding or a debutante ball, but *whoa*!"

———

Alma stared incredulously at the heaping plate of food in front of Evan.

"Are you going to eat all of that?"

"Yeah, probably. Why, do you want some?"

"Uh, no. That's just a lot of food."

"It looks so good—what are these things?"

"Tamales."

Evan picked one up and brought it toward his lips.

"Uh, Evan, you have to take off the corn husks on the outside before you eat them."

"Aww, damn," Raúl called out, breaking into their conversation. "You should have let your white boy eat the husks!"

"Just ignore my stupid brother," Alma said as she reached over to take the tamale. "I'll show you." She peeled the husk off the tamale and placed it back on his plate, pushing aside a huge pile of enchiladas in green chile sauce. "You should eat it with a fork. If you pick it up, it will fall apart."

Evan looked at her sheepishly and picked up his fork. "So, Raúl says you didn't have one of these?"

"A *quinceañera*? Absolutely not. It's a crazy waste of money. I made my dad start a college savings account for me instead."

"Bummer. I would have liked to see footage of your 'surprise dance.'" Evan laughed and nudged her with his elbow.

"I don't think so, Evan. I mean, there's a reason they made me Snow White tonight."

"What? Snow White can't dance?"

"No." Alma leaned in closer and whispered, "You know, I'm, uh, pure as the driven snow."

Evan's eyes sparkled, and he laughed a strong, hearty laugh.

The entire table turned to look at them.

"What's so funny?" Maritza asked.

Alma looked firmly at Evan, trying to convey that her "Snow White" status was not the business of the entire table.

"Alma's trying to teach me how to eat tamales, and I'm making a complete idiot of myself," Evan replied, grinning.

Everyone fell back into conversation, and he leaned toward Alma. Pressing his hand gently against the stiff blue tulle just above her knee, he whispered, "There's nothing wrong with that, Alma."

She felt his lips gently graze the soft skin just below her ear, while the warmth of his hand radiated through her body. She closed her eyes and tried not to sigh out loud.

Maritza's voice broke her swoon.

"I'm ready to *dance*! Who's with me?"

Mary Catherine tugged on Evan's arm. "Come on, y'all, let's dance."

"There's not a chance you'll get Alma on the dance floor," Maritza said. "She's too sophisticated to dance at a *quinceañera*."

"*Quinceañeras* are patriarchal," Magda said, mocking Alma.

"Silly," added Maritza.

"A waste of money and time," Raúl chimed in.

Alma stood up. "Are y'all finished yet?" she asked. "Because I'm getting kind of thirsty. Can I be excused from the hazing to get a drink?"

"You aren't going to dance?" Evan asked. "What else are you going to do? Watch old guys shoot tequila?"

He glanced across the room at a table full of grandfathers in cowboy hats gathered around a half-empty bottle.

"She won't dance," Maritza replied.

The music changed. A hip-hop remix of some eighties song came over the speakers.

Evan suddenly dropped one hand to the ground, keeping his knees bent as he pulsed his hips and one of his arms to the thumping beat of the music. It looked like some kind of eighties break-dance move.

Alma stared at him, horrified, as the others clapped and squealed with delight.

"How can you resist *that*?" Mary Catherine yelled above the squeals.

"OK, Evan, you win." Reaching her arm toward him, she cried out over the music, "I'll dance with you if you promise never to do *that* again."

Evan hopped up effortlessly. "You've got yourself a deal, Miss García."

Alma skipped onto the dance floor and began to spin, her silly blue skirt billowed around her. She concentrated on nothing but the melody of the song, coursing through a synthesizer. It was so strange, but she felt great dancing, and she didn't care what anyone thought—not even her dad. She had been trying to do the right thing for so long, to act as expected, that she had ignored how she actually felt. She wanted to let it go. All of it.

She suddenly recognized the eighties song. She stopped spinning, threw her arms around Evan's neck, and blurted, "Don't you want me, baby!"

Evan came to a standstill and grinned his perfect grin.

"Come again?"

She leaned in closer, only a little embarrassed. "That's the name of the song, Evan."

Evan wrapped his arms around her and pulled her in close. Their bodies moved together, keeping rhythm with the thumping bass. She felt his hands on the small of her back and his chest pressed against hers. She trailed her fingers through the hair above his neck as she gently arched to look up at him. His hands slid deeper into the curve of her lower back. The music seemed to slow, and the room around them blurred. A diffuse, warm energy coursed through them both. They continued to move together with focused intensity. The deep, sultry voice of a female vocalist hovered over the booming rhythm of the bass.

One of Evan's hands moved slowly up along her spine and onto her bare back. Pausing for a moment at her shoulder, he lightly grazed her collarbone and the skin above her chest. As their fused hips moved together, Alma arched back farther and let her head drop. Evan leaned in and pressed his lips against her neck.

She thought she might melt into a puddle right there on the dance floor when a strong grip jerked Alma out of their trance. She found herself face-to-face with Raúl. His eyes darted toward a table adjacent to the dance floor, where Alma's father sat poised at the edge of his chair, staring at her intently, hands perched on his knees like he was about to pounce.

Alma smiled weakly in her father's direction and then glanced toward Evan. Mary Catherine was whispering in his ear, and a dull remorse seemed to spread across his face. Raúl pulled Alma to his own chest, shifting her mental focus into the footwork of a rapid merengue, but the deep longing ache remained.

After what seemed like a sufficient amount of time, Alma glanced again at her father, who had turned his back to the dance floor to talk with the other men around his table. She looked for Evan, and he wasn't very hard to find. He led Mary Catherine with ease, twisting and turning, pulling her close into his body and then spinning her away. He dropped her into a sudden dip, and they both laughed delightedly when she popped upright and spun back in toward him. Alma realized, smiling, that many eyes were on this beautiful couple, the only couple on the dance floor not moving in a tight merengue; the only white couple on the floor—or, for that matter, anywhere in the San Francisco Banquet Hall.

The song ended, and Evan and Mary Catherine made their way toward Alma.

"What *was* that? I mean, the dance you were doing?" Alma asked.

Mary Catherine looked at Evan. "I don't know. Uh, swing? Shag? It's just dancing."

"You two looked so *good* doing it. I mean, did you take lessons or something?"

Mary Catherine and Evan both laughed. "Yeah. I guess," Mary Catherine said. "If you call cotillion lessons. I'm actually a terrible dancer, but Evan could lead a cardboard box and make it look good."

She nudged Evan toward Alma. "You should try."

Alma glanced at Evan skeptically. She wasn't sure that her hormone-riddled body could handle dancing with Evan again, not with her father glaring from his perch nearby.

"I vow to keep at least six inches of distance between us at all times," Evan said.

"Promise you can do that?" Alma asked.

"I can promise," he said with a crooked grin, "but can you?"

Raúl took Mary Catherine by the arm and looked sternly toward Evan. "I hope y'all both can," he said, "or my dad will go ballistic on you."

Evan gave Raúl a serious nod, and then Alma was twirling. Their arms twisted smoothly in and out of complicated pretzel-like maneuvers, while Alma's feet spun beneath her. Mary Catherine was right. All she had to do was feel the gentle tug on her arm, or the light pressure at the small of her back, and she would move in unison with Evan. He did all the work.

"You're good," he called out as she spun into him.

"I have no idea what I'm doing!" Alma replied, laughing.

"Yeah, but you follow well."

"Don't get any ideas," she replied. "I only follow on the dance floor!"

Evan smiled a wicked smile and slung her into a dip. She gasped and popped back up.

"So, really, where'd you learn to dance like this?" Alma asked.

"I spend a lot of time escorting my mom to charity events. There's not much else to do but dance."

"Does your dad dance?"

"Yeah, but he's pretty much bailed on the party circuit."

He spun her out and back again.

"So, you go as your mom's date? That's cute, Evan."

"I guess."

Taking both of her hands, he threw one arm behind his head in a pretzel maneuver, and then drew her back to him.

"I'd like to see that sometime."

"I don't know. You might get jealous," he said with a wink.

He rested his hand against her back and she fell into another low dip.

"All the ladies love to dance with BeBe's sweet boy," he said, holding her suspended in midair.

———

Coming out of the dip, Alma's expression suddenly changed and her body tightened. She took Evan by the forearm and began to pull him off of the dance floor, weaving through other couples.

"What's up?" Evan asked. "Did I screw up again?"

"No," she said. "It's just my cousin, he's coming toward us. I don't feel like dealing with him."

Out of nowhere, that guy from the parking lot a couple of weeks earlier was standing in front of him in sagging jeans and a wifebeater. This wannabe gangster was Alma's cousin? Evan felt the adrenaline release into his veins.

"So, did you and Mr. Country Club actually do it out here on the dance floor, or was that just foreplay I saw earlier?"

Evan took Alma's hand and pulled her closer.

"Don't you have anything better to do than study my moves on the dance floor, Manny?" she replied.

The loser looked directly at Evan. "I saw you pull up in that girly car."

"What's your point?" Evan growled.

"I'm gonna find out who drives the Hummer, and when I do, you'll be the first to know."

What was his obsession with Conway's Hummer?

Alma grabbed the guy by his arm and yanked him toward her. They shifted into a rapid exchange in Spanish, spitting words at each other. Evan wanted to break in and defend her, but he understood nothing. Feeling like an idiot, he just glared at the guy across from him.

Mary Catherine stepped between Alma and her cousin.

"Uh, hi. Excuse me, I just need to borrow these two for a second?"

She said it tentatively, as if she were asking his permission, but Manny slouched away toward a group of rough-looking guys.

"Sorry to interrupt, Alma, but I have to go, and I was hoping Evan could walk me out. Dillon wants me to go with him to a concert. He's picking me up now."

"Who's Dillon?" Evan asked.

"A new friend. I met him at the Dripolator. He's *nice*."

"How old is he?"

"I don't know, Evan. Quit acting like my father."

"Seriously, Evan." Alma said. "We'll both walk you out."

"OK, just give me a sec. I've got to primp in the bathroom first."

Mary Catherine headed away, and Evan and Alma were left standing in silence.

"So, that was my charming cousin Manny." She shook her head slowly and continued, "I told you about him. Remember?"

Evan didn't remember. All he could think about was the heated exchange in the parking lot.

"You know, the one with a chance at citizenship. God, what a waste."

Evan figured she didn't need to know about their earlier encounter. She was angry enough already.

"I'm sorry if I've caused trouble for you tonight," he said.

"No, Evan. This is the first *quinceañera* I've ever actually enjoyed—and I've been to way too many to count." She squeezed his hand lightly. "Don't worry about Manny. I think he has you confused with someone else. Anyway, he's an idiot. And my dad, well, he's just going to have to get used to us."

"Us. I like that," Evan said.

Evan wrapped his other arm around her waist and stepped close. He let his eyes close and his face dip into her hair. He breathed her in, and all of the tension released. He was breaking the six-inch barrier, but he didn't care. He didn't care about Alma's cousin; he didn't care that her dad might be watching. All he cared about was that he and Alma—finally—were "us."

Mary Catherine, back from the bathroom, stepped between them. "So, do you two lovebirds realize that just about everyone in the room is staring at you?"

Evan looked up sheepishly and realized she was right. He tried to drop Alma's hand, but she just squeezed it tighter.

"Let's go," she said, and she led him off the dance floor by his hand.

They waited outside for a long time. Apparently Dillon wasn't the punctual type. Raúl eventually joined them, clearly hoping to convince Mary Catherine to stay with him. The four sat on a curb and watched cars pass, Evan holding Alma's hand in his lap while Mary Catherine and Raúl shamelessly flirted.

Eventually, a black BMW coupe pulled up. Raúl took Mary Catherine in his arms and whispered something in her ear. She threw her head back and laughed, then gave him a peck on the cheek. Evan and Alma watched as they walked together to the BMW. He opened the door and helped her in. As soon as the door closed, the BMW sped off.

"So what's up with M.C.?" Raúl asked.

"I don't know," Evan said. "She has strange taste in men."

"Yeah," Raúl said.

Evan wished Mary Catherine had decided to stay. Being with Raúl would be good for her. Evan knew he would treat her well, but Mary Catherine didn't seem to be into the kind of guy who treated her well.

As they made their way back toward the building, two guys came bolting around the corner and entered the hall. If Evan had to guess, he'd say they weren't sober. Evan saw Alma and Raúl glance nervously toward each other, and Raúl pulled out his cell phone.

Within moments, the doors to the hall burst open and several bodies lurched through the door, fists flying. Without thinking, Evan dragged Alma to the corner and pinned her body against the brick wall as they watched a fight unfold. Raúl disappeared around the corner, cell phone to his ear.

By the time Raúl returned, the sound of sirens filled the air. Two guys went running in different directions, but two remained locked together on the concrete. Raúl ran by, grabbing Evan's arm as he passed.

"Help me out, man."

Evan watched as Raúl grabbed one of them from behind and wrenched him away. Raúl nodded toward the other, and Evan leaned down and forcefully yanked him to his feet, holding him in a tight grip. Raúl spoke in Spanish to the guy in Evan's grasp, and then yelled at Evan to let go.

He took off running just as the police cruisers turned the corner and pulled to an abrupt stop in front of them. Raúl dropped his arms, and Evan realized that he had pulled Manny from the fight.

A flashlight shone brightly in Evan's face.

A deep Southern voice boomed, "Evan Roland? What the hell are *you* doing here, boy?"

Evan shielded his eyes from the glare of the flashlight, trying to see the source of the voice. He slowly stepped to the side as the flashlight's beam hovered beside him. It was Logan's cousin Troy.

"Troy, man! You're blinding me," he said, laughing as he walked toward the police cruiser and away from that asshole Manny. "Put down the flashlight, for chrissake!"

He glanced over at Raúl, who looked petrified—like a deer in headlights.

———

"Alma, Raúl, this is Troy," Evan said, as if he were introducing an old buddy—as if the cop standing in front of her didn't have the power to throw Raúl in jail, even without evidence that he had done anything wrong. "He's Logan's cousin—we go way back."

The cop reached out to shake their hands—to shake their hands! "Nice to meet you folks."

This was all getting too weird. Alma remembered a time on the soccer field when tempers had flared and a fight broke out. The police came, and they definitely didn't shake any hands. They never even gave the guys a chance to explain. They just threw them in the back of the cruiser and took off.

The siren squealed on the police car, and the cop looked back toward the cruiser. "All right then," the cop said, punching Evan gently in the arm. "I'm headed back to work. Y'all stay out of trouble."

The cruiser drove away, sirens blaring again.

Raúl breathed a loud sigh. "Evan, man," he said, "I don't know how to thank you."

"For what? I didn't do anything."

Alma felt a sudden wave of sadness sweep over her, catching in her throat and threatening to well up into tears. How could she begin to explain to Evan what this meant? Wasn't his certainty that the world was a good place—that cops were fair and friendly, that people were kind and charitable—one of the things that made Evan who he was?

Suddenly exhausted, Alma leaned against the side of the building. "Are you OK?" Evan asked.

"Yeah. Long day, you know? I mean, the hair alone took two hours to sculpt." She smiled weakly.

"Any chance you'll let me take you home—I mean, now that we're going public and all."

Alma motioned her head in the direction of the black stretch Hummer parked next to the curb. "And deny me the opportunity to ride in *that*?"

Evan laughed, looking at the beast of an SUV. "Yeah, I guess I can't compete."

Raúl came to join them.

"Thanks again, Evan," he said.

"No, man. Thank *you* for taking care of M.C. all night. She can be a handful."

"Yeah, no problem. She's pretty cool."

"She has crappy taste in guys, Raúl," Evan said.

"Whatever. Hey, you should come out to Grant Park tomorrow to watch my dad's team. We lost a lot of players this fall, so we sort of suck, but it's fun."

Raúl left out the part about the players being arrested and deported. That probably was a good idea. Evan didn't need to know.

"I'm there!" Evan said, not even trying to conceal his excitement.

"Our game is at one. Bring your cleats. We can shoot some."

"Definitely," Evan replied. "Are you going?" he asked Alma.

"Yeah, if it's at one I can go. I have a meeting to go over scholarship applications tomorrow afternoon, but not until three."

"Alma's meeting her new best friend," Raúl replied. "She's a retired middle school counselor."

"Damn," said Evan. "I thought I was your new best friend. But I mean, how can I compete with a retired middle school counselor?"

"Shut up, y'all," Alma said. "I am just trying to get somewhere in life! Like, maybe, out of this town for starters."

ELEVEN
Goal!

"*¡Gracias a Dios y a la Virgencita!*"

Alma's *abuela* Lupe called out to her from across the phone line.

"*Buenos días, Abuelita,*" Alma said, smiling as she imagined her grandmother talking from the courtyard of her little *tienda* in San Juan. Alma hadn't seen the *tienda* or her grandmother in a very long time, but after fifteen years of phone calls, videos, and photos, she felt like she knew them both well.

"I'm going to get my visa!" her grandmother replied in Spanish.

Alma knew that *Abuela* Lupe had not yet been to the consulate. She laughed heartily and asked, "And how is it that you know this, *Abuelita*?"

"The signs are all there, *mi vida*! I talked to the consulate and my appointment is set."

Alma didn't want to disappoint her grandmother, but for Mexicans, getting a tourist visa was a lot harder than just getting through to the consulate to make an appointment.

"December ninth at midday—twelve o'clock."

"That's great, *Abuela* Lupe, but—"

"Which means, *por supuesto*, that Juan Dieguito and *la Virgencita* are praying for me."

"I don't follow—"

"December ninth? *Ay, mi vida*. The feast day of Juan Dieguito. Aren't you going to *misa* anymore?"

"Yes, *Abuela*, I still go to church, but—"

"He's a saint now, you know? It's official. And since *la Virgencita*'s feast day is December twelfth and my appointment is at twelve, the signs are all there."

Alma felt a smile curl the edges of her mouth, or maybe it had just been plastered there since last night.

"*¡Imagínate!* We all will be celebrating *Las Posadas* together in Georgia this December, *muñeca*."

If this miracle actually did happen, and they all were eating *posole*, drinking warm fruit punch, and processing through the streets together for the nine days leading up to Christmas, Alma knew it was likely to be the first and last time. If *Abuela* Lupe was right about *la Virgencita*, she would be granted the visa in December, which would give her six months. *Tía* Pera and *Tío* Rigo would return to Mexico and set up their new lives there, while *Abuela* Lupe would stay with Alma and her family. But in June, right after graduation, *Abuela* Lupe, Isa, and Selena would have to return to Mexico for good.

Alma couldn't help but catch the wave of excitement. After last night with Evan, Alma was feeling so optimistic that she was almost tempted to share in her *abuelita*'s certainty that a future of good fortune lay ahead.

———

Evan never exactly enjoyed sitting through church with his family. None of it seemed real. It was just a show that everyone dressed up on Sunday mornings to put on.

Look at us. We are a happy family. The family that prays together stays to-gether.

All Evan wanted was to get it over with—to see Alma again. Plus, Uncle Sexton and Aunt Maggie were in town with all of their kids, which spelled family drama. When Whit excused himself before the sermon to go to the restroom, Evan knew what was coming. Ten minutes later, his aunt gently nudged him.

"Evan, sweetheart," she whispered, "can you please do me a little favor and check on your cousin? He's been gone for quite a while."

Ugh.

Evan knew where to find him. He went to the balcony and edged into the space between the organ pipes and the stained glass window. Whit was there, taking a long swig from his flask.

"What's up, Evan?" Whit asked casually, as if it were perfectly normal for him to be hiding out behind the organ getting drunk.

"You shouldn't be drinking in here," Evan said. If that wasn't stating the obvious, Evan didn't know what was.

Whit took another swig and shrugged.

"In case you haven't noticed, it's before noon on a Sunday," Evan said, "and we're in church."

"I've noticed," Whit replied. "But I need to prepare myself for this afternoon's public display of filial piety." He pulled a container of prescription pills from his pocket and examined the label.

"I have no idea what you're talking about, Whit," Evan said.

"Of course you don't, Evan. You and your mother live in a state of domestic tranquility, and—as far as I can tell—your dad basically no longer exists to either of you."

As always, Whit was wrong. It was Evan's dad who seemed to have forgotten about them.

"Let's go, Whit," Evan said, reaching out to pull Whit to his feet. "I've been sent to retrieve you."

Whit stood and followed Evan, and they both slid back into the pew just before the benediction.

When church ended, Evan felt elated to be leaving alone rather than following his family to the club—that is until Whit rushed over to join him.

"So, Evan," Whit announced, "as you know, my parents and I can't be alone together for more than five minutes, and it's a ten-minute drive to the club."

"What's your point, Whit?" Evan asked, getting into his car.

"I need to ride with you."

"I'm not going," Evan said.

He started to close the door, but Whit grabbed it and held it open.

"Not fair!" Whit exclaimed, thrusting the car door open. "What's your excuse?"

"A soccer game."

"Granted, I don't know much about high school sporting events," Whit said as he pulled the flask from his pocket, "but I know you're not in season yet."

"It's a city league," Evan replied, grabbing the flask from Whit's hand and shoving it under the seat of his car. "A friend and her brother invited me. And, *Christ*, can you please not drink in the parking lot of our church?"

"What friend?" Whit asked.

"You don't know them."

"Try me."

"Alma and Raúl." Evan knew there was no way Whit had crossed paths with Alma's family.

"Wait, you're not going to watch the Liga Latina are you?" Whit asked.

Evan's jaw dropped. How would Whit know about this league?

"You *are*!" Whit exclaimed. "Can I come, too? Please? Please, please?"

"You've got to be kidding me." Evan said as he started to slam the door shut.

"OK, then." Whit announced, wedging himself into the car and reaching down for the flask. "I'll just hang out at the club and finish this bottle before this afternoon's televised interview."

Evan rolled his eyes and let out a long sigh.

"Hand over the bottle. And the pills," Evan said. "Let's go."

Whit released a squeal and thrust the flask into Evan's hand. "I *love* cultural experiences."

This had the potential to be bad.

———

Standing at the edge of the field, Alma saw Evan walking toward her with another boy she didn't know. They both had on khakis and white button-down shirts. Evan also wore a strange look on his face. Maybe embarrassment.

"Hey, Alma," Evan said as he approached. "This is my cousin Whit. He's visiting from out of town. I'm on babysitting duty."

So this was the delinquent cousin. In his preppy clothes, he sure didn't look like any delinquent Alma had ever met. And he was way too old to need babysitting.

Whit threw out his arms and lifted her off of her feet, in apparent defiance of his beanpole frame.

"Look at you!" he commented, holding her at arm's length. "You're ravishingly beautiful."

Evan stood beside her awkwardly.

Alma laughed. "You're not so shabby yourself," she replied.

It was true. Whit had a beautiful, broad jawbone and a long, angular nose. His dark hair and dark eyebrows set off creamy skin. The only blemishes on his near-perfect face were the puffy, dark bags under his eyes.

"She thinks I'm sexy," Whit announced triumphantly to Evan.

Just then a whistle blew and they turned to watch the game.

Evan stood with his body inclined slightly forward, leaning into the field. His eyes focused with laser-sharp precision on the ball, occasionally darting across the field to take in the position of the goalie or an open player. He seemed completely oblivious to everything and everyone around him, including Alma and her little cousin Selena, who, to Alma's surprise, had sort of nuzzled up against him like a stray puppy looking for someone to feed it.

Alma was actually glad Evan had brought his cousin along. Whit didn't seem to care a bit about soccer. He knelt down beside Selena and engaged her in intense conversation.

"Man, your brother is good," Evan said, not even looking at Alma. "Who's that small kid—the striker? Number twenty-three?"

"You mean the guy with long hair? That's Ramiro."

"He's pretty good, too. Where does he play?"

"Right here. He's not a kid. He's, like, twenty-five. He's a framer."

"A what?"

"A framer. You know, he frames houses. That's his job." Then, trying to make conversation, or maybe just to pull Evan out of the trance he seemed to have gone into, Alma continued, "He's got twelve brothers and sisters back in Oaxaca."

"Oaxaca?" Whit asked, standing up. "Does he speak an indigenous language? I read that there are sixteen surviving indigenous languages in Oaxaca."

"Actually, I think he does," Alma said. "Mixtec." Alma was impressed. Evan hadn't told her the delinquent cousin was smart.

"Pass. Pass the ball," Evan cried out. He turned to look at Alma. "Who's the midfielder? Number ten?"

"I don't know his name. He's new." The new guy had stepped in a few weeks back to replace Rafael—one of the casualties of the Silver Ribbon raid.

"He has no idea what he's doing," Evan replied. "How do you say 'pass' in Spanish?"

The whistle interrupted and the referee called halftime. The score was 3-0. The Diablos de Daxthi were in the lead, and there was no chance that the Santos de San Juan would pull it out.

Number ten jogged over toward Alma's dad on the sidelines. They watched as he said something to Alma's dad, who then buried his head in his hands. Number ten walked toward the parking lot. Alma's dad called his team over to consult. The players shifted on their feet and flailed their arms. They were not happy. Raúl said something that seemed to calm them, and then he jogged toward Evan and Alma.

The whole team watched as he approached.

"Hey, man. Rough match." Evan said.

"Yeah, we lost some players, so we've got a bunch of novices out there."

"This is my cousin," Evan said, nodding toward Whit.

Whit thrust out his hand toward Raúl. "*Encantado de conocerte,*" he said.

Whoa. He spoke Spanish with a perfect Castilian accent. That was the Spanish of the elites. Until now, Alma had only heard it on television.

"Good to meet you, too, man," Raúl said, taking his hand. "Thanks for coming out."

Raúl turned to Evan. "So, Diego—one of our midfielders—he just got called in to work. We're short a player. We probably should forfeit since we're getting crushed out there. But I thought you might, uh . . ."

Evan's face lit up. "You want me to step in?"

"If you're up for it," Raúl said, shrugging.

"Hell, yeah!" Evan replied. "Just give me a sec."

He jogged over to his car and rummaged around in the trunk. Then he slid into the backseat.

"Where'd you learn the Spanish, man?" Raúl asked Whit.

"Salamanca," Whit said. "*Estudié un semestre en la Universidad de Salamanca—en España.*"

"No way," Alma said. "How did you pull off a semester at the best university in Spain?"

"My parents find ways," Whit said. "They prefer for me to be as far from Georgia as possible."

Alma laughed nervously, not sure how to respond.

"Damn," Raúl said. "I wish I could get myself in that kind of trouble."

"Let me know if you need some help," Whit said. "It's my special talent. Evan scores goals; I score DUIs."

Raúl laughed and glanced toward Evan's car. "Looks like he's ready."

Evan emerged wearing cleats and soccer shorts. Alma had never seen him look so good. It wasn't just his body. It wasn't even the way he pulled his long bangs off his forehead and secured them back so that she could see his entire face, with that beautiful smile that spread across it. He just looked so confident, like everything in this moment was *right*.

"Let's go," Raúl said.

"Wish us luck," Evan yelled over his shoulder.

Seeing Evan and Raúl jog toward the team, she had a feeling they weren't going to need it.

Evan pulled his white undershirt over his head and let it fall to the ground.

Swoon.

Alma's dad handed him a neon-green team jersey. He shrugged it on too quickly and stepped into the huddle.

"Oh, my God," Whit said, pulling Alma out of her Evan-induced trance. "Your brother just made Evan's day."

Alma decided not to tell Whit that he had made her day, too.

Watching Evan play soccer was disconcerting. He left his easy-going, friendly self crumpled on the sidelines with his discarded under-shirt. He stripped himself down to something else, something more elemental. Evan was a very aggressive player. He taunted the player whose unfortunate job it was to defend him. He threw his elbows and body in ways that Alma was sure would earn him a yellow card, but he seemed to know just where the limits were.

"People are starting to gather," Whit said, nudging Alma and point-ing across the field. "I think they're baffled by the gringo boy."

He turned away from Alma, striking up a conversation in almost flawless Spanish with an elderly grandmother sitting next to them.

Yes, Whit was surprising.

Intrigued by the transformation of Evan's character on the field and by his odd cousin, Alma almost didn't notice that he and Raúl were dom-inating the game. The spectators around her began to point and com-ment. Seeing Evan through their eyes, she realized that Evan was good, really good. He and Raúl seemed to read each other's presence, to sense the other's next move. Evan carried the ball up the sideline, passing two defenders, and then slid a left-to-right pass across the top of the box to Raúl, who sent an arcing shot over the head of the Diablos' goalkeeper and into the top right corner of the goal.

Five minutes later, Evan sent another effortless pass to Raúl, who neatly tucked away their second goal. The crowd along the sidelines grew, and the newly energized fans of the Santos de San Juan began to yell and hoot for the dynamic duo. Even Alma's dad was smiling. His body involuntarily hopped when Evan set Raúl up in the box, positioning him perfectly to send the ball cruising into the left corner of the net, bringing the game to a tie.

Evan felt them watching him—the white kid dominating field eight. He didn't care. Playing with Raúl was such a rush that even if spectators had been screaming, "Get off the field, gringo," he would have ignored their jeers.

There were only three minutes left in the game, and defenders were all over Evan and Raúl. Evan tried to deflect them by sending a few passes to the other forward. He was pretty good at finding Evan's passes, but not the goal.

With the clock down to forty seconds, the Diablos' best player fell to the ground, clutching his knee. Whistle blown.

Evan yelled out in frustration, "Oh, come on! The guy barely touched him."

This would take them into stoppage time.

While the opposing player rolled around on the pitch, feigning an injury to catch his breath, Evan jogged to the sideline. Mr. García yelled out instructions in rapid and completely incomprehensible Spanish. Evan jumped in, hoping his brash behavior wouldn't put him on Mr. García's bad side. Evan described a play that he and Raúl had used at GHS. It required very little help from their teammates, except the defender Ramiro. He was good. Raúl translated, and the other players nodded in agreement. Mr. García—amazingly—smiled and nodded, too.

Another whistle blew, and Evan felt his body shift back into focus. Surrounded by energy from his teammates and the crowd, he felt aggressive but calm. He took in the position of the players around him, motioning for the defenders to adjust.

The other team put the ball back into play. A Diablo sent an errant pass in Ramiro's direction. Ramiro executed the play just as they had planned. He dribbled up the middle and crossed the ball to Evan. Evan drove it down the left sideline and then crossed it into the penalty area. Raúl received the ball, but he couldn't get a shot off. He glanced around as the clock continued counting down. Evan motioned for Ramiro to move forward, into the midfield. Finding him open, Raúl sent a long pass back to Ramiro, who then tapped it across to Evan. Scanning the field, Evan realized that the defenders were so busy covering Raúl that they'd left the goal open. From fifteen yards, he sent the ball airborne, and nailed the top left corner of the goal. It wasn't the plan, but it worked.

Spectators charged the field as teammates piled onto Evan, cheering and hugging. Evan felt the familiar rush of exhilaration, the thrill of the win. His eyes scanned the crowd to find Alma, who stood on the sidelines with a bemused grin.

He looked around. The frenzied crowd was acting like the team had just won a state championship, not a midseason match in a rec league.

Evan untangled himself from the players and jogged over toward Alma.

"First win of the season," she said, smiling serenely. "Thanks."

"Hell, Alma," he said, "You don't need to thank me. That was more fun than I've had in a long time—and your brother is crazy good."

"He's not the one getting all the attention," Whit said, glancing around at the people pointing and gawking at Evan.

"Yeah, it's a little weird," Evan mumbled.

People gathered around, offering congratulations—some in English and others in Spanish. Trying to be polite, Evan responded with "Thanks, uh, *gracias.*"

Whit leaned in and mimicked his accent, "Graaciaas, mew-chas graacias."

Throwing a dismissive glance toward Whit, Evan wrapped his arm around Alma and turned away.

"Your cousin speaks great Spanish, you know. Maybe you should take lessons from him," she said.

"Never gonna happen. You might as well get used to being embarrassed by your gringo boyfriend."

Alma laughed and threw her arms around his neck. Neither of them cared that he was sweaty, or that there were dozens of people gathered around them. He just hugged her in tight.

Evan saw Whit watching them. He was smiling in an odd way, almost genuine. Whit seemed happy here, so far away from their world. Evan was happy, too.

Overjoyed, in fact.

Alma led Evan over to where Raúl and Mr. García stood, beaming from ear to ear, with a group of men who looked to be Mr. García's friends.

"Very good game, Evan. You are a very good player," Mr. García said. He glanced at Raúl, an encouraging expression in his eyes.

"My dad wants you to join the team," Raúl said. "But I told him you probably didn't want to risk injury for the regular season."

"Really? Your dad wants me on his team?"

"Uh, *yeah*," replied Raúl, as if this were totally self-evident. "It would be awesome, but it's no big deal if you can't."

Evan glanced at Alma, whose eyes were sparkling. He'd done it. He had earned the trust and maybe even the admiration of Alma's dad. All it took was a few plays on the soccer field.

"I'd like that, Mr. García. Thank you so much," Evan said.

"Welcome to the team," replied Alma's dad. "Now, we celebrate!"

"Everybody's going to Tres Hermanos on Pine Street," Raúl said. "Wanna come?"

"Yeah!" Evan replied.

"Hey, I hate to ruin the big celebration, but somebody has to drop me off at the Krispy Kreme in a half hour," Alma said. "Remember?"

Raúl rolled his eyes, and Alma's dad smiled a patronizing smile.

"Oh, yeah. Your middle school counselor." Raúl chuckled. "Alma's getting a head start on her college applications."

"I can take her," Evan blurted out, "and then meet you at the restaurant?"

"Thank you, Evan. That is very good." Mr. García said.

Evan's heart started to beat fast, but then he remembered Whit. He had been so close to having Alma alone.

"Hey, Raúl," Whit said, "I need to meet my parents downtown. Can I catch a ride with you?"

Evan was shocked. Whit was trying to help him out.

"Sure, man," Raúl said. "If you've got time, you can come hang with us at the restaurant first."

"*Mil gracias,*" Whit replied. "I love the *posole* at Tres Hermanos. *Muy sabroso.*"

Evan and Alma watched, stunned, as the others turned and walked toward Mr. García's Bronco.

TWELVE

Too Sweet

Realizing that they were alone—or as alone as they might ever be—Evan and Alma grasped hands and ran toward a large grove of poplar trees.

They stumbled and fell, tumbling over each other into the thick bed of leaves—those stubborn poplar leaves that coated the ground every September, not noticing that the heat of summer was far from subsiding.

Evan buried his hands in Alma's long hair and pulled her toward him. They kissed, clinging to each other urgently in the soft bed of dry leaves.

Evan pulled back and held her face in his hands. "I can't believe this is happening."

"I know," Alma said. "Believe me . . ."

Alma ran her hands along the contours of his jaw and interlaced her fingers behind his neck. Evan touched his lips gently to hers, noticing the faint sweet scent of her breath. When he couldn't take it any longer, he pulled her on top of him and kissed her again, hard.

They kissed like that for a while until Evan felt his hands leading places that he knew they weren't ready to go. He pulled her lips away from his, sighing deeply.

"We have to stop," he said. "I mean, I need to stop."

Alma nodded and rolled to the ground. They lay on their backs, holding hands, watching the blue sky through the poplar branches; brown leaves floated gently and landed softly on their still bodies.

Alma turned to face him, propping her head in her arm, and reached across his body to take a leaf from his chest. Then she stood and let the dry leaf fall to the ground.

"Time to go," she said, reaching out to pull him up.

They walked silently to Evan's car, fingers entwined, not caring or even noticing who might be watching. Evan opened Alma's door and watched her slide into the seat of his car. He walked slowly around to his side, in quiet wonder that she was there. He got into the car, leaned toward her, and pulled a crushed leaf fragment from her hair.

They drove, suspended in silent reverie, until they arrived at the doughnut shop. Evan pulled into a nearby space and stepped out of the car. When Alma emerged, he was there to meet her, taking her hand and pulling her gently out. They paused, bodies almost touching, with Alma's face lifted toward Evan's. They kissed again, and Alma turned to go.

Mrs. King sat waiting in her Buick, windows rolled down, watching.

——

"You *do* know who that boy is?"

Mrs. King sat across from Alma, glaring as she shook a doughnut in her fist.

"Yes, ma'am." Alma replied.

"You're telling me that you know who his people are? You know his family?" She slammed the doughnut onto the table, releasing a cloud of powdered sugar.

"Well, I don't actually *know* them," Alma said. "I mean, uh, I haven't met them yet." She stared at her coffee.

"I don't expect you ever will," Mrs. King said.

"Mrs. King," Alma said, staring down at the table where she'd left a trace of powdered sugar, "Evan's great, and I *trust* him."

"Alma, sweetheart," Mrs. King said, reaching out to squeeze her hand, "I know you have good judgment, but sometimes judgment can be clouded by feelings."

"Watch," she commanded. She took the lid off of Alma's black coffee and opened a small container of vanilla hazelnut creamer.

"You like your coffee black, right?"

"Yes, ma'am, unless it's cappuccino."

"Well, sweetheart, Krispy Kreme is not known for its espresso bar, now is it?"

"No, ma'am."

"So this black coffee sittin' here between us, it's clear and strong, just like your intentions. Do you follow?'

"Uh, I think so."

"This coffee has a future; it has a plan." Mrs. King lifted the creamer and pointed toward it. "And this here? This is your Evan." She slowly poured the creamer into Alma's coffee and lifted the cup out toward her. "It's nice and sweet now, but it's *real* cloudy—so cloudy you can't see your way through it."

Wow. Not only did synthetic sweetener ruin Alma's coffee, it was also killing her mood.

"Evan knows about my goals," Alma said. "I mean, he even knows I want to be an anthropologist—and he supports me."

Mrs. King shoved half a doughnut into her mouth, chewed fiercely, and swallowed.

"I see," she said, lifting a napkin to wipe the sugar from her lips. "Then it looks like I'm going to need to be more direct."

Alma bit her lip and waited.

"Three issues," Mrs. King announced, putting her elbow on the table and gesturing toward Alma with three fingers outstretched. "We'll start with the obvious."

"Point one," she said. "Latinas have the highest teen pregnancy rates of any group in the U.S."

Yikes. Alma felt her cheeks turn red, remembering the feeling of her body pressed against Evan's.

"Why is that, Alma?" she continued. "Do Latina girls have more premarital sex?"

This was obviously a rhetorical question.

"No, of course not," Mrs. King said. "So let me ask you, Alma: If you and Evan decide to—quote—carry your relationship to the next level, will you take birth control pills?"

Alma shrugged. She knew where this was going, but she had no desire to go there with Mrs. King.

"All right then. If you get pregnant, will you consider terminating—?"

"No," Alma broke in. "I would never . . ."

"That's right," Mrs. King said. "You're a good Catholic girl, aren't you? So are most of the forty-four percent of Latina teens who get pregnant before the age of twenty."

"But, Mrs. King, I don't even know if Evan and I are gonna—"

"Have intercourse? I'd say just about every one of those pregnant girls said the same thing."

Alma's face fell to her hands. This was utterly humiliating. She desperately needed a black coffee.

"So, let's move on," Mrs. King said. "Point two." She threw two fingers into the air and shook them once.

Ay, Dios mío.

"As I recall, your Evan is a senior, and a soccer star."

How did she know so much about Evan?

"Yes, ma'am."

"Do you expect that, come next fall, he's going to stay here in Gilberton and play soccer for North Georgia Technical College? Or maybe for the community college?"

"No, ma'am. He wants to go to Berkeley."

"Well, that's a mighty fine school, isn't it? So, come September, he'll be clear across the country. And you two will be history."

"But what if—"

"What? Are you gonna get on a plane and go visit him? Not without any identification, you're not. And you can't get a license, can you?"

"No, ma'am." Alma figured she didn't need to add to the strength of Mrs. King's argument by explaining that she and every undocumented immigrant she knew were afraid to step foot inside an airport. Airports were swarming with border patrol agents.

"So let's move on to my final point."

Alma was desperate. She took a gulp of vanilla hazelnut coffee and tried not to retch as the sweetness slid down her throat.

"Mrs. King," she said, "Evan's important to me. He's *different*. I think we can make it work."

"I don't want to hurt your feelings, sweetheart." Mrs. King said, shaking her head slowly. "I want you to be happy. But I know this boy. I know his family. And you need to stay away."

"Why? Because of his uncle?"

"You may not know this," Mrs. King said, leaning back in her seat. "I came to Eastshore Middle School from Hines."

Hines was on the other side of Gilberton—the rich side.

"Really?"

"Yes, ma'am. I gave that school thirty-seven years of my life. And in my thirty-seventh year, I got to know a brilliant young man by the name of Sexton Whitfield Prentiss the Third."

"You mean Whit?" Alma asked. "He's Sexton Prentiss's son?"

How did Alma not put that together? She had so many cousins that she never thought to connect the only one of Evan's uncles she knew to the only cousin she had met.

"The very one," Mrs. King said. "Whit was one of the smartest children ever to come through Hines Middle School, but come up around eighth grade, he started makin' some trouble."

"Yeah," Alma said. "I can believe that."

"He was just a confused boy, afraid of who he was. But then he took a liking to alcohol, and pretty soon after that, he started stealing pills from his momma." She paused and drew a long sip of iced tea through her straw. "I cared about that boy. I still do," she said, looking past Alma, through the window, "like I care about you." She carefully placed her tea back on the table. "So, naturally, I devised a plan."

"Why does that not surprise me?" Alma asked, grinning.

"Therapy, drug and alcohol treatment, regular meetings with the family—nothing extreme. But we were going to have to put together a team, and his parents would need to be involved in the process. They would need to accept who he was."

She paused to take a sip of sweet tea.

"So what happened?" Alma felt pretty sure the plan hadn't worked.

"His momma and daddy—they wanted nothin' to do with it. One morning before school, the two of them marched on into my office and threatened me, telling me to mind my own business, and not to dare make any of their family's private concerns public."

"Senator Prentiss did that? He marched into your office?"

"Yes, ma'am. And then they pulled him out of school, that very day. I went over to their house to try and talk some sense into them. They didn't hear a word I said. The next day, Whit was gone—shipped off to boarding school. No treatment. No counseling. Nothing at all but a big-name boarding school overflowing with drugs and alcohol."

"Is that why you left Hines?" Alma asked.

"A couple weeks after I went to their house, I got my transfer notice. I was sent on over to Eastshore without a word of explanation." She shook her head and exhaled slowly. "After thirty-seven years."

"Oh, wow. You must have been furious!"

"Well, I met you on that first day. So it wasn't *all* bad."

"Yeah," Alma said. "I remember that—when you came into the cafeteria and handed out those little squares of peanut butter pie."

"Mmm-hmm. The way to an eighth grader's heart is through her stomach."

She took Alma's hand again and squeezed it tightly.

"Alma," she said, looking directly into her eyes, "if that family made their own son disappear to keep up appearances, imagine what they'll do to you."

PART TWO

THIRTEEN

Lovefool

Alma glanced around, making sure she was alone, and stepped out of a pair of silver Manolo Blahnik pumps. Her calves relaxed, and her bare heels sank into the satisfying softness of the carpet. A sigh of relief escaped her lips.

Four-inch heels.

She felt like the lead character in a bad movie—one of those flicks that play on cable all the time. Girl from the wrong side of the tracks uses her ingenuity (or, in Alma's case, her connections with a rich friend and her mother's closet) to achieve a total makeover. She finds herself standing in front of a gilt-edged mirror, staring at the reflection of someone who looks like she belongs in a place like this.

There was no shortage of mirrors in the ladies' lounge of the Chickamauga Country Club. Seeing her reflection was utterly unavoidable. Alma had to admit that this little black dress, with fitted bodice and tulip skirt, was fantastic in its simplicity. The strand of pearls around her neck, the small pearl studs in her ears, and the smooth twist that Mary

Catherine had produced with three quick sweeping motions all created a look that M.C. called "classic beauty."

Alma just called it strange.

It was March 14, 2008—Evan's eighteenth birthday. In a week, Alma and Evan would celebrate their six-month anniversary. Since one of Alma's cousins always had to tag along on dates—if they wanted to go to a movie, or the mall, or even to get coffee—they spent most of their time together at Alma's house. Evan was an amazingly good sport about it, and he loved the food.

Alma's *abuela* Lupe was living with them now. As predicted, *la Virgencita* came through and scored a tourist visa, and she had arrived just in time for *Las Posadas*. Evan tried every food *Abuela* Lupe put in front of him, even *patitas de puerco*. When Raúl showed him how to pick up the pigs' hooves and suck the marrow between the toes, Evan launched right in. He and *Abuela* Lupe were incapable of communicating in words, but he found other ways to express appreciation for her food. In all this time, Alma had been inside Evan's house twice, and aside from his mom and Whit, she had met none of his family.

It was a compromise. Incapable of staying away from Evan, Alma had decided to quietly avoid Mrs. King. She assured herself that there was plenty of time to worry about scholarships and college—she was only a junior. She told herself that it was OK, for once, just to let herself be happy. She was still taking honors and AP classes, and she was still keeping up her GPA. But she could not set aside Mrs. King's warnings entirely. So she had invited Evan into her world but stayed far away from his.

Until tonight.

She heard the heavy door swing open and rushed to shove her feet back into the pumps. Whit's sister Lucy lurched into the room, balancing her rail-thin arms ever so gently against the door frame. They had been together all evening, sitting at the same table for dinner.

"Oh, my God, Alma. Look at those Manolos!"

Apparently, Lucy liked the little torture devices.

"I borrowed them from Mary Catherine's mom," Alma said, rinsing her hands under the faucet, "and the dress, too."

"It all looks perfect—just like it was made for you," Lucy said. She flung herself into a cushy upholstered chair. "Oh, God. My head's, like, spinning. I think I had too much champagne."

Lucy's eyes fluttered shut for a moment, giving Alma a chance to scan the marble countertop around the basin in search of something to dry her hands. Its contents were baffling. She saw a cut glass decanter filled with bright green liquid. It stood next to lotions, combs, and neatly folded towels. Her hands dangled, dripping over the sink, until she noticed a neat hole cut into the countertop. She peeked through the hole to see a pile of used white towels. It seemed a little extravagant, but Alma went for it. She grasped at a towel just as Lucy lurched forward from the chair and stumbled toward the row of solid oak doors separating each toilet from the ladies' lounge. A moment later, Alma heard the unmistakable sound of retching.

"Are you OK?" she called out tentatively, tossing a damp towel through the hole.

Lucy stepped out of the stall.

"Way better, now," she announced, reaching toward the decanter filled with mysterious green liquid.

Alma watched as Lucy poured the liquid into a paper cup, tossed her head back, lifted it to her lips, and swished it around her mouth. Lucy grasped her tastefully highlighted hair and leaned over the sink, aiming the green liquid toward the drain.

"Mouthwash," whispered Alma, pleased that she had solved *this* mystery at least.

Lucy leaned against the flowery wallpaper.

"God, I so hate puking." Lucy said. "But on the upside, now I can dive back into the desert table without any guilt."

Gross.

There was a lot that Alma wanted to say to that stupid comment, but she kept her mouth shut.

Over the past three and a half hours, Alma had become an expert in avoiding judgment, anxiety, shame, and bafflement. She promised herself that, for Evan, she would do her best to blend in, to appear as if she were perfectly comfortable in the grand ballroom of an exclusive country club. She forced herself not to gawk at the crystal chandeliers, the elaborate ice sculptures, the balls of roses on a stick that she had learned were called topiaries. Alma, always the master at observation, discerned the purpose of each of the six utensils framing her gold-rimmed plate. She barely skipped a beat when the waiter, a black man in his fifties with whom Evan seemed chummy, whisked the white napkin from her hands and placed a black one on her lap.

Alma became an anthropologist—a "participant observer." She viewed the party as a form of cultural learning, with the added bonus of picking up a few new vocabulary words.

Senator Prentiss, to her initial horror, sat next to her at the head table. But he was perfectly pleasant. She chatted amiably with the senator and his wife throughout the dinner. Watching how he grasped Evan's shoulder lovingly and offered his careful attention whenever Evan spoke, she even began to appreciate Evan's uncle. It was easy, really, to separate this kind man from the "catch and return" senator she had seen on a Web site so many months ago.

"Soooo," Lucy said loudly, stepping forward to wash her hands, "everybody is talking about you—especially my parents."

Alma let out some sort of squeak in response. The calm escaped her body, replaced by a prickly anxiety.

" 'Isn't she beautiful? So exotic! Her hair is like silk! Just look at the way Evan gazes at her. Young love. So sweet.' "

Lucy paused to let her words settle.

"And that's just Mom. My dad was totally lecturing Whit about you: 'What a gal! So well mannered and polite. And smart as a whip, too. Lord, son. Why can't you find yourself a girl like that?' "

Alma laughed at Lucy's perfect impersonation of Senator Prentiss's deep Southern drawl. Plus, if she laughed, she wouldn't have to reply.

"Poor Daddy. I don't think he's figured out that girls aren't Whit's type." Lucy said, and then she burst into laughter.

Lucy was right. Whit didn't seem to be into girls, but he wasn't showing many signs of being all that into boys either. Alma was pretty sure that, at this point in his life, Whit was just really confused.

The door flew open and a silver-haired lady tottered in. "Let's get out of here," Lucy mumbled under her breath. "I'm so ready for the after-party."

When Alma stepped into the hallway, Evan was waiting in his tuxedo and gleaming black shoes. His hair was pushed back from his forehead, and his smiling eyes locked in on hers.

Swoon.

Alma's heart fluttered and her fingertips tingled. She felt the blush rising to her face. But her cynical mind was starting to find ways to crash the hormone fiesta. How long was this blundering idiocy going to last? How many times would she have to see Evan walking toward her before she quit feeling weak in the knees? Apparently a half year was not long enough.

He glanced around, pulled her into the corner, and drew her into a kiss that sent electricity all the way down to her toes.

⊷

Evan's phone vibrated in his pocket.

He pulled away from Alma reluctantly and glanced at the screen.

Then he grabbed Alma's hand to lead her outside through a set of French doors.

"It's your brother," he said. "We're not supposed to have cell phones in here."

Alma leaned against the wall, hugging her chest. She looked jaw-dropping in that short black dress. She also looked cold. He pulled her toward him and wrapped his tuxedo jacket around them both.

"What's up, Raúl?" He felt her arms encircle his waist.

"Not much, man. Are you anywhere near my sister?"

"Yeah, you could say that," Evan replied. Alma giggled, which made him smile and hug her in tight. He loved to hear her laugh.

"Ask her where the hell her cell phone is."

Alma glanced down toward her dress, suggesting the obvious.

"She doesn't exactly have a place to put it. I mean, the dress is, uh . . ."

"*Damn*, man. I don't want to hear that," Raúl said. "Just let me talk to her."

Bantering with Raúl made Evan wish they had found a way to get him to the party. They had become good friends over the months, especially since Evan spent so much time at Alma's house. Raúl even trained with Evan to get him ready for the season. You learn a lot about a person when you train with him every day. But tonight Raúl had to cover for Alma. Alma's dad didn't know she was here. He might have let her come, but her curfew was ten, no matter what. Evan's parents were going to Lake Rabun to recuperate after the party. Evan was taking advantage of the empty house and hosting an after-party and he wanted Alma to be there, so they had come up with a lie.

Hearing the stress in Raúl's voice, he was beginning to feel sorry they'd done it.

"How's it going?" Alma asked.

With Alma pressed close in to his chest, Evan heard his reply.

"I'm on my way to Uncle Alvaro's now. Dad's already there. He thinks you and Magda are in Atlanta at the band concert."

"It's not a band, idiot. It's an orchestra. Her cousin's in the Atlanta Symphony Youth Orchestra," Alma teased.

"Not important," Raúl quipped.

"So he thinks we're staying with Magda's cousins tonight?"

"Yeah, I'm pretty sure he bought it."

"Thanks, Raúl," she replied. "I owe you."

"No big deal," Raúl said, "though I gotta say I never thought I'd be lying for my straight-ass little sister!"

"Funny," Alma said, deadpan.

"I just wish I could be there to keep an eye on *him*," Raúl replied.

Alma looked up at Evan and smiled. "Who, Evan?" she asked, feigning innocence.

Feeling Alma's body pressed against his, Evan didn't blame the guy.

"Just lie to me and tell me you're staying at M.C.'s house, OK?"

"I *am*, Raúl. No lie. Are you jealous?" Alma laughed.

Evan struggled to stay quiet, hoping that Raúl wouldn't know he could hear the entire conversation.

"Whatever, Alma. *Cuídate*, OK? Just take care of yourself."

"Stop worrying. I'll be fine. Have fun with *los tíos borrachos*, but don't drink much, Raúl. *Tío* Alvaro's is a long drive from home."

"Yeah, I won't," Raúl said, "and *please* keep your cell phone on you. If Dad goes all suspicious on me, I'm gonna call you back."

"Yeah, OK. I owe you big."

"*No te preocupes, hermanita.* Pay me back by finding a way to get *me* into Mary Catherine's bed someday. And tell your boyfriend to keep it in his pants."

Evan couldn't contain his laughter.

"You're such a pig," she said before hanging up.

Alma handed Evan the phone. "How's that for a double standard?"

"Aw, Alma," Evan said, taking her back into his arms. "He's just being a big brother."

"And a *machista* prick."

"You wanna tell me what a *machista* prick is?" he asked, pulling back to look her in the eyes. "I probably should know in case you ever call me one."

"Never mind," Alma replied, twisting out of his grip. "Let's get out of here."

When they left the party, Alma's first act of celebration was to remove the silver torture devices from her feet. Then, keeping her promise to Raúl, Alma took the phone from her purse and tucked it into her bra.

She propped her mangled feet onto the dashboard of Evan's car.

"Good Lord, Alma!" Evan exclaimed, glancing over at her blistered toes. "What the hell happened to your feet?"

"A pair of three-hundred-dollar shoes happened to my feet," Alma said. "Aren't they great?"

"That's just plain stupid," replied Evan. "When we get home, we're gonna find you a tube of Neosporin and some flip-flops."

"Do you really care about my feet," Alma asked, "or are you looking for an excuse to get me alone inside?"

"Uh, both?" Evan said.

Alma had no trouble imagining making love to Evan, but she couldn't shake the image of waddling around pregnant, or pushing a spit-up-covered baby through Walmart, stroller laden with diapers and bottles. As much as she hated to admit it, Mrs. King was right. There was no room for dreams and ambitions in that picture. Alma hadn't worked so hard, against so many odds, to put her future aside for a baby. She reminded herself that Evan understood how she felt, and he wanted to be sure it was right. But on nights like tonight, she sometimes wished she could forget about consequences, that she could just live in the moment.

Evan's car eased down the driveway toward his darkened house. Alma saw a crowd of people gathered around a dark figure sprawled across the front lawn. Whoever it was did not appear to have any interest in moving.

Evan stopped the car and lunged out.

"What the hell, y'all? Can't you even make it to the backyard before somebody passes out?" Evan's voice had an edge that Alma didn't recognize.

Peavey looked up from where he was standing with Conway and Caroline. "It's Whit again," he replied offhandedly. He turned back toward the other two and said something that made them all burst into laughter.

Whit hoisted his body onto one arm. He was beyond wasted. "Evan, darling! I've brought you a birthday present!"

He fumbled in the pocket of his tuxedo pants and drew out a bottle of prescription medicine. Lucy was nowhere to be seen, but his other sister, Annabeth, stepped forward and thrust her hand toward him.

"Give me the bottle, Whit." She spoke with calm authority, but anger came through in the slight tremor of her voice.

"Y'all go on back to the guest house before the neighbors call the cops," Evan said to the spectators. "And *no one* goes in the main house. My mom will kill me if we trash her house."

The crowd dispersed. Evan and Annabeth stood above Whit and scrutinized the writing on the prescription bottle. Alma sat in the car with the door wide open, unsure of whether she should try to help them, or whether this was something only Whit's family should be a part of.

Mary Catherine arrived at the car door and tugged on Alma.

"Don't worry, Alma. This happens all the time with Whit," she said, interlacing her arm with Alma's. "Evan and Annabeth will drag him inside and make him puke, and he'll be good as new . . . or as new as Whit's wrecked body can be."

Alma grabbed the torture devices in her free hand and started off, barefoot, toward Evan's guest house.

She saw Lucy then, skipping toward the guest house, her arm gripping the stiff arm of her boyfriend, whose name Alma had not yet been able to glean. Everyone just called him the Inman boy. As Whit had explained, the name signaled his position in the Atlanta Coca-Cola dynasty. It reminded Lucy and everyone else that this handsome, dull boy would make an extremely desirable match. Each time she heard him referred to as "the Inman boy," Alma felt like she'd been transported into *Amor Real*, a bad telenovela about the Mexican aristocracy, set in the nineteenth century. Her *tía* Pera had been obsessed with that show—she loved all of the Victorian costumes and romantic plot twists. When it was released to DVD with English subtitles, her aunt found the perfect excuse to watch it obsessively—she said she was working on her English. Because phrases like "remove your corset" are really important to know these days.

But when she walked into the guest house with Mary Catherine, she knew this was not a scene from *Amor Real*. Alma had seen her share of drunken people over the years, almost always men, but this was different. The dozen people inside already had razor-sharp focus on one and only one pursuit, an almost magnetic draw toward the sources of their release. Alma couldn't begin to imagine what it was they were all so desperate to escape. Their lives seemed pretty darn easy to her.

Mary Catherine led her in the direction of the kitchen table, around which were splayed her least favorite of Evan's friends: Peavey, Conway, and a skinny kid named Paul.

"Pull up a chair, ladies," Peavey called out, with much more volume than was necessary. "You're just in time to get acquainted with my good buddy Seen-yor *Pay*-tron,"

He lifted a full bottle of tequila to the table. With his free hand, he patted the seat of an empty chair at his side, urging Mary Catherine to take it. Logan and Caroline came to join them with a sleek stainless steel saltshaker and thick slices of lime arrayed haphazardly on a cutting board.

"Aowwll-lma," Peavey exclaimed, gesturing toward her, "you ready for one of these?"

Alma shook her head in silence, wondering whether Peavey still didn't know how to say her name, or whether he exaggerated the Southern drawl to be funny.

"I don't really drink," Alma replied.

"Come on, Aowwwllma," Conway jumped in. "We're celebratin'."

"Just give her a beer," Logan said, gesturing toward a cooler by Conway's feet.

"Take the beer and nurse it," Caroline whispered in her ear. "He'll leave you alone."

Alma shrugged. "Sure, Conway. I'll have a beer."

"Ahh," he exclaimed as he lifted a dark beer out of the cooler and gazed at the gold label. "Negra Modelo. It's even named for you."

"What the hell are you talking about, Conway?" Logan asked.

"You know, man. She's not quite as black as a nee-gra," Conway said, shrugging, "but she's hot like a model."

Nausea overtook Alma. Hot bile rose from her stomach and stung the back of her throat.

Caroline stared hard at Mary Catherine, as if they were having some sort of conversation without words. Then she yanked the beer from Conway's hand and pulled Alma to her feet. As Caroline handed her the beer and led her away from the table, Alma heard Mary Catherine speak.

"Shut up and pour me a shot, Conway."

Caroline plopped down on the couch and motioned for Alma to sit next to her.

"He's just one of those guys," she said to Alma. "You know?"

No, Alma didn't know.

"I mean, if he decides you're the one, he'll follow you around all night and try to get you drunk."

"The one?" Alma asked, darting her eyes toward Conway.

"Listen, Alma," Caroline said. "Just keep your distance and keep a drink in your hand. We'll make sure he leaves you alone until Evan gets back."

Alma wrapped her arms around her chest and slouched over. She felt vulnerable, and she hated it.

"Relax, Alma," Caroline said. "We're here to have fun, remember?"

Evan needed to come back. Now.

—

Annabeth's cool control was gone. Evan watched, dying of frustration, as Whit's older sister pleaded with him.

Evan stepped in. "For God's sake, Whit. Just make yourself puke so I can get back to my party."

"If you don't," Annabeth said, "I'll take you to the hospital and you *know* what will happen." She shoved Whit in front of the bathroom mirror. "Do you want to end up on the cover of some supermarket tabloid looking like *this*?"

Whit fluttered his eyes open and took a long look, his vanity more powerful than his stubbornness. He leaned over the toilet and stuck his finger down his throat.

He missed the toilet entirely. Evan volunteered to help Annabeth sop it up with a towel, and then he wrangled Whit out of his vomit-covered tuxedo and took everything downstairs to the washer. Struggling to discern the meaning of the dozens of buttons surrounding the washer's electrical display, it crossed Evan's mind that a tuxedo should be dry-cleaned, but what dry cleaner in town would be open? And would a dry cleaner take a puke-covered tuxedo? Even if they could find a place, the risk of it becoming a newsworthy event—"Sexton Prentiss's partying son goes overboard . . . again"—was not worth taking. These were the sorts of things Evan always had to think about when he was with his mom's brother and family. They lived their lives under an intense public watch. Every mundane decision and private event had the potential to become public property.

When he had mashed enough buttons to make the washer start, Evan was free to go back to his own party.

"I'm heading back to the party," he called out. "Are you coming?"

"Evan," Annabeth replied, anxiety coursing through her voice, "I think you need to come up here."

Conway stared Alma down. It felt like he was standing in front of her in full camouflage, like she was a deer that he chased in the predawn hours. Maybe he didn't chase at all. Maybe he waited, silent and still, crouched in high grass until the unsuspecting creature wandered into firing range.

Alma stepped out of the bathroom and tried to squeeze past him. He was standing alone in the doorway, holding a small paper cup. He wouldn't let her by. He casually blocked the passage with his outstretched arm.

"I saved you a Jell-O shot," he said, smiling.

"No, thanks," Alma replied. She hoped he couldn't tell that her voice was shaking.

"Just take it, Alma," he said, thrusting the paper cup toward her. "It's cherry. Yum."

She watched him slowly lick his lips, and her heart started to race. She had to get out of this hallway.

She took the cup and gulped down the glob of red gelatin.

"Thanks," she said as he dropped his arm from the wall and she slid past him.

She needed fresh air.

Alma rushed through the French doors and collapsed onto the edge of a pool chair. She held her head in her hands and breathed in the cool March air.

A pair of arms wrapped around her.

It was Evan. *Thank God.*

"You all right?" he asked.

"I am now," Alma replied, leaning into his chest. She suddenly felt warm and light-headed. "Where have you been?"

"My cousin was puking blood. I had to take him to the hospital. Annabeth stayed with him."

"Do we need to go back?" Alma asked.

"Definitely not," Evan said. "This shit just happens with Whit. He'll get over it. Are you having fun?"

"Not really," she said, nodding toward the guest house. "It's sort of weird in there."

He tugged her gently from the chair and she stood unsteadily.

"Were you drinking?" Evan asked, looking at her with concern in his eyes. He knew she didn't drink.

"A couple of beers," she said, shrugging.

How many beers did she drink? Her mind felt hazy and she couldn't concentrate.

"OK." He pulled her close and whispered into her ear, "If you don't wanna go back to the party, then let's go take care of those feet."

Wrapping his arm tight around her waist, he led her toward the main house. He fumbled with the key and she clung to him, feeling the charge of his body against hers. The door flew open and they tumbled through, tripping over each other as they made their way up the stairs and into his room.

Alma's head hit the shimmering mound of pillows, and her hands found the buttons of Evan's white tuxedo shirt. He shrugged out of it and then paused, hovering above her. Their movements slowed. Her fingers traced the ridges of his chest, ribs, and abdomen, searching down toward the black line of his waistband. She wrapped her arms tightly around him and pulled him toward her.

He pushed her hair back from her face and kissed her forehead, her eyes, her cheeks, and her chin. His hands searched her body, tentatively, over the heavy black satin. When he discovered the cell phone tucked inside her bra, they both laughed, breaking the intensity for a moment.

Evan tossed the phone to the floor and her bare feet entwined with his. Alma realized that the sting had left them, and with it had gone all her childish preoccupations and worries.

Maybe she was ready, after all.

FOURTEEN
The Clock Is Wrong

The high-pitched noise reverberated through Alma's head, careening through the space between her ears, persistent and pestering. She opened her eyes to the darkness. Her tongue felt swollen and distorted, pressing its pasty thickness against the roof of her mouth. Her stomach gurgled and lurched. She needed water.

She sat slowly, her eyes adjusting to the darkness, her mind struggling in the silence to shake off confusion. The shrill noise resumed. Alma closed her eyes, registering a faint recognition. This terrible sound was the unrelenting ring of her phone.

As she leapt from the bed and reached toward the vibrating object, Alma's mind came into focus. She recalled where she was. She remembered Evan's hands searching her body, their bold laughter as he had grasped the phone from her bra and tossed it aside. The queasiness swept through her again, settling in the pit of her stomach.

She remembered nothing more.

Alma looked at the screen.

Saturday, March 15. 6:02 a.m. HOME.

The sound of footfalls above him coaxed Evan from a dreamy half sleep. He opened his eyes and tossed onto his side, gazing toward the lake. Morning light drew a line across the horizon.

The grandfather clock churned loudly and then chimed twice. Looking at the gray horizon, Evan's mind faintly registered that the clock was wrong.

Footsteps continued above him, faster. Someone was opening and closing doors, one after the other, in the upstairs hallway. Glancing across the pool, past the crumpled cover toward the guest house, where several lights were still on, he realized that Alma was the only other person in the house.

Evan set out toward the back stairwell.

He saw her standing in the doorway of his parents' room, wearing his baggy white undershirt. Evan's heart filled with warmth and his body with subtle desire. At least this morning the desire was mild——not the overpowering, consuming feeling that he had struggled so hard to control the night before. He knew she must be looking for him, but why the urgency? Was she embarrassed, ashamed?

Her slim silhouette, outlined by the frame of the door and the light from his parents' room, suddenly folded in on itself. Evan rushed toward her crumpled body. As he stretched his arms to hold her, she stayed perfectly still and let out a deep, quiet sob.

"I need you to take me home. I need some clothes."

"OK, Alma," Evan replied gently, "I can take you home, but please tell me what's wrong."

Alma leaned against the door frame.

"My dad and my brother. They're in trouble." She let her head fall to her knees. "I should have been there. I should have been with them." Alma released another dry sob. "I shouldn't be here."

"What kind of trouble?" he asked. "Where are they?"

"Jail."

Jail? Evan couldn't imagine Mr. García and Raúl doing anything that would send them to jail. And what in the world had landed them both there on the same night? DUI? He knew that Raúl drank a few beers occasionally but never excessively, and he had never seen Alma's dad drinking. Maybe a fight at the party they went to? Manny and his loser friends causing trouble again?

Alma's phone, clutched tightly in her hand, began to ring. She walked away from him, but he could hear her speaking quietly in Spanish. Evan waited, hesitant, at the doorway. Should he follow her?

He went into his mother's closet to find some clothes for her. Her own clothes were next door at Mary Catherine's, where she had planned to spend the night.

———

Alma grabbed a towel from the neatly folded stack beside the sink and brought it to her eyes. The crisp scent of fabric softener filled her nostrils, temporarily assuaging the nausea. She carried the towel with her to the bench where Evan had laid his mother's clothes. She sat down unsteadily and pulled his white undershirt over her head, recognizing his spicy odor. Taking in his scent induced another intense wave of nausea. She slumped to the floor and lifted the white towel to her face.

She wanted to make sense of the void left where her memory should have been. Did she drink enough beer to feel so cloudy? She tried to count back: one, maybe two beers, and then the horrible sweet-salty

Jell-O shot. It didn't make sense. Alma tried to tell herself that it didn't matter. She had more important issues to deal with.

She struggled into a padded sports bra, slipped on a pair of stretchy yoga pants, and shrugged on the chocolate-brown T-shirt. The snug, fitted T-shirt was the type she often saw on rich women who were running errands in their workout clothes. This one had "tough cookie" written in cursive, under a drawing of a broken chocolate-chip cookie.

Something about being in this over-the-top bathroom and wearing the silly T-shirt brought another sob tearing through her chest.

She wanted out of here.

"Alma, can I come in?" Evan asked, tapping gently on the door.

"I'm ready," she said. She wiped the tears from her eyes and stepped out to face Evan.

Evan drove in silence as Alma tuned the radio to a Spanish pop station that he knew she didn't like. When the music stopped, she turned up the volume and listened intently to the booming voice of the male announcer. Then the radio cut to a commercial.

"He said it was road blocks. My dad and Raúl probably got stopped at the one on Athens Highway."

"Who?"

"The radio announcer."

"How would the radio announcer on VIVA 101.5 know about road-blocks in Gilberton?"

"I don't know. I guess people call in. There's never been one here, but down in Shale County . . ."

Alma's voice trailed off. She looked down at her hands and studied the lines on her left palm. He wanted to take her hand, but something prevented him. She was building a wall around herself, a fortress.

"Was it for DUI's? Were they doing Breathalyzers?"

"I don't know. My dad wouldn't get a DUI."

Evan started to ask about Raúl, but then the announcer's voice came back. She brought her finger to her lips and leaned in toward the radio, concentrating hard.

"More than two hundred people taken in since midnight."

Alma's phone rang. She picked up and listened silently. She said a few words and hung up.

Evan glanced over to see her squeeze her eyelids shut. She kept them closed for a few moments and then turned directly to Evan.

"We can't find my dad's brother or his wife. My grandmother and Isa even tried tracking Manny down to see if he'd go, but he's in South Carolina, working or something."

She looked down at her hands, and Evan focused his attention forward as the car sped across a bridge and the lake opened out below them.

"We need your help, Evan. We need you to go to the county jail to post bail."

"Yeah, definitely," Evan replied without hesitation. "I can do that."

He had no idea how to post bail.

"I'm sorry, Evan. I didn't want to drag you into this, but we don't have anyone else who's, you know, legal."

Alma started to cry quietly.

Evan frantically sought the right thing to say.

"It's OK, Alma. I'll figure it out. Maybe your dad just left his wallet at the party, or maybe his insurance expired or something. I'm sure it's no big deal."

Alma looked up at Evan, not even trying to hide the tears streaming down her face.

"Raúl doesn't even have a license, Evan."

She went silent.

"Yeah," Evan said. It would cost a lot of money to get Raúl out of jail if he was the one driving. Peavey got caught driving without a license when they were fifteen and his parents had to pay a thousand dollars.

"But my dad . . . it doesn't make sense. I wish I had been at home when they called. My grandmother was so confused . . ."

Her face fell into her hands.

"I'm sorry, Alma," Evan said.

"I should have been with them."

The sun rose, revealing one of those too-bright March mornings with crystal-blue sky and crisp, cold air.

She had him drop her off in a neighborhood near the jail, in the circular drive of Maplewood Elementary School. Evan had never seen the small school tucked into this modest neighborhood. He'd never had a reason to be here.

They got out, stepping under a bright yellow banner that read, "Welcome/*Bienvenidos*." He took off his parka and wrapped it around her. She held up her phone.

"Text me as soon as you know something."

He nodded. He wanted to hold her, to stand with her and comfort her. But she seemed so distant. He knew, as she'd made it clear all morning, that she didn't want to be touched. He was worried that something had changed for her last night, that they had crossed some threshold. He wondered whether they would ever get back to their easy intimacy.

He wanted to be back there.

Alma stepped under the banner, frozen in the entryway she had passed through hundreds of times as a child. She saw herself and her brother,

Maritza, and Magda, hunched from the weight of their backpacks, walking to school from the apartment complex across the street where they'd grown up. She heard their laughter and teasing, the plans they made for after school, with hours of free time stretched out before them. She saw Maritza and Magda tumbling down the hill, sweaty and giggling, with bits of green grass sticking to their bare arms and legs. She felt the loud thump of Raúl kicking a soccer ball, over and over, against the building's brick siding.

She walked slowly along the road that led from their apartments to the Boys and Girls Club. She imagined that it was summer—that she was no longer shuffling under the weight of Evan's oversized parka. Instead she was running, fast and light, in her favorite turquoise bathing suit with the lime-green piping, racing Maritza to the pool behind the Boys and Girls Club.

As the building came into view, she saw the familiar words painted on its side: "The ideal place for kids to grow up/*El lugar ideal para los niños crecer.*"

Back then, it *had* felt ideal. It had felt just right. Maplewood Elementary, Terrace Trace Apartments, the Boys and Girls Club—they all welcomed Alma and her family. In their bilingual signs and their encouraging mottos, in their friendly staff and their pleasant grounds, they took in Alma—and so many others. No one questioned whether they were supposed to be here, whether they were allowed to stay.

It was simply their home, their place.

And then she remembered middle school, and how everything had changed. She remembered going with her father to visit Mrs. King after the incident with Mario, when her dad finally broke down and let her move to Atlanta. She recalled Mrs. King's house, a yellow bungalow down the road from the Boys and Girls Club. Alma wondered whether Mrs. King still lived there, and whether Mrs. King would let her in if she showed up at the door again. Alma tried not to think about the scholarship applications she hadn't finished or the college brochures she'd set aside. She tried not to think about the unanswered calls from Mrs. King. The lies to her father. The party . . .

It was too much.

Evan slowly turned off Brady Road, following a line of cars into the parking lot. The lot was surrounded by a wasteland—fenced-in plots of unnaturally gray soil with abandoned cars and trucks strewn across. Amid such harsh terrain, the county jail seemed out of place. It was a new building made of red brick with tinted-glass windows gleaming below a large bronze sign that read "Office of the Sheriff, Gilbert County Jail."

The lot was full. He had to circle twice before finding a spot. He waited, idling behind a cab with "Taxi El Palmar" written across the sides. An elderly woman emerged and shuffled toward the door. He parked near a line of deputies' cars, aware that he was being watched. He glanced toward the brick building, looking for the visitor entrance. It wasn't hard to find. Dozens of people gathered around the glass door, pressing in to read notices taped to the inside.

Alma had been right. This was not good. His eyes closed briefly against the bright morning light. He let out a deep sigh and headed toward the throngs of people.

There was a subtle shifting of bodies, and anxious conversations fell silent around him. He felt the gaze of curious eyes as the crowds parted to let him through. Posted on the door was an alphabetical list titled "Current Detention Center Population," with hundreds of names, almost all of them Spanish. When he arrived at *G*, his eyes fell upon the names he didn't want to see:

García, Eduardo

García, Raúl David

A young officer opened the door from the inside.

"We need an orderly, single-file line, folks. Sign in on the clipboard and take a seat."

Evan went in and waited for the clipboard. By the time his turn came to scratch his name onto the list, the pencil had been worn down to a nub. He considered asking the young officer to sharpen it, but he sensed the urgency of the people pressing behind him. He turned to hand the pencil to a small woman wearing a housedress embroidered with bright flowers.

Then a door slammed behind him and an arm caught his shoulder. Evan turned, startled by the grasp. Sheriff Cronin stood looking at him with a broad, silly grin spread across his face.

"Evan, my boy, what the hell are you doing here?"

Evan, confused by the sheriff's jovial tone, was unable to produce an answer.

"Aw, hell, son," he exclaimed with a long Southern drawl. "Don't you go tellin' me that the after-party over at your place got out of control."

Evan shook his head slowly. He couldn't produce a word.

"I know, son. I was young, too," he said, jostling Evan's shoulder lightly. "I guess it's time for you to call in a favor to your old Uncle Buddy, huh?"

His eyes swept across the crowd gathered in the waiting room.

"You picked a hell of a day to do it." He scratched the back of his head. "So which one of your partners in crime landed himself in the slammer?"

Sheriff Cronin ushered Evan through a door, and they sat down on molded plastic chairs.

"What's the matter, boy? Cat got your tongue?"

Evan looked down at his feet and grasped the edge of the chair.

"Don't worry, son. Old Uncle Buddy has seen just about everything. Hell, remember those stories your momma used to tell?"

Hope flickered in his mind. Uncle Buddy *could* help, couldn't he? He was, after all, the sheriff. "Uh, nothing happened last night at the party, Uncle Buddy."

"Go on and spit it out, boy," the sheriff said.

"It's my friend Raúl. He and his dad are here. I need to figure out what happened and try to post bail."

"Well, where the hell is the rest of his family, Evan? You don't need to get caught up in this."

"Like I said, his dad's in here, too. He doesn't have a mom. I mean, she died a long time ago, and his sister, Alma, uh . . . You know, my girlfriend? She asked me to come."

Sheriff Cronin leaned back in his chair and shook his head slowly.

"It was a mistake, Uncle Buddy. They're good people."

"Your girlfriend's daddy, huh?" He spoke slowly, processing the information coming through Evan's anxious words. "You're talking about your momma's gardener, right?"

"Uh, yeah," Evan replied, "Mr. García has a landscaping business. He does our yard."

"Damned shame," Sheriff Cronin replied, shaking his head again. His jovial Uncle Buddy tone was gone. He had shifted into his Sheriff Cronin voice.

"What the hell was your momma thinkin' hiring an illegal to do her yard?"

Evan shrugged.

"Doesn't she know what a mess this will be for Sexton?"

Suddenly, the word "illegal" surged into Evan's awareness, bringing on a bout of vertigo. *How did he know?* He leaned back into his seat and held on.

Sheriff Cronin stood up.

"Well, son, I can take you back there to see them, but don't waste your time postin' bail. We'll have to keep 'em here till Immigration comes."

Evan's throat produced a sound he didn't recognize. "But what did they *do*? What *happened*?"

The sheriff held the door open and urged Evan out of the interrogation room.

"I haven't got a clue, son. All I know is they're here because they don't have the paperwork to prove that they're in the country legally. It's my responsibility to make sure they get on back to where they belong."

Evan felt his muscles begin to twitch as the heat rose to his face.

"Since when is it your responsibility?" Evan's anger surprised him. "You're the local sheriff. You can't just go and deport people for no reason."

A smirk spread across Sheriff Cronin's face.

"You've been brushing up on immigration law, have you?"

"I don't know much," Evan replied, struggling not to raise his voice, "but I know that immigration is a federal issue, and you're a county sheriff."

"So you think I'm gettin' too big for my britches, huh?" Sheriff Cronin asked, chuckling softly. "Look, son. I need you to keep this quiet for now because we don't want to stir up commotion. But our county and a few others in Georgia are gonna start helping ICE deal with this illegal-immigration problem. You know what ICE is?"

"Immigration and Customs Enforcement," Evan said slowly.

"Some of our deputies got trained by ICE, and they're gonna make sure that anyone who we pick up in Gilbert County has permission to be here. If they don't have permission, we'll turn 'em over to ICE and they'll be deported."

Evan stood up and ran his hand through his hair. "So, you're saying that Raúl and his dad broke a law?"

Sheriff Cronin stood and reached out to grasp his shoulder. "Evan, son, I'm real sorry that your friend and his dad got mixed up in all of this. I'm sure they *are* nice folks, but if they're here in my jail, it's because they're illegal. With any luck, they'll be back home in Mexico in a few weeks."

Evan tried to imagine Raúl in Mexico, to reconcile the words "home" and "Mexico" with everything he knew about his friend.

He pulled away, anger coursing through him. "So, no favors today?"

"Son, you know I'd do just about anything for your family. But *this* I simply cannot do. You have no idea the shitstorm it would cause if I released your girlfriend's family from this jail. I can guaran-damn-tee you that I wouldn't be doin' nobody any favors, especially not your Uncle Sexton."

Evan's phone emitted a high-pitched noise. He looked down to see the text.

Any news?

Evan wanted to shove the phone back into his pocket, but he gestured for Sheriff Cronin to wait and typed a quick reply:

It's not looking good. I'm so sorry. On my way to see them now.

Evan tried with all of his might to keep the tears from coming.

FIFTEEN
Hometown

Terror surged as Alma processed the words in Evan's text. She squeezed her eyes shut and forced herself to imagine the serene face of Our Lady of *La Leche* while she said a silent prayer. She saw the black eyes and pink cheeks, and the way she held tightly to her son.

Dios te salve María, llena eres de gracia . . .

If Evan, the eternal optimist, was acknowledging that things weren't good, then they must be very bad. Alma slumped to the ground.

El Señor es contigo.

Trying to calm her mind, she walked along the road in front of Maplewood Elementary and made a mental list—a list of any facts that could possibly offer hope. Her father had a valid driver's license.

Bendita tú eres entre todas las mujeres . . .

It would expire soon, and since the laws had changed in Georgia, he wouldn't be able to renew. But it was still valid—for now.

Y bendito es el fruto en tu vientre, Jésus.

Neither her father nor Raúl had ever been in trouble with the law—not even a speeding ticket.

Santa María, Madre de Dios . . .

Alma's phone rang. Evan. She fumbled to answer.

"Evan?"

"Nah, Alma. It's just me. Sorry to disappoint."

To her surprise and relief, Raúl's voice came through the line.

Alma placed her hand over her heart, trying to calm the rapid beating. This was good, right? If Raúl was talking to her on Evan's phone, then he wasn't in jail.

"Raúl? You're out. What happened? Where's Dad?"

"Alma, slow down. We're not out. Your boyfriend must have the hookup with the cops cuz they brought him back here to us *and* they let me use his cell phone to call you."

Raúl chuckled. He was trying hard to calm her with his cheerful tone, but Alma heard worry pressing through his voice.

Instinctively, she began to pray again silently. *Dios te salve María, llena eres de gracia . . .*

"Evan said you heard about the checkpoints on the radio," Raúl said.

"Uh-huh," Alma replied.

"Dad came up to one on Athens Highway."

"I knew it," Alma said.

"I was on my way home, too, in the work truck. I left a few minutes after him. He called to tell me I should turn around. They were checking for driver's licenses, so Dad got through. But while we were talking on the phone, he said a cop was trailing him with his lights flashing."

Raúl paused, and Alma slumped deeper, staring at a crack in the pavement.

"We hung up, and he pulled over to talk to the cop. I didn't know what happened to him until I saw him here a couple hours later. I turned around and went the back way, you know, toward the lake. But there was another checkpoint back there."

"Oh, no," Alma said.

"I got stopped for not having a license. I'm telling you, Alma, they had the whole neighborhood blocked off. There was no way out."

"So do you have to pay a fine, or something?"

"That's not all, Alma. You know the machete—the one dad keeps behind the seat?"

"Yeah."

"They said it was a concealed weapon, and I'm supposed to have a permit."

"The machete? Did you tell them it was just a gardening tool?"

"Yeah, they didn't buy it. They said if it was for gardening, then why weren't there any other landscaping tools in the truck?"

Every Friday afternoon Alma's dad took the tools from the bed of the truck to clean them. This Friday had been no exception.

"But it's not like it was hidden. It's just there so it doesn't rattle around in the back."

"They charged me with a misdemeanor, Alma. They weren't all that interested in the details."

"I can't believe this is happening," Alma said. "What about Dad?"

"The cop stopped him because something was wrong with the Bronco."

"Dad's Bronco?" Alma asked, incredulous. He kept it in impeccable shape.

"Yeah. You know those little lights next to the license plate? There's one on each side?"

"Yeah," Alma replied, not sure whether she did, and wondering how this conversation had anything to do with her dad being in jail.

"One was burned out, and they stopped him because of that." Raúl's voice thickened as he continued in a low growl. "They were just looking for a way to stop us, Alma. They were trying to find any excuse."

"Oh, God." Alma said.

This was bad.

"Everyone's freaking out in here. People are saying they've called ICE to come and get us. They're not even allowed to do that, are they?"

"No," Alma replied, dazed. "I don't think so."

"We'll get out of here when they figure out they screwed up."

Alma heard a rustling on the other end of the line.

"Hold up a sec, Alma."

Muffled voices crossed the line, and whoever was speaking seemed angry.

"Listen, I've gotta go," Raúl said anxiously. "People are getting pissed that I'm using Evan's cell phone. They're asking the guard why they can't use theirs."

"But can't I talk to Dad?"

"Later, OK? He's fine, Alma. Don't worry."

"Give Dad a hug, OK?"

"Yeah, sure. *That* will help me make friends in here—if I go hugging on other men."

Alma had to smile. He had a point.

"Good to know you're still a *machista* prick," she replied, teasing. "Stay safe."

"I love you, Alma."

The line went dead.

Why had he said that? Why had he told her, with soft vulnerability in his voice, that he loved her? He never said things like that. Never. Hot tears burned her eyes and slid down her frozen cheeks, and she collapsed onto her knees.

Alma barely registered the rattling noise coming from behind, but she did hear the loud thud that followed. Without thinking, she turned to look. An elderly black woman stood next to her garbage can, holding a bulging bag.

She gazed at Alma curiously.

"Are you lost, sweetheart? Can I help you?"

Alma replied, wiping the tears from her eyes, "No, ma'am. I'm not lost. I'm just, uh, wandering around."

The woman continued to look at her curiously as she dropped the bag into the can.

"I mean," Alma stuttered, trying to make sense, "I used to live over there, in the apartments. Uh, this is my hometown."

She heard the words come from her mouth, the acknowledgement that this place—whose cops had just trapped and jailed her own father and brother—was her only real hometown. It was more than Alma could handle. Her breath came hard and fast, her shoulders hunched and a dry sob emerged.

She started to run, and she didn't stop until she was standing in front of Mrs. King's house, where she collapsed on the front stoop.

The door flew open and Mrs. King stood towering over her in a plush blue bathrobe.

"What in heaven's name?"

"I'm sorry," she heard herself mutter. "I just need . . ."

"Come on in this house right now. You'll catch your death o' cold out here."

She reached out and took Alma's freezing hand, and tugged her into the house. Alma was crying so hard that she could barely breathe. She thought she might suffocate from the pain of it. Her back pressed against the wall, and she slid to the floor.

"I'll be right back," Mrs. King said. "You just stay put."

Mrs. King walked into her kitchen and came back with a mug. She sat next to Alma on the floor, so close that Alma smelled her Ivory-soap scent. She hoped Mrs. King didn't smell the beer that must be oozing through her own pores. Mrs. King carefully placed a steaming mug of black coffee on her knees. Alma lifted the coffee to her nose and took in its soothing, bitter scent.

"Now, I see you have a cell phone there in your hand." Mrs. King said, with soft kindness in her voice. "I'm going to take that phone from you, and then I'm going to call your father, you hear?"

"You can't," Alma choked out, and then she released another long sob.

"All right, Alma. Then you just tell me who should I call."

She didn't want to admit it, but she was deeply relieved that someone else was taking over—that another person was telling her what to do with her mess of a self. She felt the urge to nestle into the soft blue quilted gown wrapped around Mrs. King and stay there until it all was over. Instead, she placed her phone on Mrs. King's lap. Between the sobs that had surged through her, she squeaked out one word.

"Evan."

Mrs. King held the phone up. Evan's face was framed in the screen. He was smiling and looking away in the photo. The light caught his auburn hair and skirted the edge of his chin.

"And I'm gonna go on and guess that he's the reason you've been avoiding me?"

Alma looked up and released a low noise she barely recognized.

"My, my." Mrs. King shook her head slowly. Then she looked directly into Alma's eyes. "You ab-so-lute-ly sure about this? Wouldn't you rather I call your family?"

Alma just looked into her eyes, pleading.

Mrs. King pressed a button and lifted the phone to her ear.

———

Evan knew he had to go to her. She was waiting, worried. He had to tell her what he knew. But he was paralyzed, sitting in the parking lot of the county jail, his forehead pressed against his steering wheel.

His phone rang.

"Alma?"

"No, young man. Your lady friend is here on my sofa and she has asked me to call you."

"Is she OK? I mean, is she hurt?"

"Well, Mr. Roland, I'm not sure I can answer that question. I'm thinking *you* might have the answer for me."

This angry voice sounded stern and accusing, but also strangely familiar.

"I *do* intend to ask you to come for her, but before I do that, you and I need to get one thing clear, Evan Prentiss Roland. This is Mrs. Bernice King. I've known you since you were a boy. I know your family. And I promise you, young man, that if you don't do right by this beautiful child, I'm going to let your momma and anyone else I can get ahold of in on your little secret."

The recognition settled on him now. Evan had no idea what little secret she was talking about, but he knew exactly who she was.

"Mrs. King? Is that *you*? From Hines Middle School?"

"Why, yes, child. Of course it's *me*," she replied, with a scolding tone.

"And you're with Alma?" The whole thing was baffling. What was Alma doing with his middle school counselor?

"I believe we've covered this, Mr. Roland."

An image of Mrs. King came to Evan's mind. Evan was a freshman in high school, and his mom had sent him over to Whit's house to pick up a box of party invitations. As always, Evan went right in without knocking. Uncle Sexton and Aunt Maggie argued by the stairwell. Whit sat crying on the living room sofa, and Mrs. King sat beside him, gently rubbing his back. Evan had never seen Whit cry. He'd never seen his aunt and uncle fight. He couldn't believe they would do all of this in front of the middle school counselor. The Prentisses were a very private family.

"I'm sorry, Mrs. King," Evan said, "but why is Alma with *you*?"

"Well, if you need to know, Alma and I go way back. She was working with me to apply for scholarships—until she met *you*."

Evan remembered dropping her off to meet with a counselor at the Krispy Kreme many months earlier, but Alma never talked about her.

"Mrs. King, is Alma OK?" he asked. "Is she hurt?"

"Child, you *know* she's not OK. Just go on and answer me this: Is Alma in a motherly way?"

It took a moment for the question to sink in, but when it did, Evan remembered all that had happened the night before.

"No, ma'am. Alma isn't pregnant."

He smiled, and it felt good. At least this was one worry they didn't have today.

He heard a soft "mmm-hmm" on the other end of the line.

"Mrs. King?" he asked, trying to express in his voice the genuine respect that he had for this woman. "Would you please tell me where you are so that I can come for her?"

"Against my better judgment, I can. But you'll need to make me a promise."

"What's that?" Evan asked.

"You'll be sure to make right *what*ever or *who*ever has made such a mess of this young woman."

Through his swirling confusion, he heard himself make a promise he had no idea how to keep.

"I will. I promise."

SIXTEEN
Satellite

Evan eased his car to the curb, unable to draw his attention away from Alma. She was waiting for him on the stoop, her face wet and blotchy and her body wrapped in a dull wool blanket. Mrs. King stood bent on the stoop, urging Alma to stand. Evan walked toward them. He knelt at Alma's feet and took her face in his hands. He only wondered briefly what Mrs. King would think. Then he pressed his lips to Alma's eyes, her cheeks, her mouth. He felt her lips warm against his, and the wind chimes that hung from the porch made a faint tinkling sound. Evan let himself imagine that the two of them were being transported, together, to some other place and time. But cold, hard concrete pressed against his knees, anchoring him now in this place.

"We'll be going on back inside now," Mrs. King announced. "Or the neighbors will get to talkin'."

Evan lifted Alma to her feet and guided her gently through the door into a warm room that smelled of Pine-Sol. He led her to an old-fashioned sofa, with pretty pink upholstery and deep wood trim. She leaned against him, seeming barely able to balance on her feet. She let him support her weight almost completely as they landed on the firm cushions.

Mrs. King wandered off to the kitchen. Evan and Alma sat silently, their bodies intertwined, staring at the screen of an incongruously large flat-screen television. The sound was turned down too low to hear, but news images of an unmanned satellite careening through space flashed across the screen.

Mrs. King returned and carefully rested a plate of thick-sliced banana bread on the table. She handed Evan a glass of milk.

"I'm brewin' more coffee," she said. She eased her body into a wingbacked chair.

On the television screen, the image shifted to reveal the blue-green Earth, shrinking as the satellite hurtled toward some distant planet.

Everything in this small shotgun-style house seemed too large—the television, the furniture, the rugs—too grand for the modest space. Evan peered through the kitchen door to see a small, fully updated kitchen, with bright tile floors and thick wood countertops. The house was neat and orderly, freshly painted and scrubbed clean. He wondered if this was how all of the houses in this part of town looked on the inside. Though he'd never admit it, he had always imagined these houses shabby and sagging.

Evan sat forward and took a piece of banana bread from the plate. He swallowed it in two large bites. He hadn't realized how hungry he was, and the bread tasted delicious and warm. He followed with a second piece, and then a third, washing them down with long, deep gulps from the glass of milk. Finishing the milk, he rested the glass on the table and paused, realizing that Alma and Mrs. King were staring at him, incredulous.

"You'll have to excuse Evan's manners, Mrs. King. I guess you'd say he has a healthy appetite," Alma said with a smile. A smile he was relieved to see.

Evan wiped his mouth with the back of his hand.

"Your banana bread is delicious, Mrs. King.

"Thank you, Evan," Mrs. King said.

What do you put in it?" he asked.

"I'll never tell. But we're not here to swap recipes, are we?"

Evan shrugged and took another gulp of milk.

"Alma has filled me in on her family's terrible predicament," Mrs. King said. "I *know* you two will be relieved to hear that I have a plan."

"Well, that's real kind of you, Mrs. King," Evan said, "but I think I need to tell Alma about what happened at the jail." He clenched his teeth, absently ran his hand through his still-uncombed hair, and continued, "Uh, the 'predicament,' as you call it, is worse than it seems."

"You don't have to explain," Alma said. "I know. I know they're going to be sent to the detention center. I know ICE is involved."

Evan replied, "You know? How?"

"I've been paying attention, and it's already happening in a couple of other counties around here—the roadblocks, people going to jail for practically no reason and then not being allowed to post bail."

She paused and looked down at their intertwined hands.

"I should have known Gilbert County would be next."

"Lord have mercy on us," Mrs. King said. "Sounds to me like Sheriff Bull Connor come to town."

She looked at them both and continued, "You *do* know who he was—Bull Connor?"

"Yes, ma'am," Evan said. "He was a sheriff in Alabama."

"In Birmingham," Alma said, "back in the civil rights days."

Mrs. King started to walk toward the kitchen, but then turned around and continued.

"Alma telling me her story, well, it sure reminds me of those days—the bad ol' days, as my daddy called them."

Mrs. King chuckled while Alma nodded her head vigorously. Evan sat perfectly still. For the first time in his life, he was feeling more than a little uncomfortable in his white skin.

"Enough about that," Mrs. King said, returning from the kitchen with a fresh pot of coffee. "Let's talk about this plan of mine. It has three parts, just like our Lord's Holy Trinity. Three's *always* a good number for starting out."

She looked to them as if they might have a response.

"Yes, ma'am," Evan said tentatively.

"Part one: We all three will get down on our knees and pray. Now, I'll be headin' to that little church over there." She pointed out her front window, toward a white clapboard building with a tall steeple that stood catty-corner from the house.

"First Iconium Baptist Church. And you two children can be sure I'll tell everyone gathered there tomorrow about what I heard from you. Won't be the first time we gathered ourselves together and called on God to let justice roll down like waters and righteousness like a mighty stream."

Evan had no idea how talking about rolling waters and mighty streams would help. He hoped the next stages of the plan would be a little more practical.

"Now, how about you two?" She seemed to be speaking to them both, but she looked directly at Evan.

"I know your momma and daddy must still take you to that fancy Methodist church downtown?"

"Yes, ma'am, First Methodist," Evan replied. He couldn't begin to imagine going to his staid and proper church and sharing what he had learned today.

Alma, on the other hand, felt certain that all fifteen hundred members of her church, Santa Cruz, would, without a doubt, be praying about this tomorrow. Alma and Mrs. King, it seemed, shared an entirely unreasonable expectation that going to church and praying had anything at all to do with fixing this problem.

Evan could feel an undercurrent of rage beginning to surge through his gut. He grasped onto the edges of the sofa and, without willing it, imagined what it might feel like to approach Uncle Buddy's favorite corner table at brunch tomorrow. He would ask the Sheriff whether stealing a boat was less of a crime than driving with a broken taillight, whether driving drunk and crashing into the side of a house was somehow more noble than crossing an invisible border to feed one's family. All of these stories his mom had laughed about over dinner—the stories of good ol' Buddy's crazy days—ran through his mind. Evan now understood them for what they were: hypocrisy.

———

Strangely, Alma was feeling hopeful. Sitting in Mrs. King's cozy, warm home, sipping a fresh cup of coffee, nibbling sweets—it all was almost enough to make her think that everything would work out. Alma looked at Evan, wanting to share her unlikely hope with him, wanting to hold his hand. The lines of his jaw were hard, and the muscles throbbed, pulling in taut ropes along his neck. His cheeks burned red, nothing like the endearing pink splotches that appeared when Evan was nervous or wanted her. His eyes were thin slits surrounded by lines of tension.

This was not a face of hope.

"Evan, are you okay?"

He turned to her but seemed to look past her.

"Let's just get to the rest of the plan," he replied.

"Well, all right then," Mrs. King said. "Part two: You, young man, are going to make a little visit to your Uncle Sexton."

Alma's bright optimism began to fade. Sexton Prentiss had no intention of helping her dad and Raúl. Going to visit him would make things worse before they'd make things better.

"Mrs. King," she asked, "I don't mean any disrespect, but do you think that's a good idea—for Evan to talk to his uncle?"

"Honestly, Alma," Mrs. King replied, "I'm not sure what to think. But he's a powerful man, and if he wants to, he can make things happen."

"It's worth a try," Evan said. "He and Aunt Maggie went out to the lake after my party,"

"Lake Rabun?" Mrs. King asked.

"Yes, ma'am. We can go out tomorrow to talk to him."

Alma was glad to see the hard lines soften on Evan's face, but she was far from glad to hear that he expected *her* to accompany him on a visit to the "catch and return" senator.

"Uh, by 'we,' do you mean you and I?" she asked tentatively.

"Yeah, Alma. He *loves* you. Remember? He wants to clone you so that he can make a match for Whit."

Mrs. King laughed a hearty laugh.

"I think we can put that into the past tense, Evan," Alma said. "I'm pretty sure he doesn't want his son dating a *mojada*." Both Evan and Mrs. King stared blankly. Alma translated. "A wetback. An illegal."

"You mean an 'undocumented immigrant,'" Evan said, grasping onto her knee. "Remember?"

Alma smiled and shook her head. "Yeah," she said. "I remember."

"So, it's settled. You two will make a drive out to Lake Rabun tomorrow," Mrs. King said.

She walked toward an old-fashioned telephone table, complete with a real phone book and a bulky cordless phone that looked like it must be older than Alma.

"And so we come to part three. This is my part," she said. "I'm gonna pick up this phone and call my son, Reginald. Little Reggie's a partner at one of those fancy law firms down in Atlanta, and you can be sure they've got somebody down there who can help your daddy and brother."

She lifted the heavy black receiver and waved it into the air as she spoke. "Problem is, those people, they charge a king's ransom. You children wouldn't believe how much they get paid, just to talk to a person on the telephone."

She shook her head as she dialed. "Don't you worry, though. I'm gonna tell my little Reggie that he better find you a lawyer, and a *good* one, without charging a penny."

She disappeared through a doorway, phone cradled between her ear and shoulder.

"Lord knows those people can afford it," she said as she closed the door behind her.

Alma looked at Evan to see whether he was as awed by this amazing good luck as she was. He smiled and shrugged. Then he pulled her into his chest and ran his hand slowly through her hair while they turned their attention back to the television, where the satellite now floated weightlessly beyond the atmosphere.

SEVENTEEN
Sins of the Father

Alma picked nervously at the mound of chicken salad on her plate. Her stomach was in knots, and she wasn't sure how she would manage another bite of the sweet, creamy concoction. She used her silver fork to stab a mayo-slathered pineapple and washed it down with a gulp of oversweetened iced tea.

Whit sat glowering next to her at the table. He didn't even pretend to eat. That left Alma, Evan, and his aunt Maggie and uncle Sexton to try to make conversation. Alma and the senator both seemed unable to meet the challenge, but Evan and Aunt Maggie were doing their best.

"Did you get a chance to talk with Emma Jane Watson at your party?" Evan's aunt asked.

"Yes, ma'am. She seems to like Suwanee."

"And her mother told me that she'll be coming out this summer," Mrs. Prentiss said.

Coming out?

Alma shot Whit a glance. He rolled his eyes and mouthed, "Debutantes."

Alma catalogued the phrase in her mind, surprised to learn that there was another meaning for "coming out."

"I'll ask your mother if she'd like to host a tea for Emma Jane in July. You know, her mother hosted a lovely party for Lucy and Annabeth when they came out."

Whit leaned in to whisper in Alma's ear. "I'm still waiting for my party."

Alma lifted her napkin to her mouth, stifling a giggle. Maybe she was wrong about Whit. Maybe he *was* sure about his identity.

It felt good to hold back a laugh, to get her mind off of the real reason they were here—even if only for a minute. On the drive to Lake Rabun, Evan had assured Alma that everyone knew why they were coming. So why were they having a polite meal filled with meaningless chitchat? Wasn't anyone going to get to the point?

Aunt Maggie's chair scraped lightly across the floor. She stood to clear the table, and Alma stood to help. They silently removed the china plates, crystal glasses, and heavy silver cutlery. This was not exactly what she had imagined for a casual Sunday lunch at a "cottage" on Lake Rabun. She was expecting maybe fried chicken and coleslaw on paper plates.

To get here, they drove along country roads, Southern style—the kind with dilapidated double-wide trailers and rusted-out trucks up on blocks in weedy yards. Eventually, the trailers gave way to stately homes that had to be about a hundred years old. Apparently these houses had been in families for generations. They all stood on rolling, manicured lawns, across a small lane from the lake. On the other side of the lane, each house had what Evan called boathouses, but what any normal person would describe as full-sized homes built on stilts over the lake.

Alma thought that she had seen over-the-top, but this was new. It was a tasteful, chicken-salad-on-china-plates, old-South opulence that would scoff at ostentation. Part of her longed to spend a summer afternoon curled up in one of these white Adirondack chairs, reading a good book beside the lake. Another part of her felt nauseated by this wealth-saturated beauty smack in the middle of poverty. Or maybe there was just too much mayonnaise in the chicken salad. Alma hated mayonnaise.

She returned from the kitchen to find that Evan and his uncle were no longer at the table. They were nowhere to be seen.

Aunt Maggie spoke to her, gently.

"Alma, dear, Evan and his uncle have gone into the library to talk. May I offer you some more iced tea?"

Anxiety rose in her chest. What would she do in this house without Evan?

"No, thank you," she replied politely.

"There's no reason to keep Alma locked up here, Mother," Whit announced. "Won't you allow me to show her the sights?" He spoke as if this were a cruel joke.

His mom shook her head vigorously, but he continued, speaking slowly, as if to a small child.

"Alma, darling, can you promise my mother that you will not permit me to ingest any, ahem, substances while we are on our little tour?"

Mrs. Prentiss's face went red.

"And that you will not permit me to enter Mr. Wilson's drugstore to purchase any cough syrups, et cetera?" He drew out the "et cetera."

Alma realized that Whit was the one being held prisoner here.

Mrs. Prentiss looked directly at Alma and forced an everything-is-just-fine smile.

"As a matter of fact, I *do* need some Aleve. I just ran out and my tennis elbow is flaring up again. Alma, would you like to walk with Whit down to the drugstore?"

Alma nodded. "Sure," she said.

"It does seem to have warmed up quite a bit from yesterday," Mrs. Prentiss said. "Fresh air probably would do you both some good."

At this, her first acknowledgement that anything was actually wrong with Alma, that any crisis at all had occurred in her life, Mrs. Prentiss reached into her purse, gave Alma a twenty-dollar bill, and walked away.

"Free at last," Whit said. "Let's get out of here before she changes her mind."

She and Whit rushed from the house. It was a nice day, sunny and cool but not biting cold as the day before, and the air felt good pumping through her lungs.

"So, you're under house arrest?" Alma asked.

They walked along the winding lane that hugged the shoreline.

"Yes. After my visit to the hospital Friday night, my parents decided that I need another twenty-eight-day vacation. Until that fun begins, I'm imprisoned here in socialite hell with my mother."

"Rehab?"

"Mmm-hmm."

"But you don't want to go?"

Whit stopped walking and whipped his head toward her, eyebrows raised.

"You've obviously never experienced the joys of the twenty-eight-day program."

"No."

"Well then, suffice it to say that no, I am not inclined to go back to rehab."

Alma wondered how many times a seventeen-year-old kid could have been in rehab, but she thought it might be weird to ask.

"You know, Whit," she said, "this little prison of yours isn't so shabby. You should see where my dad and brother are hanging out."

"I heard about their situation," Whit said. "What a debacle." He shook his head. "Only in Gilbert County, Georgia—imbecile capital of the world."

"Actually, it's happening all over the country, especially in the South,"

Alma said. "Looks like Gilbert County's got some competition for that title."

"And this, uh, strategy is intended to solve *what* problem, precisely?"

"The problem of people like me hanging out with people like you, I guess."

"Ah, well, that makes perfect sense, then. They definitely should continue on course."

His deadpan delivery was flawless.

Alma knew he was a mess, but she loved being with Whit. He was eccentric, sarcastic, and inclined to use big words. All of these traits, in her estimation, were assets.

"Wanna see the dam before we go on your little errand for my mother?" Whit asked.

"Sure," Alma replied.

They turned off the lane and onto a gravel road. Whit pulled a beat-up pewter flask from his waistband, unscrewed it, and took a deep swig.

"Am I supposed to take that away from you?" Alma asked.

"Most certainly, yes." Whit replied. "Do you want some?"

"No, thanks. I'm still getting over Friday night."

"Me, too," Whit said. "Thus the need for my friend here."

He lifted the flask toward her, and she saw that it was engraved with "SWP III."

"It has your initials?"

"Sexton Whitfield Prentiss the Third," he said.

Who carried an engraved flask around? And what kind of name was Sexton Whitfield anyway? Alma marveled that the name had survived three generations, even without any discernible first name embedded anywhere in it.

"Was that like a Christmas present or something?" she asked.

"Yes, to myself, three years ago. Since then, it's been a constant companion."

The gravel road ended at a narrow bridge. On one side of the bridge, sparkling waters filled the crevices between sloping mountains, forming Lake Rabun. On the other side stretched a void from which emerged the deafening roar of falling water.

"Mathis Dam," Whit announced. "It feeds energy to the Terrora Power Plant."

Whit took Alma's elbow and pulled her toward the dam.

"I've always liked that name," he said. "I mean, Terrora power. There's something poetic about power and terror in the same name. You know?"

Then he led the way onto the narrow bridge that separated deep waters from nothingness.

———

Evan hadn't wanted to leave Alma alone out there, but when his uncle took his arm and sternly led him into the library, he didn't seem to have any choice.

"Evan, son," he began once he had closed the door behind them, "I'm very disappointed in you. You've shown poor judgment bringing *her* into our home."

So Alma had been right. Thirty-six hours and the revelation that his girlfriend was an "illegal" produced a complete reversal in his uncle's opinion of her. She was no longer the "great gal" who charmed him at the country club. She was "*her*." And she was not welcome in his house.

Evan's uncle went to a mahogany table, lifted a glass decanter, and poured himself a drink. Bourbon, probably.

His uncle stood and sipped, gazing out the window toward the lake, while Evan began describing all that he knew about the García family's situation.

His uncle listened patiently. Then he sat next to Evan in a wing-backed leather chair and asked, "Son, are you still escorting your mom to all those charity events?"

"Yes, sir," Evan replied, confused.

"And how's that working out for you?"

"OK, I guess. What's this got to do with anything?"

Evan had no idea where this conversation was intended to take them.

"I don't want to be unkind, son. But I do want you to recognize that children pay for the mistakes of their parents. That's just how life works, whether we like it or not."

Evan didn't want to grasp the connections that his uncle was working to establish.

"Uncle Sexton," Evan said, "my dad is a selfish ass who refuses to grow up. I know that."

"Well, at least we can agree on that today," his uncle replied, taking another sip.

"But I *choose* to fill in when he abandons my mom. It's my decision." He remembered Alma sitting on that bench at school, telling her story. "Alma and Raúl, they didn't get to make a choice, and Mr. García is about as far from a selfish ass as any man can be."

"But he made a bad choice, Evan. And now he and his family have to live with the consequences."

Evan felt the anger rising. He turned to face his uncle, who stood and walked slowly back toward the window.

"How can you say that, Uncle Sexton? It was the only choice he could make if he wanted to give his kids a future. He gave up so much for them." Evan could almost feel Alma's body, brittle against him, after she had told him the worst part. "Alma's mom *died* in the desert for this,"

Evan said, his voice rising. "She *died*. Do you have any idea how many people die in the desert trying to get here?"

His uncle turned to face him squarely.

"Yes, son. I know all too well. And I'm very sorry for your friend and her brother. But I need you to listen carefully to me. There's not a damned thing I can do about this. If I were to help your friend, the entire state of Georgia would be on that lawn outside my office tomorrow, waving their signs and yanking their votes. It would be political suicide, son."

Furious, Evan stood and tried to speak, wanting to ask his uncle who the selfish ass was now. But Uncle Sexton held up his hand to pause Evan's interruption.

"But more importantly," he said, "I have sworn to support and defend the Constitution of the United States and to represent the people of Georgia, Evan. It's my job to understand their interests and to make those known in Washington. And the people of Georgia want an end to illegal immigration."

Evan's head was spinning. He slumped back in his chair and rested his forehead on his hand.

"And what about family?" he asked, unable to look up. "What about your responsibility to your family?"

Evan's uncle sat down next to him and touched him lightly on the arm. "Evan, I love you like a son. You *know* that." A subtle trace of emotion rose in his uncle's voice. "I want what's best for you. But I also need for you to know this: being part of a political family means we sometimes sacrifice our own wants and needs for the wants and needs of the people."

"Even when the people are wrong?"

"I don't believe the people are wrong about this, Evan. But yes, sometimes even when the people are wrong. Your mother and I have known that for a long time."

"How?" Evan exploded. "How can you possibly not see the ugly wrongness of all of this, Uncle Sexton? I just don't get it."

His uncle gazed out over the lake, saying nothing.

"Do you know that I went to the jail yesterday? I went to post bail for Raúl and Mr. García."

"I know, Evan. Your Uncle Buddy called to tell me."

"And did he tell you," Evan asked, emotion rising in his voice, "did he tell you that when I came in, he patted me on the back and said not to worry. He told me 'boys will be boys' or some bullshit like that."

"No, son. He told me you were upset, though."

Evan slumped deeper into the chair. He felt like screaming and crying at the same time. He felt completely out of control.

"He told me he would get my friends out, but that was before he knew who my friends were."

"What's your point, son?"

Evan tried again, this time cutting to the chase.

"Maybe the sacrifices you and Mom keep making, maybe they're a mistake. Maybe they're the mistakes that my mom is paying for, that I'm paying for." He paced in front of the window. "Maybe they're just eating away at our whole family." He stopped and looked directly at his uncle. "I mean, hell, look at your own son."

Evan involuntarily tossed his head toward the room where Whit, messed up out of his head at noon on a Sunday, recently sat slumped in a chair, eating nothing, saying nothing.

"Listen to me, boy. I'm not sure what you're trying to say, and frankly I don't think I want to know," his uncle almost whispered. "But I am sure about this: It is time for you to end this thing with Eduardo García's daughter. It's time for our family to move past this particular set of mistakes before we have to live with some ugly consequences."

"No," Evan said simply. "I'm not abandoning Alma for 'the good of the family.'"

He turned his back to his uncle and stared out the window.

"I know it must seem a hard thing to do *now*," his uncle said, moving beside him. "But you're young, and you've got a lot of life ahead of you." His uncle lifted a hand and placed it on Evan's shoulder. "In a few months, you'll be far away from all of this, playing soccer, enjoying college." He wasn't looking at Evan. Both of them had eyes fixed on the horizon. "You'll forget all about this mess."

Evan pulled away from his grip.

"It's way too late for that, Uncle Sexton," he said. "Alma and Raúl, Whit and I—we're already living with the ugly consequences of a bunch of mistakes we never made. We can't escape them. I mean, damn, look how hard your son tries." Evan stepped toward the door. "But I'm not Whit, and I don't want to escape them. I want to fix them, and I will." He paused and then corrected himself. "Alma and I, we will. Together."

He turned his back on the only real father he had ever known, and walked away.

EIGHTEEN
Terrora Power

Alma and Whit stood close, leaning over the railing to watch the water tumble into a concrete slab at the base of the dam. It was mesmerizing. There was a violence in it that Alma couldn't turn away from.

"He's not going to help you. You understand that, right?" Whit spoke, raising his voice over the thundering roar of water.

Alma didn't look up.

"You mean your dad? Of course I know, Whit. I wasn't born yesterday. But Evan and Mrs. King seem to think he will."

"Bernice King should know better. She's in on all of our family's dirty little secrets."

"Mrs. King is amazing," Alma replied. "I completely blew her off when she tried to help me last fall, and she still rescued me yesterday."

"She's good at that," Whit said.

"Yeah," Alma replied.

"Does she still live in that little house in the crappy neighborhood?"

"You mean the shotgun house?" Alma asked, turning to look at him.

"And by the way, that crappy neighborhood is where I grew up. It was great, actually."

Whit laughed. "Sorry, but you must admit that some of the homes in your old neighborhood are in need of attention. God, talk about rescue! She takes me in sometimes, when my father starts in on me."

Whit's dad? Laying a hand on him?

"What do you mean?" she asked, sounding stressed out.

"Oh, God, Alma. Don't get all worked up. He doesn't *beat* me or anything. He just constantly insists that I be someone I'm not. You know?"

Whit laughed, a sort of high cackle.

"He wants me to be Evan, or he wishes Evan were me. It's exhausting."

They both fell silent as the roar of the water started to ring in her ears, and Whit took another long swig from his flask.

"I'm sorry," Alma replied, and she meant it.

She didn't understand any of it, but she knew just by looking at Whit that he was tired, very tired.

She decided to change the subject—to let him in on some of her own vulnerability.

"So, Whit, since you seem to be sort of a professional in the alcohol department, I have a question for you."

"My, what a lovely compliment, Alma."

Alma pressed on, knowing she might lose her nerve if she waited another moment.

"Friday night, while Evan was dragging your drunk ass home, I drank for the first time."

"Really?" Whit drew out the word, almost singing.

"Yeah, really."

He turned to face her, sizing her up with his gaze.

"I'm not surprised. I mean, look at you. You're the Virgin Mary, all dressed in blue, sweet and innocent."

"I am *not* sweet," Alma replied, belligerently.

"All right, maybe not sweet, but definitely virginal."

"Yeah, I think that might be gone, too," Alma said.

Was she about to confess to Whit that she wasn't sure whether or not she had lost her virginity to the love of her life? Until now, she wouldn't even let herself think of the possibility. There were so many other stresses in her life, and Evan had been so consistently himself with her since Friday—nothing so monumental could have happened. It would have changed things, right? But once she said the words out loud, she knew that her anxiety was real.

"Which brings me to my question," she said. "I'm sure I only had a couple of beers. But I can't remember anything about that night, except landing on a bed with Evan."

"So, you think you blacked out, and that precious moment that's supposed to last a lifetime is forever gone?"

"Something like that, yeah."

"Alma, darling, you are tiny, but even a tiny person isn't going to black out after a couple of beers."

"Oh, and a Jell-O shot," Alma added, "a gooey blob."

Whit looked at her, eyebrows arched. "And now, I presume you're going to tell me this shot was delivered by Conway?"

"Nice job, Sherlock," Alma replied, feeling sort of confused.

"OK, then you definitely blacked out. I don't know what he puts in those shots, but it's not alcohol, and it's strong."

"Oh, God," Alma said. Her head was starting to spin. "Do you mean, like, drugs?"

"Yes, Alma. I mean, like, drugs. So, did you bleed?" Whit asked, nonchalant.

"What?" Alma called out, too loud.

"Did you bleed? Are you sore?"

She started to blush. She could feel it rising in her cheeks.

"I can't believe we're having this conversation."

"You didn't, then."

"No."

"And this is Evan we're talking about? The one who you think may have deflowered you?"

Alma wanted to crawl under a rock.

"Of course!"

"And he was more or less sober, thanks to me?"

"Yeah, he was sober."

"If you'll permit me to be Sherlock Holmes once more, I'd say this is elementary, my dear Watson. No blood, no soreness, and a sober boyfriend who is almost as saintly as you. Your virtue is intact."

He grabbed Alma's arms and turned her body to face him. "Alma, there's no way Evan took advantage of you if he was sober and you were as wasted as you say you were." He dropped his arms and shrugged. "So, you two can go on and gather up the rose petals."

"What are you talking about?" Alma asked, both relieved and confused.

"You know," he said, "bed of rose petals strewn across a blanket under a moonlit sky? You and Evan can do it the way everyone fantasizes it will be the first time."

"Yeah, OK. Can we stop talking about this now?" Alma said, stepping back. "I'm *really* sorry I brought it up."

She wasn't sorry, though. She was relieved. Whit was right. She no longer needed for this anxiety to linger amid her other, more concrete concerns.

They both leaned over the railing again and watched the waters fall.

"Wanna hear about my first time?" he asked, nudging her.

"Not really, but I don't think that's gonna stop you," Alma said.

"It was just *too* romantic," he began, his voice dripping with sarcasm.

"Wait," Alma said, "was this with a girl?"

"Yes!" Whit exclaimed. "Well, let's just say a girl was involved."

This was going to be good, but Alma wondered whether she was too much of a prude to handle it.

"Conway and I, we broke into your boyfriend's house after a party where Conway, incidentally, had been passing out those wicked Jell-O shots. He only gives them to a select few—always girls. It doesn't take Sherlock Holmes to figure out what he's up to with those."

Alma stepped back and hugged her chest tight. "Wait," she said. "You mean he's purposely *drugging* girls?"

Whit just raised his eyebrows in a gesture that, Alma thought, was meant to convey something along the lines of "Duh."

"And you all just *let* him do this?" Alma asked.

"I don't *let* him do anything, Alma. He's not exactly mine to take care of."

She felt nauseated and confused. She wanted to be alone all of a sudden, but she had no idea how to escape.

"I didn't even know you and Conway were, uh, friends," Alma said quietly.

"We weren't, and we definitely aren't now. He won't even look at me."

Whit leaned farther out over the dam, and then allowed his body to ricochet backward.

"But we were so far gone, or at least I was," he continued. "Evan and his mom were in Greece. God only knows where his dad was."

Whit spun around and leaned against the wall, looking up at the sky. "I told Conway I remembered where they hide the key—under the big white planter by the guest house. So we stumbled into Conway's god-awful Hummer and drove there from a party at Paul's house. We had a girl with us. She was so wasted she could barely stand, and young. Christ, she was young."

Whit seemed to be trying hard to make the story sound funny, but it clearly wasn't funny, and below the humor was a sort of trauma pushing its way out. He looked down at his feet.

"We ended up in Aunt BeBe's bathroom, the three of us. I don't remember much else."

He turned and leaned out over the railing and rocked back and forth.

"I don't even remember her name. I'm pretty sure I never knew her name."

Alma felt like she might throw up.

"She was Latina, like you. She had tons of curly hair. Thick. And she was so young. I guess I already said that. She let us take turns, and then she passed out, and we didn't know where to take her, so we left. We just wandered off and left her on the floor of Aunt BeBe's bathroom."

"*Let* you?" she asked, her voice rising in anger. "There's no such thing as 'letting' in that situation, Whit. You know that, right?"

He looked directly at Alma, his eyes glassy and bloodshot, rimmed in red with purplish circles underneath.

"It's marble, Aunt BeBe's bathroom floor. It must have been cold," he said.

Alma felt dizzy. She grasped the metal railing and held tight.

"Say something," she heard him plead.

"What do you want me to say, Whit?" she asked, looking away from him.

She wanted him to know that his story was the exact opposite of funny. She was horrified to think that she might know this curly-haired Latina, that Conway might have drugged her. She probably did know the girl. Gilberton was a small town, and in the Latino community, everyone knew everyone.

But it didn't matter. Whether she knew the girl or not, what Whit and Conway had done was wrong in so many ways that Alma didn't even know where to begin.

"God, I'm a mess," she heard him say.

"Yeah."

She watched Whit bury his face in his hands. He sat down on the gravel bridge and started to sob. His battered pewter flask fell onto the gravel beside him.

Alma didn't know what to do. She was too disgusted to touch him, too angry to lean down and try to comfort him. As far as she was concerned, Whit deserved to be in agony. So she left him crying on the edge of the dam and wandered off in search of his mother's Aleve.

———

Evan went to the lake, searching for Alma. He saw her on the dock in front of Mr. Wilson's drugstore, balanced on a piling like a tightrope walker, with a half-empty plastic bag dangling from her hand. Her back was turned away from him, and she was surrounded by an almost perfect silence.

Alma extended her leg behind her and let it dip around to the side. She moved slowly and methodically.

A loud grumbling punctured the silence as a sleek antique speedboat pulled away from the marina.

The next thing he saw was Alma tumbling toward the black water. She had lost her balance. Without thinking, he ran across the dry grass and onto the dock. He hurled his body toward where she had fallen, toward the white plastic bag that slowly began to drift.

Evan grasped Alma's hand, and they both paddled frantically through the freezing, murky water. They heaved themselves onto the dock and collapsed together.

"Good Lord, that's cold," Evan exclaimed as he shook his head vigorously, releasing the frigid water from his hair.

Alma hugged herself tightly and replied through chattering teeth. "You shouldn't have come in after me. Did you think I was gonna drown or something?" She sounded angry.

The boat pulled up beside them and the driver called out.

"You two OK?"

"Yes, sir," Evan replied, "A little cold, but OK."

"You got somewhere to go and get dried off?"

Evan glanced back down the road toward Uncle Sexton's house. There wasn't a chance in hell that he'd be going back there. He had an idea.

"Uh, yes, sir, but it's across the lake. Any chance for a lift? It would be a cold walk back."

The man motioned for them to climb in, and they both tumbled into the back of the boat.

Alma watched as they pulled farther out from the dock and away from her stupid mistake. How many times had she done that—balanced at the edge of the water to still her mind? She'd never even come close to falling. The white plastic bag containing Mrs. Prentiss's Aleve (and her twelve dollars and twenty-eight cents change) bobbed in the wake of the boat. She had no idea where they were going, and the wind pierced her skin like a thousand little needles. All she could think about was that Evan's aunt wouldn't get her medicine, and she'd be able to say that an "illegal" stole twenty dollars from her.

Evan talked with the driver, motioning to a point across the lake. Then he sat beside her on the rear bench seat.

"You OK?" he asked, having to speak loudly over the sound of the motor.

"I'm freezing."

"Yeah, well, at least it's not the second time in three days you've been dunked in cold water."

Alma looked at Evan, confused.

"At my party?"

She continued to stare blankly at him.

"When they busted into my room?"

Alma figured it was time to come clean with Evan.

"I guess I had too much to drink the other night. And Conway gave me some disgusting shot that was spiked or something. I don't remember anything that happened after we went to your room."

"Conway gave you a shot?" Evan asked, sounding stressed. "Who let him give you a shot?"

"No one let him, Evan. I just took it."

"Yeah, OK," Evan said, an anxious edge in his voice. "Well, anyway, there's not much to remember. Conway, Peavey, and Paul burst into my room, carried me to the pool, half naked and screaming, and threw me in."

Alma huddled more tightly into a ball, wrapping her arms around her sopping jeans.

"By the time I got back, you were pretty far gone. I got M.C. to come up and put you in a T-shirt. I didn't think I'd be able to handle it."

So, Whit had been right. Nothing happened. Alma smiled, feeling both relieved and a little sheepish.

"That's embarrassing," Alma said. "I don't know how I got so wasted."

Evan shrugged. "I think those shots are pretty strong." They were leaving things unspoken. Alma felt it. But it didn't seem like either one of them had the energy to take it on.

The boat started to slow as it came toward a large yellow boathouse.

"This the one?" the driver asked.

"Yes, sir. Thanks so much," Evan said as he took Alma's hand and helped her onto the dock. She smiled at the driver and tried to play along with whatever charade Evan had going.

They stood shivering on the dock as the boat pulled away. Evan took Alma's hand and led her toward the door.

"This is M.C.'s boathouse. I know where the key's hidden."

"What is it with you people and your hidden keys?" she asked.

Evan didn't hear her. He was rummaging around under a big empty flowerpot. Very original.

He looked back at her and turned the key in the door.

"I couldn't go back in there, Alma. I'm sorry. I couldn't face my uncle."

"I'm sorry, too, Evan," she replied softly. "I should have tried harder to convince you not to come."

———

They didn't have to say anything more. They both sensed how broken and battered the other felt, and how desperately each needed to take refuge in the other. Evan closed the door softly behind them and kicked off his shoes. Alma leaned into the door, reaching down to remove her wet socks and shoes. They stood close, peeling away the dampness. Evan pulled his sopping sweatshirt over his head. It landed heavily on the slate floor of the entryway, tangled with a white T-shirt. He turned to face her, bare-chested, and looked directly into her eyes, with a question burning in his own.

"Alma," he whispered.

She lifted her arms, and he reached down to grasp the edge of her sweater. He pulled it gently over her head. She shrugged out of it, feeling the pleasure of release from its clammy dampness.

Sunlight streamed through a wall of windows, heating each patch of bare skin that emerged as they slowly undressed each other. Almost naked, they knelt together high above the deep water. Each studied the other's body, touching it lightly, taking in its contours. And then, when the intensity of their desire threatened to overwhelm them, they tumbled together onto a soft antique prairie rug.

Their hands searched urgently as their open mouths met. They kissed hard, pressing into each other, hoping that the taste of the other might quench the fire, or at least dull the bright radiance of its heat. When the shimmering radiance refused to dim, Alma fell back and held Evan tightly while he kissed her neck and shoulders, chest and stomach. The sunlight beat down on their gleaming bodies.

Evan rose onto his knees and brought his mouth to Alma's ear.

"I don't have anything," he whispered urgently. "Is it OK?"

Alma pulled away and opened her eyes.

"Only once," he continued, pleading, "We've waited so long."

Evan leaned forward to kiss her again, but Alma propped herself onto her elbows. An image of Whit, crumpled and crying on the dam, filled her mind. What did he have to do with this? A new image forced its way in: her body lying naked on Evan's mother's bathroom floor.

"Was Conway there?" she heard herself asking. "In your room with me?"

Evan sat up.

"What the hell, Alma?" His tone almost frightened her. "What are you talking about?"

"When they threw you in the pool, was Conway there?"

She thought of the way Conway had looked at her as she stood across from him in the hallway, the urgency and anger in his voice when he offered her the shot, Whit's terrible story, Evan's account of Friday night, all that she couldn't remember. Was it all just coincidence? She didn't want to know the answer, but she forced herself to ask again.

"Did Conway carry you to the pool? Did you see him there, or was he in the room with me?"

Evan jumped to his feet and walked away from her, wearing nothing but his boxer shorts. Alma curled up, modesty descending on her like a ton of lead.

"Please, Evan, just answer me."

Evan ran his hand through his hair. "Peavey and Paul carried me. I don't know where Conway was."

"Think about it," she demanded.

"God almighty, Alma. What the hell is this all about?"

"I just need for you to remember," she said slowly. "Please."

Evan slumped onto the edge of a couch and rested his face in his hands. The sun moved behind a cloud, and the room dimmed.

"No, I guess he wasn't there."

"And when you came back to your room? Was I alone?"

"Yeah." Evan nodded into his hands.

"Was I the way you left me?"

Evan looked up.

"Was I?" Alma commanded.

"No, you took off your dress and your bra."

Alma felt cold, suddenly. She grabbed a quilt from the couch and wrapped herself in it.

"But I was passed out."

"Not quite," Evan said. "You were out of it. It felt wrong to want you so much. You were so, uh, wasted. So I got Mary Catherine to help."

It hurt Alma to look at him, to see him breathing so deeply. He was still struggling to bring his desire under control.

"She was drunk, too," Evan said. "But she said something about Conway."

Alma thought she might vomit.

"Evan, please try to remember what she said."

"She said he came out from my bathroom and told her he wanted to help. She called him a perv and kicked him out."

Alma glanced around urgently. Her stomach heaved. All she saw were closed doors, so she lurched toward the sink in the small kitchenette. She stood over the sink in her underwear. Again and again, she hurled bits of mayonnaise-laden chicken into the basin.

—

Evan turned on the heat. The light from outside was almost completely gone, but the room stayed warm. He was afraid to turn on the lights. He didn't want anyone to find them. He gave Alma a glass of water and wrapped her in the quilt. He wrapped himself in a towel and put their wet clothes in the dryer. Then he sat on the couch, watching Alma shrink deeper and deeper inside the quilt on the other end. The dryer tumbled repetitively in the background, and he listened to her talk. She told him about Whit and Conway and the way they took advantage of a drunken girl in his own house. She called it "sexual assault." She said the words, over and over, as if naming the act would make it disappear.

Each time she said it, he thought how strange it would be for them to have watched each other do that. Conway probably hated himself for watching Whit, or for wanting Whit to see him.

"He wanted to do it to me, Evan," Alma said.

"What? No," Evan said.

"He cornered me alone and made me take a shot."

Evan felt his chest collapse. She was right.

How did he let this happen?

"Do you see where I'm going with this, Evan? Because I don't think I can say it out loud."

Evan nodded. Prickly heat spread through his chest and his face.

"Why were you alone with Conway? Where the hell was Mary Catherine? Where was I?"

"I don't know, Evan. Don't get mad at me. I just needed to get away from him, so I took it."

"Jesus, Alma, I'm not *mad*. It's just, everyone *knows* . . ."

"Everyone *knows*?" Alma cried out. "What the hell is wrong with you people?"

He forced his reluctant mind to return to that night, to recollect every detail while Alma waited in silence.

"Alma," he said, "just calm down. You're right about Conway. He likes to fool around with wasted girls."

"It's not called 'fooling around,'" Alma said. "It's called 'sexual assault.' And if everyone *knows* then why the hell don't you *stop* him? I mean, *Madre de Dios*, are you telling me that Conway is going around *raping* girls, and everyone just *knows*?"

Alma's head fell into her hands.

"Oh, Christ, Alma. Oh, Jesus." He was starting to sweat. Evan worked hard to knit together the evidence. He grasped his elbows and rocked back and forth, trying not to let the rage and remorse overtake him.

Then it all came together.

"I don't think he hurt you. He didn't have time. I was down there for ten minutes."

Alma shot her head up and gave him a look that made it pretty clear. Ten minutes was plenty of time.

Evan started to pace. "Listen, Alma. I looked at you. I watched you for a while. I mean, when I found you almost naked in my room."

Alma hugged the quilt even more tightly.

"You had your underpants on. They were smooth against your skin, not like someone had tried to force them off or anything."

God, he hated this. He hated that the sweet memory of stealing a glance at her body was becoming evidence in some sort of investigation. Suddenly, he felt like a pervert instead of a boyfriend who was just completely in awe of his girlfriend.

"Your hair was smooth. You were kind of curled up." Evan's forehead fell into his hand. "You probably don't remember, but when they busted into the room, your dress was already halfway off, and, uh, your bra was unhooked."

"Oh, no."

"I was just starting to realize you were too drunk. I told you we needed to stop."

Alma looked down at the floor and squeezed her eyes shut. When she looked back up, she spoke quietly.

"Thank you," she said, "for stopping."

He sat down beside her.

"You shouldn't thank me for that, Alma," Evan said. He bit down on his lip. "It wasn't a favor. It was just the thing to do."

Alma nodded silently and looked away.

"He may have touched you. But I don't think he, you know, uh . . ."

"Yeah, I know," Alma said. Thank God she hadn't used the word again.

"He would have needed to take off your underpants."

"I guess you're right," Alma replied, looking away from him. "I didn't bleed. I'm not sore." She turned toward him. "All of that would happen, right?" she whispered. "I mean, on my first time."

Evan shrugged and took her hand in his. "You're asking the wrong guy, Alma."

She edged toward him and rested her head in his lap. He stroked her hair gently, as innocently as possible.

"I'm not ready," she said, in a tone that was both gentle and firm.

"We'll wait," he said, "for as long as you need to."

"OK," she said, propping herself up to kiss him softly. And then she said something really strange: "Let's hold out for moonlight and rose petals."

NINETEEN
St. Jude, Plead for Us

Sometime before four a.m., the helicopter roared through Alma's unconscious mind, shining its blinding light onto that awful scene. She awoke, panting and sweating, with the sickly sweet taste lingering in her mouth. This time, she had seen the source of the saccharine sweetness: a red Jell-O shot forced into her mouth by Evan's aunt Maggie.

Yuck.

Alma's dream was back for the first time in months, and it was worse than ever. Call it superstition, but Alma worried, wide awake in her bed in the predawn hours, that if they didn't get to the next part of Mrs. King's plan soon, everything would go to hell in a handbasket.

She texted Evan.

Are you awake
No. Why?
I need to ask a favor
At 4:15 in the morning?
No. at 7

You know I'll do anything
Take me to mass
You mean church? Tomorrow's monday.
Go back to bed
Meet me on the bench at 6:45. Catholics have
church every day
Good lord. Which one?
Which church?
No, which bench
Fortitude?
Sounds about right

Evan must have passed out because Alma's text awoke him in the guest house, his bleeding hand wrapped haphazardly in his own T-shirt and Mary Catherine wrapped in a duvet, dozing on his bare chest.

Evan held it together when he was with Alma. They waited until late and then walked the three miles around the lake to his car. She fell asleep on the drive home. He shook her awake and walked her to her front door. The moment he left her the rage overtook him. All of the insanely frustrating events of the past few days converged into an image: Conway tugging on Alma's dress. He drove recklessly through the darkness, blinded by the image, using every last ounce of his will to keep his car from steering toward Conway's driveway, to keep himself from beating Conway to a pulp. He could almost feel his hands aching with the sensation of it. Instead, he stormed into his empty house, slammed the doors loudly. He tried to take a long, hot shower, to watch pointless television, to listen to music so loud that the neighbors would hear. But even the angry screams coursing through the speakers couldn't dampen his fury.

Evan took a bottle of Johnnie Walker from the liquor cabinet in his dad's office and sucked down several long, painful swigs. When the buzz came on strong instead of mellow, Evan knew that being alone was a very bad idea. He lurched out of the house, his tense body carrying him toward Conway while his battered mind urged him to stay away.

When he saw a dim light coming through Mary Catherine's window, Evan realized that she might offer him a way out. He texted M.C. to see if she was awake. Moments later, they met in the guest house, as they had many times. Until now, it was always to deal with Mary Catherine's crises—some lame boyfriend or another who had broken her heart again.

It was Evan's turn to call in the favor.

They finished the bottle, passing it back and forth as Evan fumed. Mary Catherine listened, stunned and horrified. Evan explained the jail, his talks with "Uncle Buddy" and Uncle Sexton, and then the hardest part. He hoped desperately that she would have a way to refute his story about Conway, to come up with an alternative explanation. Instead she confirmed everything, slowly reconstructing the events of Friday night.

Evan probably frightened her when he grasped the near-empty bottle of Johnnie Walker by the neck and smashed it against the kitchen counter. Small shards of glass and the last drops of dark liquid splintered across the gleaming tile floor. But she didn't show that she was scared. Instead, she knelt with him to pick up the fragments of the bottle, seeing that his hand had been gashed with a deep wound and watching the blood flow red. He remembered burying his face in his bloody hands. Then anger finally gave way to sorrow.

Mary Catherine told him to take off his shirt. She wrapped his hand in it, and somehow, they both fell asleep on the couch.

"It's four fifteen," he said, nudging her. "You should go home."

She heaved her body across his and pulled the duvet over her head.

Evan lifted her from the couch and carried her from the guest house. The cold air jolted her awake.

"Thanks," he said. She kissed his cheek and stumbled away.

Evan knew he wouldn't sleep again, so he went inside, threw his bloodied shirt in the trash, and took another long, hot shower. He pulled the glass from his wound, bandaged it, and waited for morning to come.

He arrived at school long before Alma's bus, so he sat waiting on Fortitude, holding a cooling double cappuccino. When the bus came, Alma walked toward him and took the cup.

"What happened?" she asked, noticing his bandaged hand.

"Stupid accident," he said. "The knife slipped when I was making a peanut butter sandwich last night."

She shrugged and led him to the car.

His head was pounding so he didn't mind the quiet as they drove to Santa Cruz. They went into the church, and Evan sat with Alma in the second pew of the almost empty sanctuary. He couldn't believe he was skipping calculus for this. He had no idea what was going on since the entire service was in Spanish. All he knew was that there was a lot more standing, sitting, and kneeling here than in his church. He was pretty impressed that the three old ladies sitting in front of them kept up. His head still ached and his bandaged hand throbbed. How had he ended up feeling so ruined?

The faint smell of incense combined with the warmth and the dim light created a perfect atmosphere for sleep. He wasn't sure how much longer he would last.

Hoping to enhance his appearance of piety, Evan made the mistake of closing his eyes. Why couldn't he shake the image of Conway standing over Alma, tugging her dress up around her narrow hips?

Alma nudged him. She was standing, watching the priest walk out of the church. At last, it was over. Alma dug in her purse and pulled out a candle—the kind you see in the "ethnic foods" section of the Bi-Lo. She motioned for Evan to follow as she walked from the sanctuary and into a room crammed full of statues and paintings and flickering candles.

She placed her candle in front of a plastic statue of a bearded man in a white robe. He had a green drape over one shoulder. With his left hand, he held what looked like a big gold coin in front of his chest. His right hand had a long staff, like the one Jesus held on his preschool coloring pages of the "Good Shepherd." There was a weird little flame over his head.

"Is that Jesus?"

"It's St. Jude. Wanna light the candle?"

"Um, OK," he said, looking around for a pack of matches. She took a long stick that had been burned on one end and balanced it over the flame of the adjacent candle. That one had a weird image of a toddler all dressed up like a Spanish conquistador or something.

Alma handed him the stick, and he touched the flame to the wick of Alma's candle. They watched it flicker in silence for a while. He felt lighter, surrounded by dim flames and unfamiliar images.

"So, did I just participate in some sort of voodoo ritual?" he asked.

"No, it's not quite that exotic," Alma replied. "You made a prayer to St. Jude. Or I guess it would be more accurate to say that you asked St. Jude to plead to God for us."

"Plead? Wow."

Evan struggled to keep the heaviness from descending again. They both glanced around the room, taking in the dozens of images and statues that surrounded them. "Why'd you choose him?"

"He's the patron saint of hopeless causes."

"That sucks," Evan said.

"Yeah," replied Alma, "it does."

He took her hand in his good one and they stood together a little longer, watching the candle flicker alongside many others, each making a silent, impossible plea.

—

They probably would have arrived on time for second period. But Evan offered to stop at the Dripolator on the way back. Evan could always be counted on to feed her addiction. They both stopped by a trash can in an empty hall of the school. Alma sucked down the dregs of her second double cappuccino, and Evan noisily pulled the last droplets of water through a straw. Just as they were about to part ways, Alma heard a deep male voice call her name. She turned to see Mr. Massey, the principal, walking toward them.

Busted.

Alma and Evan tossed their drinks into the garbage.

"Mr. Roland," the principal announced with a firm voice, "shouldn't you be in a classroom somewhere instead of loitering in the hallway?"

"Uh, yes, sir," Evan replied shakily. He caught Alma's gaze and shrugged. "I'm on my way now, in fact."

He turned and walked away, leaving Alma stranded in the hallway with Mr. Massey.

"I'd like for you to come to my office, please, Alma."

Alma followed Mr. Massey. Did he already know about what had happened to her father and brother this weekend? Was he planning to offer condolences? Or was he just eager to start the process of transferring her files to the nonexistent high school in her family's hometown in Mexico?

He motioned for her to sit down in the fake leather chair across from his desk.

"Alma, I've just received some very exciting news."

She wondered where this was going.

"You have been named a finalist for Youth of the Year by the Boys and Girls Clubs of Georgia."

This had to be some sort of cruel joke.

"We're very proud of you, Alma. This is a wonderful honor for you and for the school. I know that you and Mrs. King worked very hard toward this."

He was wrong. Alma had given up on it months ago. She had submitted most of the application in the fall, but she never turned in the teacher recommendations. She was too in love to face Mrs. King and her judgment, so she quit and tried to forget about it. Alma told herself that she could come back to scholarship applications senior year, when they mattered more. But Mrs. King was not a quitter. She must have submitted the recommendations for Alma.

Mr. Massey lifted a letter from his desk and read, " 'High school juniors who show exceptional qualities of scholarship, leadership, and citizenship—' "

This *was* a cruel joke.

" '—are guaranteed a one-thousand-dollar college scholarship, and are eligible to compete for the regional and national awards next spring. Those awards carry scholarships of up to fifty thousand dollars.' "

Fifty thousand dollars. She was speechless.

Mr. Massey thrust the letter into her hands, and Alma skimmed it.

"Youth of the Year, a year-round development program, honors Boys and Girls Club members as outstanding scholars, citizens, and leaders. Criteria include poise, public speaking, and demonstrated ability to overcome obstacles."

"This year's theme is 'The Face of Promise,' " Mr. Massey said. "They're even planning to put your photograph on billboards throughout north Georgia. It's all very exciting, Alma. We're so pleased for you."

She stared at the letter, unable to draw her attention away from one phrase: "Demonstrated ability to overcome obstacles."

He thrust another sheet into her hands. It looked like some sort of acceptance letter or release form. Her eyes scanned the orderly rows of blank boxes, each waiting to be filled with the relevant information.

"You'll just need to fill out this form, and we'll be sure to return it today."

She found the space on the form that always eluded her—the nine small boxes that would remain empty. Once again, the absence of a string of numbers on a flimsy blue piece of paper stood between her and her dreams. Alma would not overcome the obstacle of the Social Security number. This was one ability she simply could not demonstrate.

She slowly lifted her gaze to look toward Mr. Massey, who gave her an encouraging smile.

"I guess the cat got your tongue, huh? It *is* a lot to take in."

She searched for a way out. "Yes. It's a lot. I need to get to class, Mr. Massey. There's, uh, a quiz I can't miss. Can I bring the forms back later, maybe?"

Mr. Massey seemed genuinely surprised. "Yes, uh, sure. I mean, that will be fine."

Alma stood to leave, but he thrust his hand out to stop her.

"Alma," he said, "I'm very pleased that you decided to come back to Gilberton High School this year. We all believe this is a good place for you. But please be careful. Don't let yourself get distracted. You can't afford to make any mistakes."

Alma nodded slowly.

"I know that you and Evan Roland missed first period today, and I'll let it slide this time, but whatever it is that you two are doing, you need to think long and hard. Consider the consequences."

If she told him what they'd been doing, he'd never believe her.

Conway was coming toward Evan, with Logan and Peavey. He knew it would happen eventually, and he knew that it would not be pretty. But the force of his rage still surprised him. It almost launched him from the ground. He stumbled back into the wall, his mind urging his body to move in the opposite direction from its instinctive thrust.

"Dude, what's up?"

Evan felt the cool wall pressing against his back. He leaned in farther.

"Have you heard?" Conway asked. "Logan's dad's like a national hero."

"Huh?" Logan asked, clueless.

"Your dad totally filled the jail with illegals, Logan. I went down there with my cousin Bo last night. It was awesome—everybody's out there holding signs about how great Sheriff Cronin is."

The cool wall no longer pressed against his back. Evan's body seared with heat. He imagined hurtling forward. Conway would hit the ground below him, and his head would produce a satisfying *thud* against the concrete floor. Evan's useless right hand would make painful contact with Conway's chin.

"Get out of my way," Evan growled.

Logan's hand was on his shoulder. "What's going on, Evan?" he asked, pushing Evan away from Conway.

"For starters, he *drugged* Alma."

"What the hell are you talking about?" Logan asked, confused. "You two are making *no* sense this morning."

"I didn't *drug* Alma," Conway said dismissively.

"You cornered her and gave her a Jell-O shot."

"I don't know what you're talking about," Conway said. "Your little Mexican *chiquita* is making up stories."

Evan barely registered his voice. He was struggling out of Logan's grip, lurching toward Conway.

"Back-assed redneck son of a bitch! You *drugged* my girlfriend!"

A teacher leaned through her classroom door.

"My girlfriend was catatonic on my bed. You *drugged* her."

"Evan, man. Keep it down," Peavey said in a loud whisper.

Evan stood up straight, glared directly into Conway's eyes, and said, "Don't. Go. Near. Her."

Logan pulled him away and he didn't resist. He found himself in Dr. Gustafson's classroom, face-to-face with the old man. Logan closed the door.

"Mr. Roland," Dr. Gustafson announced firmly, "I don't know what Davey Conway did to you, but whatever it was, that boy is *not* worth it. You have got to pull it together."

Evan nodded.

"Do you understand what I'm telling you?" Dr. Gustafson asked, with an authority that had an oddly calming effect on Evan.

The bell rang.

"Logan," he heard Dr. Gustafson say, "take Evan to his sixth-period class, and stay with him until he sits down. If you need a late pass, come back to me for it."

"Yes, sir," Logan replied. "And, uh, thanks."

He took Evan's arm and led him out of the room. They walked in silence to Evan's classroom, Logan's grip remaining firm on Evan's forearm.

"Christ, Evan," Logan finally said, "You almost got yourself suspended—thrown off the team! What the hell were you thinking?"

Evan didn't speak.

"Jesus, Evan." Logan took a long pause. "What is *up* with you?"

Evan turned away and walked into his classroom. What could he say? He barely recognized himself.

Arriving late to Evan's game, Alma scanned the bleachers, looking for a friendly face. She saw Evan's uncle sitting beside his mother in the front row, and immediately devised a plan to avoid them.

She looked up at the scoreboard. Halftime, and Buford was winning 2-0.

Maritza called her over.

"Hey, y'all," she said to Maritza and Magda, scanning the field for Evan. Evan was standing in what looked like stunned silence as Coach Nelson screamed and gesticulated wildly in his direction.

"What's the news on your dad," Maritza asked, "and your brother?"

"No news," Alma said. "We're just waiting to see what happens. It looks like they'll get picked up by ICE. We have to get a lawyer."

"That sucks," Maritza said. "I can't believe . . ."

Two girls they didn't know squeezed into the seat next to Alma.

"We'll talk about it later," Maritza said.

"Yeah, OK," Alma replied.

"It's not good out there, Alma," Magda announced. "Your boy already earned himself a yellow card."

"Evan?"

"Yeah. He was offside a couple of times, he's been missing tackles, and he can't seem to get off a pass or a shot," Magda said. She was into soccer—always good to have around for explaining technical rules.

Alma hunched over on the bench.

"Good thing you missed the first half. It was pretty painful," Maritza added.

"Do you think Coach Nelson is going to pull him out?" Alma asked.

"I don't think he can," Maritza said. "Buford is *good*."

The whistle blew and the players took to the field. Alma was relieved to see Evan jog toward the half line, but her relief lasted only moments. As soon as the play started, she knew that something was wrong. He always played aggressively, but his aggression was usually controlled and focused. He knew the limits. Not today.

After eighteen painful minutes in which Evan continued to melt down, a Buford player tackled him just outside the penalty box, and Evan faced a wall of opposing players, poised for a penalty kick. He stepped up and drilled the ball directly into the wall.

"Oh, my God!" Maritza cried out. "What is he doing?"

Alma stood up, shocked.

Two stunned Buford players hit the ground. Another defender cleared the ball out of bounds. Evan turned in tired resignation to face his coach, who called him to the sidelines. Substitution. Evan was taken out of the game.

Evan didn't fight it. He didn't resist at all. He lowered his head and jogged off the field, ignoring his teammates.

"Evan Roland riding pine," Alma heard Magda say. "I never thought I'd see the day."

Alma sat in pained silence and watched as Gilberton High School finished its first game of the season without a single goal. She tried not to look at Evan slumped on the bench, but her eyes kept wandering to his back, her heart lurching toward him. Maritza made several valiant efforts to explain away Evan's strange performance, but Alma knew the truth.

When the match ended, Magda and Maritza stood up. "Hey," Magda said, "tell Evan not to worry. Everybody has sucky days."

"Wanna walk home with us?" Maritza asked.

"No. I think I better wait for Evan."

They pulled her in for a hug. "Yeah, well, call if you need anything, OK?

"Yeah, OK."

Alma stayed in the bleachers as they emptied, watching Evan and his teammates walk slowly toward the lockers. She saw Senator Prentiss approach him and watched as Evan turned away, leaving his uncle shaking his head in what looked like disbelief.

She waited on the hood of his car. It took a long time for Evan to come out, and when he did, she almost wished she hadn't waited. She realized—watching him approach her with wet hair and sunken eyes— that she had no idea what to say to him.

"I'm sorry," she said.

"Don't apologize," he replied without emotion. "It's not your fault."

Alma felt confused.

"I wasn't apologizing. I was saying that I'm sorry you lost your first game of the season."

She wished that she could explain in Spanish. The difference between apology and sympathy was so much clearer in her native language.

Evan squeezed his eyes together and brought his bandaged hand to his head. He reached out and stroked her face with his other hand. His eyes looked so tired.

"Hey," she said, "did you know that you're touching 'The Face of Promise'?"

"What?" he asked.

"I got offered a scholarship from the Boys and Girls Club. It's called 'The Face of Promise.' Mrs. King put in the application."

"That's amazing!" he said. "Why didn't I know about this?"

"Doesn't matter. I probably can't take it," Alma said.

Evan squeezed the back of his neck and winced, like he was in pain.

"Can we talk about this later, maybe? I need some sleep. I think I'm getting sick or something."

"Probably all those icy swims," Alma said.

TWENTY
Voluntary Removal

Evan sat up in bed. It was spring break, and he didn't need to be up, but he couldn't sleep. He heard the door to his parents' room open and the familiar rumbling of suitcase wheels against the wooden floor. His mother spoke, and the rumbling ceased just outside his bedroom door.

"Will you be back?" his mother asked calmly.

"I'm not sure," his father replied in a low voice. "I'll stay in the condo in Atlanta. It will be easier that way."

"Then you'll need to move forward with the plans to open the clinic there," she replied.

"I've called Jim Watson about the financing already. I'm sure he'll spread the word around the club."

"And you've got an agent to help you find a lease?"

"Yes, we're targeting the area around Northside Hospital."

"I think you should consider Midtown Hospital. It's . . ."

". . . farther away from Gilberton." Evan's father completed his mother's thought. "You're right. I need a good reason to be staying down there instead of commuting. I'll look into it."

"Evan doesn't need to know yet," his mother said. "No one should know. And you'll need to come back on Sundays for church and brunch at the club."

"Right," his father said.

A silent pause, and then the wheels began to roll toward the stairs. Evan heard the door to his parents' room close gently, and then the tap of their bathroom sink.

His mother was brushing her teeth.

His father was finally leaving them.

Evan waited in his room until he heard the roar of his father's SUV. Then he scurried out quickly, not wanting to see his mother. Today would be difficult enough. He didn't have the energy to construct more lies with his mother, to pretend that his family actually existed intact.

Evan got into his car and drove toward Alma in silence.

When he arrived, Alma sat perched on the front stoop, holding a blue gift bag with gold tissue peeking from the top.

"What's this?" he asked as she stretched onto her toes and enfolded him in a hug.

"An early Easter gift, I guess," she said, shrugging.

She thrust the bag into his hands, and he pulled out the tissue paper to look inside.

"It's great," he said as he examined the small blue-and-gold window decal with "Cal" written in cursive script. "But you probably should have given it to me in a plastic egg, and a bunny costume would have been a nice touch."

Alma flung her arm out to hit him, but he caught it and pulled her into a kiss.

How could he leave her? In four months, he would be on his way to California to play soccer for one of the best teams in the country.

"Your car will definitely fit in over there," Alma said, leaning back to look at him. "You may need to add a few leftist bumper stickers, though."

"Why don't you bring me one every time you visit?" Evan asked, nudging her.

Alma stepped away and looked directly into his eyes.

"You know that won't happen, right?"

"What, you're planning on dumping me when I go off to college?" he asked, trying to force a smile.

—

Alma didn't need to answer. They both knew how uncertain her future looked. If Alma returned to Mexico with her family, she could never get a tourist visa to come back to the States and visit Evan; if she stayed in Georgia, she'd never risk going to an airport with border patrol agents around every corner. Just the thought of it made her shiver.

Alma's dad and brother had been in the Gilbert County jail for three weeks. Everything was a mess there: Gilbert County sheriff's deputies had filled the jail with "illegals," but Immigration didn't seem particularly interested in taking the next step. As a result, the jail was overflowing with people who had rolled through stop signs, failed to use turn signals, been driving without valid licenses. The sheriff just kept packing them in, hoping each day that the charter buses would arrive to take all of these "criminals" to a federal detention center and off the hands of Gilbert County.

In the meantime, someone needed to take responsibility for the García household. Alma's grandmother was still staying with them, but in the eyes of the government, she was just a visitor passing through. All of her dad's assets—the trucks, the house, the business, the bank accounts—would be frozen unless he gave a U.S. citizen something called power of attorney.

It was almost impossible to believe, considering how many birthday parties, baptisms, and *quinceañeras* Alma had endured over the years, but they were having a hard time finding someone. They had a broad network of friends and family in Gilberton, and everyone was willing to help the family out in this time of crisis. They had received so many meals that the fridge was overflowing with *caldos* and casseroles; they had prayed so many novenas that *la Virgencita* had to be completely sick of hearing the García family name. But hardly anyone was a legal resident.

The only exceptions were Manny and his parents, who had just been busted by the IRS for failing to pay federal income taxes. They forgot—for a decade. So they were off the list of potential candidates. Honestly, Alma's dad wouldn't have trusted them anyway.

Technically, Evan could do it, but an eighteen-year-old kid with a trust fund was not really the best candidate to sell a house, a car, and a business. They hoped Alma's dad would be released from detention so that he could take care of everything, but in case he wasn't, they had to find someone. Mrs. King—master problem solver—stepped up and offered her services. They were on their way to pick her up now.

"Well, Evan, I got a call from your cousin yesterday," Mrs. King said as she opened the car door and sank into the passenger seat.

She had just gone through cataract surgery, and though it clearly pained her to be separated from her Buick, she had to accept rides for at least another few days.

"Whit'll be headin' back to us in a week, now," Mrs. King said.

"Is he going to live at home?" Alma asked. "Please tell me he isn't going to another boarding school."

"No, Alma. His momma and daddy finally got some sense up in those heads of theirs. He'll be living in Gilberton in a group home for recovering addicts. It's called a three-quarters house."

"I think it's gonna work this time, Mrs. King." Alma said. "I honestly do. We talked a few days ago, and he seemed—I don't know. He seemed centered, or something."

Alma wasn't sure why she had decided to forgive Whit on that afternoon he showed up at her house, a few days after she left him on the edge of Mathis Dam. She had been selfishly relieved to see him standing on her front stoop, with his tired eyes and beautiful, angled face. He had seemed so desperate when she left him, and it crossed her mind more than once how easy it would have been for him to lean out too far over the edge and plunge into the churning waters. Instead, he came to her and apologized. He gave her the pewter flask, and he told her that it wasn't such a good friend after all. He wanted to get well, and she wanted that, too.

Whit had turned back from the edge of the dam and faced the future that made him so afraid. There was something to be said for that.

After driving south for about an hour, they pulled off the interstate in the crisp light of a beautiful spring morning. They drove along a broad avenue, flanked on either side by parks filled with hot-pink azaleas and flowering dogwood trees that looked like wispy clouds hovering just above the ground. Even the high-rises of midtown Atlanta were clean and gleaming, new towers buffed to a sheen.

Mrs. King's son, looking distinguished with his gray suit and close-cropped hair, emerged from a bank of shining double-glass doors. He took Mrs. King's arm in the crook of his elbow and then turned toward Alma.

"Do you think you're ready for this?"

"As ready as I'll ever be?" she replied. She had tried to sound confident, but the statement came out as a question.

"Let me assure you, Alma," he said, "Sue Chen is the best immigration attorney in this city—and one of the best in the nation. You're in good hands."

Evan took her hand and squeezed it lightly. Alma smiled faintly and headed into the building.

"Are you OK?" Evan whispered in her ear.

"Yeah, why?"

"You look a little dazed."

He rested his hand lightly on her lower back and gently guided her toward one of several long banks of elevators. Alma forced her attention toward the precise point where his hand touched the fabric of her shirt. She let his warm touch fill her senses. The elevator rose so fast that Alma's stomach lurched. By the time they arrived on the forty-eighth floor, she felt queasy and off balance. As the others walked out, she grasped onto the polished bronze railing behind her, feeling it cool and smooth against her hand.

"Are you sure you're OK?" Evan asked.

"Just nervous," she said.

"Alma, she's a good lawyer," Evan said. "Good lawyers fix complicated problems."

Holding the door open with his foot, Evan reached for her hand and pulled her into his chest. She wasn't sure who might be watching, and she didn't care. She let herself listen for the steady beat of his heart.

"Everything's going to be fine," he said. "You'll see."

———

Voluntary removal.

Evan struggled to understand how these words were being used together. The lines of a silly song from elementary school ran through his head, reminding him that there was a term for this: oxymoron. According to Ms. Chen, this oxymoron explained why his friend Raúl was on his way from a prison cell to a bus bound for Mexico.

Evan was completely lost. Ms. Chen appeared to be extraordinarily capable. She sat erect at the head of this table in a handsomely furnished conference room, sipping her Diet Coke, wearing a dark suit and a simple strand of pearls, her jet-black hair pulled into a smooth bun.

She had been explaining for an hour, but none of it made any sense.

The good news was that Ms. Chen had gotten Raúl's misdemeanor charges dropped. Apparently Sheriff Cronin stepped in and determined that the machete in Mr. García's truck was actually a tool and not a weapon. Evan wasn't really in the mood to thank his Uncle Buddy for this "favor," especially not after he heard the other "good news" (Ms. Chen actually used this phrase). Raúl and Mr. García had been transported from the Gilbert County jail to the Stewart Detention Center, a huge prison in some south Georgia town Evan had never heard of. This took them out of limbo and into the custody of the Department of Homeland Security.

Weren't those the people who dealt with terrorists? That's what Evan wanted to ask, but he kept his mouth shut.

Evan wasn't sure that he got all—or even most—of what Ms. Chen was telling them, but he was pretty sure that Raúl had waived his right to a hearing in front of an immigration judge. Ms. Chen explained that Raúl would take this thing called "voluntary removal," to avoid having a felony on his permanent record. That seemed sort of reasonable to Evan, until Ms. Chen also explained that Raúl would be unable to reenter the United States for ten years, with or without the felony.

Ten years! Could that possibly be right?

He glanced across the table at Mrs. King's son, Reginald, who started pacing, running his hands over his short-cropped hair.

"Now, Sue, there must be some avenue we haven't explored."

"No, Reginald," Ms. Chen responded patiently.

"You mean to tell me that this boy—who came here when he was *five* years old, graduated from high school with honors, played on an all-state soccer team, and has never so much as gotten a ticket for jaywalking—you mean to tell me that there is *no way*, none at all, that he'll be able to return to the United States until he's thirty years old?"

"Yes, Reginald. That's right." Ms. Chen responded matter-of-factly.

Reginald was a lawyer, but he didn't specialize in immigration. Evan took some comfort in the fact that he seemed just as baffled as Evan.

"*Nothing?* Not a *damn thing* we can do about this?" Reginald asked.

"No, Reginald. But if Raúl doesn't attempt return and keeps a clean record, he will be able to apply for a visa—if he qualifies—after the ten-year period is up."

"And what sort of visa would he qualify for?" Reginald asked.

"That's a tough one," Ms. Chen replied. "Raúl is an intelligent young man," she said, shrugging. "If he gets an advanced degree in Mexico—perhaps in engineering or computer science—he may be able to return on a temporary work visa . . . eventually."

Who was this woman kidding? Alma had explained enough to Evan that he knew Raúl probably wouldn't even be able to find a job there. How was he going to afford college and graduate school?

"But if he refuses to take voluntary removal, the felony on his record will, in effect, make his bar on reentry permanent." Ms. Chen said.

"Lord have mercy," Mrs. King muttered under her breath.

"So he would never be able to come back?" Reginald asked.

Ms. Chen nodded.

"Well," Reginald replied, "that's just plain crazy."

Evan couldn't even look at Alma, who was slumped silently in the chair beside him. He didn't have to. He felt the despair releasing in soft waves from her body.

Ms. Chen launched into more legal gibberish, this time about Alma's dad.

Thankfully, Reginald stepped in again.

"So, let me be sure I've got this," Reginald said. "Mr. García will not waive his right for a hearing. And we are aiming for the judge to grant him permission to be released from custody for a couple of months to get his affairs in order, sell his business and his home."

"That's right, Reginald," Ms. Chen said.

"And he would buy his own ticket back to Mexico, and then give the court proof that he left the country before a certain date?"

"Yes," Ms. Chen said. "This option is called 'voluntary departure.' But if he doesn't leave by the date agreed upon, he will be put back into detention and 'removed,' with a felony on his record."

There was that word "voluntary" again. Wasn't that supposed to mean doing something because you *wanted* to?

Ms. Chen leaned forward and looked at Alma intently.

"Alma," she said. She spoke softly, reaching her hand out across the table. "There is something difficult that you will need to prepare for, if your father is released from custody."

Something difficult? Ms. Chen must be a complete hard-ass if she didn't think *all* of this was difficult.

Everyone was looking at Alma now, but Evan couldn't do it. He couldn't take seeing her so upset. Ms. Chen said that if Mr. García was fortunate enough to be granted "voluntary departure," he'd be wearing some sort of device around his ankle.

Suddenly realizing what she was talking about, Evan blurted out, "Do you mean a *LoJack*?"

Ms. Chen glared at him, her eyes casting darts. He actually shuddered.

"Excuse me, Ms. Chen," he said, looking down at the table. "I'm sorry I interrupted."

Ms. Chen said that Mr. García would also face the ten-year bar on reentry, an "unavoidable consequence" of having been in the United States continuously for more than a year without permission.

Suddenly, Evan felt a terror coursing through his body. He closed his eyes and heard Reginald ask the awful question forming in his own mind.

"For whom, exactly, is this a consequence, Sue? *Anyone* who has been in continuous residence? Regardless of age?"

Would they kick Alma out? Would they make her wait ten years to come back? Those were the questions Evan knew they needed to ask, but he couldn't bear to hear the answers.

Ms. Chen said something about "extraordinary circumstances," and then Mrs. King broke in. She had barely spoken at all until now.

"Lord have mercy," Mrs. King said. "You are just going to have to slow down, Ms. Chen, and we're gonna need for you to explain all this in laymen's terms."

Thank God for Mrs. King.

"I'm sorry, Mrs. King," Ms. Chen said. "Let me just give you an example. Let's say Reginald, here, falls in love with an undocumented immigrant from Mexico and they go off and get married."

Reginald chuckled.

"Well. Wouldn't we all be praising the good Lord for that?" Mrs. King said. "It's about time for him to settle down, don't you think?"

Ms. Chen flashed a faint smile and continued, "We'd need to hope he wants to settle in Mexico because his new bride will have to return there for a while."

"How long?" Reginald asked.

"If she's been in the U.S. for more than a year without permission, it's likely to be ten years before Reginald can apply for her to come back and live with him here.

"Good Lord," Reginald said. "That's gotta be tough on a marriage."

"Mmm-hmm," Ms. Chen said. "Although, Reginald, if you had some sort of 'extraordinary circumstance'—for example, you were being treated for cancer, or you already had a child with this woman and the child was severely disabled . . ."

"Well, this just keeps getting better, doesn't it?" Reginald said, shrugging.

"In that sort of case, you could get a waiver—so she *would* be able to stay with you in the U.S. But these waivers are *very* difficult to get. You have to show what's called 'extraordinary pain or suffering' for the citizen if the alien spouse is returned to the country of origin."

Was she calling Alma and her family aliens? What was it with this woman?

"All right, Sue." Reginald said. "We get it. But now, it's time to move away from hypotheticals. Let's talk about Miss García, here. What are Alma's options?"

—

"Excuse me, Ms. Chen?"

Alma tried to speak, as if she had control over the haywire synapses in her brain. She had to hold it together, if not for herself then for Evan. She knew that the last thing she should worry about right now was how *Evan* felt about all of this, but she *was* worried. She couldn't bear watching him taking in these new realities, seeing the way they challenged everything he thought he knew about the world. She wanted to go back to the beginning. She wished she had kept her resolve not to pull him into all of this.

"I know you are very busy, and I'm so grateful for your time, but I, uh, I think I need to stretch my legs."

"Of course, Alma," Ms. Chen replied, with just the slightest hint of softness entering her voice. "I need to check in with my paralegal on a matter."

Ms. Chen walked to the door. Alma swerved her chair toward Evan, whose face was buried in his hands. She gently touched his arm, feeling his biceps tense through the fabric of his shirt. He dropped his arm and turned to face her, running his fingers roughly through his thick hair. Even now, her stomach fluttered. As his sad eyes met hers, she remembered, for the thousandth time, why she hadn't been able to walk away all those months ago.

She leaned in toward him.

"You should go, Evan. This has gone on for too long, and you're going to miss practice."

He didn't respond.

"If you leave now, you can get there in time, as long as there's no traffic."

His face changed then, breaking into a broad, beautiful grin. He reached out and tousled her hair.

"This is Atlanta, Alma. There's always traffic."

The familiar lightness had returned to his voice, but the sadness stayed in his eyes.

"Please, Evan," she pleaded weakly. "How are you going to explain this to your coach?"

He pushed her hair back from her face and rested his hand lightly on her shoulder, pulling her in softly for a kiss—in front of everyone. Then he whispered, "It's just a game, Alma. It doesn't matter. *This* is what matters."

He sprang to his feet.

"I'm getting you a coffee," he announced cheerily. "Who else needs one? Mrs. King? I think there's sweet tea over here, too."

As Alma's eyes followed his sudden motion, she realized that the others were watching, too. They probably had been all along. Even Ms. Chen hadn't yet left the room. She stood leaning against the doorway, looking at Evan with a sort of starry-eyed grin. Alma realized that they probably all thought it was sweet, the way that she and Evan loved each other, the way they looked out for each other. But Alma knew better. It wasn't sweet. It was painful and hard. And it was only going to get worse.

She had to *do* something. She had to find a way to release Evan from all of this.

He handed her a black coffee, and she silently savored the bitterness until the conversation resumed. Alma didn't want to hear what was coming next.

Ms. Chen sat and grasped her chin. She looked like she was thinking hard. "If Alma were to stay, her father's parental rights would likely be terminated. There is a chance that the Division of Family and Children Services would put her into protective custody—foster care—since she'll have no legal guardian when her father leaves the country."

"What if someone else took guardianship?" Reginald asked. "A relative or friend?"

Alma didn't have the heart to tell him how few people in her life would be able to do that.

"Guardianship is not the primary problem, Reginald." Ms. Chen said. "When's your eighteenth birthday, Alma?"

"August thirty-first."

"That's soon. On August thirty-first, Alma will begin to accrue unlawful presence. If she were to finish high school before turning eighteen and a half, she might be eligible for a student visa, but unfortunately that's not an option. Unless her father is granted relief, and that's un-likely, Alma's best course of action will be to return to Mexico before she turns eighteen and a half. At eighteen and a half, everything will change for Alma."

Halfway through her senior year.

Mrs. King and her son launched in, firing questions and hypo-theticals. Alma heard but barely registered their words. Then Evan spoke quietly.

"What if she graduates early?" Evan asked. "She already has a lot of college credits." He reached under the table and took Alma's hand. "Right, Alma?"

Alma recalled the most recent meeting with her so-called adviser.

"I still have to take health if I want to graduate, and a couple of other electives. That's what my so-called adviser said."

"We can look into that," Alma heard Mrs. King say. "But it will be tough to graduate early if she's missing those, and if she goes for a GED she'll lose eligibility for some scholarships."

Alma couldn't really hear them anymore. All of the "What if—" and "If only—" formulas coming from the lips of these people, all of these people who cared deeply about Alma and her future. They spoke of scholarships and student visas; they spoke of the difference a few months might make.

"What if—"

"If only—"

And none of it mattered. None of it mattered because she was, as she had always known, one of the kids stuck in between.

Evan wasn't sure why he did it. When the meeting was over, he made up some lame excuse to return, leaving Mrs. King and Alma waiting in the snack bar across the street. Alma probably thought it was because he needed to get away from her. And there was some truth to that. The way she held her shoulders, the weariness around her eyes, her stubborn silence. All of these suggested resignation, a defeat that Evan would not, could not, accept. So here he was, arriving again on the forty-eighth floor.

When the brass doors slid open, Sue Chen was standing with a small group of men, waiting for the elevator. Surprise registered on her face.

"Have you left something?" She reached into her purse for her cell phone. "I can have my assistant help you."

Evan inhaled deeply.

"No. I was hoping to speak with you, Ms. Chen."

She glanced at her phone and motioned for him to follow her. They stood around the corner from the elevators, alone in the small alcove that opened onto an emergency exit.

"What can I do for you, Evan?"

"I'm not sure," he replied. What was he doing here?

"I know that meeting was difficult for you," she said.

Her voice sounded hard. It had been a mistake to return.

She pushed open the exit door and motioned for Evan to enter the emergency stairwell with her.

Figuring he didn't have a choice, Evan followed. He sat down next to her on a cold concrete step.

Ms. Chen turned to face him.

"As a lifelong feminist and an immigration lawyer with fifteen years of experience, I can't believe I'm about to say this. But there's something about you and Alma that is simply breaking my heart."

Evan stayed quiet.

"There may be a way out of this, and it involves you—to put it mildly. But first, I need to know—do you love her?"

Was this the same Ms. Chen he had been sitting across the table from for two hours? The woman who shot poison darts from her eyes? Who delivered terrible news as if she was reciting the daily specials at a restaurant?

"More than you can imagine."

"And if she weren't in this mess, would you still feel the same way about her?"

It was an odd question, and it took a while for him to formulate an answer.

"I don't really know what our relationship would be like, but I can't imagine not loving her."

"And you're eighteen?"

"Yes, ma'am."

"Don't call me ma'am." Her voice was cold again. But then she smiled and continued, "It makes me feel old."

"Yes, ma'am," he replied, instinctively. He quickly corrected himself, "Uh, OK."

"Do you have any money of your own, in a bank account or a trust?"

What did this have to do with anything?

"Um, I know that there's a trust. I mean, my mom has told me that, but I don't think I have access until I'm older. And I have a bank account, but there's not a lot of money there. Maybe ten thousand dollars."

"Evan, sweetheart, to most people ten thousand dollars *is* a lot of money." She chuckled and shook her head. It made Evan feel stupid and childish.

She was completely transformed, calling him sweetheart, smiling and laughing. She looked intently into his eyes, making him feel extraordinarily uncomfortable.

"If you were to marry her—"

"Marry her?"

Evan was in total shock. This all-business lawyer, perched on the edge of the steps in her dark suit and black pumps, was telling him to marry a seventeen-year-old girl?

"Yes. If you were to do it now, it's possible—but not certain—that she would become an LPR before she turns eighteen and a half."

She was starting to talk legalese again.

"An LPR?"

"Yes, Lawful Permanent Resident, with a green card."

"And a Social Security number?" He conjured an image of Alma's face, just as it had looked when she'd told him the news of her scholarship, and of the nine little boxes she would have to leave blank.

"Yes."

"And all I have to do is marry her?"

"No, you have to prove that you have money to support her, and you have to prove that it's not fraudulent. But you have the money, and I can't imagine anyone sitting in a room with you two for more than sixty seconds and not seeing that you love each other. You would have to live together, of course, at least for a while."

How would they live together? He was on his way to Berkeley, and she was trying to get a Georgia scholarship. His mother would have a heart attack if he moved in with Alma. And, *oh, Christ*, his uncle Sexton. Evan pushed them out of his mind. He needed to focus.

"What about the penalty?"

"You'd need to get married immediately, Evan, and then hope for rapid processing. Normally, they are able to schedule an appointment within nine months."

"What appointment?"

"With the Immigration officer. They basically just interview you to make sure that you are legitimately married. They ask you to show photographs of where you live together, of trips you've taken. They ask sort of silly questions, too, like what kind of toothpaste Alma uses. They'd just want for you to talk about your life together."

Their life together—Evan wanted that so much.

"You would need to do it at the consulate in Ciudad Juárez."

"Where?"

"In Ciudad Juárez—it's a city on the border."

"We can't do it here?"

"It would be best, in your case, to go there. It's more expedient. She would need to be there for a few days, at least, before the interview. It would all need to happen before Alma turns eighteen and a half."

"What if it took longer?"

"Then the bar would apply. She'd stay in Mexico for at least three years."

Evan tugged at his bangs. "Three years? So, we'd be married and she'd be in Mexico for three years?"

"Yes, that's right, unless she stays here for more than a year without permission. Then the bar increases to ten years."

"This is a little overwhelming."

"I know. And you need to keep in mind that, if she goes home now, she may still be able to come back here for college, legally, as an international student."

Home. That was such a strange way to describe it.

"But how would she pay for it? I mean, would she be able to get financial aid or scholarships as an international student?"

"I doubt it, Evan. Of course, she wouldn't qualify for federal financial aid, and most scholarships are for citizens or lawful residents, but not all of them."

"If I married her, she would qualify?"

"Yes."

"And could she apply for her dad and brother?"

"Yes, after she's twenty-one, but the penalty is almost certain to hold for them both."

"So they'd have to wait ten years?"

"Yes."

"When do we need to figure this all out?"

"If the two of you decide to marry, you should do it immediately. Her birthday is coming fast."

"OK. Well, thanks, uh, for the information."

Ms. Chen rested a cool hand on his forearm. Her fingernails were manicured, with little white tips.

"Evan, I know this is confusing and overwhelming."

"Yes."

"Please promise me that if you two move forward, it's for the right reasons."

"What are the right reasons?"

A deep silence filled the space between them.

"I'm not sure, to be honest." She lifted her hand from his forearm to her temples as the muscles in her face tensed. "I still can't believe I've even suggested it as a possibility. As a lawyer, it's irresponsible, but I'm not your lawyer, technically. And I thought you should know."

"Are you married?"

"Yes."

"Why?"

"I don't know exactly."

"OK. That's helpful."

Ms. Chen smiled. "I'm just being honest with you, Evan."

"My parents, they're married for the wrong reasons. A lot of people I know are."

"Yes, I'd have to agree with that. But Evan, knowing when it's wrong is a start to understanding when it's right."

"Do you think that loving her is enough?"

"Probably not."

They sat together in silence for a few moments.

"I have to get to court now, Evan. Call me if you want to discuss this further."

She pulled a business card from her jacket and then dug around in her purse to fish out a pen. Writing a phone number on the back of the card, she said, "This is my cell. You can call me anytime."

She walked through the door, leaving him alone in the emergency stairwell.

TWENTY-ONE
Fishing Without a License

"It sucks."

Alma had gone *way* off script. She glanced around the room at all of the earnestly smiling people.

"It totally sucks, but I can't be here any longer. If this place doesn't want me, then I don't want it. I'm going home. I'll finish this school year, and then I'm going back to Mexico."

There. She said it.

It was a little weird that she was unloading this *here* since she didn't have the nerve to tell Evan or any of her friends in Gilberton.

"And it will be good. I want to know more about my country, my culture. I've heard so much about it, but I've never been there—not since I was two. And my family can be together, and we won't have to worry all of the time."

She made the mistake of finding Mrs. King in the crowd. Instead of smiling encouragingly or scolding Alma with her eyes for ruining yet another opportunity, she was just staring at the wall behind Alma, tears streaming down her face.

Crap. Do not cry. You will not cry.

"It's not fair, though. My dad and my brother and I, we have done everything right. We have followed all of the rules. But we're being sent away while my tax-evading uncle and his good-for-nothing son get offered citizenship. It just doesn't make any sense. But . . . whatever."

Fantastic.

Not only had she said a sort of bad word in front of the scholarship people, she was rambling and divulging family secrets. Why couldn't she just stick with the script?

Alma was the second of the three finalists to speak at the "Face of Promise" luncheon. The room was filled with business leaders, chairs of nonprofit organizations, and lots of other important people from across Georgia. They were here to listen to the heartwarming stories of "underprivileged" high school juniors who had overcome the odds. They expected to be inspired by teens who surmounted any obstacles that stood in their way. Alma had worked for weeks to prepare just such a story: nice young girl, the "model immigrant" sharing her tale of hard work and achievement.

Then, yesterday, she had met with Ms. Chen. The whole system seemed to be such a mess—random and unfair. This morning, Alma woke up furious. She had to *do* something. So she pulled out her speech and started to revise. She decided to tell everyone about her status—to "come out," to quit being afraid and ashamed. She would win over the crowd with her story of hard work. But then she would ask them all to help her, and others like her, reach their American Dreams by seeking fair immigration laws.

She had a script. It was pretty good. But then Alma walked into the room and saw *her*—Evan's mom, sitting front and center. How could Mrs. King not have warned her? Alma knew she went to lots of fundraisers, but *this one*? She was falling apart, and her eyes wouldn't focus on the words.

Alma had to find a way to get through this. She could not look at Mrs. King, and she would not dare look toward the front row, so she tried to make eye contact with a stranger in the crowd. Her gaze fell on a white-haired lady in the center row. Bad choice. She was wiping her eyes with the sleeve of her sweater. Alma looked toward the back of the room and saw another woman with tears in her eyes. She frantically searched for a man in the crowd, under the assumption that men are less likely to cry in public. No luck. The man she locked eyes with in the crowd was teary, too.

Damn. This was getting embarrassing.

"But it's OK. In many ways, this country has been good to us. My brother and I got a great education. We got to live in a good house in a great neighborhood. We are bilingual and bicultural. And no one can take that away from us. We will be fine."

A quiet sob escaped from Mrs. King's lips. How could she do this to Alma? She was dependable, strong—a solid rock.

Crap. Crap. Crap. Alma was going to have to wrap up quickly—before any more public displays of sympathy.

"So, I invite you all to come and visit me in Mexico anytime!" She forced a big, friendly smile. "I'll even throw in a free Spanish lesson."

As she scurried back to her seat, Evan's mom caught her gaze. The room was erupting into frantic applause, but Mrs. Roland just looked hard at her. She wasn't teary; she wasn't smiling. She showed absolutely no emotion at all.

—

Evan sat in the parking lot and tried to get up the nerve to go in. He ran himself through the pep talk one more time: You're in Atlanta. No one knows you here. You don't have to buy anything. Just go in and browse.

He took a deep breath and stepped out of the car. There were several other cars in the parking lot, so he knew the store would be busy, too busy for the salespeople even to notice him, right?

Wrong.

The glass door swung shut behind him. Evan looked up to see a dozen eyes on him. There was not a single customer in the store, and standing at attention behind the long cases that lined each of the store's walls were six unoccupied salespeople. Their eagerness pulsed through the air like electricity.

Evan felt like he'd been thrown to the sharks. He locked eyes with the least threatening-looking of them, a compact Indian woman with long dark hair, and headed in her direction.

"I'm just looking," he said.

"Ah, wonderful. Because I'm just here to help," she replied cheerfully, in a lilting accent. "Do you seek a gift? Maybe something for a special young lady friend?"

There was a gentle teasing in her voice that made Evan squirm. Maybe he should have chosen the burly black guy at the counter across the room. He wouldn't tease about a "lady friend."

Too late.

"Yes, ma'am. I'm looking for a ring for my girlfriend."

"Do you have anything special in mind? Her birthstone, perhaps?"

A plan took shape in his mind.

"Uh-huh. But, um, do you have, like, a birthstone chart or something? Uh, I don't really know what her birthstone is."

The truth was that he had absolutely no idea which month was assigned to the diamond.

She led Evan across the room, toward a display case filled with rings.

"That won't be necessary, young man," she said, shaking her head. "When is her birthday? I know these things."

"Oh, right. Of course." He looked down at his feet.

Feeling something nudge against his shoulder, he looked up to see the burly black guy thrusting a laminated sheet toward him.

"Here you go, man. This should help."

It was confirmed. Evan definitely should have picked that guy. He frantically searched the sheet to find a diamond.

"April. Her birthday is in April."

"Indeed? What a fortuitous coincidence. My birthday is also in April," the saleswoman said, grinning broadly. "Which day?"

"Uh, the thirty-first."

Alma's birthday was August 31. He figured he could lie about the month but still be honest about the day.

"Hey," said the helpful black guy, in a deep, sonorous voice, "I think you mean the thirtieth."

Right. Of course. There was no thirty-first of April.

"In any case, perhaps you should consider a necklace with a lovely diamond pendant, or a bracelet possibly?" She pulled a gold necklace with a diamond chip from the case.

"Uh, that's pretty. But, uh, she likes rings."

What a joke. Alma wasn't exactly into sparkly jewelry.

Another salesperson joined her behind the counter—a chubby woman in her fifties with perfectly coiffed white hair, pink lips, and lots of eye makeup.

"What she means to say, sweetheart, is that a diamond ring might give a girl the wrong message. Do you get my drift?"

"Oh, yeah. Uh . . . right," Evan stammered.

"Ladies!" The black guy broke in, arms crossed on his chest and voice booming. "Enough. If the man wants to buy a diamond ring for his girl-friend, then show him some diamond rings, for God's sake."

Both women shot him a surprised look. Now it was their turn to seem embarrassed.

"Well then," said the saleslady, "shall we take a look at the engagement rings?"

Without meaning to, Evan let out an audible sigh.

"Sounds good," he said. "Let's do that."

———

Leaving the event in Mrs. King's Buick, Alma broke the uncomfortable silence.

"I'm sorry."

"For heaven's sake, Alma, what do *you* have to be sorry for?" Mrs. King asked.

"You've worked so hard to help me, and I ruined it."

"*You* did not ruin this. And while your speech may not have been pleasant, you were speaking from your heart. That's always the right thing to do."

"I can't be the poster child, Mrs. King."

"I'm not sure I follow."

"I'm sick of it. I'm so tired of standing up there and acting all perfect, as if I need to *earn* the right to be here—as if my good grades and sweet demeanor make me somehow *worthy*!"

It felt good to get these nagging thoughts off her chest.

"Well, your good grades do in fact make you worthy of a scholarship, but as for your demeanor, I can't say I've ever thought of it as *sweet*."

"Well, I'm done," Alma said. "This town's going to have to find itself another model immigrant."

"So, it's decided?"

"What? That I'm leaving? I don't have another choice. And even if I could find a way to stay . . ."

"And what does your Evan think?"

"*My* Evan?" She heard herself say. Alma closed her eyes and tried to push the image of Evan—fretting beside her in Ms. Chen's office—out of her mind. "Oh, Mrs. King. I hope his mom doesn't tell him! I just haven't figured out a way to break the news, you know? He's so determined to fix it. And he's so damned naive."

"Are you perhaps being a little naive, too, Alma? I mean, to think that you can make a life for yourself back in your parents' hometown? It's going to be hard."

Alma's voice rose to a shrill pitch. "Oh? And this *isn't* hard?"

"Of course it is, Alma." Mrs. King almost cooed her response.

She slowly eased her car into Alma's driveway. Alma needed to pull it together. There was no reason to take this out on Mrs. King.

"Do you want to stay for dinner?" Alma asked. "Whit's here."

"I'd love to see Whit, but I wouldn't want to impose."

"I promise, it would *not* be an imposition. *Abuela* Lupe had nine kids, and she still cooks gargantuan amounts of food every day. I think Isa has gained fifteen pounds."

Isa had definitely left her hunger strikes behind. Since the moment her parents left for Mexico, she had been making up for lost time. While stuffing her face, she was fond of proclaiming dramatically that, back in Mexico, they'd probably all be too poor to eat, so she might as well enjoy good food now.

"Well then, I suppose it's my duty," Mrs. King said, stepping out of the car.

Entering the house, they were greeted by an unusual combination of smells—burnt sugar, roasted tomatillos, and sautéed garlic, maybe? Isa and Selena were chasing each other around the couch, fighting loudly over the TV remote. In the kitchen, *Abuela* Lupe stood on one side of the stove, vigorously chopping onions. Their neighbor *Señora* Jimenez was sitting at the kitchen table with her three children, shoving their feet into an array of new shoes that were laid out across the table.

The sliding doors were thrown open to the deck, where Whit balanced in a headstand on his yoga mat. Since leaving rehab and moving into the transitional house, he had spent almost all of his free time here. Whit came out of rehab clean, centered, and with an obsessive need to practice yoga. His zeal for it was verging on evangelical, and he had Alma in his sights. The day before he somehow had convinced her, for the first time since elementary school, to plunge into a full backbend. According to Whit, this particular contortion promoted an attitude of surrender—openness to any circumstance.

He and *Abuela* Lupe immediately developed a strange bond over shoes of all things. *Abuela* Lupe was an entrepreneur. For the past dozen years, *Tía* Pera had been sending her clothes from the clearance racks in Gilberton, and Alma's grandmother sold them for a profit in her little *tienda* in San Juan. When she came to Gilberton in December, she brought three suitcases full of leather shoes from Oaxaca—shoes that sold for practically nothing there. The first time Whit visited Alma after rehab, he saw the shoes, heard her plan, and immediately found a calculator and a pencil. He and *Abuela* Lupe worked profit margins together on a regular basis. According to Evan, Whit was the kind of guy who, at age nine, tracked the value of his stocks on homemade graphs posted on his bedroom wall. Alma didn't know nine-year-olds could own stocks. She also wondered how he went from being that smart, motivated kid to becoming the seventeen-year-old addict sprawled on Evan's lawn.

"See what I mean?" Alma asked Mrs. King, raising her arm toward the chaos.

Mrs. King chuckled and headed into the fray. Alma rushed into the kitchen and flipped a switch on the wall to start the vent, adding a loud rattling hum to the cacophony.

Then she texted Evan. She was going to have to get this over with—
Alma needed to tell him before *she* did.

Come for dinner. Beef in salsa verde, your favorite.

Alma threw the door open and flung herself into his arms. She held on
tight and whispered in his ear, "Mrs. King's here, and Monica just came
over."

She took his hand and yanked him toward the kitchen, where a table
was strewn with plates and cups. Mrs. King, *Abuela* Lupe, and Isa sat
gathered around Monica, who was speaking rapidly in Spanish. Whit
sat by Mrs. King and translated.

"He was fishing," Whit said.

"Fishing?" Mrs. King asked, incredulous.

Alma leaned into Evan. "Monica showed up about fifteen minutes
ago to tell us the news. Her uncle was picked up by ICE for fishing
without a license."

Evan stepped back. "Fishing? Are you friggin' kidding me?"

Mrs. King looked over at him and shook her head slowly. She didn't
greet him. She was too focused on Monica and her seething anger.

"Yeah," Alma said. "There's this protest over at the North Georgia
Detention Center. *Padre* Pancho told us about it. Monica wants to go,
but she needs a ride. She's pretty mad."

Whit stood up suddenly and pushed his seat back from the table.
"Let's do it," he announced. "I'll drive."

That was a very bad idea, but Evan wasn't sure he knew how to stop
Whit.

"Whit," Alma said, glancing at the wall clock, "your curfew."

"Oh, Christ," Whit replied, reaching down to grab his yoga mat from the floor. "If I'm not back at the transition house in fifteen minutes, I'm back in rehab."

He gave Monica a big hug and rushed out of the room.

Monica stood up and clenched her jaw. "We have to quit sitting here. We can't just let this keep happening. We have to speak up!"

"Monica's right," Isa said. "I was watching TV, and there were a bunch of teenagers who called themselves DREAMers on *Cristina*. They said we have to quit hiding. They said we should come out of the shadows and just tell people who we are, you know?"

"Yeah," Alma said, "I know." She looked at Mrs. King and smiled, as if they had some sort of inside joke.

"All right then. What are we waiting for?" Evan said.

"Are you sure?" Alma asked, grabbing onto his hand.

Evan smiled and squeezed her hand. "As long as I can get my beef in salsa verde to go."

Alma's grandmother threw together two soft tacos and handed them to Evan wrapped in a paper towel. Alma, Monica, and Isa piled into Evan's car, and they took off toward the detention center as he munched on the tacos dripping with green salsa. When they got to the parking lot where people were gathered, they headed toward a man standing with a bullhorn.

"We will walk in silence to the center," he commanded. "And then we will stand in silent solidarity with our detained sisters."

Alma whispered, "This detention center is just for women."

"Is it a jail?" Evan asked.

"No. But it basically functions like one. You'll see."

They filed in line behind a man holding a sign. They walked for about twenty minutes, before arriving at a two-story building surrounded by a high fence. The building had no windows. They stood across from an empty parking lot. Then the man with the bullhorn crossed the street and stood at the gates.

"No more profits off our pain!" he called out. "Shut the North Georgia Detention Center down! Stop separating women from their children!"

Everybody just stood there for a few minutes, then walked back to their cars.

"That was kinda boring," Isa said. "Can we go to Dairy Queen now?"

Evan pulled the car onto the highway and headed toward Dairy Queen. He wasn't sure what he had expected from his first protest, but it wasn't this.

That's why he was so surprised the next evening when his mom freaked out on him.

Evan fumbled with the keys and slowly opened the front door, willing his mom not to be home. He moved through the quiet house and tiptoed up the stairs.

His mother's cheerful voice broke the dense silence. "Pumpkin? Is that you?"

He slowly descended toward the kitchen.

"Hi, Mom."

She stood at the door to the garage, surrounded by large shopping bags.

"I picked up takeout from the club. Are you hungry?"

"Sure," he said, nervously fingering the soft velvet box in his pocket. He had left it in the glove compartment the night before. Now he needed to figure out a way to stash it in his room. "Any of that stuff for me?"

"Yes, sweetie. I got you some shorts—you know, the cargo shorts that you like—and a new tie for Easter, and a few button-down shirts."

"Cool, thanks. I'll take them upstairs." Normally, it was only a little embarrassing that his mom still did all of his shopping, but today it made him feel different. Feeling the ring in his pocket and thinking about what it meant, he felt a nostalgic sort of sadness welling up in his chest.

"What's your hurry, sweetheart? Let's sit down and eat before our food gets cold."

He pulled out a stool and sat at the breakfast bar while she pulled two takeout containers from a paper bag. She handed him a Sprite from the refrigerator and then poured herself a large glass of chardonnay. Evan opened the first container to find a dainty salad.

"This must be yours," he said.

"Yes, sweetie. I got you a steak."

She carefully transferred their food onto china plates and placed each on a freshly ironed linen placemat. They ate in silence. Evan wondered, not for the first time, whether this arrangement was better—not having his dad around. At least, between Evan and his mother, the silence was usually companionable. But tonight, his mom seemed different, as if there were something she wanted to say.

She stood up and poured herself another glass of wine. Then she pulled a newspaper from the drawer next to the sink and paused, her back turned to him. Evan's mom wasn't one to read the newspaper at all, and never during dinner.

"What's up, Mom? Is everything OK?"

When she turned to face him again, he noticed it. Her eyes were rimmed with red. His mother had been crying.

She glanced down at her abandoned salad, barely picked over. "Your father will be here tomorrow afternoon. He looks forward to seeing you."

"I won't be here, Mom. I'm taking Alma down to see her dad. He got moved to the federal detention center."

She took a long sip of wine. "Oh, Evan, pumpkin. That's not a good idea. You need to stay here and go to church with us on Sunday."

"Mom. I'm sorry, but she needs to see him before his court date. It may be her last chance."

"Well, isn't there someone else to drive her there? An aunt or an uncle? This is something her family should be dealing with, honey."

"Maybe, but I'm going to take her. We're coming back late tomorrow night."

Evan figured now wasn't the time to explain how all of her family and friends were afraid to drive down there, and terrified of going into the detention center with ICE agents swarming the place. Plus, it didn't matter. He needed to be there, too.

"I have to be back to go to the tournament anyway," he said. "Remember? The bus leaves Sunday at one. I'll go to church with you and Dad if that's what you want."

So absurd. Evan didn't understand why they had to keep up the whole charade, but this wasn't the time to get into it.

"That's not my only worry," she said.

Evan's mom picked up the open newspaper and placed it down in front of him.

"Evan, your uncle Sexton called me today from Washington. He's very concerned."

She pointed to a large photo on an inside page of the *Gilberton Examiner.* In the photo, Evan stood next to Alma and her friend Monica on a street corner. A hippie-looking guy with dirty long hair was standing behind her with a sign that read, "No human is illegal!" Monica was looking away, and Alma wore a calm expression. Evan looked sort of lost.

"Wow," he said, trying to break the tension. "That's kind of a bad picture of me, huh?"

He remembered the moment, but he hadn't noticed anyone taking photographs. No big deal.

Except, apparently it *was* a big deal, at least to his uncle.

"Read the caption," his mother said, icily.

Evan Prentiss Roland, nephew of U.S. Senator
Sexton Prentiss, participating in a protest of federal
immigration policy at the North Georgia Detention
Center for Women.

He looked up at his mother. "Whatever, Mom. I bet, like, twelve
people read the sixth page of the *Gilberton Examiner*."

"Well, Evan, that's not what your uncle and his chief of staff believe."

He pointed to Monica's image in the photograph.

"I don't mean any disrespect, Mom, but do you see this girl?"

"Of course I do, sweetie."

"Her name is Monica. A few days ago, Monica's uncle was fishing down
at Trout Bend Creek—fishing!—and the DNR officer asked him for
his fishing license. When he said he didn't have one, they threw him in
jail and called ICE. He has three school-age kids who are citizens of this
country, and he's about to be deported for fishing. I mean, what is *up* with
that?"

"Well, Evan, is Monica's uncle an illegal?"

Now he was almost yelling at his mother.

"Do you know what they are saying, Mom? They're saying that this
new program is supposed to target people who 'pose a threat to the security of our communities.' Did you know that?"

"No, Evan, I didn't."

"Since when, Mom, does *fishing* threaten our safety?"

"Evan," his mother said calmly, "you need to stop yelling. My point
is simply that your uncle and his chief of staff are disappointed."

He snapped.

"They're disappointed?"

"Yes, Evan."

"They're disappointed. A few days ago, one of the coolest guys I know

was dumped off an armored bus in some crappy Mexican border town and told, basically, never to come back. Now, I am about to take my girlfriend to see her dad, who wouldn't hurt a fly, in a high-security federal prison, maybe for the last time in a decade, and *they* are disappointed?"

He was filled with such rage that he could barely see. He stood up and slammed his hands hard against the counter. A searing pain tore through his hand, still wounded from the bottle incident. He clenched his teeth and groaned.

"Evan, calm down," his mother whispered, taking his good hand and pulling him back into the seat. "You need to begin the process of disentangling yourself from this situation. She won't be a part of your life forever, Evan. You need to let her go."

"You don't get it, Mom. You just don't understand."

"We have asked you to do it, but now we are telling you. You have no other choice. Do you understand?"

"You know what, Mom?" Evan said, pushing his chair back again. "You can tell Uncle Sexton and his chief of staff that I don't give two shits how they feel! And, no, I do *not* understand."

He spun away as her arm reached out to touch him. Shrugging her off, he stalked out of the kitchen.

"Evan," his mother called out in a pleading voice. "Evan, please."

He didn't turn back. Instead he bounded up the stairs two at a time.

TWENTY-TWO
Crossroads

Maybe this was a mistake.

Alma sat in the backseat of Evan's car and watched his hands grip the steering wheel. The flesh around his deep wound was still raw, and both hands trembled visibly.

"I can't believe I left my license in my jeans. It will only take a minute," he said.

"It's no big deal, Evan," Alma said. "It only takes four hours to get there, and as long as we're there before one, they'll let us visit today."

Evan turned the car into his driveway and came to an abrupt stop.

"Just wait here, OK? I'll be right back."

Alma's *abuela* Lupe looked puzzled in the front passenger seat. Evan stepped out of the car and slammed the door behind him.

"*Olvidó su licencia,*" Alma explained.

"*¿Ésta es su casa?*" *Abuela* Lupe asked, disbelief in her voice.

"*Sí,*" Alma said.

"*¿Para tres personas?*" *Abuela* Lupe was shaking her head slowly.

"*Sí,*" Alma replied. "*Nada más tres personas.*"

She stepped out to get some air and saw Evan's mom heading straight toward her.

"Hello, Alma. I'm just on my way to water the impatiens. Why don't you join me?"

Alma followed Mrs. Roland to the flowerbed that wrapped around the patio, wondering how she was surviving the change of season without Alma's dad around to keep up the yard. Who planted the annuals for her this year?

Mrs. Roland picked up a prissy little watering can and sprinkled droplets on the new plantings.

"Should I bring over the hose?" Alma asked, trying to be helpful.

"No, thank you, Alma. This will do just fine." Her voice was cold and hard. "You should know, Alma, that I do not approve of this."

"Excuse me?"

Admittedly, Alma rarely interacted with Evan's mom, but this tone was new to her. Was it because of what Alma had said in front of all those people? Alma knew that Mrs. Roland hadn't told Evan about it. He would have said something. Or she would have seen it in his face. He was no good at hiding secrets.

Alma still hadn't gathered the courage to tell him about her decision, but he didn't seem to notice her anxiety. Maybe she was better with secrets. She had lived with one for so long.

"I told Evan not to go today."

"You did?" Alma heard the surprise in her voice. "I, uh, I'm sorry, Mrs. Roland. I didn't know."

Mrs. Roland looked up from the impatiens and smiled weakly. "My Evan, he has a kind spirit."

Alma nodded.

"Just the other day," Mrs. Roland said, "as I was cleaning out the game room . . ."

Alma tried to imagine Evan's mom cleaning. She couldn't.

"I remembered one of my favorite stories about Evan. It was a few days after Christmas, and he was just a little boy. Maybe six or seven."

She put down the empty watering can. Alma felt sorry for those impatiens. There was no way they would survive the heat of the summer with Mrs. Roland trying to care for them.

"I took him into his playroom and I gave him a large cardboard box. I explained that since he had just been given so many wonderful gifts from Santa, he should consider giving away some of his old toys."

Alma stared at the suffering impatiens and listened silently.

"At first he was confused. I told him that some children don't have parents, and others have parents, but their parents don't have enough money to buy them toys. Then I left the room. When I came back, the box was filled with all of his new toys. He was crying. He said he wanted the children to have the good toys, that he would keep the old ones."

"That's a nice story," Alma said.

It *was* a nice story. It captured something about Evan's spirit.

Mrs. Roland turned and looked directly into her eyes.

"Don't confuse mercy for love, Alma."

She lifted her watering can and walked toward the house, abandoning Alma and the thirsty flower seedlings. Alma felt as if she'd been punched in the gut.

They drove for hours—through Atlanta, past the airport, and then south on an almost empty highway. But no matter how far they drove or how hard Evan tried to make small talk, Alma couldn't get his mother's words out of her head.

When Evan stopped at Chick-fil-A, Alma stayed in the car. She felt paralyzed. He brought her fries and a Coke, and she sipped on the Coke to settle her nervous stomach, but she just watched the fries get cold, wondering—even though she hated herself for thinking so—whether he had bought her food as an act of mercy.

The closer they came to the detention center, the more desolate the roads became. They drove in silence through a deserted town square. A courthouse stood in the center with paint peeling in large sheets down the sides. Leaving the square, they passed by several sagging trailers propped up on cinder blocks. They made their way along an open stretch of road. Evan saw it first, a large sign that read "Correctional Facility" with an arrow pointing down a narrow street.

"It's not a correctional facility," Alma said, her heart beating fast. "A correctional facility is a jail."

Evan turned and approached another sign. This one read "Stewart Detention Center."

"I don't know, Alma. I guess this is it," he said, sighing.

They turned a corner and a building came into view.

"It's huge!" Alma exclaimed.

And it was.

The windowless white fortress stretched out behind a broad expanse of asphalt, separated from the parking lot by four long rows of chain-link fence, each topped with curling loops of razor wire glinting in the noonday sun. The glare was so strong that Alma threw her hands up to cover her eyes.

"Oh, good Lord," Evan said.

Abuela Lupe turned toward her and spoke rapidly. She asked whether maybe they had come to the wrong place? Perhaps there was a different building for the noncriminal detainees?

"*Madre María,*" she said. "*Mi hijo no puede estar aquí. Mi hijito precioso no debe de estar aquí.*"

And she was right. Alma's dad didn't belong here.

"Alma, look," Evan said.

A row of police cars lined the edge of the parking lot. Along their sides were printed the letters "ICE."

Her heart lurched as the memory of the raid at the poultry plant came tumbling back. She felt her breathing speed up.

"But Ms. Chen told us ICE isn't here on the weekends," she said be-tween deep gulps of air. "She said that it would be OK for me to come."

"She said they *usually* aren't here on the weekends, Alma. Remem-ber? She said they probably wouldn't be looking to arrest anyone here. It should be OK. You have your school ID, right?"

Evan's words were not exactly inspiring confidence.

Alma got out of the car and followed the others, on shaky legs, toward the barbwire fence. A young pregnant woman wearing a bright red shirt and matching lipstick stood alone. She pressed a buzzer and waited. They were joined by an old man with an oversized baseball cap covering his sun-damaged face and a younger man neatly dressed in khaki shorts and a button-down shirt. A woman—she must have been his wife—walked toward them with three small girls, each of whom had her hair neatly brushed and braided. They all were Latino except for Evan.

The younger man pushed the large red call button again.

"Identify!" a voice barked from the small speaker.

"Visitors," the man said.

The pregnant woman turned to speak to Alma. "Are you here to visit family?"

"My dad," Alma replied.

"First time?"

"Yeah."

The young woman glanced over at the three small girls, the youn-gest of whom was clinging to her mother's leg.

"I couldn't do it," she whispered, gesturing toward the mother and her girls.

"Do what?" Alma asked.

"You know, bring little kids to see their dad here—talking on a tele-phone through a glass wall. I wouldn't want them to see him that way, you know?"

Alma was confused.

"I thought we got to go in a room with them," Alma said anxiously.

"Nope. You sit in a cubicle and talk on an old-fashioned telephone—just like in the movies."

A loud buzz broke through Alma's stunned silence, and the first gate churned open. They stepped into a holding area and waited for the gate to close. When it did, they were all enclosed in a narrow space, waiting for the second gate to open. Alma could feel the anxiety radiating off of the group. It was torture to stand here, trapped.

"Her dad is a nonviolent offender," Evan said. "I'm sure it's different for them."

"My husband's here because of an expired driver's license," the woman shot back angrily. "There are no contact visits. Not for anyone."

"Sorry," Evan replied sheepishly. "I mean, I didn't mean to . . ."

"It's OK," the woman replied. "It's just that, I hate the way they're treated like criminals. I get sort of emotional, you know?"

Yes, Alma knew. She was using every ounce of energy to keep from crying. At least, thinking of her dad inside this awful prison, she could stop obsessing over the conversation with Mrs. Roland. *When was the gate going to open?*

Alma had an overpowering urge to run, or to climb the fence or something. She needed to calm down. She needed reassurance.

"Can I ask you a question?" Alma said to the pregnant woman. "It's personal."

"Sure," she replied.

"Are you, uh, legal?"

"Yeah, I was born here. In California. Aren't you?"

"No."

The woman glanced over at the ICE vehicles lining the entryway.

"I've never seen them bother anyone, but still . . . aren't you a little worried?"

Another buzz and the second gate churned open. Alma stared ahead at the fifty feet of sidewalk she would have to traverse before entering the building, her heart thumping wildly. If she stepped through the second gate and felt it close behind her, she would full-on panic.

Alma yanked Evan's hand and pulled him in close to her.

"I can't do it, Evan," she whispered urgently. "I can't go in there."

She lunged forward and mashed on the red button next to the first gate. Nothing happened.

She heard Evan's voice, but it sounded like it was coming through a long, narrow tunnel.

"Alma, it will be OK."

She glanced back at the row of police cars. "I'm sorry, Evan. I just can't."

Her eyes were losing focus, white spots swarming the corners.

"But what about your grandmother?"

"You have to take her in." She grabbed onto the fence to steady herself.

"I'm not leaving you, Alma."

Was this another act of mercy? Alma's head suddenly cleared. She needed to be strong. The gate stopped and the others walked toward the facility. Alma sucked in a deep breath and spoke with authority.

"Take *Abuela* Lupe in and get started on the paperwork, Evan. I'll wait in the car."

"No!" Evan said firmly. "I can't leave you out here."

"You have to," Alma said calmly. "I won't go in there."

"Please, Alma," Evan pleaded. "Let me stay with you."

"I'm not going, and she needs to see her son. She needs your help."

Evan grabbed Alma's hand and squeezed it. His palm was sweating. Alma looked at him and forced a single nod.

With that, he released her hand and jogged toward the entrance while Alma stood trapped between two barbwire fences, watching the gate slowly close.

—

By the time Evan and *Doña* Lupe had finished filling out the forms, Alma still hadn't come in. Evan had no idea what to do. He wanted to check on her, but he had to see Mr. García.

Evan heard the guard call his name. He stood up and walked with *Doña* Lupe toward the metal detector. A dozen people passed through security together. The guard led them through several sets of barred gates and into a long, narrow visitation room, where five desks, separated by thin partitions, looked across thick glass. Five men dressed in blue jumpsuits sat awaiting their visitors.

It felt cold in the room, but the whole place was so awful and sterile that Evan couldn't be sure whether the chill in his spine was because of the temperature.

Evan watched as Alma's grandmother found her son on the other side of the glass. She sat down in a molded plastic chair and took the phone in one hand. Evan sat against the wall at the rear of the room and waited with several other people.

The family that had entered the prison with them was taking turns talking with a young man. The wife waited next to Evan with one of the children on her lap. The other two children sat on the floor at her feet.

"Where are you from?" the woman asked.

She spoke in slightly accented English.

"Gilberton. We're here with my girlfriend, but she didn't want to come in. This is her dad."

"It's nice that you came," the woman replied.

Evan's heart skipped a few beats, remembering why he was here and the conversation he would need to have with Alma's dad.

"How about you?" he asked. "Where did you come from?"

"North Carolina," she said. "Near Charlotte. We're visiting my husband's brother." She nodded at the child on her lap. "This is his little girl, Jessica."

"Hi, Jessica," Evan said. He almost asked *How are you?* but considering the circumstances, he figured it was a dumb question.

"How old are you?" he asked instead.

She looked shyly into her lap and held up three fingers.

"Three. Wow. You're a big girl."

"The other two are mine," the woman said.

Alma's grandmother stood and gestured for Evan to come to the phone. With his heart lurching, Evan waved at the little girls and walked to the booth.

When his turn came to take the telephone, Evan realized that he needed a translator—desperately. For the first time in his life, he wished Whit were around. The phone line crackled and buzzed so much that Evan barely heard Mr. García. It was going to be tough to understand his limited English.

Evan beat around the bush for a while. He asked about the conditions inside and tried to explain why Alma wasn't with them. It wasn't surprising that Alma's father was stoic and calm. He assured Evan that everything was fine, that he was being treated well, and that no matter what happened, things would turn out OK.

The guard stuck her head in and told the visitors that they only had five minutes left.

It was now or never.

Evan leaned in and cleared his throat.

"Mr. García, I'd like your permission to ask Alma for her hand in marriage."

There. He said it.

Alma's dad involuntarily dropped the phone, leaving it dangling at the end of a heavy silver cord. Evan fidgeted nervously as he fumbled to pick it up.

Mr. García returned the phone to his ear and stammered, tripping over his words.

"I, uh, I . . ."

"What is it, Mr. García?" Evan asked.

"This is very difficult, Evan. We must talk, and I cannot make the words."

His head fell into his hands.

"I don't understand," Evan said.

"I want to make the words in Spanish," he said, looking up, "in my language."

This was not going well.

"I'm so sorry, Mr. García," Evan said. "But can you please try?"

Mr. García sighed and then dropped one hand to his belly.

"Is she . . . ?" He made circular motions with his hand.

"I don't understand, Mr. García," Evan said. "Is she *what*?"

He just kept gesturing.

Feeling panicked, Evan glanced around the room.

The woman from North Carolina was watching him. She placed her niece on the chair beside her and rose to her feet. She leaned in to whisper, "I think he wants to know if his daughter is pregnant."

"What?" Evan asked.

By now, he probably shouldn't have been shocked, but he was. Evan was pretty sure his face had turned crimson. The chill in the room was gone, and he felt sweat pooling under his arms.

"Thanks," he said, shrugging. He turned back and shook his head. "No, Mr. García, she's not, uh, pregnant.""

This was so humiliating.

"Why?" Alma's father asked.

"You mean, why do I want to marry her?"

"Yes," he said.

"Because I love her," he said, speaking fast, "and because I can't imagine living without her even for a day. And because I don't want her to lose everything she has worked so hard for—everything *you* have worked so hard for."

"Can you say again?" Alma's dad asked, his face crumpling in frustration. "Slowly."

Evan felt a tap on his shoulder. The nice woman was still standing there.

"Let me," the woman said gently. "I can tell him that."

"OK," Evan replied. "Thanks."

Watching her speak to Alma's dad in fluid Spanish, tears gathering in the corners of her eyes, Evan didn't even care that she had been eavesdropping. It was all just too much. He had the urge to stand up and bolt out of the room. Instead, he balled his wounded hand into a fist and focused on the pain pulsing through it.

After a few moments, she turned to Evan. "Her father wants you to know that he and her mother got married when they were your age, and that he has no problem with how old you are. In that way, he thinks you're ready."

Evan nodded slowly. Maybe he would say yes.

"But he's very concerned that you may be feeling pressure to do this, and he doesn't want you to feel that way," the woman continued. "He wants you to know that it's hard—being married," she said, leaning forward to look directly into Evan's eyes.

Of course Evan knew that. At least, he knew it was hard for his parents. But Evan and Alma were nothing like his parents.

"It's hard under the best, uh—what's the word?—under the best *circumstances*" the woman said. "And these, these aren't the best, uh, circumstances."

"I know," he said, looking down at the ground. "Believe me, I know."

The woman reached out to touch Evan gently on the knee. He looked into her eyes, brimming with tears.

"But if Alma will agree to it—that's his daughter's name, right?—then he gives his permission."

Evan exhaled deeply and took the phone from the kind woman. He pressed it to his ear. "Thank you, Mr. García. I promise, I won't let you down."

"Yes," Alma's dad said, nodding slowly. "I know."

———

Alma knew what she had to do. She was absolutely certain now. And because she knew, it pained her to look at Evan. Still, she couldn't tear her attention away from him.

He stepped through the gate and walked toward her, his oxford button-down clinging to his chest and shoulders. She wanted so much to be able to turn away, not to watch as he ran his fingers through his hair, pushing his shaggy bangs out of his eyes. But she couldn't resist him.

As *Abuela* Lupe climbed into the front seat of the car, Evan leaned down and cupped her face in his right hand, the one that wasn't hurt. He pulled her lips to his, and she let herself melt into them, but only for a moment.

"I couldn't do it," she said. "I'm sorry."

He wrapped his arms around her waist. "It's OK, Alma. Are you hangin' in there?" he asked.

She nodded slightly. "Did you explain to my dad? I mean, was he upset that I didn't come?"

"No." Evan touched her hair, pushing it behind her ear. "He seems fine. That place—it's not as bad as it looks. I mean, it's so overwhelming from the outside, but—"

She stood up, and he followed. He was standing so close that she caught the sharp metallic scent of his sweat. She knew, from his scent, that he was anxious.

He kept talking.

"I mean, I just wish you had been able to see your dad, you know? He wasn't . . . It wasn't . . ." He paused. "I'm rambling. I should shut up now."

He took her left hand in his and studied it. Alma placed it on his chest and felt his heart beating fast.

"You're nervous," she said. "It's over now. You can relax, Evan."

"Yeah," he said. "OK."

"I met a woman while we were waiting," Alma said. "She invited us to have lunch before we go back. She has a house—like a place for people to stay."

"That's kinda weird, Alma," Evan said.

"I know," Alma replied. "It's like a church group or something. She's nice. You'll see."

Evan shrugged and got into the car to drive. He was starving, and too exhausted to challenge her. Plus, there was nowhere to eat around here. There wasn't even a gas station in this little town.

Before long, Evan was digging into his third helping of turkey tetrazzini, allowing the animated conversation to wash over him. Honestly, he barely remembered how he got here. Maybe it was some sort of post-traumatic stress response. All he knew was that the food tasted good. By now, he was accustomed to sitting around a table where everyone was speaking a language he didn't understand. He usually felt frustrated, but now he just felt relief—he had an excuse to shrink into himself and focus solely on the creamy spaghetti making its way down his throat.

"Evan," Alma turned and spoke to him.

"Yeah?"

"Claire has invited us to stay tonight so that I can visit dad tomorrow. She says ICE is never there on Sundays."

There was no way in hell Evan would leave Alma and her grandmother with a stranger in this creepy town.

"Alma, I have to travel for a tournament tomorrow," Evan said. "I have to get back tonight. I'm already on the verge of getting kicked off the team."

Alma sighed. "I know. I don't want you to miss it, but—"

Evan broke in. "I have to be there, Alma. I'm really sorry."

Seeing Alma's face, Evan struggled to work out another solution in his head. Maybe they could stay in a hotel in Columbus. He counted the hours backward, trying to find a way for Alma to visit and for him to get back in time. The detention center allowed visitors at nine. He needed to be on the team bus by one.

"We have to leave tonight. I can bring you back next weekend."

"Claire lives in Cumming, and she's going back tomorrow. She offered us a ride."

Alma smiled at the volunteer, who nodded eagerly.

Evan's heart sank. Claire was very kind, and even though this house was small and the furniture was sort of worn-out, she and the other volunteers were so friendly, the place felt kind of homey. He just hated the thought of leaving Alma in this pathetic town. She seemed so vulnerable here.

"How will you get from Cumming to Gilberton?"

"I can take them, Evan," Claire said. "It's only a half hour out of my way."

"And are you sure it's safe? I mean, for Alma to go to the detention center? How will she fill out the paperwork?"

"We can't be *sure* of anything," Claire replied.

"She explained the risk," Alma broke in, "and I'm willing to take it to see my dad. I just sort of freaked out today. I'll be fine."

"And what does your grandmother think?" Evan asked, looking toward *Doña* Lupe, who was dousing her noodles with hot sauce.

"She supports whatever decision I make," Alma said.

Claire stepped away from the table and went into the kitchen. She returned with a container of homemade chocolate-chip cookies. As she offered them around, Alma stood and cleared the plates from the table.

"You should go soon," she told Evan. "You need a good night's sleep tonight."

Glancing at the clock on his phone, Evan nodded. "Yeah, OK."

Evan felt so wrong about this, but he knew he wouldn't be able to convince Alma to leave with him.

"I'll walk you out," Alma said.

———

Evan leaned against his car door in the dusty gravel driveway and pulled Alma into him. The deep ache welled back up in her chest as she struggled to focus.

"I'll miss you," he said.

She needed to say it. How was she going to do this?

"I'll miss you, too," she began tentatively. "But it's probably a good thing. I mean, we need to start getting used to this, you know?"

Evan glanced around. "Getting used to what, exactly? Cuz I don't think I can get used to *this*."

She knew he was trying to make a joke. He was talking about the neighborhood. It was a ghost town, with abandoned trailers and dilapidated houses. Irrational anxiety welled up in her—was this what it would be like to live in Mexico? She had never been in a place this poor. In Mexico, she knew, they called towns like this *triste*—sad. She understood that now. This little town made her so deeply sad.

"We need to get used to being apart, Evan," she said. "I'm going home."

Her mind lingered on the last word.

"Home?" Evan asked, as if reading her thoughts. "What do you mean?"

"I mean, I think you know I'm going home soon, back to Mexico."

He dropped his hands from her waist. She heard them land on the car door with a dull thud.

"Since when is Mexico your home?"

Alma stepped back so that she no longer felt his body against hers.

"It's always been home, Evan. You know that."

"Like *hell* I do!" Evan said, standing up straight. "This is your home, Alma. You belong here."

Alma couldn't help releasing a harsh laugh. She gestured toward the hulking detention center a half mile down the road. "Yes. I guess I *do* belong here, technically. But they have a different prison for women. Remember?"

"You know what I mean, Alma."

His back fell against the car door again and he lifted his hand. She knew he would run it slowly through his hair, as he always did when he was worried or confused. She turned her gaze, not letting herself see it.

"You should go, Evan. We can talk about this later, OK?"

She tried to walk away.

"Alma," he said.

She didn't know how to keep from turning back toward him. It was so natural and unavoidable, like the pull of gravity.

"I don't belong here," Alma heard herself say. "I understand that now more than ever. I want to go home with my family."

"We can fix this, Alma." He was pleading. "I want to help you."

Don't confuse mercy for love, Alma.

The words surged through her mind, and she hated them.

"God, Evan," she replied. "You have *got* to stop lying to yourself. We'll never go up against *that*." She nodded involuntarily in the direction of the detention center, with all of its barbwire and windowless walls. She couldn't see it from here, but she felt its stifling presence.

Evan reached into his car.

"Just give me a second, OK?" he said.

He rummaged around in the glove box. When he stood to face her, he was holding a small black box covered in velvet.

"What are you doing, Evan?" she asked. Her heart was pounding. He couldn't possibly be doing what she imagined.

"Ms. Chen," he said. "She told me how to fix it. She said we can get married, you know?" He was talking fast, tripping over his words. "It has to be soon—like *now*. She said it would work—or at least, she was pretty sure it would."

"What?" she asked.

He was walking toward her, with the little black box still tightly shut, teetering on the edge of his trembling hand.

"We can get married, Alma." He spoke anxiously.

"You're kidding, right? And what? I'll go live in your dorm with you?" she asked.

"No, we'll stay. I mean, I don't know——"

Alma remembered the conversation with Mrs. King so many months before. She should have known better. She should have stayed away.

"You've lost your mind." Alma shook her head in disbelief.

"Wait, let's just back up, OK? I'm screwing this all up." Evan stumbled over his words. "Can we just start over?"

He opened the box to reveal a gold ring with a shimmering diamond perched at its center. Alma was speechless. She stepped away involuntarily.

"I want to marry you, Alma. Your dad already gave me permission."

Her dad? Hot with anger, she screeched a reply. "You asked my father's permission? Without even asking *me* what I think about this insane plan?"

"I just want to fix this, Alma. And I don't want you to leave me."

"And when," Alma asked, her voice filled with angry sarcasm, "has two teenagers getting married *ever* fixed *anything*? Tell me that."

Evan looked into Alma's eyes and walked toward her. He reached out with his empty hand—the one without the ring, the one that was scarred and wounded.

"Alma, why are you so angry?"

This was easy. Thanks to his mother, and to those words she couldn't forget, Alma knew exactly why.

"Because, Evan, you seem to think that you and your perfect life can just come in and save me, swooping down like some knight in shining armor or something. This isn't a fairy tale, Evan. You're not my handsome prince, and I'm definitely *not* your charity case."

"My. Perfect. Life." He enunciated each word slowly, almost growling. "Who the hell are you kidding, Alma? Have you been paying any attention at all? Have you noticed anything at all about *my perfect life* lately?"

He turned back toward the car and slammed his closed fist onto the hood. She stared at him and realized that she was afraid. She wasn't afraid *of* him, not worried that he would hurt her. She was afraid *for* him. She had never seen him like this, so out of control.

"I haven't slept for weeks because every time I close my eyes, I see Conway on top of you. I got wasted trying to forget and gashed my hand on a broken liquor bottle, and now the damn thing refuses to heal. I completely suck at soccer now, the only thing I love, the only thing I used to love."

He sank down to the ground, pulling his knees toward his chest.

"My father left us, for real this time, and by the time I get back to Gilberton, I'll probably be disowned by the rest of my family."

He looked up at her, and her heart broke open.

"Christ, Alma. I'm falling apart. Can't you see that?"

"I didn't know, Evan," she whispered. "I didn't know any of it."

"You didn't ask," he replied coldly.

Alma struggled to find the right thing to say. She refused to ruin another person's life by bringing him permanently into her mess, especially not the person she loved so deeply. He didn't love her that much, though. He couldn't. His mom had it right. He felt sorry for her, and she didn't want his pity.

"Evan," she said slowly, "what we have—all of this—it can't be love."

He looked up at her. "What are you saying, Alma?"

"It's not love, Evan. Look at you! Love doesn't destroy people."

"Are you saying you don't love me?"

How would she bring herself to say it? She couldn't even nod her head.

"Are you?" he demanded, standing up slowly.

"I guess so," she said quietly.

"Say it! Say you don't love me."

She couldn't breathe. She needed to take in air, but her body refused to comply. She pushed the words out weakly. They slurred together with the last bit of air in her nearly empty lungs.

"I don't love you."

He spun around and lurched into his car.

"I'm done," he said as he slammed the door shut.

He backed the car away and sped out onto the empty road, leaving the black velvet box on the driveway, covered in a fine gray dust and half buried in weeds.

It was still open.

PART THREE

PART ONE

TWENTY-THREE
Flowering Cactus

Evan let the water run cold. Closing his eyes, he splashed it against his cheeks, feeling the shock run through his otherwise numb body. He lifted his face and covered it with a towel. It had been forever since he left Alma standing on the streets of that pathetic town, but he still couldn't look at his own reflection in the mirror.

Five weeks.

Thirty-five days.

Eight hundred and forty-four hours.

How else could he mark the passage of time? He could count the number of minutes between classes—the short stretches of time when he studiously avoided her, ignoring the pain. He had pushed it so deep inside that it was as if, somewhere near the pit of his stomach, he had grown a new organ—one that processed the toxic waste of love not returned.

He could mark time with the forty-five minutes that split each week-day into two equal halves: the slow hours of quiet dread that came before they were in class together, and the quick bursts of anger that came after. Or he could measure those forty-five minutes when he sat so near her that he could smell the clean scent of her shampoo, could see the outline of her bra underneath her shirt, could almost taste her on his lips.

He had wanted to switch seats, to move to a far corner of the room. Maybe from there, their classmates would disperse the energy that pulsed between them. But he didn't move. Was it just part of his struggle to save face—to make it seem that this was easy for him? Or was it because he needed to feel the sweet pain of her presence, the only thing that could remind him he was still alive?

No, not the only thing. He would measure the time in another way:

Seven games.

Six hundred and thirty minutes.

Five goals.

Eleven assists.

Three perfect penalty kicks.

Only on the field could he focus fully and completely on the present. Only there could he forget the past and shield himself from a future without her.

He slowly buttoned his shirt and lifted the collar. He pulled a tie from his top drawer, looped it around, and tightened. For a moment, it felt like a noose, pulling against the thick cords of his neck.

Downstairs, Evan took his mother's keys and pulled her Escalade around the driveway, letting it idle loudly at the front door. His mom never wanted to ride in his hybrid, so he drove her car instead. He used to complain about having to drive it, but he didn't complain anymore. It didn't matter.

Mrs. Roland opened the door and gracefully lifted her small body into the passenger seat, her tall heels tapping quietly against the running boards. She was so thin that she seemed to float in the broad cushions of her SUV's leather seats. Evan told her she looked nice even though he barely noticed what she was wearing.

They arrived at the hotel, and the valet carefully helped his mother down from her perch and then pulled away. Evan watched the car descend into the garage, abandoning him to another night, another party. He took his mother's arm and led her into the hotel.

This was his penance. This was how he apologized to his mother, without ever saying a word.

Three charity auctions.

Eight Sprites.

Two chicken breasts in cream sauce.

One poached salmon with asparagus.

One ugly painting for his mom ($1,100).

One signed Chipper Jones jersey for him ($400).

One ski trip to Jackson Hole for his parents, who no longer spoke to each other ($3,500).

—

The room still looked like Raúl's. She'd been living in it for months, but the baseball caps still hung in neat rows across the far wall, the soccer jerseys and ticket stubs stayed tacked above Raúl's bed. Not even the books on his desk, reminders of the community college courses he never would complete, were out of place. Moving anything seemed like a betrayal.

But in a few short minutes, he would call and she would have to beg him not to return. How would she do it? What could she say to make him stay in Mexico?

Alma took the phone from her bedside table to check the time. Evan gazed at her from the screen, lips curved into a sly grin, as he did from that photo each time she touched her phone. Why hadn't she erased it? Every day she allowed herself to study this image only once. She had so many opportunities to speak to Evan, but she didn't know what to say.

Would she tell him she still had the ring buried deep inside a drawer? If only she could bury her regret there, too. But there was no space.

Evan had forgiven her so much, but she felt certain he would not forgive her this betrayal. She had revealed so many of her bruises and scars, and she thought he had loved them, too. But maybe he had only wanted to blot them out, to make her right, so that she would be able to live in his world.

But she didn't want to live there, and neither did he. She knew that much.

———

It was the only luxury hotel in town, and he rarely came here. Usually the benefit parties were held at the club. The venue was different, but everything else was the same: same people, same silent auction items, same music, same arrangement of tables.

He looked around the room, trying to avoid eye contact. He knew almost every person here, and had no desire to talk to anyone. He walked over to the bar and ordered a Sprite for himself and a chardonnay for his mother. The bartender looked him up and down and questioned whether he was old enough to order wine. This was a difference, he guessed, between coming here and going to the club. At the club, all the bartenders knew that he was BeBe's regular date, that it was his responsibility to supply her with a steady stream of chardonnays since his father couldn't, or wouldn't.

His mom approached and spoke discreetly with the bartender, who handed him the glass of wine. Did the bartender seriously think that if he were trying to order himself a drink, he would order a *chardonnay*?

He led his mother to their table and sat down. She placed her purse on the linen-covered chair and wandered off to find Aunt Maggie.

A waitress came to the next table and filled the water glasses. She wore combat boots, and he wondered if that was against the employee dress code. She looked him over and delivered the kind of smile that meant she intended to pay him special attention. Evan had seen it before. He knew the drill.

Besides the combat boots, she wore the required uniform of the waitstaff, but her black skirt was noticeably shorter than the others' and her T-shirt was snug. She had a plain face, but her body more than made up for it; she carried herself like she knew it. Her auburn hair was piled on top of her head, exposing the back of her long neck and, curving around its side, the tip of what appeared to be a very large tattoo.

"It's a flowering cactus," she said, tugging down her shirt to reveal a bright red bud. "It's soft and beautiful but protected by thorns. It thrives in the desert because it can store up water, you know?"

Obviously she wasn't from around here.

"I didn't mean to stare," he said.

"Tattoos are meant to be stared at," she replied, smiling again.

She reached across him, holding the pitcher out to his glass.

"Thirsty?" she asked.

"Yeah, thanks."

Filling his glass slowly, the girl whispered in his ear, "Just find me if you need something stronger. I'll take care of you."

She turned and walked away before Evan could reply.

He stared into his glass, relieved that he was thinking about someone besides Alma, and wondering where on this girl's body the fragile tips of the cactus roots might begin.

——

Alma had spoken with Raúl many times, first when he arrived in Ciudad Juárez and later when he reached the little town in Oaxaca. It was strange, but he seemed so close. Ricocheting across the satellite feeds, his voice came through clear and strong. He could have been calling from a work site in Lakeshore Heights, or from the dining hall at the community college. He could have been calling to tell her what time he would pick her up after class, or asking her to get some SunnyD at the Bi-Lo. But he wasn't.

He was telling her things she didn't want to hear.

At first, Raúl was amused by the "return" to San Juan. He described its beauty, the way that the green mountains unfolded around it. He said it was even prettier than the photos they had seen over the years. He told her about the cool, deep river where he would swim, and about the return of the *pochos*, all the guys like him, who—according to the locals—spoke Spanish with a funny accent and acted like gringos. He made her laugh with stories of eccentric relatives: their great-grandfather Berto, who'd been a farmworker in California when he was Raúl's age, regaled him with stories of his bachelor days; their great-grandmother Mama Carmela concocted healing teas and pomades from the herbs in her garden. He had been entertained, at first, trying exotic new foods like crickets spiced with hot pepper.

But when the newness wore off, things changed. He explained how Mama Carmela ground herbs to cure his melancholy, and how *Tía* Pera lit candles for him every day, adding to the black soot that covered the feet of the Virgin Mary in the church on the town square.

Alma assured him that things would be better when she and their father arrived. They would have their own place, and Dad would be able to help him find work. He explained that the house had only concrete walls and no roof, and that they wouldn't be able to come up with the money to finish it since every day new people returned from *el norte*. Even before the return of the *pochos*, no one had work here.

And then he had told her about a nineteen-year-old who came back from Washington, DC, with two tears tattooed on his face. Alma had read about those tears and what they meant, but she didn't believe this kid showing up in their hometown was a real gangbanger. She assured Raúl that the boy was probably just a poser, like their cousin Manny and all the wannabe gangsters in Gilberton. But Raúl said she was wrong. He was a permanent legal resident of the United States, with all his papers in order. He had lived in Washington practically his entire life. He didn't even speak Spanish. But he was busted for gang activity and deported.

According to Raúl, the kid was dangerous, and he didn't belong in this sleepy town. And though she didn't say it out loud, for fear of making the melancholy worse, Alma knew that Raúl didn't belong there either.

———

Evan felt a tap on his shoulder and turned around to find Whit standing behind him in a seersucker suit.

"Sulking?" Whit asked.

Whit was, quite possibly, the last person in the world he wanted to see right now, unless he counted Alma. But he was trying not to think about her at all—trying to pretend that she didn't exist.

"Yes," Evan answered. "And I'd prefer to sulk alone."

Whit ignored him and pulled out the chair next to him.

"Nice shoes," Evan said, gesturing toward the saddle oxfords on Whit's feet.

"Just doing my part to keep up the esteemed Southern tradition of wearing ridiculous clothing to ridiculous events."

"Since when did you get on the charity circuit?" Evan asked.

"I have a deep concern for the well-being of our local waterways," Whit said dryly.

"Is that what this party's for?" Evan asked, not caring.

"And I'm working on my fourth step," Whit announced.

"That's cool," Evan replied, hoping not to sound interested.

Whit made a sweeping gesture across the room. "Because, really, what better place than here to make a searching and fearless moral inventory of myself?"

They sat for a while in silence, a pretty remarkable feat for Whit.

"Is there anything you want to ask me, Evan?"

"About your moral inventory?" Evan replied. "Absolutely not."

"About *her*," Whit said.

Evan felt his heart beat fast as the subtle stinging sensation met the corners of his eyes.

"No," he said.

Evan stood up and looked around the room, suddenly desperate to find someone else to talk to. He knew Whit would tell him, whether or not he wanted to hear.

"They denied his request for voluntary departure," Whit said. "Her dad can't leave the detention center. He'll be deported soon."

Evan turned to walk away.

"She's leaving, too," Whit said.

He spun back and looked directly into Whit's eyes.

"When?" he heard himself say too loudly, with too much anxiety in his voice.

"As soon as school ends. They're all going back."

Evan slumped back into the chair before his knees gave out.

"How is she?" Evan asked. Immediately, he wished he hadn't.

"Miserable. Bereft."

"Yeah," Evan said quietly.

Was it his fault? The question that haunted him returned. What would that night have been like if she hadn't lied to be with him at his birthday party? Would her father have been driving through the checkpoints? Would Raúl have been there?

He had to stop this train of thought. It was torturing him.

"I've gotta find my mom," Evan said.

Where was the girl with the cactus tattoo?

———

"I can't stay here," Raúl said.

"Yes," she said. "You can and you will."

"You don't understand," he said, pleading. "You don't get what it's like here, Alma."

What could she say to make him stay?

"This is what I understand," she said. "I understand that if you come back, and if you are caught, you will have committed a felony."

"I won't get caught," he replied.

"You don't know what it's like *here* now, Raúl. Every day people are being detained. They're getting deported for fishing without a license, for God's sake!" Her voice was urgent. "And even if you don't get caught, even if you live here until the day you die, you'll never have a real job, never finish school. You'll have to build your life around lies. You'll never be able to tell the truth, to be honest about who you are. You will have to put together a false life with fake papers or, worse yet, no papers at all. You will be without identity."

Silence.

She tried one last time. "You will live a dead-end life full of lies. Is that what you want?"

"I'm coming back, Alma."

"You can't come back. Please, don't come back."

"You don't understand," Raúl said sadly. "I've told you so many times, but you still aren't hearing me. I can't live here."

"No," she replied. "*You* don't understand. You'll never be able to live *here*—at least not legally."

"At least there I have a life. I can get a job. I have friends. Down here

I'm just freeloading and hanging around a bunch of strangers from other places with too much time on their hands. That's a bad combination, Alma."

"You'll make friends. You'll find work."

"Alma, listen to me. People get mixed up in some serious shit when they're bored and have nothing to lose. Or, worse, when they're desperate."

"Do you hear what you're saying? You're in *San Juan*, for God's sake. It's a quiet little country town. There's nothing to get mixed up in."

"Not yet," Raúl replied. "But I'm telling you, Alma, things are going to change here—and not for the better. I can feel it."

"But you won't, Raúl. I know you won't change."

"That makes one of us," he said.

Evan found her at the edge of the ballroom; she seemed to be waiting for him. Without speaking, she took his hand and pulled him into the kitchen. Reaching under a stainless steel prep table, she pulled out a bottle and two plastic cups. She poured them both a shot of vodka, and then another. They drank silently, watching each other. Then she screwed the cap back on.

"I need to get back to work," she said.

He nodded and watched her walk away. Then he slipped into the empty seat between his mother and Mrs. Watson, grateful for the warm buzz making its way through his body.

The lies and half-truths slipped off his tongue. Together, he and his mother wove a seamless story. They built a life for their family that did not exist. In this life, everything was going as planned. They carefully steered the conversation away from the dangerous terrain of Evan's absentee father and toward the smooth path of Evan's future. He went along with their banter, joined in on their jokes about how he would be going to college on the "left coast," laughed amiably as they warned him not to inhale the marijuana fumes or inadvertently find himself marching in the Gay Pride parade in San Francisco. This could be another way to measure time—a better way.

Three months, one week, one day.

It seemed impossible that he would be, in that short amount of time, hurtling through the sky on a plane—away from this place—and then touching ground on that narrow stretch of land that juts into the San Francisco Bay. In the meantime, Evan smiled and laughed, cheered and cajoled as the live auction got under way. Tipsy women with flushed faces coaxed their husbands' hands into the air, and the men eagerly went along, as if in some ancient ritual display of masculinity. Evan joined in at his mother's urging.

It was easy, and made even easier by the spiked Sprites that the tattooed girl kept silently placing by his side, each time gently grazing his shoulder as she walked away.

He let the vodka guide him as one of the final auction items came up for bid—a three-day vacation at a Ritz-Carlton south of Tucson, Arizona. As the auctioneer enthusiastically described the dry, hot climate, the golf course dotted with large cacti, Evan called out absurd sums of money. Four thousand, forty-two hundred, forty-five hundred, five. The crowd roared with delight to see the teenage boy go head-to-head with Dr. Richards, and then "win" a trip he didn't want to take.

———

"Do you remember Uncle Tico?" Raúl asked Alma. "He's our mom's second cousin or something?"

"No, why?"

"He's a coyote. He's bringing some people across soon, and I'm coming with them."

"No! Raúl, Dad will *kill* you if you do that!"

"By the time he gets here, I won't be around for him to kill, Alma."

"You're such an idiot. How will you pay for it? I thought you had no work, no money."

"I've still got my savings."

"You mean your college savings?"

"Yes."

"Shut up!" she cried out. "Stop! Do you hear what you're saying? You're going to pay a coyote to bring you back to *this* with your college savings?"

"Yes."

"It's too dangerous," she said. "Haven't you heard the stories? Haven't you paid any attention at all?"

She was angry, and she heard the anger in his voice, too.

"What are you talking about?" he asked, accusingly.

"Crossing. The desert. The border. It's all too dangerous."

"You're kidding, right?" His voice was escalating to a high pitch. "You're asking me if I've *heard the stories* about crossing the border?"

"Yes," Alma replied. "I mean it just keeps getting worse, you know?"

"I don't need the stories, Alma. I was there," he yelled. He paused for a moment. "It can never be worse than that time," he said.

Alma was confused. His voice had gone so soft, and she could hear the pain surging through the phone line.

"What?" she asked quietly.

"I was there, Alma, with Mom, and so were you." His voice was calm, almost soothing. "We were there."

"That's not true," she said, anxiety rising like a flame through her chest. "We were waiting in a hotel room. We went separately."

"Listen to me, damn it," he commanded. "We were with her. She refused to leave us. She wouldn't let us cross with *Tío* Osvaldo. She wanted us to stay together."

"You're lying," she cried out. She felt as though she were suffocating. She needed to breathe.

"Alma, we were there."

"No," she screamed, trying to drown out the pounding in her chest. "We went in a car, through the checkpoint. We used the papers—the birth certificates."

"We did. But that was later. *Tía* Pera said that you shouldn't know, that you didn't need to know. She said we wouldn't tell you. But I was five. I remember."

"It's not true!" She was still screaming as the flames of anxiety engulfed her.

"We went with her, the first time. We tried to cross with Mom. We drove through with *Tío* Osvaldo a couple of days later—after she died."

"You're lying. Why are you lying to me?"

"We were there when she fell, and when the coyote left her in the desert. The border patrol found us all there, together."

"No! Stop saying that." She shook her head violently.

"Alma, it's true."

Alma sucked in a deep breath. She felt an eerie calm descend, a strength that she didn't know she had. Then she spoke in a low voice. "We wouldn't have survived either. How would we survive and not her?"

"You were still little, Alma. She was nursing you, you know? So, she nursed us both. I didn't want to drink it, but she made me. It saved our lives."

"I don't believe you, Raúl. I can't." Alma could think of nothing else to say.

"I was there, Alma. I remember. I remember when the helicopters came. I remember the dogs and the lights. I remember how she couldn't get up, but we could."

"No." As her mouth formed the simple word, her body collapsed onto the bed.

"And one of the border patrol agents, he was Latino—I mean, he looked Mexican. He took us away from her." Raúl's voice was strained. "He had a huge gun hanging from his shoulder, but he was nice. He hugged you, and I know this sounds weird, but he gave us both a lollipop, and told us everything would be OK."

Lollipop. Alma closed her eyes and tasted it. The sweetness rushed to her mouth. The dream—the dream that had been jolting her from sleep for as long as she could remember—it finally made sense.

She knew that it wasn't just a nightmare she'd been enduring for so many years. Well, yes, it *was* a nightmare, but it was the worst kind of nightmare. It was the memory of her mother's death. It was true.

———

The tattooed girl came back and put another "Sprite" in front of Evan. She plopped down next to him, poked his arm, and said, "Hey, Big Spender." Her hand was on his thigh and it felt good. She'd be off of work at midnight, she said, instructing him to ditch his mom and meet her at the service entrance. She'd supply the drinks and the entertainment. All he had to do was show up.

From across the room, Whit leaned against a pillar and watched.

I know regret, and you are going to regret this. That's what Whit was telling him, without saying a word.

Evan stood up and balanced himself against the table. His head was spinning. He walked over to Whit and handed him the keys to the Escalade. Whit took the keys but said nothing. Evan turned away, dismayed that it had come to this, that he and Whit now knew each other so well they didn't need words. But he was nothing at all like Whit. That was what he told himself as he headed toward the service entrance.

He had a new way to measure the passage of time.

> Six (or seven?) shots of Vodka.
> One tipsy mom passed off to his cousin because he was too drunk to drive.
> One girl with a cactus tattoo.

Alma knew how she would tell the story. The next time she was invited to offer her inspiring testimony, she would agree to go. She would stand in front of the crowd, the perfect image of the model immigrant, and she would begin:

When I was two, my mother brought my brother and me across the border. She tried to carry us through the Arizona desert and into the land of opportunity. But my brother and I sucked the life out of our mother in that desert, and we left her, in search of a better life.

Then, while all the earnest scholarship people stared at her in shock and disbelief, she would ask—no, she would scream, at the top of her lungs:

Have I earned it? Have I earned it now?

TWENTY-FOUR
Sweet Georgia Rain

"You have *got* to stop sulking," Whit proclaimed. "It's *so* tedious."

Alma knew he was right. She needed to move on, but she had no idea how.

"And I need your help, desperately." He plopped a stack of yearbooks onto the kitchen table. "Look through these and find the Latina girls for me, OK?"

Alma grimaced. She should have been offended, but she knew why he was obsessing over the yearbooks. He was on his fifth step, and the time had come for him to make amends with the girl, the one from the night with Conway. The problem was that he still wasn't sure who she was, or where she might be. The Gilberton High yearbooks seemed a good place to start.

"Whit," Alma said, "thirty-two percent of the school is Latino. Any chance you could give me something more specific to look for?"

"I told you: curly hair," he said. Then, looking at the floor in an unusual display of shame, he continued, "Young. We should start with the freshmen."

Alma silently opened a yearbook as Mrs. King came and joined them at the kitchen table, a mug of coffee in her hand. She was meeting with the real estate agent in an hour to put their house up for sale.

"Are you children up to trouble again?" she asked.

The beautiful thing was that they were up to no trouble, and she knew it. Whit had been sober for sixty days, and he'd just been given a small gold chip to memorialize it.

"I'm trying to find a girl to make amends, Mrs. King," Whit said. "But it's not proving to be easy."

"Amends," Mrs. King said, nodding her head slowly. "Well, that sounds like a fine idea." She looked directly at Alma. "How 'bout you give it a try, Alma?"

"It wouldn't do any good, Mrs. King," Alma said. "How can I apologize when he won't talk to me? He doesn't even look at me."

Alma glanced over at the stack of boxes lining the walls of the living room. In two weeks, she would be leaving this town—and Evan—forever.

"Did you talk with Ms. Chen yesterday?"

"Yes, ma'am."

"And she told you about the academy in Mexico City?"

"Yes, ma'am."

"What's this all about?" Whit asked.

"There's an excellent academy in Mexico. Ms. Chen spoke with the admissions office at her alma mater and they suggested that Alma try to enroll there. Alma sent her transcripts down, and the academy is willing to accept her for next year."

"That's great, Alma," Whit said. "Now you're sure to get into Princeton."

"Yeah, Whit," Alma said sarcastically. "It's, like, a done deal."

"It's a wonderful opportunity, Alma." Mrs. King said. "You should feel grateful."

Alma was grateful, but none of it seemed real. She was in, and she had distant cousins whom she could live with in a town near Mexico City, but she didn't have the money to pay tuition. Ms. Chen and Mrs. King had assured her they would find a donor. But even if they found tuition money, she would have to scrape together enough to pay bus fare to and from the city, to buy books and uniforms. And before going to an elite school in Mexico, she would need much practice reading and writing Spanish.

"When will you speak with the academic adviser?"

"About Spanish? I talked to her yesterday. There are some classes I can take in Oaxaca this summer, at a language institute in the city."

"You're taking Spanish classes?" Whit asked. "What the hell?"

"Watch your language, young man," Mrs. King commanded.

"Uh, yeah, Whit. I've never actually studied Spanish. It's an international school, so I will take classes in English, but some of my academic work will be in Spanish—obviously."

Alma could kick herself for having taken Latin all these years. She thought it was what the smart kids did. So stupid. Here she was, a perfectly fluent Spanish speaker, and she didn't even always know where to put an accent mark. The Spanish classes were going to cost money, too. Money their family didn't have.

"I'll help!" Whit said, jumping to his feet. "I'll give you lessons—starting tomorrow."

"I can't believe this is my life," Alma said under her breath. Then, reluctantly, she looked up at Whit. "Thanks," she said. "I could use a head start."

"And I could use a project. So the benefits abound," Whit said. "But there's one condition," he said, leaning in toward her. "You *must* stop sulking. Now."

He shoved another yearbook in her face.

Alma's phone vibrated on the table. Whit looked at the screen and smiled.

"See," he said, thrusting the phone toward her. "Maritza agrees with me."
Alma read the text from Maritza.

> Stop feeling sorry 4 yourself
> Help us figure out a way 2 get 2 Atlanta 4 the
> game
> Last chance 4 u 2 c a bunch of Latinos kick private
> school boys' asses without getting thrown in jail
> Lol

"Go brush your hair and change out of those pathetic pajama pants. I'm taking you and your friends to the event of the season," Whit said.

Mrs. King stood up, hand on her hip. "And what might that be, young man? Because you are not going to any parties on my watch."

"I wouldn't dream of it, Mrs. King," Whit replied. "Alma and I are going to a completely dry state championship soccer match. GHS head-to-head with Wolford Academy in Atlanta—it should be priceless. A ragtag bunch of immigrants, mixed in with a Southern boy or two, facing off with Atlanta's best and brightest."

"*¿Qué pasó?*" *Abuela* Lupe called in through the kitchen door. "*¿Adónde van?*"

She was separating dollars into neat stacks on the coffee table, surrounded by a few boxes of still unsold shoes.

"*Un partido de fútbol, Abuelita,*" Alma said. "*Pero no quiero ir.*"

"Oh, yes, you want to go, Alma," Whit said. "Just admit it."

"That sounds like a real nice time," Mrs. King said, faking an innocent voice.

"I can't go, Whit," she replied. "Seriously, I can't."

Abuela Lupe walked toward the kitchen door, nodding and shooing her along with her hand. "*Véte, mi corazòn. Véte. En el nombre de Dios, no puedes quedarte llorando aquí todos los días. Te vas a enfermar, m'hija.*"

Abuela Lupe insisted that Alma go, said she was going to make herself sick if she just hung around and cried all day, but her grandmother had no idea how sick Alma felt at the thought of seeing *him*.

"It will do you a world of good to get out of this house," Mrs. King interjected.

"Just pretend he's not there," Whit said.

It would be impossible not to notice Evan on the field. When he was playing well, his energy and intensity drew the attention of every spectator. Alma had heard he was playing better than ever.

"How am I supposed to do that, Whit?" Alma asked.

"Lesson one about popular sporting events," Whit said. "One does not attend to watch the game. That's simply tedious. One attends to see—and be seen by—the spectators." He pulled her from her chair and pushed her toward Raúl's room—her room now. "So hurry along my little *señorita*," he said. "Go get cute and meet me at the car in twenty minutes."

It was useless for her to protest.

———

"We're both free men, Evan."

Logan stepped out of Conway's Hummer into Evan's driveway. "Caroline and I ended it—for real this time."

"I'll believe it when I see it," Evan said dryly.

A free man.

Six weeks

Forty-two days.

One thousand and nine hours.

But who was counting any longer?

"Why are you driving Conway's Hummer?" Evan asked.

"Mine's in the shop. Can I leave it here? He said he'd come get it after the game."

"I guess so," Evan said.

Evan and Conway hadn't spoken since the morning after Lake Rabun, but he still hadn't told Logan the whole story. He didn't have the energy for it, and he wasn't really sure the story was his to tell.

"I mean it, Evan," Logan said as they climbed into Evan's car. "You and I are going to have an amazing summer. We'll call it the summer of no strings attached. We'll be floating free in a universe of beautiful women."

Evan thought of Ingrid, the tattooed girl from the hotel, and of the cruel "freedom" that he had earned against his will.

As promised, Ingrid had been waiting for him at the service entrance, still dressed in her black work clothes and combat boots, her auburn hair hanging in messy waves around her shoulders. She was wearing black eyeliner and a deep-red lipstick that made her face look almost translucent. Ingrid was attractive in a sort of harsh way, unlike any girl he knew.

Maybe that was her beauty. She reminded him of nothing and no one he had ever encountered.

They headed to her apartment in a complex next to the highway, not far from the hotel. On the walk there she pulled a half-full bottle of vodka from her giant purse, and took a deep swig as they crossed the empty parking lot. Then she passed the bottle to Evan. They crossed diagonally through two gas stations and the drive-through of a McDonald's. She told him it was a shortcut. The landscape followed the contours of the interstate, carving spaces at each exit that were, really, no place at all—just pauses on the way to somewhere else.

She was hungry, so they went into a convenience store, where she bought a huge Coke and chocolate Ho Hos—she liked the white, creamy swirls in the middle.

When she kissed him on the concrete slab outside the convenience store, her mouth tasted like processed sugar.

He tasted the kiss, but he didn't feel it.

Evan looked back at Logan who was climbing into the passenger seat of his car. "All I can say is this, Logan: before you start 'floating free in a universe of women,' you'd better play some wicked defense," he replied.

—

Alma was growing very anxious, but not because they were headed toward Evan at eighty miles an hour. It was Whit. More specifically, it was Whit's bizarre silence. At first he had joked around with them, but around the time that Magda squeezed into the backseat Whit fell completely silent. It was getting creepy.

They pulled off the interstate, and within a few minutes, they were turning into the leafy green campus of Wolford Academy. Beautiful brick buildings stood in orderly rows at the edge of broad, impeccably manicured lawns.

"Is this a high school?" Monica asked.

"Technically, it's a day school," Whit answered. "Pre-K through twelve. It's almost impossible to escape a place like this."

Alma wasn't exactly sure what he meant, but she was glad to hear his voice.

Waves of heat shimmered off the black asphalt of the parking lot. It was May, but it already felt like midsummer. As they got out of the car, Alma looked up at the hazy sky to see storm clouds gathering.

Whit grasped her arm. "Alma, wait."

"What's up?" she asked.

"I think that's her—your friend. I think she's the one from that night."

"What? Which one?"

"The one with the curly hair. Magda," he said.

"No way," Alma said. "That's impossible."

"She looks so familiar."

Alma shook her head. "What? So now all curly-haired Latinas look like the girl. Get over it, Whit. Racial profiling doesn't suit you."

"I know," he said. "It sounds absurd, but I think it's her."

"You're wrong," Alma said. "She was acting totally normal. She wouldn't have been acting normal, Whit."

"Yeah, I guess you're right."

"Plus, I'm pretty sure she's a virgin." She paused. "I mean, I don't think she'd lie about that."

"OK," Whit said. "Just forget I said anything."

They walked toward the packed stadium. In Gilberton it would be impossible to draw a crowd like this to anything but a football game.

Apparently Wolford Academy was for elites of many backgrounds, and even though there didn't seem to be many Latinos at the school, there were enough Asian, Indian, and black students that no one seemed to think twice about an obviously rich white kid heading toward the bleachers with a group of Latinas. Alma felt transported back to North Atlanta High, but with more designer labels.

She felt it before she saw it—Evan's presence on the field. She wanted not to look, but she did. He wore a black leather strap, a home-made necklace with some sort of bead in the center.

The opposing team kicked the ball into play, and then Evan easily took control, the necklace pulled taut against his neck. Alma refused to let herself wonder where it had come from. Already, it pained her to watch his fierce beauty, to see his intensity unleashed, literally airborne.

The Red Elephants were on fire, and Evan was the one who kept stoking the flame.

———

Evan's entire body buzzed with adrenaline. He was fully present on the field, entirely aware of how his teammates were arranged in space. They were playing possession football at their absolute best. If he had to make a prediction at that moment, he would say that their best was good enough to beat this team—but he was too superstitious to let himself think about the outcome. He just played his heart out, and it felt fantastic.

When the buzzer sounded, there were still eleven minutes left in the second half, and the Red Elephants were up 3-0. Evan hadn't noticed the gathering clouds, the distant thunder coming closer. Rain delay. He jogged off the field reluctantly and followed the rest of the team back to the locker room.

He saw her standing under an overhang, pressed against a brick wall, looking up at the sky. Sheets of rain separated them. It was amazing, and infuriating, how quickly she could drag him away, how relentlessly present she was in his head. Alma was the image he saw when Ingrid had tried to kiss him again on the tattered couch at her apartment, her roommates playing video games on the floor in front of them. And then he saw Alma again, in the kitchen, when he'd gone to pull another beer from the refrigerator. He had wanted alcohol to numb him, or maybe to blur his vision of her in his mind.

He'd *wanted* to want Ingrid, but he didn't. And each time she wrapped her arms around his waist and pressed her lips against his, Evan saw Alma just as she looked standing here—her eyes distant and face serene.

Evan should have been thinking about the final minutes of the championship game. He should have been entirely focused on strategy, but as he passed by her, trying not to look, he remembered standing in the middle of Ingrid's kitchen in tears, a can of beer gripped tightly in his hand.

He told Ingrid his sad story, and she cried, too. She led him into her living room, and they sat on the dumpy couch, drinking and playing video games until they both passed out. The next morning Ingrid wove him a necklace out of thick straps of leather, with a golden citrine stone knotted into the center. She tied it tightly around his neck and told him that citrine had healing properties—that it worked well for depression.

Evan insisted that he wasn't depressed, but Ingrid gave him a look and insisted otherwise.

Fingering the smooth stone at his neck, Evan followed his teammates to the locker room and the air-conditioning rushed out to hit him. Something about that jolt of cold air made him realize it: He had to turn around. She was leaving, and he had to say good-bye. Maybe if he told her good-bye, she would get the hell out of his head.

Evan jogged through the rain toward Alma. She watched as he came nearer but showed no expression. And then they were nearly face-to-face.

He needed to say something, but he couldn't find words. He wanted to reach out and touch her, but his body wouldn't let him.

"You're amazing out there, Evan," Alma said. "The best I've ever seen you play."

"Thanks," he replied, holding her gaze. His chest ached.

"Cal will be so lucky to have you," she said.

"I can't wait to get there," he replied, dragging his gaze from her eyes to his feet.

"I miss you," she said.

His chest collapsed and his head started to spin. This was a mistake. He should be in the locker room, focused on the last few minutes of the championship game, not out here in the rain letting his heart break open again.

"Be safe getting down there," he said, forcing himself to look up.

And then, because it hurt too much to look at her, and because he wanted to change the subject, he told her, "When you get there, say hi to your brother for me. Tell him to keep playing."

"He's like you, Evan," she said. "He can't stop."

She was right. Evan couldn't stop, especially not now. He had to get back into the locker room—back to the one thing that would protect him from this pain.

"I've gotta . . ."

"I know," she said, "Focus. Go out there and crush them, OK?"

Evan didn't reply. He turned away and jogged back through the rain to the locker room. As soon as he got there, he thrust earbuds in and listened intently to the last song in his pregame mix. He had to focus. He would force every fiber of his being into the game.

When the rain delay ended, Evan led his team back onto the pitch. With the Red Elephant mascot revving the crowd, they took to the field, and they dominated. It felt awesome.

Evan heard the buzzer and then felt the crush of bodies against him. Fans mobbed the field, chanting and yelling. Evan's team had shut out their opponents, with a final score of 5-0. Evan scored two of those goals, but only with perfectly executed assists from his teammates. Only three of the guys on his team had access to prestigious soccer academies, and no doubt the Wolford players had trained at these kinds of places since they left diapers. Still, the Red Elephants dominated. Evan was so proud that he screamed at the top of his lungs while his teammates lifted him into the air.

Alma stood still in the bleachers as the fans rushed the field. She watched Evan, perched on the shoulders of his teammate, raising the hulking trophy toward the sky. She imagined the trophy joining all the others in the entryway of Gilberton High School, and she knew that another photograph would hang on the wall where she and Evan used to sit on rainy mornings. She imagined walking into the building on the first day of her senior year and standing in front of it, her eyes searching the row of kneeling bodies to find Evan. She knew exactly how he would be smiling, and how the edges of his eyes would crimp the slightest bit.

It was a relief to know that she would never have to see the photograph.

TWENTY-FIVE
Sabotage

"These burgers taste like rubber," Maritza said. She took a deep swig of Coke and swallowed dramatically.

"And the French fries are vile," Magda added.

Whit turned to face them in the backseat. "Why are you looking at me? The Varsity was *not* my idea."

"OK, *flaco*, it wasn't your idea," Maritza replied. "But you should have stopped us. I mean, here we are trying to give Alma something to remember when she goes back, and all she has to go home with is *this*?" She reached forward and grabbed a silly red-and-white paper cap from Alma's head.

The Varsity was not just a fast-food restaurant. It was an Atlanta institution. So as they drove back to Gilberton from the game, Monica, Maritza and Magda insisted they stop at the big red *V* for a celebratory dinner. In their opinion, the food was mediocre at best. The only consolation was that meals came with free paper hats, just like the ones worn by the cooks.

"Give me that hat," Monica said, lunging toward Maritza. "This little *salvadoreña* is goin' in there to teach those people how to make a burger."

"It's not *that* bad," Alma broke in. "I mean the Frosted Orange is actually pretty good."

"You've gotta be kidding me," Monica said. "How can that thing pass for a milk shake? It's like drinking crushed-up baby aspirin."

"Yes, but Alma's a good girl," Whit said. "She likes to take her medicine."

"Y'all get off my back," Alma said. "You're supposed to be feeling sorry for me, you know."

"No," Maritza said. "We're supposed to be cheering you up. But obviously, we suck at it."

"It's not your fault," Whit said. "I think it would behoove us all to simply endure her brooding lament. She's morose, but she's still Alma."

Magda looked at Monica. "Do you have any idea what he just said?" she asked.

"Dang, Whit," Maritza added. "Have you got an SAT prep book up there in your head?

They all laughed. Alma wasn't exactly having a good time, but she was glad to see that Whit was coming back to himself. He must have decided that she was right about Magda. She couldn't be the wasted girl from last summer.

They were still laughing when Magda glanced at her phone and started texting rapidly. It didn't surprise Alma. Magda was the kind of girl who always had her phone within a few inches. She obsessively checked her texts.

"Uggggh," Magda groaned, and continued texting without letting any of them in on the conversation being tapped out in fragments on her phone.

"I've gotta get back to Gilberton," she announced. "My cousin is freaking out."

"Who, Flor?" Maritza asked. "I thought she was in South Carolina."

"Yeah, she was. She came back a couple of days ago."

"With her baby?" Alma asked.

Flor's parents had completely lost it when she finally told them that she was pregnant. Her father almost had a heart attack, her mother went into a depressive slump, and within days Flor was seen leaving the house, suitcase in hand. According to rumor, she went to *Padre* Pancho and he intervened, convincing Flor's parents that, instead of disowning her entirely, they should send her to live with an aunt in the country. There had been much speculation on the local rumor mill about who the father might be, but no one knew for sure.

"Yeah," Magda said. "She was born in April. She's super cute. Flor treats her like a baby doll."

"I guess that's what happens when you have a baby at fifteen." Maritza sneered.

"Sixteen, now," Magda said. "She turned sixteen a few days ago."

"Sweet sixteen," Maritza mumbled under her breath.

"She's actually doing pretty well with the whole thing. She's got a lot of help," Magda said, giving Maritza an eye.

"Where's she living?" Monica asked. "I thought her parents kicked her out."

"Yeah, they basically did." Magda answered. "She's living with her boyfriend. I mean, he's the dad, I guess. They're getting married next weekend, so we figure maybe then her parents will start speaking to her again."

Magda leaned forward in her seat.

"Alma," she said, "this is weird. I've been trying to find a way to tell you."

"What?" Alma asked.

"The dad—the guy who is marrying her—it's your cousin Manny."

"What?" Alma cried. "He's twenty years old. And plus, he doesn't even live here anymore. He's in—"

"South Carolina." Magda finished her sentence. "He moved to be near her while she was pregnant. He paid for the doctors and everything. When she turned sixteen, they decided to get married and move back to Gilberton together."

Alma shook her head.

"I know you think he's a loser, Alma," Magda said, "but he's been great. He's gonna work the night shift as a supervisor at Silver Ribbon so she can go back to school."

"A supervisor? Are you sure that we're talking about the same Manny?" Alma asked.

Manny doing shift work at the poultry plant. Taking care of a baby. It killed her that he got a job as a supervisor when he'd barely managed to get a high school diploma. That was the difference having legal status made—and speaking English.

"Because he has never in his life done a single responsible thing," she continued. "Ever."

"Yeah," Magda said. "I saw him yesterday. They're living in his parents' basement." She looked around at Maritza and Monica. "It was the weirdest scene, y'all. Flor was, like, hanging flowery curtains, and Manny was sitting at the kitchen table, studying for the citizenship test with the baby asleep on his chest."

"Manny? A citizen?" Alma asked.

"Yeah, if he passes the test." Magda said. "He wants to help Flor get papers, you know?" She looked back down at her phone. "Hold on a sec," she said as her fingers moved frantically across the keyboard.

"Bastard," Maritza said, filling the silence left by Magda's distraction. "I don't care if he's stepping up now, he was way too old to be fooling around with her. That's, like, criminal."

"Technically, it *is* criminal," Whit said. "At least until they get married. Fortunately for them, our enlightened state of Georgia allows children to marry at age sixteen, as long as they have consent from their parents."

Alma felt her stomach contract; Whit's words dragged her thoughts back to Evan's proposal.

Magda looked up from her phone. "Flor's losing it. Something happened, and Manny went ballistic. He took off and she's stuck there alone without a way to find him. She thinks he's gonna hurt someone."

"Yeah," Alma said, nodding. "That's starting to sound more like my cousin."

"Whit," Magda said pleading, "can you take me to her house, like, *now*?"

Whit eased his car back onto the interstate and pressed hard on the gas.

"Ooohhh, the drama!" he exclaimed. "Tell her we'll be there in forty minutes—maybe less."

———

The party was under way by the time Evan arrived with a carload of his elated teammates. Santiago had old-school hip-hop blaring from the speakers, and Miguel and Jonathan were half standing in the backseat with their torsos hanging out of the windows. They sang at the top of their lungs. Evan watched them in the rearview mirror, and he was happy for them. He wanted to feel their unbridled joy, but he felt nothing. The numbness was good. He knew that his only choices were this or overwhelming sadness. Even tonight.

Evan eased into an empty space as Miguel and Jonathan hoisted themselves out of their respective windows and landed on their feet. The door of the truck in front of them squealed open, and Conway, Peavey, and three junior girls tumbled out.

Peavey leapt into the air and gave Miguel and Santiago high-fives, while the junior girls mobbed Jonathan with a group hug. Evan hung back, but Conway was headed straight for him.

"Great game, man." Conway punched him lightly on the shoulder. "Y'all kicked some serious city-boy ass out there."

Evan didn't respond.

"And that defender—what was he, like, Indian or something? He couldn't touch you, man."

Seeing Conway in front of him, Evan felt a spark of the hatred that had engulfed him for so many weeks, but the spark wasn't enough to bring back his fire. It was too late. Evan had worked so hard to forget, to pretend that none of it had happened, or at least that none of it mattered. Maybe all of that work was paying off because now he didn't want to fight Conway. He didn't really want to do anything except go home and stare at the walls, but his team had just won a championship, and he was going to celebrate whether he wanted to or not.

—

The door flew open, and Flor rushed out, her curly hair wild and her eyes swollen and red. She bounced a screaming infant in the crook of her arm. The baby's face was nestled into her mother's chest. Alma saw a shock of dark-brown hair, interspersed with a few pink barrettes.

Magda stepped forward first, reaching her arms toward the baby.

"Calm down, Flor. We're here. And give me that poor child."

Magda took the screaming baby, who immediately fell silent.

"Football hold," Magda announced as she entered the house. "Works every time."

Alma, Maritza, and Monica followed, but Whit held back, standing frozen by the car. Alma was too concerned about Flor to worry about

Whit. She watched Flor stumble into the house and fall onto a red brocade couch. She slouched forward and buried her head in her hands.

"Oh, God. What have I done?" she asked. She seemed to be speaking to herself, so no one answered.

"We don't have much time," Flor said, looking up. "We need to find him before he does something stupid. We're getting married! He's taking the citizenship test! What if he screws up and gets deported?"

Alma knew it was possible. Manny had his green card, but he could be sent back to Mexico if he committed a felony before becoming a citizen. Manny definitely was capable of committing a felony.

"Just calm down and tell us what happened, Flor. He won't get deported," Magda said gently.

"I messed up. Again," Flor said. "I mean, Manny, he's been so great about it all. In the very beginning he wanted to know, and I just said it was one of the country-club kids, and it didn't matter because I loved Manny and it was a mistake. A big one. But now we have Jasmine and she's so beautiful, and it doesn't even feel like a mistake, and she's his—even though she's not."

"You're not making sense," Magda said. "Slow down."

Flor looked at Magda and said, "Manny and I, we have been together since I was fourteen, but since he was so much older we never told anyone. But we weren't like, uh, *together* together. And then last summer—please, you have to promise not to tell anyone this." They nodded vigorously. "Last summer, I got wasted at a party. I woke up the next morning alone in a fancy house by the golf course. I didn't remember anything, but I was pretty sure—you know. A month later, I was peeing on a stick."

"Oh, God," Monica said. "That's horrible."

"Manny was so mad at first. I was supposed to be saving myself for him, you know? He demanded to know who it was, but I wouldn't tell him. He started to harass all of my friends about it. Yazmín told him that I left the party in a black Hummer, but that was all he knew until now."

Alma felt light-headed. Her heart was hammering in her chest, and blood rushed to her ears. A series of snapshots ran through her head: Manny confronting Evan at the *quinceañera*, the strange things he said about a Hummer, Whit standing at the edge of Terrora Dam. It was all beginning to make sense.

"In South Carolina, he almost forgot about it all," Flor said. "He promised me that it didn't matter, that the baby would be his."

"So, what happened?" Magda asked.

Alma had to stand up. She walked toward the door and inhaled the warm night air.

"Something about coming back to Gilberton set him off. He said that before we get married, he has to know who it was. I told him I don't know." She began to cry.

"But he wouldn't let it go," Magda surmised. She stood with Jasmine peacefully sleeping in her arms.

"No," Flor replied. "So I just took him by the house. The Hummer was parked in front. As soon as he saw it, he sped home, practically threw me and Jasmine out of the car, and left. He didn't say a word. I think he knows who lives there. He's going after whoever it is."

Alma leaned against the door frame to balance herself. She wasn't sure that she would be able to produce sound, but she tried.

"Where was the house?" she asked.

"In Lakeshore Heights, on a dead-end street near the country club."

"A big brick house on the lake? With white columns?" Alma asked quietly. "And white rockers on the front porch?"

"Yeah," Flor said. "Do you know who lives there?"

"Yeah," she said. Alma felt herself sinking to the ground.

At the moment her body touched the ground she realized two things:

Evan was in real danger, and Whit was still outside. She turned to look out the window. It was dark, but she saw Whit in the glow of the street lamp, slowly pacing in front of the car. He held something in his hand, and his thumb rhythmically rubbed across its surface.

Seeing him, she knew. Alma and Whit were the only two people with the information to piece together this puzzle—unless she counted Conway, and she refused to think of him in the presence of that precious sleeping baby.

She forced herself to stand up.

"Just stay here," she said. "Don't follow me."

Alma ran outside and Whit looked up.

"Is it his?" Whit asked. Alma knew that he meant the baby.

"No. But we can't think about that now. Evan's in trouble."

"What? Evan? Why?"

"Manny made her tell him who the dad is. She couldn't remember, but she showed him the house."

"Evan's house? Oh, Jesus."

His hands fell to his side, and a gold chip landed on the asphalt. He breathed too quickly, his chest heaving.

"Give me your phone," Alma said.

"That's the girl, Alma," he said, handing over his phone. "It's her. I knew it as soon as she opened the door."

Alma dialed Evan's number and put the phone to her ear.

"I know, Whit," she said. "But you have to hold it together." Evan wasn't picking up. She dialed again.

"I think I'm going to faint," Whit said.

Still no answer. Alma hung up and handed Whit the phone.

"You are *not* going to faint," Alma replied sternly. "You are going to get in that car, and you are going to drive like a bat out of hell to the team party. We need to find Evan." She took his chin in her hand and lifted his eyes to meet hers. "Do you understand what I'm telling you?"

Whit nodded, crouched down to scoop up the chip, and then jogged toward his car.

———

The party was in full swing. Peavey was trying to do a keg stand, but he was too drunk to get up on his hands. Evan watched, mildly amused, as Peavey gave up and sucked the beer directly from the tap. Behind him, Logan and Caroline stood pressed against a wall, making out.

So much for the summer of no strings attached.

Evan sat on a chair in the kitchen, nursing a warm beer. He was bored. He had no interest in being here, but he also didn't have the energy to come up with an alternative. So he sat and watched from a distance as everyone else celebrated.

His phone rang. Whit. Evan ignored it and shoved the phone back in his pocket. It rang again, but he didn't even look. Whit was the kind of guy who called a million times before giving up. Just another way that he annoyed the hell out of Evan.

Mary Catherine tumbled into his lap and wrapped her arms around his neck. She was wasted. Her already short skirt rode up practically around her waist. He tugged the skirt down far enough to cover her powder-pink undies.

"You take such good care of me," she crooned in his ear.

"You should stop drinking," he replied.

"Or maybe you should *start*," M.C. said. "We're all celebrating *you*, and you won't even celebrate."

"I'm here, aren't I?" Evan asked.

"Barely," she replied. She ran her fingers along the back of his neck. Evan closed his eyes and tried to focus on the feel of her touch. He didn't feel a thing.

Mary Catherine rested her forehead on his shoulder.

"I need some air."

She stood up unsteadily and tugged at his hand, and he followed dutifully out the front door. Evan wrapped his arm tightly around her waist and guided her down the porch stairs. She leaned into him, barely able to stand.

At the bottom stair Evan looked up.

There was a sort of charge in the air. Something felt very wrong.

"Evan Roland."

Evan heard the voice first, and then he saw its source. Alma's cousin Manny was standing a foot away, leaning against the railing.

"So there you go again," Manny growled, gesturing toward Mary Catherine, "taking advantage of any drunk girl that falls into your arms."

Evan had no idea what Manny was talking about.

"Does that make you feel like a man?" Manny asked.

Seeing Manny standing so close, with his wifebeater and ugly tattoos, Evan felt an overwhelming rage.

"Because you're not a man," Manny said roughly. "You're a scared little boy."

Manny stepped forward, and Evan released Mary Catherine, who sank to the ground. Evan lunged toward Manny, and then he felt it. An intense searing pain radiated through his right hand and then hurtled into his gut. He stumbled backward.

Just to *feel* was so good.

He lurched forward again, his shoulder and face slamming into Manny's chest. In the space where his teeth met his gums, he felt a tingling sensation. Warm blood coursed from his nose, and he tasted its saltiness on his lips. The blood was thin and watery, but it tasted intense and real. It tasted like the truth.

Manny took a step back. "You're scared," he said. "And you should be."

And then Manny's body pounded into his, again and again. The blunt sensation shot through his nerves as he hurled fists, elbows, shoulders into Manny's soft flesh and angular bones. It didn't matter that he had no idea why they were inflicting such awful pain on each other. He knew, somehow, that both were diluting the acid bile of anger and frustration, helplessness and paralysis, with the blood and spit and hate of the other.

Another hit to his gut, and Evan was airborne. His shoulder crashed into the stairs, but before he could register the pain, he was floating free again, legs dangling. Someone was pulling him backward, away from Manny. He twisted his torso enough to see that it was Conway, tightly pinning Evan's elbows back, dragging him to the grass. Evan saw that Manny was being pulled away, too, in a chaotic tumble of red and blue flashing lights.

Two sheriff's deputies dragged him away from Evan. One was Troy.

Evan heard himself call out, "It was me. I started it." He tried to wriggle away from Conway, his heart pounding in his chest. "Listen to me, damn it. I started it," he yelled, louder this time, twisting away from Conway's grip.

Peavey stood over him. "Shut up, Evan," he commanded. "Shut the hell up."

Suddenly Evan saw it—what Alma always insisted was there but he had refused to see. They wouldn't arrest him. They would only arrest Manny.

Evan watched as Troy's partner pulled handcuffs from his belt and drew them open.

Still struggling to break free, he called out again, "Troy! Why are you leaving me here?"

"Evan, shut up!" Peavey demanded. Logan was standing next to him now, and all three hovered in his face.

"Do you want to go to jail?" Conway asked, struggling to hold him back.

Evan fought to pull away from them. "Goddamn it, Troy," he yelled across the lawn. "Listen to me! It was me!"

No one listened.

They shoved Manny into the backseat of the cruiser, and then Troy walked slowly over to Manny's red Corvette. By now, the entire party had spilled out onto the lawn, so everyone saw when Troy pulled a small black revolver from Manny's glove compartment.

"Busted," Peavey said.

"Adios, amigo!" Conway called out, releasing Evan's arms to cup his hands around his mouth for more volume.

Evan ran toward the cruiser. He slammed into Troy, thrusting his bare wrists at Troy's face.

"Cuff me, for chrissake!" he demanded. "I started it."

Troy turned away from him and stepped into the cruiser. "Go home, Evan," he said. "Sleep it off. You did not start this, and you'll never find a single person to say that you did."

Evan turned toward the house. Dozens of people stood watching from the lawn.

"I started it," he growled at Troy.

Troy pulled out his loudspeaker. He barked at the crowd, "Step forward if you witnessed the beginning of this fight."

Everyone stood perfectly still.

"If you have any information," he said, "please step forward."

No one moved except for Evan. He stumbled backward and collapsed to the ground.

And then, through the sweat and blood and tears, he smelled the sun. The buttery warm scent filled his nostrils, overpowering the metallic odor of his blood. By some miracle, Alma was falling with him.

TWENTY-SIX
Broken Parts

Alma burst out of the car. She wanted to catch him before he fell. She was too late, so she tumbled to the ground with him, shielding his crumpled body with her own.

"I'm so sorry, Evan."

She whispered into the place where his shoulder pressed against his ear. "I tried to get here in time. It's my fault. It's all my fault. I'm so sorry."

He sat up and wrapped his arms around her. She pressed her face into his bloodied sleeve. Sorrow and relief, confusion and pain, joy and longing and love—all of these feelings welled up inside her, and she finally gave them room.

No one came near them. Alma pulled Evan gently to his feet. She led him to Whit's car, and the crowds of onlookers stepped back to let them pass. They climbed into the backseat and sat with arms and legs intertwined, curling so closely into each other's bodies that they seemed to merge into one. From there, they watched as a truck sped along the road and pulled up next to the police cruiser. Flor flew out of the truck and threw her body against the window. Manny looked at her through the window and spoke, but Alma knew that she couldn't hear him through the thick glass and the sound of her own anguished cries. Magda was leaning over an infant car seat in the truck, cooing at the baby. Maritza sat in front. Her father was driving.

Whit sat frozen. His hands clutched the wheel so tightly that his knuckles were white.

"What's her name?" he asked.

"Flor," Alma replied.

"And the baby?" he asked.

"Her name is Jasmine," Alma said.

"That's a pretty name," Whit said.

It was such an earnest statement, not the kind of thing Whit usually said.

He turned back to the scene unfolding on the other side of the windshield, his hands still gripping the steering wheel. They watched as Magda approached Flor and gently coaxed her away from the police cruiser.

"Will he get deported?" Whit asked.

"Probably," Alma replied.

"Even though he's got a green card?" Whit asked.

"It doesn't matter. If he committed a felony, he gets deported, and he probably committed two tonight."

Evan sat up, and Alma hated to feel him pull away from her.

"I attacked him," he said. "He didn't do it."

"It doesn't matter," Alma replied. "No one will believe you."

Whit turned to look at Alma and Evan. "I can't make this situation right," Whit said, "but I can make it less wrong, and I will."

He started the car and drove slowly away from the scene.

Alma couldn't imagine how Whit must be feeling right now. But she knew that some part of what he felt was genuine remorse. Although it would be impossible for him to repair the damage he had caused, he deserved a chance to make it better.

"I don't think there's anything you can do Whit," Alma said, trying to express sympathy.

"Yes, there is something," Whit said firmly. He sucked in a deep breath. "Fortunately for us, my father cares about nothing more than protecting his reputation, our reputation. I'm going home right now to tell him what I did, and then I'm going to threaten to go public with it if he doesn't get Manny's charges dropped—tonight."

"Do you think he'll do it?" Alma asked, trying to hide her eagerness.

"Is Flor legal?" Whit asked.

"No," Alma replied. "Why?"

"That's good," Whit said. "He'll never let it come out that, at the tender age of seventeen, his son fathered a so-called anchor baby."

"Anchor baby?" Evan asked.

"That's what the anti-immigrant people call babies born in the United States to undocumented immigrants," Alma said.

For the first time in months, Alma felt something akin to hope. Whit was right. Senator Sexton Prentiss would want nothing to do with Flor and her baby.

"He won't believe you," Evan said. "He'll think you're just pulling a stunt to piss him off."

"I'll threaten to take a paternity test and make it public," Whit replied.

"But what about Conway?" Alma asked. "What if the baby's not yours?"

"He can't ever know about Conway," Whit replied. "No one can. I was the only person with her. I borrowed Conway's Hummer and drove her to your house. Conway stayed at the party."

"Do you think it will work?" Evan asked.

"Yes, I know it will," Whit said.

"Conway can't get away with this," Evan said.

"I know," Whit replied. "I'll think of something to get him busted, but he can't have anything to do with this."

"OK," Alma said. "I trust you."

Evan struggled to lean forward, wincing as he reached out to grasp Whit's shoulder.

"Whit, man," he said, "I never thought I'd say this, but I trust you, too."

Whit shifted in his seat uncomfortably.

"First things first," he announced, almost cheerfully. "I'm dropping you two off at the marina."

"The marina?" Alma asked. "Why?"

"Because it's time for you to make up, before you drive us all crazy. And there's no place better than the open water to get your shit together."

Alma stared out the window, afraid to look directly at Evan. Was he ready for this? Did he even want it?

"I need to get back to my car, Whit," Evan said.

He wasn't ready.

"Like hell you do! You are in no condition to be driving," Whit replied.

"It's late, Whit," Alma said.

Whit dug around in the center console. He lifted a key and tossed it toward Evan. Evan caught the key and then grimaced and grabbed his shoulder. Alma sat forward and tried to break in, but Whit shut her down.

"I refuse to come back until you have worked through all of your basically nonexistent issues and made up entirely," Whit said. "So I'll pick you up in the morning."

"The morning?" Alma cried out. "My grandmother will kill me."

"What's she gonna do?" Whit asked. "Ship you off to Mexico?'

He had a point. It didn't matter anymore.

"Listen, Alma," he continued. "I have a lot of experience in this department. I'll come up with some excuse."

"I don't know," Evan said. He carefully studied the key chain, as if it might offer some guidance. "I don't want to risk getting her in trouble."

"Believe me when I tell you, Evan, it's not a risk. The risk is that I will strangle you both if you continue sulking," Whit said.

Evan looked into Alma's eyes with a question in his own. Even through his swollen cheek and bloodied lip, she saw him. She really looked at him for the first time in so long, and she knew that she would not let him go.

She didn't have to explain this. She didn't have to tell him that she wanted to be with him, that she had no choice but to go with him.

"For God's sake," Whit said, "I absolutely insist. If you won't do it for yourselves, you *will* do it for me. You can't expect me to endure your misery forever."

Alma shrugged and Evan smiled. Then he rested his head in Alma's lap and closed his eyes, his body trembling slightly. The three of them rode together in silence as Whit turned onto the highway and sped toward the marina.

———

That night, the lessons Evan gave Alma so many months ago were put to use. His shoulder was hurting, and he'd had a couple of beers at the party. So he sat in the passenger seat and Alma eased the boat away from the dock. It felt amazing to drive, just fast enough that the wind blew through her hair as she steered out into the open water.

Evan sat, watching her. When they reached the center of the lake, he touched her arm.

"Do you want to swim?" he asked. "I'm sort of a mess."

Alma nodded and cut the engine.

Evan walked to the rear of the boat and threw the anchor. He didn't speak. He pulled off his bloodstained T-shirt and shorts and stood at the edge of the boat, waiting. Alma did the same and then stood beside him. The air felt scrubbed clean by the afternoon's storm, and the clouds had all passed on. Alma took his hand, and they fell together into the cool water. When they floated to the surface, they were still holding hands. Evan tugged Alma, pulling her through the water toward him. She felt his other hand on her back.

They kissed, treading water.

The feel of Evan's lips sent such relief through her body that she released his hand and floated to the surface. She felt Evan's touch move from her back to her hip and along her torso. He held onto her waist and swam behind her. He pulled her on top of him so that they floated, staring up at the clear, moonless sky, her body wrapped into his.

"Are we really alone?" Evan asked.

"Yes," Alma said.

Evan kicked slowly, and they floated toward the edge of the boat. He dived under the water and emerged near the engine. She watched the silver streams glide down his back as he lifted himself out of the water and climbed the ladder. He took a towel from under the seat and held it out for her.

Alma stepped forward and placed a finger on his chest, where a spot of blood was beginning to spread.

"You're bleeding," she whispered.

"I know."

Alma dabbed his chest and then traced the red marks with her fingers, mapping the wounded places with the motion of her hand. Even in the dark, she saw them. She grazed the swollen skin under his eye, the tender spot above his cheek, the small cut at the base of his chin, the bruise on his collarbone. They watched in silence as her fingers continued to his ribs, where the swollen, red flesh was beginning to turn purple.

He winced and then closed his eyes.

"Does it hurt?" she asked.

"Yes."

"Should I stop?" she asked.

"No."

He stood perfectly still. Her touch filled them both with longing and relief.

"Alma?"

"Hmm," she replied, lightly running her finger along his abdomen.

"You were wrong." His voice was tender, not angry. "It's not our love that's causing all of this."

"I know," she said. "I'm sorry."

He reached out to stroke her hair.

"I thought it would be better for you if I found a way to make you leave," she said, "but . . ."

"It wasn't," Evan said simply, leaning down to kiss the soft skin of her neck.

"I just wanted to make things right," Evan said. "I just didn't want you to hurt anymore."

"I know," Alma said. "But I guess things can't always be right."

Alma gently stroked his bruised cheek with the back of her fingers.

"I love you, Alma," he said.

"I love you," she said, looking up at him. "You know that, right? I lied when I said I didn't love you. I think maybe I've loved you from the moment you landed on my lap, in my dad's stupid truck. Or, at least, I wanted to know what it would be like to love you."

Evan smiled. "I'm sorry I spilled your precious coffee."

"I forgive you," Alma said. "And I'm sorry I lied to you."

She took his chin in her hand and led his lips to hers. They kissed slowly, allowing their bodies to remember it all—the touch and the scents and the quiet sounds that they had created together so many times before. But it was different this time. They weren't afraid—maybe because they were alone; maybe because there was nothing left to fear.

He knelt in front of her and leaned his forehead into her chest. Warm energy spread through her body.

"Evan," Alma said, "I'll always think you're beautiful, even if these bruises never go away. I think maybe the broken bits are good, too, you know? Because they're part of us."

"Let me see your broken parts," he whispered, placing his hand on her stomach.

"They're all inside," Alma said.

They lay intertwined at the bow of the boat. Alma told Evan of the fears and the memories that came to her in the dark of night, and Evan whispered the truths that his family held silent. With the touch of their hands and the sound of their voices, they explored each other's broken parts, and they coaxed each other back into the light of day.

TWENTY-SEVEN

Home

"Mom," Evan said from across the breakfast bar, "are you absolutely sure that you know how to start my car?"

"Of course, pumpkin. It's just a car," she replied, pressing a button on the blender. The churning of her morning smoothie reverberated off the kitchen's marble surfaces.

The school year was over. Evan was a high school graduate. And, now that summer was here, Evan's mother was on her way back to boot camp at the club with Aunt Maggie in honor of swimsuit season.

For a brief moment, Evan thought about how nothing ever seemed to change, but he knew that was wrong. Everything was different.

"Would you like a detox smoothie, honey?" she asked.

"Sure," he said, trying to hide his reluctance.

She split the smoothie into two tall glasses. Evan took one from her, and they both gulped in silence. He wouldn't exactly describe it as good, but it wasn't terrible. It tasted like cilantro, which was a little weird this early in the morning.

"Your uncle Sexton called from Washington," she said. "He tried your cell, but you didn't pick up."

Evan wasn't ready to talk to his uncle. "I was probably in the shower or something."

"Well, he just wanted to say good-bye. He said to call if you need anything."

"OK," Evan said. "Thanks."

"He cares about you very much, Evan. You shouldn't push him away."

"I know, Mom," Evan said. "I'll call on the drive. I promise."

Evan meant it. It was pointless to blame all of this on his uncle. Uncle Sexton had the power to help make things right, but he wasn't the one who made them all so wrong. At least, he didn't do it alone. Plus, he had helped Manny and Flor—a lot. He got all of Manny's charges dropped, expedited his citizenship process, and even found Manny a paralegal to fill out the paperwork for free. He also gave Evan a Spanish-English dictionary and a guidebook to Mexico for graduation, along with a big check. It was pretty cool of him. Evan figured that was Uncle Sexton's way of saying, "I'm sorry."

He walked around and took his mother's hand. "Come on," he said. "I'm going to show you before I leave."

"The car? My goodness, sweetheart," she said. "How hard can it be?"

He slung a large duffel bag over his shoulder and led his mother, still protesting weakly, into the garage.

The garage door began to grind open, slowly flooding the space with dim light. Propped against the wall was a metal "For Sale" sign.

"What's that?" he asked his mom.

"Lord, Evan. I have no idea," she replied, looking at the sign as if it were some sort of foreign object. "I came home from lunch with Aunt Maggie yesterday, and a strange man was standing in the middle of our yard, hammering away at that ugly sign."

"The house is Dad's?" Evan asked.

"Mmm-hmm," she replied. She walked over and touched the edge of the sign. "Metal," she said with disgust. "Good heavens. Who uses metal signs any more?"

"So, you took it down," he said.

"Why, yes, pumpkin. The last thing we need in our lives is an ugly sign announcing your father's financial troubles."

For their entire marriage, Evan's mother and father had maintained completely separate finances—twenty years of split dinner bills and separate checking accounts. Evan learned this two nights after graduation. His mother had explained that his father's finances were tumbling into free fall as a result of several risky real estate investments. She told Evan not to worry. Her own, more conservative investments remained rock solid.

"But, Mom," Evan said, "if Dad needs to sell the house . . ."

His mother broke in. "If your father needs to sell this house, then I'll just buy it from him. There's no need to make all of this public."

He led his mother to the car and handed her the square key. She eased into the driver's seat and daintily lifted the key to inspect it.

"Where's the key?" she asked, turning it in her hand.

"Remember, Mom?" he said patiently. "There's not a metal key. No ignition, either. You just have to keep that in your purse, or in the car somewhere, and the car will start when you push this button."

He leaned across and pressed the power button. "And your foot has to be on the brake, or else the car won't start."

"Well, isn't that interesting," she said.

Evan shook his head slowly. "I'm glad I showed you," he said as he took his mother's hand to help her out of the car.

"Yes, pumpkin," she replied. "So am I. I would have been looking for a key inside that little black box for a very long time."

"We have to stop pretending, Mom," he said.

"I know," she replied, stepping out of the car. "I'm going to try."

"You should put the sign out," he said.

"Maybe you're right, sweetheart," she replied. "I don't need to rattle around in this big house alone. And I certainly don't need the trouble of maintaining the garden. I'll call the agent, whoever he is, and tell him to send out a more attractive wooden sign."

Evan pulled her into a hug, and she buried her face in his chest.

"Thank you," he said.

He knew that all of this was confusing for her and hard to accept. But she tried her best to understand, and now she was letting him leave.

She rested there for a moment and then pulled away.

"Now, go," she commanded, shooing him with her hand. "I'm sure they're waiting for you."

He got into his mother's SUV and cranked the engine.

"Call me twice a day," she called out. "No texts. I want to hear your voice. And be sure to put premium gas in the Escalade."

Evan nodded obediently, but where he was going, he wasn't sure premium gas would be an option.

Could it really be morning? Alma sat up in the makeshift bed she had created on the floor of her brother's room. She counted the days backward in her head—fourteen nights since she'd told Evan about her recurring nightmare. Those fourteen nights had been filled with deep and dreamless sleep, restful, like nothing she had experienced before.

She got up and wandered into the kitchen. The counters were bare, save a coffeepot and one mug neatly placed alongside it. She pulled the milk from the otherwise empty refrigerator and poured herself a cup of coffee. She wandered into the living room, cupping the warm mug between her hands, wishing it were an espresso drink from the Dripolator instead of her grandmother's cheap Nescafé. But this would have to do.

The house was still and silent. All of the others were gathered in the driveway, busily preparing for the journey. Isa struggled to lift lawn chairs into the trailer. She hoisted them high in the air as Mrs. King and *Abuela* Lupe called out instructions in two languages. Selena sat on the edge of the driveway and sifted carefully through the neat pile of her most cherished possessions—a scruffy stuffed pig, her backpack, and a small case filled with DVDs. Manny secured the concrete blocks that held the trailer's wheels in place on the steep driveway. His car was parked on the street, and Flor stood beside it, gently rocking the baby with one hand while she cradled a telephone in her ear. Pelé the dog curled around her ankles.

And then she saw Evan. She smiled as he hoisted the U-Haul trailer onto the Escalade's hitch, and then carefully removed the neat stack of stones that held the trailer in place. Evan drew two long chains from underneath the trailer to connect it to his mother's SUV. Manny handed a padlock to Evan, and he secured it into place. It gave her a strange sense of comfort to see the U-Haul and the Escalade so sturdily connected, and to know that her near future, at least, was securely linked with Evan's.

Alma marveled at how much could change in a couple of weeks. Selena, Isa, *Abuela* Lupe, and Alma would not be boarding a bus today. They would not depart on a several-day journey bearing only the possessions that would fit into a small suitcase. They would not leave two decades' worth of accumulated family possessions in the hands of an unscrupulous relative who offered, for an exorbitant fee, to ferry their items back to Mexico in his truck, bit by bit over the course of the next several months. Instead, they would pile into Mrs. Roland's white Escalade, and Evan would drive across the border, through the interior of Mexico, and—in a few days—to San Juan, the place Alma was now expected to call home. He would stay with her family for four weeks. He was already enrolled in intensive language classes at the university in Oaxaca, an hour from her family's small town, and the credits would transfer to Berkeley in the fall. After four weeks of Spanish, they all hoped, Evan might finally be able to keep up at the dinner table.

She knocked gently on the window to get his attention. He stood up, wiped his hand across his brow, and smiled broadly.

"Good morning, sleepyhead!" he called out, loud enough that she heard it through the glass. "There's a double cappuccino from the Dripolator waiting for you in the microwave. It was hot when I brought it an hour ago!"

How strange it was that something so simple as a double cappuccino could fill her heart with joy.

***

Flor approached Evan, holding a map in her hand.

"My dad says you should cross at Harlingen—don't go to Reynosa." She hoisted Jasmine over one shoulder and then spread the map onto the hood of the Escalade and pointed to the far eastern edge of Texas. "The lines at Reynosa can take, like, thirty-six hours."

Who knew so many people were trying to get into Mexico?

"And you shouldn't try to cross today. Stay in Houston or Corpus Christi tonight and go down to the border early in the morning."

"Thanks, Flor," Evan said.

"I marked the map with the best route," she said, offering it to him. "My dad knows it well."

"I have a GPS," Evan replied, waving the map away.

"You should take it just in case, Evan. You never know about signals."

"You're right," he said. "I might need it."

Manny approached them, carrying a four-pack of Rockstar energy drink. He offered the drinks to Evan. "You're definitely gonna need these, man."

"Thanks, Manny, but, uh, I don't drink caffeine."

"Dude," Manny said, "you're about to drive two thousand miles with Isa whining in the backseat. Trust me, you'll want caffeine."

Evan took the drinks and let them dangle in his hand. He knew that Manny was offering more than caffeine for the drive. He was offering an apology, and Evan felt ready to accept it.

"Thanks," he said, giving Manny a quick pat on the back.

Whit's instincts about his dad were dead-on. Manny had been released from jail without charge three hours after his arrest. The next morning, Whit visited Flor to make amends. He did not speak of Conway or of their hunch about the Jell-O shots. He never explained why Flor couldn't recall the events of that night.

Whit had different plans for Conway. Two days before graduation, Troy arrived at school in his cruiser, accompanied by two narcotics officers and a drug-sniffing dog. The dog headed straight for Conway's locker, where the officers found a synthetic "date rape" drug called gamma hydroxybutyrate, also known as GHB or "Georgia Home Boy." Conway fought the entire way to juvie, insisting that he had never even heard of GHB. Maybe he hadn't. Whit always enjoyed fooling around with chemistry, even as a kid.

To protect Flor and Manny, Whit apologized, but he also hid the full truth. Then he figured out a way to keep Conway from causing the same problem again. This solution made Evan uneasy, and maybe it had been the wrong one. But if Evan had learned anything over the past few months, it was that doing the right thing is not always as simple as it seems. Seeing Manny and Flor together with that baby, Evan felt pretty sure that keeping Manny here was right.

———

Alma took an empty box from the hallway and wandered from room to room, looking for items left behind. She filled the box with a pair of Selena's flip-flops, a heavy wool sweater that must have been her father's, and a mug from the bakery on the town square. She wandered into Raúl's room, folded the blankets, and stacked them in a neat pile. She shoved them in the box, and on top of them she laid a small black book. She thought about the family's last night together in the house; she wanted the memory imprinted on her mind.

Manny and Flor understood that Whit's dad had arranged for Manny's release. Even though he was grateful, Manny still didn't trust himself near Whit. So when Manny and Flor offered to help Alma's family prepare to leave, Whit knew he would need to stay away. He came to the house to say his good-byes the night before.

They all sat on the bare floor and ate *sopes* from paper plates. Whit distributed gifts: a SpongeBob DVD for Selena, a stack of gossip magazines for Isa, and a dessert cookbook for *Abuela* Lupe, who had developed a fondness for American pies. To Alma, he offered a small journal with lined pages and a black leather cover. He said that it would be her friend—a much better friend than the pewter flask he had given her months ago. He instructed her to fill its empty pages whenever she felt despair. Alma joked that, next fall, the journal would return with her, its lined pages still blank. She'd use it instead to take notes at Princeton, or whichever fabulous university she decided to attend after they fought over her for a while, throwing her scholarship money and begging her to choose them.

Her phone vibrated and lit up with a picture of Raúl's face. She hesitated to pick it up, not wanting to hear what he was about to tell her.

On the fourth ring, she answered.

"Hi."

"Are you all packed and ready to go?" he asked, cheerfully.

"Pretty much. Where are you?" she replied.

"Juárez."

She held the phone more firmly to her ear, trying not to picture Raúl in Ciudad Juárez—that dangerous city carved from the edge of the desert.

"Alma, are you there?" Raúl asked.

"Yes."

"I'm sorry I won't see you."

"Me, too," she said. "When will you cross?"

"Tomorrow morning. I should be in Gilberton by Friday."

"Be careful," she replied. There was so much more to say, but Alma couldn't find the words.

"You'll be back soon, too, Alma," he said. "I know you will."

She didn't respond to that. Instead she said, "Call me when you get to Phoenix."

"I will," he said. "I promise."

When the line went dead, Alma wandered to the kitchen and poured herself a glass of water, clear and cold, from the tap. Without thinking, she offered a sort of prayer for Raúl, pleading for him to find water when he needed it. A part of her hoped they might be able to reunite at the border before their futures moved in opposite directions. But she knew that would be impossible. Alma was crossing the border in the easy direction. She would be going through a gate at a busy checkpoint on the far eastern edge of the border, safely enclosed in an air-conditioned vehicle. Raúl would need to travel the hard way. He would cross on foot, as far as possible from a checkpoint, in a burning stretch of hot desert beyond the border wall.

She hoped he would make it back to Gilberton safely, but she didn't want to come back to this town—maybe not ever. She would not give up on her future, though, and she had a lot of good people pulling for her. Ms. Chen had found someone with deep pockets to pay most of Alma's tuition at the academy in Mexico City. The donor insisted on complete anonymity. Ms. Chen wasn't even sure who it was. The donor also insisted that Alma and her family contribute 10 percent of the tuition. According to Ms. Chen, this anonymous benefactor wanted to be sure that she would take personal responsibility for her success.

Beginning in September, Alma would live with cousins outside of Mexico City, but she would need to find a job to pay for bus fare, books, uniforms, and the rest of tuition. She would try to work after school so that she could spend weekends with her dad in Oaxaca. And she reminded herself that Oaxaca would be a great place to study anthropology. She even had discovered an institute where she could take Saturday classes and learn the indigenous languages of the region.

She wandered back into the living room. There was only one thing left to do. *Abuela* Lupe had insisted that they not disturb the *altarcito*— the corner of the room where all of the statues and images of the saints and the Virgin Mary were arranged around a perpetually burning candle. Alma thought it seemed silly and superstitious for *Abuela* Lupe to protect this altar with such devotion. If there were a bunch of saints up there praying for her family, would they mind being packed in a box for a few extra days? According to *Abuela* Lupe, the answer was a firm and unequivocal yes. So Alma had left this corner of the house untouched until the very last moment.

She stretched onto her toes and blew out the candle.

The Escalade was loaded. Selena tumbled around in the backseat as Isa ran her fingers along the smooth calf-skin leather.

"This car rocks!" Isa announced, settling into the deep cushions.

Selena reached up to the roof to release the small television screen. "Can we watch movies?" she asked.

"Yeah," Evan replied, standing beside the open door. "Lots of movies. It's a long drive."

Isa whistled loudly, and Pelé bounded into her lap.

"The dog? Really?" Evan asked.

"She's all my dad can talk about," Isa said. "Every time he calls or writes, he asks about Pelé."

"It's true," Selena said. "He's dying to see her."

Evan grumbled from the front seat. "My mom will kill me if she finds out."

"Pleeeaaaasse," Selena said, clasping her hands as if in prayer.

"Yeah, OK," he said. "What's one more passenger?"

Selena hurled herself out of the car and threw her arms around Evan's neck. "I'm so glad you're back!" she said, her body dangling two feet off the ground. "I missed you."

"Is the U-Haul ready to close?" Manny asked, from behind the trailer.

"I'll check inside," Evan called out, prying Selena's hands from his neck. "Just to make sure there aren't any more boxes."

He jogged toward the house.

"Alma, we're ready."

He saw her sitting cross-legged on the floor of the living room, clutching a statue of the Virgin Mary.

"Are you OK?" he asked, crouching beside her.

"Yeah," she said, looking up at him with clear eyes. "I was just thinking about this statue. She's called Our Lady of *La Leche*."

"Can I see?" he asked.

She handed him a statue of a frail, white-faced woman with a massive gold crown perched impossibly on her head. She was covered from head to toe in draping gowns, with one exception: one of her breasts was exposed with a chubby little half-naked baby attached to it.

It was pretty weird.

"She's always been my favorite," Alma said. "I guess now I know why."

Evan thought about the story she had told him on the boat, about her mother and how she died. It was so terrible it made chills run down his back.

He sat down on the floor across from her.

"Where did it come from?" he asked, taking her free hand into his. "I mean, the statue."

"I got it with my *tías* in St. Augustine a long time ago. They saw it in a gift shop. They were totally obsessed." She shook her head and sighed. "They made me wander around the streets of the tourist district asking where to find the Virgin *dando pecho*—breastfeeding."

Evan smiled and his heart filled.

"Utterly humiliating," Alma said. "Every time I said 'breast' to a shop clerk, I felt my face turn bright red."

Evan reached out to touch her cheek, trying to imagine her as a bewildered child, before she became this amazing, confident person. A person he couldn't bear the thought of being away from.

"Alma," he said quietly, "you can't leave."

"I have to," she said, her voice faltering. "You know that." She put the statue down between them and took his other hand.

"Let me marry you, Alma," he said. "I want you to stay." He leaned forward so their foreheads touched.

"We promised that we would stop trying to fix each other," she whispered. "Remember?"

"I don't want to fix you," Evan replied, looking down at their intertwined hands. "I just want to be with you—always."

"I want that, too—more than anything," she said. "But always can't start like this, not as a half-truth. And *not* here." She leaned back and glanced up at the empty living room.

"It's just, I mean." Evan pressed his hands tightly against hers. "Oh, God, Alma. What if you leave and you can't come back?"

"Please understand," she said. "We can't get married to keep me here. And Gilberton, it can't be home for either of us, not anymore."

"You're right," he said, looking directly into her eyes. "I know you're right." His head dropped and he squeezed his eyes shut. "Please just promise me we'll find somewhere else."

"I promise," she said quietly, lifting his chin so that he would meet her gaze.

"OK, then," he said, opening his eyes to look at her. He stood up and watched Alma take the strange little statue back into her hand, and then he pulled her to her feet. "Let's get out of here."

Acknowledgments

I always thought of myself as a practical person. That changed on the morning I sat down to start writing—of all things!—a novel. Believe me, I had plenty of other activities to fill my time. And every single one of them was more sensible. But, here I am, publishing a novel. Let this serve as just another reminder of how crazy-unpredictable life can be. It's quite a ride.

I'll start by thanking those who gave me the courage to do such a wildly impractical thing: Lee Taylor, my first reader. She is the least judgmental person I know, and she also happens to be a kick-ass sister. Elizabeth Friedmann, my extraordinary mom, and my first and best writing instructor. She'll never know how my heart soared when she first told me she loved this story. Carroll Ann Friedmann, who currently is my sister, but who just might become my guru someday. Her life is a beautiful example of how we thrive when we embrace the unpredictable. Mayra Cuevas, my critique partner. I'm not sure how it happened that we were born across an ocean from each other, because I'm quite certain she was meant to be my sister. (Clearly, cosmic error.) Without Mayra, Alma and Evan would still live in a tiny world filled with exclamation points, and this book would be gathering virtual dust in a virtual folder somewhere deep in the bowels of my laptop.

And now to the people who made my own teen years so vividly memorable that I have an endless well of experience from which to draw: Emily Arthur, who continues to bring extraordinary beauty into my life; Jamie Brigman, whose *18 Songs from JRB*—inexplicably—gave me this story; Cheryl Hall; Trey Tune; Holly Smith; Laura Kachergus; and Trip Nesbitt, my oldest friend. I love you all so very much.

For all the ways they made this novel better, I want to thank the talented Jita Fumich, Katie Beno-Valencia, Veronica León, Juan Ramirez (for extensive knowledge of machetes), Araceli Martinez (for great stories and cherished friendship), Karol Ramos, and Erin Harris, who so gracefully took me on. And, while on the topic of grace, I'm just going to go ahead and say that my editor, Laura Chasen, is one of the most gracious and generous people ever to come into my unpredictable life. Having edited my work, Laura knows that I am a woman of *many* words. Yet, I find no words to express my gratitude to her for believing in this project and for shepherding me so gently through the process.

Most importantly, I want to thank Lorena, Lalo, Yehimi, Carlos, Loreli, Felipe, and every single DREAMer whose story I have ever had the honor to hear. My love and respect for them is what pulled me out of bed before dawn every morning to write this story. They have inspired me, again and again and again, and I am awed by their courage and tenacity. It is my most fervent hope that, after reading this book, more people will seek out their remarkable stories.

To Mary Elizabeth, Nate, Pixley, and Annie: Thank you for showing me every day how to love this wild ride that we call life. For more than half of the ride, I have been strapped in next to Chris Marquardt, a poet, a dreamer, and a just plain beautiful man. If I know anything about what it means to love and be loved, if I can say anything real about love's extraordinary power to overcome, it is because we taught these things to each other. *Pura Vida*.